Tina Moon was born on January 16th, 1976, in Slovakia and graduated from a secondary medical school in the field of pediatric nursing. In primary school, she devoted herself to the artistic recitation of poetry and prose. Later on, in addition to her studies, she played in an amateur theater and worked with young people and children. For 14 years, she has been one of the leaders of the amateur theater-dance group *Alimah Fusion and Alchemy Theater*. She founded the project *Aphrodite's Balance*, in which, together with other members of the group, she taught belly dancing. With her dance-theater group, she performs at various cultural and social events where they present their theater-dance performances. She worked as a senior caregiver in Austria for several years. She has two adult sons and today, she lives and works as a nurse in a retirement home in Germany.

D1665878

I dedicate this book to all human beings, celebrities, and anti-celebrities who are looking for or have already found all four levels of love.

Tina Moon

Four Levels of Love

The Hidden Gifts

Austin Macauley Publishers™
LONDON * CAMBRIDGE * NEW YORK * SHARJAH

Ordering Information
Quantity sales: Special discounts are available on quantity purchases by corporations, associations, and others. For details, contact the publisher at the address below.

Publisher's Cataloging-in-Publication data
Moon, Tina
Four Levels of Love

ISBN 9781647501969 (Paperback)
ISBN 9781649795427 (ePub e-book)

Library of Congress Control Number: 2022906679

www.austinmacauley.com/us

First Published 2022
Austin Macauley Publishers LLC
40 Wall Street, 33rd Floor, Suite 3302
New York, NY 10005
USA

mail-usa@austinmacauley.com
+1 (646) 5125767

I would like to thank Soraya because without her effort, it wouldn't be possible to publish the book in English, and without her practical help, I would not be able to achieve many things.

I would like to thank my whole family, my sons, my sisters, Lucia, Beatrice, Katarina, our trainer Libor, and all current or former members of my theater and dance family, all friends, acquaintances, colleagues at work for their support and love.

Chapter 1

A council of the Olympian gods was held in the palace in the grand hall. All the gods convened there regularly to confer on important matters of the Olympian pantheon and earthly issues as well. The grand hall was one of the most beautiful rooms in Olympus. It was supported by robust columns of snow-white marble around which ivy leaves of pure gold twined. The vault was transparent and provided a wonderful view of a multitude of constellations and other worlds separated by millions of light-years. The throne of Zeus was made of pure diamond, and as the light of the eternal lamps that were arranged around the hall was refracted, it sparkled with wonderful rays that were showering on the hall around. Scenes of human and divine tales that have lasted for ages were portrayed on walls. Love played the main role in all of these legends and tales. The whole journey of mankind has been a quest for the path back to the paradise, wherefrom the mankind had been expelled. Zeus raised from his throne and all the gods present in the council bowed. The ruler of Olympus and of the gods approached the Book of Life lying on the ivory pedestal and sighed: "One handsome man down there troubles me a lot. He has got a good heart, but he could use a little bit more humility."

In the meantime, he turned to Apollo and continued: "What fate awaits him further into the future?"

Apollo answered with a surprised look on his face: "Zeus, the whole world is in a mess. The earth is shaking. Riots, famine, diseases, and death is everywhere. And the worst thing is that people are not destroying the Earth that feeds them, but they are also destroying, with their selfishness, the most precious gift they have been given. Love. And you are interested in the fate of some man. Why?"

Zeus gave it thought and said: "You are right, Apollo. That is exactly why I am interested in the fate of one man, who needs to recognize more deeds of compassion and mercy."

Zeus continued contemplatively while stroking his beard: "We call these deeds; the Deeds of Pearls, because for each such deed made by a human on Earth, here up, one pearl in the Pearl Fields will be added."

There, goddess of wisdom, Palas Athena spoke: "I don't understand where you are getting at with all of this, Zeus. What does it have to do with the reason, for which we have all met here today? If I am not mistaken, we were supposed to discuss something completely different. The state of pearls in the Pearl Fields is alarming and—"

Zeus interrupted her: "You are right of course. Therefore, I have chosen his fate, because he is one of the millions of human beings, who would also need to do and receive more deeds of mercy and compassion. I have chosen him, as I want to ascertain, whether or not people are still capable of loving selflessly regardless of their status, wealth, power, or fame. We simply have to find out, whether or not, the selfless love that gives out from the heart still exists. We need to see it in a living example. Only thus we can demand from human beings to commence doing the deeds of pearls."

Thereupon the ruler of the underworld, Hades, approached Zeus and noted: "You are right, Zeus. My wife Persephone is also complaining that evil deeds are accruing on the scales of justice. And the deeds of precious pearls are diminishing greatly."

Hera said quietly: "The Earth is shaking, because responding to the human deeds of evil. People forget to give, and they want to take. Mercy and compassion are disappearing from human lives like smoke. Helping a fellow man is no longer in fashion. Nowadays people learn a rule, that is ruining a whole generation. May I be well of first, and only then is the others turn."

"Due to greed and lack of compassion, there are so many blood fields on the Earth, that I am no longer able to look at them all. Poverty, hunger, and wars. All of this has its primary origin in the lack of higher levels of love, mercy, and compassion. But I like it," added the god of war, Ares.

Finally, the goddess of love and beauty, Aphrodite, spoke exaltedly: "People stopped listening to their hearts and emotions, they listen to the cold reason and calculation. More and more couples, who are initially in love, fall out of love after some time. They can't bear the loss and close the gate of their hearts. My son Eros has to exert himself more and more to endow them with a new love."

Poseidon, the ruler of the seas, contemplated: "I am not interested in earthly matters that much, nevertheless then why is Eros shooting his arrows for millennia even to such places, where they cause a lot of damage? Why is infidelity so common on Earth? Why does love appear and suddenly disappears as sea waves appear and disappear in a short time?"

Zeus replied nobly: "The world and mankind have lost perfection. Hence, they must feel the pain to find their way back to paradise. A human being looks inside itself only through pain to understand the power of love and sacrifice. If people would not fall, they would not learn to stand again. If they would not feel the pain, they would not experience happiness. Therefore, Eros torments everyone with his arrows. Because only through love will human beings realize their dark side. When in an unhappy love they come across fragments of their pain and they advance closer to themselves through understanding and experiencing that pain."

Pallas Athena asked abruptly: "Zeus, what do you actually want to do with this handsome man?"

Zeus spoke while walking in the grand hall: "In some of his acting roles, he sacrificed himself for others' sake. I want to know, how he will manage one especially difficult experience in his real life."

Hera, knowing her Olympian husband, said mysteriously to Pallas Athena: "He wants to send him love. Pure love. The one that loves from the heart. If he decides to accept this experience, he will recognize all four levels of love. We must respect his free will."

Apollo, who was silent all the time, spoke mockingly: "You say love? People ceased to value love. It is always only selfishness and call of low instincts. No love. My servants enter the fates of people and their loves in this book every day," continued Apollo indignantly while holding the Book of life, "all that people have done to love is getting back to them as a boomerang. Stupid, proud creatures have forgotten and don't want to remember, for they would have to look in the mirror of their own soul, and that is what they fear so much. Only the human being that can see itself in other human beings is capable of true human love."

Aphrodite did not give up though.

"Wait, Apollo. They are not all like that. Although I have to admit that the way in which the human world works does not give them a choice, as in addition to love, justice is disappearing from human lives as well. Therefore, everyone takes care of himself. Because they are afraid. In return to help, they get harm instead of gratitude. In spite of that, there is a possibility of finding the lost balance and contribute to Pearl Fields with a small portion. However, people have to remember first. Remember that they are created from love and for love. Not for hatred. And how else, if not through the kind of love that causes the most madness and pain. Through the love that belongs to a couple."

Ares smiled.

"So how do you want to prove that to the one handsome man who has almost everything?"

Poseidon added contemplatively: "He is permanently in love, isn't he?"

Hades said quietly: "Some people resist love and without love the soul dies. Hunger relieved by bodily pleasures will not always relieve the hunger of soul and heart. But food prepared for the heart and soul can burn. That is why there is the fear of tasting it."

Zeus sat on his throne of pure diamond and continued: "The imperfection of human beings allows the possibility of choice. So, we will give a chance to one ignis fatuus to choose. Aphrodite!"

Zeus called the goddess of love and beauty, and she stepped closer to him.

"I think the time has come for your son. He may use the love potion for his arrow. You know I don't agree with it much, but fame and wealth are always a crux. If we are to help to open his gate of heart, magic means need to be employed as well."

Hera asked: "Wait, Zeus. How do you want to choose another arrow for him? After all, he already has enough lovers."

Ares smiled.

"Sometimes love, sometimes war…"

Pallas Athena nodded.

"Love and war are sometimes the same, Ares. In many relationships, there is more work for you than for Aphrodite and Psyche."

Hera added: "Psyche will help searching in the Book of life. She knows all recesses of the human soul; hence she must select the right arrow. The rest is then up to you and your son Eros. We shall see, whether or not human love is still the greatest miracle on Earth."

Apollo frowned. He did not like interfering with the fates of people a lot, but he could not anything against the will of Zeus. Therefore, he asked: "What about his free will? You want to use magic."

Hera tapped Apollo on his shoulder and whispered: "He will be given the arrow, but he has to decide himself, what to do with it. The free will shall be preserved."

Apollo sighed, and Zeus concluded the council saying: "You may all leave for your assignments. Another council regarding Pearl Fields will be summoned by the master ruler of guardian angels. There is nothing else we can do. It is up to guardians to awake the human hearts."

All the gods, except Hera, bowed and left. When Zeus and Hera were left alone, Hera asked Zeus: "Why did you choose his fate in particular?"

Zeus smiled eerily.

"He has a hidden desire in his heart and soul."

Hera objected: "As many others have. Zeus, I don't envy the bearer of his new arrow a bit. It will not be easy for her."

Zeus acknowledged: "You must admit, Hera, it is very difficult with celebrities. He is wealthy, handsome, and famous, and his wealth may be as interesting as he is."

Hera considered: "Wait, but then you would have to return him back in time if you want to show him that he will be loved regardless of his fame."

Zeus remarked quietly: "That is not necessary. He already has friends, family, and hopefully loves as well. Besides, every famous man is only a human after all. Everyone is born and dies naked and without anything. Nobody is allowed to take his fortune to the other side. He can take only himself. Besides, the arrow bearer also ignites the light of all levels of love in his heart. A man without unselfish love is miserable."

And so, Zeus became silent, Hera left quietly. Zeus thought about how strong love can be when it joins unequal couples and they fight with such verve to break all limits and prejudices. It will be the same this time. Zeus suspected what Aphrodite did not yet. He saw the future and smiled mysteriously. He will get a piece of rare fruit of extraordinary love. Whether or not, he will like it will depend on the skills of the bearer of Eros's arrow.

In the meantime, Aphrodite, the goddess of love and beauty, hurried to Eros. She transferred herself to the beautiful residence of Eros and his faithful spouse Psyche at the speed of light. Their palace was decorated in shades of blue. Many beautiful turrets, roof inlaid with blue mother of pearls, arched windows, and a gate formed a beautiful complex. In the vast gardens, a lot of beautiful flowers blossomed, but especially roses of different colors, for rose is the flower of love. The palaces of other gods looked similarly. They differ only in small variations and in color. Each of the gods adjusted its palace to its needs and taste. Aphrodite's palace was decorated in light pink color. The residence of Pallas Athena was decorated in silver and white. The palace of Zeus and his wife Hera was gold and white, as the grand hall, where the other Olympians gods would meet regularly. The scarlet red color of another palace would show to everyone far ahead that it belonged to Ares. Artemis's palace was hidden in Olympian woods and reveled in shades of green. Poseidon, the ruler of oceans and seas, had his palace inlaid with mother of pearls in marvelous ivory color. Hermes, the messenger of the gods, had his palace decorated in vibrant yellows like the sun. Hephaestus, the Olympian blacksmith, and inventor wallowed in dull grey. The palace of Apollo reveled with the colors of the four elements of water, air, fire, earth. Sky blue, grey, red, green. Although Olympus, floating in higher spheres, could not be seen by the human eye, vibrant life was pulsating there. The gods, of whom there were many more indeed, took care not only of their spiritual matters but they also governed some earthly matters. And what is more important they fostered the human soul as well. For that purpose, the Olympian gods had many other helpers, who worked close to the people on Earth.

Aphrodite stopped for a while in the garden in front of the palace of her son Eros and his spouse Psyche. Her face was beautiful. She had long brown hair falling up to her waist arranged in light, seductive waves. Her hazel eyes could be cold as ice when she punished all those, who liked to play with the emotions of others. Her upper lip was a little thinner than the lower one, but her lips looked seductive and feminine.

She stood there and contemplated: "People are increasingly unhappy in spite of the love they are given. Earth has been seized by darkness and its helpers and there were more of them in the vicinity of human beings than of light guardians. And they were making the situation very difficult. Moreover, the human spirit has fully surrendered to matter and reason. The people did not even believe that worlds other than material one existed. And as a matter of fact, Earth could not function without these other worlds. What a paradox – it is the higher spheres that people draw their strength, energy, and inspiration from yet they proudly believe that they do it themselves. Without help."

After a long while, Aphrodite awakened from her thoughts and entered the residence of her son. She was welcomed only by Psyche. Eros has not returned yet. Once Psyche lived on earth as an ordinary mortal and already then, she excelled in great beauty. She had light long straight hair loose most of the time, captured only by a diamond headband. Green and blue eyes were lined by long eyelashes. Her nose was tiny as a button. Her mouth was not very big, but it was heart-shaped perfectly. The great rivalry between Psyche and Aphrodite over Eros had to turn into mutual respect at the order of Zeus. In the end, all three had to work together.

"Dear Aphrodite, to what do I owe your visit to our palace?" Psyche asked politely.

"We have an important task, Psyche, but call Eros first. It concerns him as well."

Psyche said: "Oh, he hasn't come back yet. Reveal to me what is about."

"We are supposed to send another bearer of Eros's arrow to one poor soul searching for a piece of true love."

As soon as Aphrodite disclosed to Psyche his name and the country where he lives, Psyche easily found the fate of this man in her Book of Living Souls. Psyche had to know the corners of the human soul very well, because when Eros hit someone with the arrow of love, Psyche made sure that a mere physical attraction developed into love that fed not only the body but also the soul. Aphrodite oversaw the whole metamorphosis, and this was getting more difficult in recent times on Earth.

When Psyche learned who was this man, she shouted with apprehension: "By gods! Whose idea was that, Aphrodite?! How are we supposed to do that? How do you want to find an appropriate woman? One shall not gamble with love."

Aphrodite calmed Psyche down: "It was the idea of Zeus himself and he allowed us to help her. Eros may use the love potion for his arrow."

That did not satisfy Psyche, for she asked: "Who do you want to send to him? Famous and good-looking people like him sometimes have trouble with love. Not only them."

Aphrodite held her own. "I am aware all of that, but Zeus is convinced of the opposite. During the time assigned by her fate to spend with him, a very tricky task awaits her. She must persuade him that he can be loved by a woman even without his wealth and fame. Hence, it will not be easy to select such a woman. Until Eros arrives, we will simply start looking in your book."

"That will be like looking for a needle in a haystack. We need some help, a hint to help us find such a woman."

"You better stop talking and call the helpers – the guardians angels – to help with the search. Bring also some ambrosia and nectar, may we refresh ourselves."

Psyche called a few guardian angel for help using telepathy, which was common on Olympus. Wonderful winged beings flew into a room, which was equally splendid as the exterior of the palace. Three beautiful female angels wearing a pink dress that was fluttering around them like breeze. Three male angels wearing a sky-blue habit. When they were flying, a multitude of tiny lights glittered around their dazzling feather wings.

Besides these beings were the faithful helpers in Olympus, a huge number of them worked down on Earth, which was an important part of their work. Every human being was given its guardian from the day he or she was born. They helped their protégés – people – on their journey of life. They joined them in their battle against dark beings who had black bodies and wings like bats and who instigated people to do evil. Unfortunately, people heard the voices of darkness much more than the voices of light guardians. The good whispered imperceptibly in the heart and soul, while the evil continuously roared in the human mind. Six helpers bowed to Aphrodite, for great respect and hierarchy dominated in the higher spheres as well.

Aphrodite rose from a chair and spoke majestically: "I am sorry to disturb you in your duties, but I am sure others will substitute you gladly. We need your help in searching."

The goddess of love and beauty did not manage to finish and one of the angels spoke: "You don't have to waste your time explaining, Aphrodite, the messenger of the gods has already performed his duty and announced it where ever possible."

Another of the guardians turned to Aphrodite: "So, tell us straight, how are we to look for her!" Aphrodite answered: "We will search in the Books of Living Souls. The woman we are looking for must be unselfish because only selfless love can do a miracle."

Another male guardian agreed: "In his case, such miracle is exactly what we need."

One of the female guardians objected tough: "There are millions of women like that in the world. This key for search will not be enough."

The goddess of love told her approaching her: "I know, but it will have to be for now."

All of them began to search at enormous speed reading the Psyche's Books of Living Souls. Then something quite unexpected happened. A female angel entered the room. Her wings were somewhat battered; therefore, she could not fly. That was why she did not come alone but was being helped by Zephyrus, a light breeze. When they saw the angel, they stopped working, Aphrodite asked a bit surprised and angry as well: "What happened? Why are you disturbing us? Don't you know only the one who has something really important to tell may disturb me now?"

The angel sunk her eyes guilty and whispered: "I know. That is exactly why I came. Namely, it concerns one wish. It is something I can't handle myself."

Aphrodite came closer: "Speak out, what is it about? But quickly, I don't have time to deal with trifles."

The angel pulled out a small ball-size translucent sphere from the fold of her pink dress and handed it over to Aphrodite. Psyche stood up from her book and sighed out: "That is a stone, a piece of human fate. As I can see, it comes from the future."

The goddess of love approached the table and the guardian angel pointed to the translucent sphere: "You all better have a good look at it."

All gathered around the table and Psyche stroked the sphere gently. In a moment, they saw images. They saw a woman walking into a chapel. She lit a candle in front of an altar, knelt, and started to pray: "Dear God, you are infinitely wise and kind. I beg you to help me. I am in love with one of the most beautiful men in the world. Regardless of how he looks, I fell that he has a pure and rare heart. I know, it is bad and he is too far away. I beg you to make me forget all about him. Make him happy!"

After a while, tears started rolling down the woman's face. She wiped them off with the reverse of the hand and whispered: "Thank you, God!" then slowly walked out of the chapel. Everyone in the room was silent. They were speechless.

The guardian of that woman begged: "Do you understand, Aphrodite, why I dared to disturb you? My protégé has already enough hardship. If this fragment of her fate will happen, I will not be able to fly anymore."

In the meantime, Psyche found the identity of that woman in her book and sighed: "Her prayer is honest. I am afraid, it will not be possible to prevent what is going to happen."

Aphrodite continued: "Strange, that you arrived just at the moment when we are searching for the appropriate bearer of Eros's arrow for the man, to whom that prayer will belong."

One of the female guardians considered: "Aphrodite, what if she is the one who will bear the arrow of your son?"

One of the male guardians objected: "Zeus would never allow this. They are thousands of kilometers apart from each other."

The guardian angel, who brought the stone of fate of that woman, explained: "That is why came. To ask you simply not to register this stone, and other ones related to this strange love, in the Book of life."

Psyche in utter shock raised form her chair and: "What is your name, please? How do you dare to request something like that?"

The guardian answered: "My name is Nolachiel. I know that I am asking for interference with fate."

One of the female guardians noted: "The human beings learn to understand themselves through hardship. Why do you want to prevent that?"

Nolachiel replied determinedly: "I know. But if there is too much of that the soul begins to feel despair and emptiness. Then it becomes more difficult for us, the guardian angels, to get close to the hearts of human beings."

Aphrodite approached Nolachiel, took her palms into her hands, and said: "Listen, Nolachiel. Sometimes, in very special cases, the god of prophecy, Apollo, may interfere to reverse certain paths of destiny. But this time, it probably won't be possible. Something tells me to let it be. Besides, people attract what happens in their lives with their emotions."

Suddenly, one of the male guardians asked: "May we continue with the search?"

Aphrodite turned to the guardians and whispered contemplatively: "Oh, yes, of course."

Then she told to Nolachiel: "Now, return down to Earth, where your place is. The tears of misery and pain that human being shed are of great value, believe me. Even difficult experiences in human life make sense. Through these experiences, human beings will understand the true price of invisible values. We cannot allow her to bear the arrow of Eros, as Zeus would not let us that. The price of true human tears is unspeakable. Especially of those shed for pure love. We will let the fate unfold as it is supposed to."

Psyche also came to Nolachiel: "Return to her. Believe me, you will handle everything."

Nolachiel had no power to oppose. She bowed and left the palace.

As she walking thoughtfully on the path to the gate of Eros's palace, she encountered Eros himself in the garden. He addressed her immediately, as he noticed her wounded wings and sadness in her face. He recognized, that Nolachiel was the guardian of human beings. Eros had beautiful golden curly hair, sky blue eyes, and beautifully shaped full lips. He was wearing a white silky habit adorned with little golden stars. The hem of the habit was adorned with a golden fringe. The habit was short and tied by a golden belt around the waist.

As soon as he saw Nolachiel, he asked: "What happened to your wings, and why are you so sad? Angels can't comfort people when they are sad themselves indeed!"

So, the fate arranged that Eros learned about that unpretentious ordinary woman before he came to his mother and Psyche. Nolachiel started talking and showed Eros the unfortunate stone of fate belonging to that woman as well. Eros was touched by her appeal and then he asked: "But how is that related to your sadness and wounded wings?"

Nolachiel sunk her eyes and whispered: "I am sad for I have failed, Eros. Her eyes shed so many tears in the past. Finally, she managed to fulfill some of her dreams. She does not need some unreal desire. For what? You know, that salt fumes of tears are dangerous to us angels. When I wanted to get to her and help her, the salty mist nearly burnt my wings. I can't fly, even here I had to be brought by Zephyrus."

Eros thought for a moment and he recalled that Zephyrus used to bring Psyche to him. He did not know why himself, but suddenly he decided to arrange that the ordinary woman would at least get a chance. He was aware of how much he would risk by opposing his mother Aphrodite, Zeus, and Psyche as well. But he liked the prayer of that woman because she was begging for his happiness, not for hers. After a while, he said to the angel: "What is real and unreal, Nolachiel? Yes, I know, famous people are almost like us, the Olympians gods. Ordinary people cannot come close to them or us. We will at least give her a chance. You must keep the secret and we will act faster than them!"

"What are you hinting at, Eros? Your mother and Psyche are searching right now!"

Eros smiled mysteriously: "I know, I know. That is exactly why we have to hurry up."

Nolachiel sighed with apprehension: "Eros, what do you actually want to do?"

He leaned towards Nolachiel, pointed at the palace, where his mother, Psyche, and six helpers were searching strenuously and whispered: "They don't want to ignore a few stones of her fate. Hence, we will try to have her appeal come true, even if only partially. We shall see how she handles the possibility of free will. Every part of a human being's life is accompanied by love, whether the people are looking for it at a given time, whether they want to forget about it, or whether they are experiencing its wonderful days. Love pursues people at every turn. Love has precious and great power. The healing angels heal with it the scars left on the hearts of people from bad deeds. Love is in fact a great sacrifice. A human being is ready to do deeds of love – Deeds of Pearls for a beloved person."

"But how do you want to arrange all this, and even faster than Aphrodite and Psyche? They are thousands of kilometers apart; he is not an ordinary man and—"

Eros interrupted her: "The god of prophecy will help us. We will meet with Apollo; he will advise something. He has the prophetess Pythia as well. At first, we must repair your wings and then we need to find the ingredients for the love potion. We will get them at the Petal fairy's palace. She is peculiar, but she will help us."

Nolachiel was startled: "Petal fairy? That fairy with whom Zeus is constantly angry with, for she rebels all the time and does not obey the rules? If I am not mistaken she had Hephaestus to fill her breasts to make them bigger. Then Zeus ordered her to remove the filling, but she did not obey. Therefore, he banned her to cross the borders of Olympus. Now, she lives close to t Earth on the border with the world of dark rulers."

"Yes, yes, that is exactly her. She revolted against Zeus, who appreciates natural beauty only. He expelled her. She is not that bad though." Nolachiel laughed quietly and Eros continued: "I think, she will help us. I will call Zephyrus."

Nolachiel asked fearfully: "What about Zeus? Won't he find out?"

"He will but don't worry, we have some time, he has other more important things to take care of. Since he entrusted Aphrodite with this task, he will be interested only in how she solves it."

Eros was consoling himself, and while he, Zephyrus, and Nolachiel were flying to Petal Fairy, Zeus, the ruler of Olympus, was looking into an Omni seeing sphere, where he observed Eros and what he was just about to do. He smiled to himself.

"The god of love has forgotten that Zeus doesn't miss anything. Well, it seems everything is going as I have expected. We shall see which of the two groups will win."

In the meantime, Zephyrus carried Nolachiel and Eros over to their destination. They were all shocked by the look of the Petal fairy's house. It was loud red, in places loud pink, just like some bawdyhouses on Earth. They noticed that the house shook from time to time. Eros told Nolachiel: "Out of all gods, only Hades, the ruler of Underworld, lives so low."

As they walked in, Petal fairy was sitting at the table reading tarot cards. Her plump breasts caught Eros's attention instantly and he blushed.

Petal fairy had thick raven-black, wavy hair, and big, blue eyes. Her mouth was just made for sinful kisses. She was simply wickedly beautiful. On the other hand, Nolachiel spotted a pile of various witchcraft books and books about magic. She glanced down the Petal fairy's dress and immediately realized what was going on. She understood, why the house was shaking. Her dress, once wonderfully pink, not only lost its shine, but it was not plain pink anymore. Here and there grey spots were striking through it.

Nolachiel shouted desperately: "Petal fairy, you are falling down, you must stop right away! We are banned from telling the future. Only god Apollo and Pythia may do that! What about those books? Don't you know, it is not allowed?"

Eros only smiled, Petal fairy finally spoke: "I knew you would come, the cards told me that. What brings you here? Nobody comes from Olympus here anymore; I am not welcome up there." Poor Eros, was backing up as she moved as close to him as possible so he could see her cleavage. He turned red like a lobster.

He remarked diplomatically and attempted to free himself from Petal fairy's captivity: "They are nice and big."

Petal fairy laughed. "Don't worry, Psyche can't see you here. So, spit it out, what you need?"

As Eros has not caught his breath yet, Nolachiel told Petal fairy everything. She was listening with interest and said: "I like the story. If they meet, I will like it even better. Hmm, so first we will heal your wings, and then we will look for herbs for the love potion. The fact that I will heal your wings doesn't mean you will be able to keep her desire inside her heart. In her case, only Apollo's flame of faith may help."

Then Eros asked: "What about the herbs, will you give them to us?"

Petal fairy winked at Eros and said lasciviously: "It won't be for free though, as I will drudge twice as much to get these dumb herbs here. We are already close to the underworld and it is cold here, hence they don't thrive here much. However dill seeds grow here the best. They enhance physical attraction."

Nolachiel laughed. "Orange tree flowers that intensify the tolerance and affinity in the potion thrive here less, don't they?"

Petal fairy sighed: "Come with me and find out yourselves."

Eros, Nolachiel, and Petal fairy entered the garden, where various herbs were growing in a sky-blue soil. At the first sight, everything seemed to thrive. At the very end of the garden, an orange tree was growing, and it was covered with buds, which were about to blossom. Nolachiel cried out: "They are going to blossom indeed! Why did you say the herbs do not thrive here? They are beautiful!"

Eros calmed the angel down: "Haven't you noticed that they ought to be protected from the cold? We are too low and that is bad for the plants. It is so because the beneficial heat from the higher spheres cools down as it descends."

Petal fairy added: "Since Zeus expelled me here, the orange tree has not blossomed even once. As soon as it gets covered with buds, the buds fade on the other day. I have tried all kinds of things. I strive to provide heat and moisture for them, but it doesn't help. Fortunately, I have enough of comfrey and marigold for your wings."

Eros was watching with interest the angel helping the Petal fairy to pick the plants for her wounded wings. Then, as they were picking the herbs for the love potion, Petal fairy remarked: "You have arrived in the nick of time. The orange tree's buds would have faded tomorrow."

Nolachiel was curious.

"As if the fate wanted them to meet after all, However, the love potion with orange tree buds only. Will it work as it is supposed to?"

Before Petal fairy could replay Eros remarked: "I am afraid we will be the first to try that out, right Petal fairy?"

She explained: "Not only the first but also the last. As you have noticed, I am sinking lower and lower. I think I won't be here next time. I am glad, that my last good deed will be for you, Eros. I have refused to adapt to the rules of Zeus, and that is a breach of Olympian laws. That is punished by Zeus, whether it is down on Earth or in Olympus."

Petal fairy became silent and Nolachiel began to convince her heartily: "So please, succumb. You have a very good heart. I don't want you to fall in completely! You don't deserve such a cruel punishment!"

Petal fairy calmed her down: "Don't worry. I know what I am up to, but I won't give up my cards and luscious curves. I don't want to surrender; I won't escape Zeus's punishment."

Nolachiel cried out: "I thought Zeus was good, but he is cruel!"

Eros silenced her: "Zeus knows what he is doing. If he tolerated, whether on Earth or in Olympus, repeated violation of laws, the balance of all spheres, the higher ones, and Earth as well, would be impaired. That would mean the end, do you understand?"

Nolachiel agreed: "Yes, yes, of course, I understand."

Petal fairy came to Nolachiel: "Don't worry about me. Now, we will heal your wings and prepare the love potion!"

All three retired to the house. Petal fairy prepared a medicated ointment from comfrey and marigold for the wings. She also added a bit of silk, so that the wings would recover the strength to fly as soon as possible. Once she applied the ointment on the wings of Nolachiel, they stretched and started shine immediately.

Nolachiel cried happily: "I can fly again! Petal fairy, you are amazing! As far as I know, the healing takes longer under normal circumstances! How did you manage to do that?"

Petal fairy only laughed, and Eros noted seriously: "Petal fairy was the right hand of my mother, Aphrodite. I think she misses her the most."

Nolachiel waved her wings joyfully and Petal fairy told her: "I prepared more of this ointment. You'd better take it; you might need it. Long months may pass down on Earth, but that will equal only one day here in Olympus. Time has different measures here."

Eros took thought: "That means we have to ask Apollo for a little more of the flame of faith. We would not make it without it. The flame of faith is energy with which humans realize their goals and dreams."

Suddenly, the whole house shook again, Petal fairy whispered: "We must hurry up, for really I don't know how long my house will stand! Well, Eros, it is time to learn to prepare the love potion. What if by any chance you will need it again?"

Eros smiled. "Do you think I will risk my neck for some other strange, crazy love again? Zeus is unhappy with me as well, but I am happy to learn something."

Nolachiel was appalled.

"Petal fairy, I thought the potion might be prepared only by Aphrodite! It is strange that you know the recipe."

"Don't speculate that much and watch as well! It will come handy for you too!"

The angel and Eros watched Petal fairy, as she commenced brewing the love potion in a copper kettle. While Petal fairy was dosing the herbs, she spoke: "Three parts of linden flower, a pinch of mandrake, one part of ginseng, and finally, two parts of orange tree flowers. Since we have only buds, we will add a little more of them. I have almost forgotten about the dill seed!"

The petal fairy stirred all herbs and added water collected from roses during the full moon. As she was stirring and both Eros and Nolachiel were observing her, she suddenly took a handful of dill seeds and poured them into the potion as well. The potion started to bubble strongly so much that a little bit of the potion spilled out of the copper kettle. Petal fairy said to explain: "Since we have too little of orange tree flowers that enable the affinity of souls, we will substitute them with the dill seed. That will guarantee at least a great passion and affinity of bodies."

Eros only laughed and Nolachiel spoke with concern: "Do you think such potion will serve its purpose? After all, the potion was meant to help him perceive somewhat more superior nuances of love not only the body and matter. We are going to attack only his body again."

Eros objected: "It is important to give her a chance to gain more time to get closer to his heart. The potion will stop working after some time anyway. Euphoria will die out and then she will have to manage herself."

Petal fairy finished; and said: "The love potion is only to stupefy him a little at the beginning so that she is able to get to him at all. If she fails to get somewhat close to his soul, the dill seed will make them have a lot of fun!"

Nolachiel shook her head in dissent: "If they only have fun, she will be only one of his trophies, nothing else."

"She will get a chance. Fate is only one of many options. Human beings have free will" Said Eros.

Nolachiel defended her protégé: "She did not pray for herself, but for him though."

Eros calmed the angel down: "I know, I know. That is why I decided we should at least try to give her a chance. Now, let's stop thinking about it, we are running out of time. We must see Apollo yet. Petal fairy, hurry up with the potion!"

Petal fairy explained: "Dear Eros, have a little more patience. The potion has to boil for half an hour and then it is ready. By the way, we haven't agreed yet, what I will get for my willingness to help you. Don't forget that willingness is paid for here in the lower spheres."

Eros turned pale, for he knew right away, what Petal fairy had in mind. She continued lasciviously, and what she said to Eros took Nolachiel's breath away: "I know it would be a vain effort to ask you to spend a night or even two with me. You are so madly in love with your Psyche that not even my new curves attract you. Even a single kiss from the god of love will satisfy me." Nolachiel started to laugh quietly. Eros gave a bothered look, approached the Petal fairy, and kissed her on her mouth lightly. Petal fairy obviously was not satisfied, as she put down a copper ladle which she was stirring the potion, pulled herself close to Eros tightly, and kissed him on the lips passionately. Nolachiel resourcefully started to stir potion so that it would not boil over and turned away decently.

Petal fairy was excited. "This was the most amazing kiss of my life. Stupid me, I should have given you the love potion as well. My own recipe – pure dill seed with mandrake. Even your stubborn fidelity to Psyche wouldn't help you."

When Eros was able to speak again, he said: "What a luck you figured it out only now. No secret is safe in Olympus. Poor Psyche would be devastated if she learned that I kissed you."

Nolachiel spoke in defense of Eros: "If it is disclosed incidentally, I will gladly testify how it happened."

Then all three laughed. When the love potion was ready, the Petal fairy poured it into a bottle of dark-pink glass. She handed the bottled and told him: "Let us hope, this botchy potion will work at least a bit. Although everyone carries the love potion hidden in their hearts. It is a pity that only a few human beings are aware of that."

Thereupon Eros and Nolachiel parted with Petal fairy. Eros called Zephyrus and before they flew away, Eros thanked the her once again: "Thank you for your help. We couldn't do anything without you!"

Petal fairy spoke with a laugh: "I have helped because in some loving relationships people are guided by uncontrollable emotion. Love is the most powerful magic. Every time two lovers are unified into one body; they give away their whole hearts and bodies. That is, they never know if this unity was not the last one. After each love relationship, very strong memory remains in the human mind. People are then inspired by these memories. Just look into human history. You will see how many artists drew inspiration for their works from love."

Eros and Nolachiel listened tensely and they parted: "What you said is really true. I am starting to doubt, whether it is worth helping that woman," sighed Eros.

Petal fairy's house shook abruptly, she urged them: "Go now. I hope you haven't forgotten to take the ointment for the wings."

Nolachiel said with tears in her eyes: "Don't worry, we have everything, the potion, and ointment. Petal fairy, don't you want to change your mind? We will miss you a lot. I will try to put in a world for you with Aphrodite!"

Petal fairy noted weightily: "After you will do what you are planning to do, you will have hard times with yourself because Aphrodite will be angry with you as well. You are about to breach the law and the violation is punished here in Olympus—"

Eros interrupted them: "We have to go. Apollo is waiting for us. Goodbye, Petal fairy!"

Zephyrus grabbed the angel and Eros and took off. Petal fairy shouted after them: "Goodbye, Eros. I think we will meet once again! You have also slipped many times. If you succeed in what you have planned, you may start falling down here as well! You are so lucky that you are the god of love, as more troubles are pardoned to you than to us fairies! Goodbye!"

Petal fairy walked into her house. Zephyrus flew away with Eros and Nolachiel. He brought them to the gardens of Apollo. They entered into Apollo's palace, who was waiting for them impatiently. He was the god of prophecy; he already knew everything. The prophetess Pythia, who lived in his palace, revealed that to him.

"Finally, you managed to leave in the nick of time. The Petal fairy's house disappeared shortly after you had left."

Nolachiel asked sadly: "Petal fairy! Oh, she sunk lower! What will happen to her now?"

Apollo consoled her: "Well, the messenger of gods, Hermes arrived to save her. Zeus has forgiven her because Aphrodite herself requested her help. As Eros has already told you, there is no more skilled fairy that understands herbs in Olympus than her."

Eros was pleased: "That is great, thank you, mom!" Eros thanked Aphrodite aloud.

Then Apollo said seriously: "Well, we know, why you are here. But in spite of that, I would like to have a look at the stone of fate of that woman."

The guardian angel of that woman, now with healed wings, handed the translucent stone of fate, to Apollo. He looked at it without saying a word. After a while, he said seriously: "I will help her. You are an expert in twisted relationships, right? Actually, I shouldn't help you, you have stirred up trouble for me with Daphne, and Cassandra also didn't care about her promise. But it is gone now."

Eros sunk his eyes with guilt, for appearance sake, and begged: "Forgive me. I thought unhappy love was hard to handle only for female souls. But, it is my job, to shoot my arrows."

Nolachiel was surprised.

"I wonder why Psyche has not taught you that already a long time ago. Male souls only pretend not to suffer. They suffer, but they don't talk about it as much as women do. They hide their sorrow—"

Apollo interrupted them: "Let us not analyze these things here now. Time is pressing on us."

At last, they followed Apollo to the most important room in the palace. They were ascending to one of the four towers on a spiral staircase. The towers were colored differently, each had one color related to one of the four basic elements: red for fire, blue for water, grey for air, and green for the earth. Each element ruled over one of the four parts that were related to the human being. Water ruled the emotions, fire the action, air the mind, earth the body. As prophecy and predicting the future were related to intuition, which in turn to emotions, Pythia was in the blue tower. When they came in, she was sitting on a triple stool against one wall that resembled the cave she once had in Delphi. On the walls of a dark blue color was depicted a sky with twelve signs of the western zodiac. The shelves in the room were filled with several oracle books and tools. There were various types of oracle cards, runes, pendulums, many precious gems, and crystal spheres of different sizes. But the most important in the whole room was the wheel of fate, guarded by the goddess of fate. Tyche. Gray hair, tied with a grey ribbon, narrow lips, and steel-blue eyes, that is how the wise goddess of fate looked like. The wheel of fate was constantly twirling and lightning with four colors of basic elements flashed from it. In the center were the symbols of yin and yang, which meant the male and female side. Around the wheel of fortune were the twelve signs of the western zodiac. While in trance, Pythia shouted prophecies, and Tyche translated them into understandable language. By the power of her thoughts, the prophecies were written in the Book of the Living souls. Tyche's clothing was in pearly grey color that symbolized the mystery of the human soul.

Nolachiel wondered: "Apollo, you don't need all these tools indeed. You have the gift of vision, and Pythia as well. Why you need all this?"

In the meantime, as Eros sat on a chair, Apollo began to explain: "From here some woman on earth took inspiration for centuries and they still do. Once upon a time, when Earth was not so immoral, people were allowed to look into their future. However, with the increasing of evil on Earth, it fell closer to the dark rulers and those clairvoyant women unwittingly began to feed not only on bright but also on dark creatures. They started using evil, so we received orders to warn them not to look into the future. In fact, a woman with a gift or ability of seeing a little bit of the future is exposing herself to direct danger in these, for Earth, such difficult times. I mean the human soul cannot distinguish from where these prophecies are coming from. You know well how little people believe in intuition and heart. They find it unreasonable and sometimes crazy to hear the voice of the heart or the intuition. They don't develop those features and therefore they resort to fortune-telling."

Eros took thought: "You are right, but people have always been fascinated with finding answers to their own future."

Apollo contemplated: "Yes, but it is not necessary. Each individual shapes his own fate by his thoughts, deeds, and decisions. For this time, we will break the rules again."

Eros asked surprised. "What do you mean, Apollo?"

Nolachiel understood immediately, what Apollo had in mind.

"You want to use dreams, don't you? They are not that dangerous."

"Yeah, that is exactly what I have in mind!" confirmed Apollo, and Eros turned to the angel:

"At first you must help Nolachiel, I hope, she can get a bit of the flame of faith."

Apollo nodded.

"Yes, of course, because a very long and painful journey between shadows of her aching soul riddled with sadness is awaiting her."

Nolachiel asked sadly: "Is it really necessary that she must fight for such a long time?"

Thereupon Eros explicated: "Every fragment of a dream is fought over for a very long time in human life. When people start asking for something, they have to fight for it. In their long journey to realize their dreams, they acquainted better with the dark side of their soul. They commence to perceive things around them, which they didn't see before. It is as if they woke up from a deep sleep and their blindness began to vanish."

Then Apollo added: "If people were given everything they wanted without struggle, they wouldn't manage to prepare themselves in order to be able to utilize properly a wish that comes true. They would take wishes, prayers, and dreams coming true for granted. Well, I think it's time to ask Pythia for their future. It will clarify a lot of us, so that we know, how to start."

Apollo approached Pythia. She was an old woman, who was not quite the most alluring. He took a vessel of a crystal-clear diamond from the table, in which there was a mixture of herbs that induced Pythia into a trance. Only Apollo knew the recipe and he always prepared it himself. Then he passed the stone of fate to Pythia without a word. As soon as Pythia, dressed in a brown habit fringed with a black order, inhaled the vapor of herbs, she started shouting incomprehensible words, which Tyche inscribed down on scrolls instantly. Tyche didn't speak almost at all. She was fully concentrated on her task. When she did speak, it always concerned a very serious matter. That is also why she disregarded Eros and Nolachiel when they entered the room. The prophetess Pythia became silent, all three waited a while for Tyche to finish the scrolls. In a moment, the goddess of fortune handed Apollo commenced reading the prophecies out.

First, he took the first scroll, which stated, "The prophecy for him: Fire that reopens old wounds shall come again, first its heat will turn into madness bewitch, but when the passion begins to burn too much again, and the annihilating flame turns into love, he shall…"

Apollo took the second scroll into his hand and continued: "She shall go astray, she wants to know forbidden, she knows what she is looking for, she takes pieces of dreams together with the invisible gifts she carries for him…"

When Apollo finished reading, he did not say a word. Suddenly, Tyche spoke in a premonitory voice: "The passion can be very dangerous."

Then she looked at Eros. Nolachiel sighed: "Maybe we should let it all be. The prophecy did not tell us much."

Apollo demurred: "It is too late. All prophecies have already been written in the Book of Living Souls. Tyche works fast. There is nothing left to be done but start acting."

Eros remarked: "Only now I realized, what will happen. We will finish it. We have to send her a sign though."

Nolachiel asked: "How? I hope not through cards!" Apollo was appalled.

"Oh, not that! You know, that tarot cards are dangerous! We will use a dream. Such a dream interpretation she will not find in any dream book. The message will be encrypted, but it will be tailored for her."

Apollo continued more calmly: "Well, I am going to prepare the flame of faith and you have to go down to the underworld. Hypnos will prepare a dream for her. Come with me."

Eros and Nolachiel thanked the prophetess and Tyche, who were not paying much attention to them anymore and, in the meantime returned to their task. In addition to inscribing the prophecies in the Book of Living Souls Tyche would add the human experiences in it. Prophecies could often change, because of human beings' free will. The most significant experiences were kept in the human mind in form of memories. They were kept on endless plantations in the form of translucent balls. Angels dressed in white clothes took care of the balls. The memories of people were guarded until their death. In the moment of death, a person was allowed to view them once again, and then almost all of them perished much like the material body. Only a few of them remained intact for endless years. When a human being would come back to Earth, he would forgets about his previous life. If he would remember something important from previous lives, it will be enabled to him. It is so, for the burden of a single life is too heavy for human beings. They would not be able to carry the burdens from their previous lives as well. On the journey through life, he should seek his spiritual mission to do good deeds.

Eros with Nolachiel followed Apollo to the red tower related to fire, which represented action. When they walked in, their eyes rested in a room decorated in light-orange to red. In the middle, there was a vessel made of a strange material that resembled gold, but it was not gold. A yellow-red flame was burning in the vessel. Such a strong blaze was coming from it that they had to cover their eyes. It blinded them completely.

Apollo explained: "I am sorry, I completely forgot to warn you that not everyone can look directly in the flame of faith. Without this flame, which blinded you so, the life on Earth would cease to exist. If people would not be getting the energy of flame, they would cease to strive to act. The cycle of life would stop. The hope is driving them forward. Without it, they would remain still and the flow of life would stop."

Eros and Nolachiel turned their eyes away from the wonderful glaze and looked up. Only now an incredible spectacle arose. They realized that the tower had no roof. A yellow-orange line was coming from the vessel continuously flowing out down to Earth. It looked like a surging fountain of light. This light was not only coming out but they noticed that a blaze darker than the one flowing out was flowing in.

Nolachiel said in amazement: "Apollo, I had no idea that the flame was so magnificent."

Eros told her roguishly: "You don't get a chance to see something like that every day. You are looking after people on Earth, and you don't have so many opportunities to look into the flame of faith. Only when, for instance, like now you can't cope with the human concerns yourselves. Appreciate what you have been allowed to see."

Apollo also explained: "Everyone, who sees the flame of faith is stunned by this sight. It is a pity we have had more worries lately. Earth and some other worlds in this level of the universe have been seized by the evil. Since people have forgotten to love one another, evil of all kind spread a lot. The flame of faith started to be misused together with the free will for evil and harmful things. For instance, if people rediscovered the true selfless love, they would stop killing each other. People are driven by the desire for material matters and the flame of faith turns into evil in their hands. This ill processed energy from the flame of faith cannot return to the vessel. It sinks down to the dark rulers. If you have a better look, you will see that there is less blaze processed to good. Zeus is afraid that if people don't learn to love again, they won't receive any energy from the flame of faith anymore."

Eros asked: "What will happen to the flame of our woman, what if her blaze won't return? For we actually don't want to help her to leave a wasteland behind her!"

Apollo objected: "Don't forget about free will. She will get the flame, but she will decide, how she will use it. People can resist the prophecies and their fate as well."

Nolachiel took thought: "That means when she will have that dream, everything may be different if she understands it."

Apollo nodded.

"Don't forget that the wheel of fortune also means change. Good or bad. When people understand its meaning, they will let the wheel be and will find the way out of it. For they will realize that events take turns in human life. Good ones are followed by bad ones and vice versa."

Eros finished: "In exceptional cases when the human spirit is completely blinded by negative emotions, the number of negative experiences will increase disproportionally compared to the good ones. It is not divine punishment. It's a possibility of waking up a sleeping man. He will begin to think about life and seek answers. When he begins to wake up, it hurts. As he starts to forgive and love, the good events will return. People are creators of their realities. Thoughts and emotions are powerful."

Eros and Nolachiel observed Apollo capturing some of the flames of faith and close it in a dark red vessel, which he handed to Nolachiel. "Guardian angels are given the flame of faith into their hands only in certain cases. People mostly receive it directly from the source. It also happens, when they begin to emit great volition due to the desire. That happened to your protégé. Now you must go. Take the scrolls with the prophecies. Hypnos will create a dream according to them."

All three walked out of the tower and Nolachiel begged: "Apollo, I would like to see the other two towers as well. Who knows when I will get here again."

"We don't have time, we must go. Besides, Psyche is waiting for me. She will find it strange that I haven't returned yet."

Apollo told Nolachiel: "You might come here again, but I will at least tell you, what is in the other two towers. They don't have a roof either. Reason rules in the tower belonging to the element of air. Grey energy that flows from it down to Earth controls intellect and reason. However, if people receive too much of it, an unbalance may occur. Emotions will be numbed in the human being. The last tower belongs to the fourth element, the earth. It controls the growth of substance, fertility, and welfare. Green energy that flows from it, enables the growths, development, and reproduction. On the other hand, if there is too much of this energy, humans will become obsessed with the pursuit of gathering abundant material objects, will cease to use the reason and emotions evenly. They will gather blindly until they will forget completely, what they need the material matters for."

Eros added: "Unfortunately, people create unbalance when they utilize these energies, because of their free will and polarity. That is to say, there is an emotion, intuition, and thought at the beginning. That is the blue energy, the energy of emotions. A human being starts to process it and decides to implement it. He will make up or find a proper method of its performance using the grey energy of reason. When he finds the method, he will commence to act. For that, he needs the most important energy – the flame of faith. He attempts to materialize the thought and desire. That is when the time comes to employ the green energy of the earth. At the end of the endeavor, he collects the fruit of his effort."

Apollo continued: "The materialization of the thought is not always successful. So, when people on Earth don't manage to materialize their dreams, the supply of flame of faith will stop and man will cease to act. However, if the thought was positive, a part of the energy from the flame would return. The unprocessed energy from negative thoughts sinks down to the lower spheres, for it is useless up here. The sequence of utilizing the energy of elements should be at least partially balanced in people."

"Why?" asked Nolachiel, who knew all the rules of Olympus indeed, but did not have the time to explore them in detail.

"I will explain it to you. For instance, if people are receiving too much blue energy of feelings and emotions, they only meditate and dream, their life doesn't satisfy them, as they experience everything only in their thoughts. These are dreamers, who complain they have nothing. Instead of trying to materialize some dreams, they pity themselves and expect that everything will come their way by itself. Those who contemplate and consider everything realistically can't process the energy of emotions by reason and the grey energy takes control over them, which prevents them from creating new dreams and thoughts. Those people turn into cold-hearted thinking machines, which have forgotten that not everything cannot be done with reason only and they are no longer capable of receiving the signs of intuition. They live day by day like machines, while they forget to see not only with eyes but also with heart. Well, and those who concentrate too much on material goods, they hoard more and more. They firstly forget why or whom they need to gather and then they cease to think rationally. For they don't know what to do with so many material goods anymore. They continue hoarding. Without emotion and without reason."

Nolachiel was listening with interest and Eros added: "Then the energy from the flame is not always processed as it should and unbalance arises."

Nolachiel contemplated: "It has occurred to me that there are many people on Earth, in whom too big volume of all energies is concentrated. Those are the people, who belong to the higher spheres of Earth. All the famous people, high ranked people, celebrities."

Eros affirmed: "The common mortals envy them naively, as they seemingly have everything. They may have many admirers and receive much of blue energy of emotions through them. Due to the fact that they are ranked high, their life becomes very difficult. They have too much of grey energy of reason from people, who manage their lives. By being on the top, they also receive extra green energy from their too large amount of material goods. Therefore, it takes them twice as much effort to stay on the top. That means also more energy of action and extra energy of the flame of faith."

Eros became silent and Apollo continued: "No wonder it is sometimes impossible for such a famous person to process so much energy. His being starts to shake and he becomes a time bomb. An explosion is imminent. That is what happens in most cased indeed. The bomb explodes. The person cannot bear the explosion of energies. Out of a sudden, he wants to make as much use of everybody as possible. This person trying to exploit the excess of all energies in the form of immoral behavior. However, when the flame of faith is mistreated this way, the energy from it does not return up but sinks down instead. The famous person is basically thrown upon the mercy of his darker side of the soul, which every human being has."

Nolachiel was startled: "Why this happens to the famous or high-ranked people?"

Apollo answered: "It is very simple. Money rules on Earth now. It is behind everything. With money people can afford everything they want. In spite of that, when some of those people awaken, they discover the reason for their great misery. Because despite the exuberance of everything, they find out they lack the most important thing. True pure love. It cannot be bought for all the wealth of the world. Since they are popular, suddenly everybody wants to be near them, but mostly only for fame and money. Some of those people know that. They do not trust anyone. They retire into themselves and compensate for the desire for true love with quick love with as many partners as possible. Today, this kind of love is such a common thing on Earth, that nobody thinks about the fact that only physical satisfaction occurs. The soul is unsatisfied and its hunger becomes more and more urgent. It is easy to numb this hunger with some drugs and alcohol. This whole carousel is spinning around ceaselessly. Fortunately, this does not happen to all people."

Apollo added: "Maybe who did not stop to appreciate the higher spheres for their dreams coming true can cope better with such dreadful life with no privacy and freedom. All people beg a lot and thank little."

Nolachiel asked with sadness in her voice: "Is there hope for people? That they will extricate themselves from this chaos of Earth?"

Apollo explained: "Well, there is a simple answer to this question. They must learn to love and pursue love again. When they discover its true nature, it will fill them with joy, which they will share with others intuitively. From this love, they will perform such deeds. They will use the energy of flame of faith properly. Such processed energy will return to the vessel. The more of it will return, the more energy of flame of faith the people will take. Fortunately, many people have already understood that. Thanks to them and their good deeds of love a balance between good and evil still exist."

Apollo concluded the conversation. Nolachiel thanked: "Thank you for your help, Apollo. Now we shall rush to Hypnos for the dream. By the way, how will I know when I should send it to my protégé?"

Apollo told her: "You will sense it yourself when the time will come. She will have the dream, and only then we will arrange their meeting."

Eros and Nolachiel parted with Apollo. Eros called Zephyrus. He was already waiting outside. Now angel Nolachiel noticed that energies were flowing down to Earth-like four-color waterfalls from the four towers of Apollo's residence. Only one waterfall was flowing in two directions: down to Earth and back to the vessel of the flame of faith. The energy of action. The energy of the flame of faith.

Nolachiel noted surprised. "Eros, how come I did not notice such beauty when we arrived?"

Eros remarked mysteriously: "Because when you entered you were blind and now you are walking out with new knowledge, you know? It happens to people on Earth often as well. They start asking and receive answers from unexpected places!"

After that response, Zephyrus transferred them to Hades, the ruler of the Underworld. Both his authority and sadness over the death radiated from his black palace. Just like Hades himself, who looked dignified and somewhat sad with his dark eyes and beard. Here in the Underworld, souls of the deceased were sorted shortly after they saw the memories of their lives in the memory plantations. A soul would carry memory balls to the scales of justice. Persephone, wife of Hades, would sort out the memories and place them on the scales shortly before boarding the boat. Good deeds to the right and bad ones to the left. The scales of justice showed accurately the side with more memories. Most human memories perish after weighing. Persephone would return the important ones back to angels in white clothing to the memory plantations. After that, each soul would board a boat according to its deeds on Earth. Ferryman Charon, the faithful servant of Hades, would transport the good souls on the river Styx to Elysian Fields, where they continued to perform the good deeds. He carries the ones, who had done much evil, in his boat of death to Tartarus. There they had to make up for their bad deeds to prepare for the possibility of a correction in the next life. The souls in the Elysian Fields would also return to Earth when they must do other tasks. Hades covered the souls going to the Elysian Fields with an Underworld mist prior to entering the boat so that they would not see the sadness in Tartarus. That is Charon would transport the souls to Tartarus first and then to the Elysian Fields. This was the cycle of life and death.

When they came to the gate, Eros said: "We have already been so close to this place today. The house of Petal fairy was nearby."

As approaching the gate, Nolachiel whispered: "I am afraid. I have never been here in the Underworld. I will rather wait for you outside, although it is cold here."

Eros objected: "Just come inside. You have already seen the higher spheres up close today. It is time to see to lower ones. People are also afraid of the transition from life to death. Some of them believe the death will put an end to everything forever. Others are afraid because they sense they will not hide their hearts here. Everyone will be given a chance to make up for the bad deeds he performed during life."

They walked through the gate. Hades came from his kingdom in the Underworld. He had no idea yet, what these two had in plan. He welcomed them surprised: "Eros, what brought you, , to this gloomy place? You are here even with one of the guardian angels! That must be something very important!"

Eros spoke in a premonitory voice choosing the words carefully so that Hades would not detect their white lie: "The god of sleep Hypnos should prepare a dream for one woman."

He was frightened Hades might be curious about the scrolls according to which Hypnos was supposed to create the dream. Strangely enough, Hades was not interested in them. He just invited them: "Well, come with me. We are going to the Underworld, although not quite there. Hypnos is the lord of sleep. He is on the very verge of life and death. He decides what kind of sleep the people on Earth are given. When their time comes, they fall asleep so deep they will not wake up on Earth. They awake in another world, here in Underworld. Some call it the another world."

Nolachiel asked with interest: "What about dreams? Why do people feel when dreaming that they have traveled all night in their dreams, while only a few minutes will pass down on Earth?"

Hades explained: "When a human being sleeps, the reason stop to act, and thus makes room for intuition and emotions only. There are different measures for time here than down on Earth. Only one day passes here, while whole weeks pass on Earth. Actually, the soul of a sleeping person travels without limits. Sometimes near my kingdom. However, it is still connected with the material body with an invisible cord. Hypnos sees to it that the soul returns to the material body in the morning again. But it takes with it the memories in the form of dreams, or at least its fragments, to the reason, to the mind. Hence the person usually remembers only the last dream, when he wakes up in the morning. Hypnos controls various kinds of sleep and dreams indeed. He may not influence how many dreams the human being will remember."

Eros deliberated: "It is related directly to the given person. If his natural intuition starts to develop, he will suppress the reason and such soul will naturally opens itself to an unthought-of insight into dreams."

He added to himself in mind: "So that is why Apollo decided to use a dream for that woman. Her desire to have an insight into the dreams will naturally open the secret door of mysteries to her ajar."

Hades opened the gate to the Underworld. A spectacle appeared that impressed Eros and Nolachiel. They felt respect. The gate of the Underworld was guarded by a three-headed dog Cerberus. He let them in with Hades without any problems. Now, they were not descending to the gate of the Underworld down the stairs, but up the stairs. The whole palace of Hades was decorated in black and grey, which evoked awe and wistfulness. The earthly journey of human beings ended here. His spirit ascended to other dimensions. Hades used the help of ethereal beings here as well as other Olympian gods. So that cycle of life was not interrupted.

Persephone was sitting on a chair – the throne of the underworld – weighing human deeds hidden in the memory balls on the scales and laid their memories of deeds on them. The scales indicated, where the spirit would go further. Many times, they awakened only in this place by the scale of justice. Here they realized what their deeds had caused on Earth. Sometimes Persephone together with Hades would watch the frightened souls, which thought nobody up there saw their evil deeds. Nolachiel wanted to greet Persephone, but Eros told her: "She does not like being disturbed at work. Just bow to her."

Nolachiel bowed to Persephone, who nodded in agreement to its sign of respect. Sadness adorned her pale, but beautiful face that looked as if it had been carved in white marble. She had dark brown hair tied with a black headband. She had nicely formed, but rigid lips and dark brown eyes. She radiated beauty despite her rigid appearance. They also greeted Charon, who was just boarding the boat to carry away another group of souls. Hades then took them further to a room, where Hypnos, the lord of sleep, was guarding the human sleep and dreams. A translucent white and grey haze was floating in the whole room decorated in grey and blue. It was making its way through a tunnel down to Earth. It was a human sleep. It could be seen from the outside as it first turned around the palace of Hades like some mist that was slowly falling on Earth. Sleep usually came to human beings at night. Sometimes sleep fell on them even by day. The lord of sleep had grey hair and a beard. He had a grey coat with black hemming. Hypnos was sitting at the table, which was also blue and grey, covered with celestial stars and constellations. Eros and Nolachiel greeted him and Hypnos stood up from his work. He had a crystal sphere on his table. He looked in it and controlled and created humans' dreams. A mysterious mist, containing sleep and humans' dreams, was raising from this crystal sphere, it passed through the roof up through a tunnel. Then it turned around the palace of Hades and finally dropped to Earth. Three Fates were sitting next to him at another table. They were weaving the length of human life waiting for the time to come to cut the string that attached the soul to the material body. The Fates were all shrouded in a black habit with a hood. Their all-white hair protruded underneath the hood and were surrounded by countless silver strings as soft as a spider web. They symbolized invisible strings that connected the soul with the body. The fates braided some of these strings further and when they received an order from the above, through Hypnos, they would cut the ones when their time had come. Hypnos would release the dreams he created along with the sleep lower to Earth, but not completely down. The dreams floated higher. The soul of a sleeping person traveled towards them during sleep. Eros asked Hypnos to create a dream for quite an ordinary woman.

Since he had to show the scrolls to Hypnos, he told him: "Hypnos, I want to help that woman behind the back of Zeus, Psyche and even my mother Aphrodite. Please, do not mention to anybody what you have seen in the scrolls."

Hypnos nodded appreciatorily as he had understood, he remarked: "I am afraid, you won't conceal it for a long time. Apollo the god of the prophecy can conceal it for a while, by not entering it in the Book of Living Souls right away, but…" Nolachiel was appalled.

"That did not occur to us! Tyche has already taken care of that. What shall we do now?"

Eros sighed: "I have taken that into account. I rely on Psyche in this case. If she notices inscribed prophecies during the search, she will know who is responsible for that as she knows me. Fortunately, she will not betray me to Aphrodite because she loves me. On the contrary, indeed, she will pretend nothing happened. She will search along with angels for appearance sake. Since Aphrodite has also other duties, she has already left for sure leaving it all to Psyche. Who would care about all those broken hearts on Earth?"

Then Hypnos read the scrolls and sank into a meditation state. He stayed like that for a few minutes. He stood up, approached a shelf full of blue vessels containing dreams, and took one of them. He came back to the table where the sphere of dreams and sleep was placed. Using magic spells, which Eros and Nolachiel did not understand, he created in his mind enigmatic symbols. He transferred them with the power of his thoughts to a piece of the mysterious haze of dream from the vessel. He put that piece into another vessel and closed it.

Nolachiel asked Hypnos: "Do you create such clairvoyant dreams for every person?" Hypnos shook his head.

"Not all people get clairvoyant dreams. Only those, who are able to comprehend them. If they awaken their intuition a little and seek answers beyond the rational explanation. The guardian angel of such a person comes here. Then I create a dream wich is the answer to that person's question. When he sees that dream he will get the answer. "

Eros thanked him and they parted. In the meantime, Hades was already sitting by Persephone. They were dealing with the souls of the deceased.

When they both bowed to them again and walked out of the Underworld, Nolachiel whispered looking at the palace of Hades around which the haze of dreams and sleep was circulating slowly: "How little people on Earth know about how much work there is up here."

Eros added: "Fortunately, everything is running smoothly. We up here must rest as well, as matter of fact. Without helpers, it would be impossible. Well, the time has come for you to return down to your warrior."

Nolachiel embraced Eros.

"Thank you so much for helping me, Eros. You risk so much for that woman!"

Eros held both her hands. "If the wish of a human being is sincere, we endeavor to fulfill it. She did not beg for herself."

Nolachiel considered: "She is so helpless... And."

"Shhh! Do not talk anymore. She will try to get closer to his heart and soul. What comes after the request is difficult to predict. People decide themselves what to do with their fates. We send signs and opportunities."

Nolachiel contemplated.

"Actually, you are right. I wanted to help her, but I am concerned, whether it is worth it. We do not even know how it is going to end."

"You heard the prophecy, haven't you?"

"I am afraid she is at a great disadvantage in spite of the prophecy. So, I better go now. You shall return to Psyche as well and explain it to her. Actually, I am to blame. Thank you, Eros, I will be waiting with her for signs from the above! When the time comes, I will send her the dream."

Nolachiel flew away to her protégé on her healed wings. Eros set out for his palace to Psyche with much apprehension. It was already dark inside when he arrived at the palace. That meant, her helpers' angels had gone to take rest and so had done Psyche. He was pleased that he did not have to explain to her anything after the exhausting day. He sneaked in quietly. He walked into a room, where they would eat divine ambrosia and drink nectar, for he wanted to refresh himself. Then he startled. Psyche sitting on a chair with her arms crossed, gave him the most furious look she was capable of. He understood immediately that she knew everything.

She yelled at him: "What are you doing, Eros!? How dare you fulfill such wishes?! When I found with horror what you had plotted with Apollo, I had to tear off their destinies from the Book of Living Souls in haste! I risk my neck here for you again, while you easily disrespect the decision of the gods!"

Psyche yelled and did not let Eros speak: "Do you realize how much you are at risk when you create another crazy, sinful relationship, from which only ruins will arise?! Why?"

When Psyche's shouting slowly turned into quite cry of fear, Eros approached her, hugged her, and whispered: "Psyche, you know, that people got a free will. We do not know, what will happen. They are creators of their realities. We are trying to fulfill their desires and dreams. They decide how they will use their opportunities."

Psyche whispered: "Maybe."

"Because she is willing to follow him among his shadows, as you followed me once, a long time ago to the Underworld to save me. That is why."

Psyche spoke silently: "Maybe it is good that you helped Nolachiel. A sacrifice for love is always very precious. However, we do not know what sort of rose will blossom in the heavenly garden on the Isle of Flowers. Yellow. Red. Pink. White. Grey."

Psyche became silent. While still holding her in his arms Eros said: "Not only bright white pearls on the Pearls Fields are diminishing. There are never enough of the precious pink tears from roses as well. Every tear, that human being sheds for love is important. You know, that angels of healing use it to heal scars on the human's hearts."

So, the stone of fate slowly started coming true. That is to say, the wish that burst from the heart will find a way of coming true. Although human beings are not always satisfied with the way it is materialized.

After some time, a beautiful being with feather wings alighted to my bed. She was holding a vessel of strange grey and blue material that looked quite like glass in her noble hands. I did not know how guardian angels look like. All that people know about them is that they have beautiful feather wings and they are gorgeous. My angel was exactly that way. A being with the face of a beautiful woman. Her hair was of light brown color and her eyes were crispy blue. They were shining with purity. Her dress was of darker pink shade. When she was floating on her feather wings, tiny stars glittered around them, which looked like tiny dots from afar. The angel with the appearance of a woman that was called Nolachiel. Although angels have not been sorted into genders, they could take the side of male or female.

Nolachiel flew down to me so that I could accept the dream while in a heavy sleep. The weirdest of all dreams I ever had. The angel Nolachiel opened the vessel, from which a greyish mist was emerging that penetrated my mind through my closed eyes. A dream made of old memories. When all the mist penetrated into the sleep, Nolachiel ascended somewhere up to the heights, where the human eye could never see, as long as it is imprisoned in the material body. The speed of her flight was unbelievable. She flew up to the palace of the god of prophecy, music, and light – Apollo.

"So, you are here, at last. Are you sure you have hit the right moment so that she would remember the dream after waking up?" asked Apollo, who was standing near the wheel of fortune that was spinning ceaselessly.

Nolachiel nodded. "Yes, of course. She will dream before the secret desire creeps into her heart." Apollo started to walk up and down the room and Nolachiel observed him.

"You know that under normal circumstances we may not interfere with the fate of people. Otherwise, they would not have the possibility to choose. If she would have the dream after meeting him, she would condemn everything connected with him in advance. This way there was the warning first, love will come later. But it will help to give her the possibility to choose. She will be thinking of that dream indeed, but since she had had it before he came, the sweet shadow of infatuation will allow to push the alert into the background."

Nolachiel stopped short: "Wait, Apollo. You want the meaning of the dream to be understood differently, right?"

"Yes. Moreover, time is important to people as well, because there is a beginning and an end on Earth. Time is different here than down on Earth. You will come back soon again. Then we may start to act. I must figure out how to arrange a fatal encounter. It must look like a coincidence. If people only knew, there is no accident in human lives. On top of that, I have told Hypnos to insert one memory into the dream. An old memory. It will help her to understand certain things. Things, which exist somewhere between heaven and Earth."

Nolachiel asked: "May I go then?"

Apollo reminded her: "Do not forget about the flame of faith. It will make her secret desire last longer than she would want it to. Without it, she will forget about him after a few weeks, but the proper time for the fatal encounter did not come yet. It will come a little later."

Nolachiel took out a vessel of scarlet-red color from the folds of her lightweight dress.

"May I get another dose, when it runs out?" Nolachiel asked.

Apollo frowned. "Try to spare it. Too much flame of faith may cause her a lot of trouble in the real life. The flame of faith takes the human soul somewhat higher. It frees it from the bonds of reasoning. The soul will gain an unprecedented flight indeed but for a too high price. So please, be careful."

Nolachiel hid the vessel again and took off. "Thank you, Apollo." She said as reaching the door of the most important room of Apollo's palace.

So, my angel Nolachiel, my guardian angel in whom I believed, moved again close to me to keep this secret desire in my heart. If the desires are very strong, although they remain unfulfilled and hidden in the secret corners of the human heart, they are still there. They wait for power. The power of the grey energy of reason, which will begin to make them true. Without action and motion, they will continue to be only dreams and fantasies. Innocent fantasies to which every human being takes recourse when it feels its real world is being filled with troubles.

Some time passed. My guardian angel Nolachiel arrived at Apollo's palace. Apollo was already waiting in the most important room where, by the wheel of fate, the Fortune wheel, the goddess of fate Tyche was sitting.

"The time to create a random encounter is approaching. Do you still have at least some of the flame of faith?"

"Not much. I should use it wisely."

"I'm going to give you some more. I hope Eros didn't lose that botched love potion and rather gave it to Psyche."

"Does Psyche know that?"

"Yes, but she wasn't excited that much. She fears what Zeus will do when he finds out about it. However, there is such chaos on Earth at the moment, that he does not know where his head stands. That is good for us now."

"I've heard that Earth has dropped a little lower, is it true?"

"Unfortunately, yes. Though there are still many good human beings and love in the world, little they care about the planet itself. Earth can no longer protect its existence and for that, it responds with natural disasters. By falling to the lower levels, it makes it easier for evil to get to power on Earth. The number of pearls in Fields of Pearls is diminishing. Zeus knows that if there are not enough of them, it won't be possible to turn away the coming government of evil in a fight."

Nolachiel asked with concern: "What fight you are talking about Apollo! Perhaps the situation can still be saved. We are doing all that is in our power to wake up love and intuition in human hearts. There is still goodness and beauty on Earth."

Apollo sighed: "It is, but the evil is spreading. Look at Earth, Nolachiel, the balance between good and evil has already been disturbed. Zeus can't wait much longer. He knows the dark rulers have a very good chance to take over Earth right now. At the order from higher levels, he ordered the angels, who care about the Fields of Pearls, to collect all the white and pink light from the pearls. That means only one thing. We will fight again. This time it will be a difficult fight because there is not enough light. I don't understand; why do we take care of Earth for centuries? I have the feeling that human beings are incorrigible. They keep repeating the same mistakes and hurt each other all over again. We have to keep cleaning the mess they create all the time."

"Zeus must also obey orders from above. You have no choice either, Apollo. And we…"

Apollo shook his head in disagreement. "We are trying to protect Earth for ages. So many times, we have turned away disasters. And human worms don't even have a clue. I would rather give it up too. Why should we save them? For what? For love? Or for them? They often misuse all the gifts they receive from us, from above."

Nolachiel tried to stand up for the people: "They received the greatest gift from the Creator. The gift of free will. With this gift, they can create reality. Be it a reality full of love or fear. If they didn't have this gift, they would no longer be able to create."

"Oh, Nolachiel, you angels have no free will, you are following the orders. We all must execute orders and adhere to the hierarchy. Sometimes I feel that the Creator has too much love for humans when he puts such a dangerous weapon in their hands. A free will."

Nolachiel tried to comfort Apollo because angel's faith in goodness of human hearts had no boundaries.

"Apollo, don't worry, you will see that everything will be fine. You know that it's the Creator's will to make people know both paths. The path of love and the path of fear. They themselves must learn to use their hearts and minds correctly. If they won't do mistakes, we in heaven would probably have no work, don't you think?"

Apollo smiled and agreed: "I admire your angelic love and belief in those good-for-nothing human worms. You're right, maybe we'd get bored here. So, let's go to work, Nolachiel, we're going to try to help create reality. Although we don't even know what it will be because of their free will."

"Do you have a plan?"

"Of course, I do, but you know how this goes. It all depends on the decisions of human beings. We have to rely on the fact that they will do the right thing with this unplanned encounter. We have no other choice."

"Apollo, let's believe that heart and intuition still have their place in human life. I do thank you for helping me. Maybe there is still some hope for humanity."

"Nolachiel, come with me, I'll give you a little bit of flame of faith. We will hope that in a few weeks that famous man will listen to his intuition and goes to the place I have chosen for him. I hope he will celebrate along with his friends the way all superstars do. With all the consequences…"

Nolachiel started to suspect where Apollo was heading.

"Apollo, do you mean a party?"

"Yes! And what a party! It is one of the largest in the country where your protégé works. This party is going to be held near her work. It's going to be a big party, and there are thousands of visitors flocking to just let the alcohol brainwash them. They will do what people do at such celebrations…painting the town red. Now, I hope, that it will work, and at this party, they will spoil everything that can be spoiled. We have to wake up that dark side in them. As soon as they start to celebrate, accidents will work for us. We must, however, notify Chasariel, the guardian angel of that famous man and his friends' guardian angels, to just keep their voices down and not earwig them the good decisions when the celebration starts. Everything will run smoothly. You know that guardian angels don't like to see when human beings ruin themselves. In such a situation they rather retreat a bit. They wait until people wake up again and call for help. At that moment, those helpers from the other dark side get the chance and they start to earwig them those bad decisions. Then, we can hope that this poisonous fluid – alcohol – will do its work. It sometimes turns human beings into easily manageable puppets who lose control over their actions."

Nolachiel listened in horror and shouted: "For God's sake, Apollo! Do you really mean that? What if something happens to them? We cannot…"

"For God's sake! Yes, that is exactly my situation Nolachiel!! Because I have let myself into this machine. When Zeus learns what I have done, Apollo will no longer exist. Shall I count to you, all the things that we will get punished for? Firstly: preparing a love potion without the boss's permission in addition to the dangerous and unverified ingredients used to make it. Secondly: the recommended dosage of used ingredients not observed. Thirdly: a high dose of the flame of faith. Fourthly: illegal use of magic against a human being who won't have the chance to defend himself. We are going to use this imperfect love potion, even though we don't know how it will work. Fifthly: illicit manipulation and interference with human destinies caused by illicit corrupt practices. We are about to ask the most loyal and the gentlest creatures, the angels, to keep their voices down for a while, just to make some other human beings make few foolish things. I have not even figured out, how to bribe these beings, that are incapable of being bribed. Shall I continue?"

Nolachiel nodded: "Oh, Apollo, it's terrible. We better stop this."

Apollo disagreed: "Nolachiel, we won't give up. Look, maybe after the war with these hell creatures, nothing will survive. Neither the heavens nor the Earth. Why shouldn't I help someone to get at least a chance before all that happens? It's not our fault that this famous man lives on the earthly Olympus. So, we have to improvise. But as you can see, we've already gotten ourselves into trouble."

"Apollo, I believe it's all good. Don't be upset. Maybe you are also missing love. The solitude does not do you well."

"For that, I can thank Eros. Crazy god who shoots arrows as he wants. Well, let's go to work, Nolachiel, you know what to do. Go to Psyche and see, she has that botched potion. We will go to the other side of the Earth to beg a couple of guardian angles not to fulfill their duties for a couple of hours in the future. Oh, I feel sick from myself. How deep I have fallen."

"Apollo, surely it won't be as bad with you as with the planet Earth. Sometimes even we have to improvise."

"Go, Nolachiel, go. Since Zeus didn't send his lightning on me, means he either does not know yet or he does not have time to deal with such petty affairs."

Nolachiel smiled. "He is trying to save the Earth so we can do our work, Apollo. Otherwise, we'll be bored and polishing pearls on the Fields of Pearls or watering heavenly flowers on the Heavenly Islands of Flowers. That would be too boring for me. What about you?"

"You're right, helping to create people's reality is an interesting job. Only if they didn't have such stupid and crazy desires occasionally. In such cases, we are forced to improvise and violate the rules."

Nolachiel agreed. "Well, sometimes things like that must happen. Don't worry, you will see, everything is as it should be. Zeus is now busy with gathering the army and light from pearls for the upcoming fight. We still have some time."

Apollo knew it was not true.

In the meantime, Zeus was going through the pages of the Book of life and was smiling. His wife, Hera, asked: "What's so funny about the upcoming disaster?"

Zeus didn't cease to smile and asked her: "Which disaster do you mean? The one that the Earth is falling down or the one that crazy Apollo has nothing else to do than to help that damn Eros in creating an unusual reality and violating all the basic rules of Olympus?"

"Zeus, this is not funny! Neither one! We don't have much time. We don't have enough pearls. We don't have enough of their light. We can't save the Earth and you are laughing? What will we do?"

Zeus took her hands and said nobly: "Faith, Hera. We have to have faith. In love and light."

"You won't punish Apollo? Everyone at Olympus is starting to do what they want, and you won't do something about it? Apollo could not fall deeper. What an idea of bribing guardian angels! That is totally unacceptable!"

Zeus shrugged his shoulders: "On Earth, people bribe all the time... And what? Apollo is desperate because he really does not want to fight. Apollo was never at ease when Earth got out of control and we got the order from above that we must interfere and fight for it. He can't understand why history must be repeated and people don't learn from it. That's why he decided to help in creating such a crazy dream. Actually, why not? Nobody wants to hurt or kill anybody in that dream. So why can't Apollo try?"

Hera shook her head in disagreement.

"What if something happens to these poor people at that party? Who will be responsible for that?"

"Hera, don't worry, we'll protect them. As I know Apollo, certainly he has a backup plan, plan B, if something goes wrong."

"Plan B? You and your damn plans B! I can see how all this will end! Does Aphrodite know what is happening? Or have you left her poor searching for a suitable female to carry Eros' arrow? What about that regular love potion that you allowed her to use for that arrow? Does she have it?"

"She does not... She does not... She's still searching for it. Let her search. In the meantime, we will observe how Apollo and Eros will be losing their heads over how to mitigate the effects of the poison that Petal fairy has created."

Hera was surprised.

"Poison? What do you mean?"

Zeus explained significantly: "Hera, love potions don't create love. The greatest magic, the real love on Earth and the heavens is the greatest miracle, and none of us, except the Creator, know exactly how it is created and how it works. Love potion just gives a little push at first. But then, when its effect ceases, it is only upon human beings whether they want to continue and try to move to higher levels of love from the initial enchantment. Even at the cost of occasional suffering. The moment when the initial enchantment fades away is decisive. Most of the short love stories crumble at this point."

Hera was concerned.

"So, you will just leave these unfortunates to do what they are doing behind your back?"

"Don't worry. Nothing bad can happen from love. Few more broken hearts at the most. As we know, rarely somebody dies because of that."

"How do you want to heal those other broken hearts when the number of pink pearls is diminishing? We don't have enough pink pearls, so they can't change to the pink light that angels use to heal the scars of these broken hearts. Moreover, on the Islands of Flowers, where roses blossom the precious dew is missing. Pink tears of human beings who understand the power of the sacrifice in love is also diminishing."

"Oh, you women, you see problems everywhere even before they are created! Look, if something happens, we will find a solution. Even now we are forced to improvise because there is lack of love on Earth. And so far, we have been successful."

Hera disagreed: "Look at poor Apollo! Look what your male improvisations and last-minute solutions did to him. And their crazy reality has not even begun yet. I am curious how you will improvise when it all falls apart, and Apollo will run out of all his B plans."

Zeus said in a quiet voice: "What will happen will happen. I will come up with something. At the end of the day, I am the ruler of Olympus. Now we must make sure that Earth does not fall to the bottom. Otherwise, all Apollo's B plans in this secret game he plays will be useless."

"Wouldn't it be better if you order Psyche to destroy that unsuccessful love potion?"

Zeus objected: "No way! Do you want to deprive me of this fun? You will see how all three of them, Apollo, Nolachiel, and Eros, will rotate like snakes in the nest when they find out what they will cause with this drink to this poor man! Just let them bear the consequences of Apollo's doing. We will interfere only if the situation is unmanageable."

"What do you mean, unmanageable?"

"Let me just remind you. A double dose of dill seed? That's how those fools are trying to create a higher love… Hmmm. I'm curious as to how those poor buds of orange flowers, which should at least try to create the conditions to create that higher love, will work."

"I'd better go to look at the Fields of Pearls. I'm trying to believe that it will be enough of them before the fight will start. I will be more at peace when I know that you don't have to improvise."

"Dear Hera, be happy that men can improvise and invent plans B. Women are immediately desperate when something is not exactly as planned. The best solutions are those that come from improvisations anyway. Well, and so it is with Olympus gods and goddesses."

Chapter 2

The golden Californian sun was warming the houses of wealthy people who settled in one of the most beautiful places to live in.

In one of those beautiful homes ringing phone woke up Rick. Famous, handsome man who could have everything he just thought of. It was his friend Peter. Rick leaned over to pick up the phone lying on the bedside table and with a sleepy voice answered the call: "Hi, Peter. Have you nothing else to do? Why are you calling so early?"

"Early? It's eleven in the morning! What did you do last night?"

Rick rubbed his eyes and muttered: "Why do you care? What is so important that it couldn't wait till let's say 2 in the afternoon?"

Peter went on: "Well, I have a great idea on how we could clear our heads this year. What would you say if the two of us went somewhere far this time?"

"What do you mean, far? Is it not enough to visit a few nightclubs here where we are? Where do you want to go this time?"

"It's been a while since we have been to the other side of our nice planet. One of my friends told me about a great festival in Germany. It's called October fest and it's cool."

"Cool? What is cool about people sitting in tents or pubs for two or three weeks, pouring beer into their throats, and eating high-calorie meals? On top of listening to their horrible folklore music. I hope you don't want me to put myself in those terrible leather trousers?!"

Peter laughed. "What do you have against the Bavarian folk costume? I don't have a problem with it. Well, we can try to dance their famous 'SHUHPLATTLER' dance. We need to learn about foreign cultures, don't we?"

Rick thought for a while and Peter interrupted him: "Hello? Are you still there? Look, it could be interesting and there are women everywhere, aren't they? You would not mind having one such chubby German, would you?"

"Give me a break with women. They are all the same. Only the cover changes."

Peter didn't give up although he didn't know why he wanted to get Rick so much to the festival. "Covers, covers. The cover is the most important thing in women, isn't it?"

"Yeah in the beginning. What's below the cover is not so luxurious though. We are all going to age, Peter. You can dance your SHUHPLATTLER dance yourself. You can also wear those leather trousers if you want to. I'm not going to make a fool of myself."

"Come on, man! What's wrong with you? You have a crisis, or what? You had no problem with that so far. To wear some costumes. Besides, your cover looks very good."

"Yeah, I had not. The luxurious cover that likes to put himself in any costume. I'll think about your offer. And who else will go? Only the two of us?"

"Well, maybe we can convince someone to join us. Such a guy's ride wouldn't hurt us, huh? You leave your girlfriends at home and we'll paint the town red. You will see, it will be great!"

Rick didn't want to go there; he didn't know why. But then why not? Maybe Peter is right, and he needs to get wild a bit and eliminate the work stress.

"Okay then, let's go. Let's try to ask if anyone will join us. It will be more fun." Finally, he agreed.

Peter was pleased. "Yes! This is the right answer! This will definitely be an unforgettable men's ride!"

"Yeah, sure it will be. Would you mind come up with a solution on how to disguise me so that not every other child will point its finger at me on the street?"

Peter laughed.

"I'm telling you we will wear Bavarian costumes. We will put hats and sunglasses."

"Hats. Sunglasses. Peter, are you sure you're okay? Did you drink something in the morning?"

"Jesus, Rick! There's going to be millions of people there. Everyone's going to be pouring beer inside them. Nobody will even notice us."

Rick just sighed: "Right. No one won't notice Bavarian costume with sunglasses."

"Okay, I don't know what we're going to do. We will come up with something on the spot."

"You see? Welcome to my reality. Everybody will recognize you right away."

Peter thought: "What about wigs? Hair can change a lot."

"For God's sake, Peter, shut up! The more ideas you have, the worse they are. Wigs? That's way too much. You put on whatever you want; I will wear my ordinary clothes."

Peter wondered with laughter: "I thought an actor would not have a problem to put on a stupid wig. Believe me, it will work."

Rick was already getting amused by this crazy idea and asked: "So, wig it will be. With or without sunglasses?"

"We'll see on the spot. We'll improvise, according to the situation."

And so, without knowing how, poor Rick signed up for this crazy stag and had no idea that it was a wig and sunglasses that will cause him many problems. Easily he managed to convince two of his friends, Will and Andy to join in. All four of them stayed in Munich in one luxurious hotel and relied on the confidentiality of the staff. They knew that would not be of much help to them. Unfortunately, the toll of glory was occasionally great. Privacy almost didn't exist. When the whole bunch of good-looking men unpacked, they wondered how best to hide their faces.

Andy eagerly asked: "So, when do we finally go out? I can't wait to see the beauties dressed in their costumes."

Will added: "Do you mean Dirndl? Well, it looks nice. Especially those corsets. It's really sexy. There are some pretty babes out there."

Peter agreed. "Of course, there are pretty chicks here. They are everywhere."

Rick shook his head in disagreement: "But you don't really care about chicks, do you? We should get some costumes. Peter may be right, we'll fit in better."

Andy sighed: "We will never fit in anywhere anymore. Everybody knows us. It's useless. We do something and the next day everybody knows."

Peter took gloriously out of his suitcase four wigs, fake beards, and mustaches. They were not only to disguise them but to make them look a little older as well.

Will looked at the arsenal and was horrified. He complained: "No way I'm going to put this on myself! This way I won't be able to pick up even some grandma! For God's sake! We have come here to enjoy ourselves. I'm not going to make fool of myself!"

Rick grabbed one of those crazy horrible wigs and smiled. "Why not? It's funny, isn't it? Sometimes we make fools of ourselves for money. And other people think how easy it is to be an actor. At least we will be safe."

Andy, the quietest of all, agreed. "Rick is right. Better than being chased and photographed and the girls will scream."

Will didn't like it. "So what? Let them scream. At least we will have a better choice. We want to have fun, don't we? And you, Peter, where did you get this awful gear from? Have you robbed a ruined theater, or did you buy it on eBay?"

"Why you always must complain? You will see, you will all be thankful for those wigs."

Andy tapped his shoulder and whispered: "We are grateful, we are. I'm just afraid that we will get even more attention in these costumes than if we were going to dress for ourselves."

They all fell silent and Rick added: "Well, Andy, you're right. Sometimes we don't know who we really are. As if every acting part left in us indelible trace and emotion. It's going to stay with us all our life. So, I'm going to dress up it's funny. Maybe we can keep our identity a secret for a while."

Peter was pleased that his great idea with wigs, fake beards, and mustaches was accepted so well and pulled out sunglasses from his suitcase.

Will exploded in laughter. "You certainly are insane!! I can understand the Bavarian costume and the fake beard, but sunglasses? Why the hell we need sunglasses? We will look like a bunch of fools."

Andy tried to save Peter: "He is right. He wants to cover our eyes. We will look like fools even without the glasses anyways. It won't help us."

Peter, who was really trying to help, gave up: "You know what? Do what you want. It's not my fault that we all look like sugar dolls."

Everyone laughed and then they ordered food. They were tired and had jet lag, so they slept like babies. The next morning a full set of Bavarian costumes with shirts and socks was delivered to the hotel.

Will desperately looked at those costumes. "We'll look like a bunch of fools."

Rick asked: "What about the Germans who have it for their national costume? It's part of their culture, that they are proud of. Do they look like fools?"

Will looked at Rick. "No, they don't but we aren't Germans, are we?"

Peter responded to Will's words: "Yes, we don't... By the way, many nations live in America, so what? Common, let's put on these Bavarian costumes and be proud of them. We'll all pretend we are Germans."

Andy smiled inconspicuously all the time, then added: "Germans are a very precise nation, and they adhere to the rules more than is necessary, right Rick?"

Rick added ironically: "Depends who, Andy... Depends who..."

They all dressed up in costumes and looked really good. Even with their hats. Will looked in the mirror and cursed: "Do we really have to spoil this outfit with these monstrosities that Peter has prepared for us? Fuck that. I don't care. With this beard, I won't be able to hook up even with a granny."

Rick sighed: "I don't know; we'll try the fake beard first. Tomorrow we'll see."

Unfortunately, poor Rick didn't know that they would not have to deal with that tomorrow. Apollo, the beautiful god of art, prophecy, and light, arranged that the coincidences that had crossed their way no longer allowed them to continue with their stag party as they would have expected. So, they went out to paint the town red unsuspectedly, relying on their wigs and fake beards to save them from revealing their true identity.

Meanwhile, Apollo was waiting for Nolachiel, and he was restless. Finally, Nolachiel arrived and Apollo asked eagerly: "So, will your protégé come over to that damn October fest?"

Nolachiel shook her head. "Her colleague was trying to persuade her all day, but she does not want to go there. She won't be able to concentrate on work the next day if she will go to bed late. And to endure to run around the department 10 or 11 hours is not easy even with enough sleep. It's not my fault. She also doesn't have Dirndl. She doesn't want to buy it. It's too expensive for her, besides she is Slovak."

Apollo couldn't stand it and said angrily: "And does it matter? Her grandmother had German roots. She could have bought a Slovak costume. Oh, yes, she does not dance Slovak folk dances but mixed oriental belly dancing. So much for the culture. She could have worn a historical dress when she does not have Dirndl. Oh, this god damn woman! First, she expresses her wish, and when her intuition sends her where she's supposed to be, she does not go. People and all their cultures. Everyone comes from one source. They all have the same hearts. Well, it is very important for human beings to adhere to tradition."

"What do we do, Apollo? Will we leave it like that?"

Apollo was a proud god. "No! We will go for plan B, which is even more dangerous, but I have no choice. We're going to finish it, Nolachiel, but we'll have more work and more problems we'll have to clean up. I need you to fly to Rick's guardian angel, Chasariel. Tell him that tonight comes the time, when he and the rest of the guardian angels, have to step down for a few hours and let those of the other dark side do their job. At the same time, they must be prepared to intervene immediately if the situation gets out of control and these poor folks will be at risk. Go now!"

"How did you bribe the guardian angels to voluntarily retreat and to quiet down the voice of heart and intuition, and thus enable the helpers from the dark side to work?"

Apollo explained in a resigned manner: "I didn't. You, angels, are pure beings. You fulfill your tasks. I had to tell them the truth and promise that none of their protégés would get hurt."

"What if something happens, Apollo? You know what all human beings are capable of when their low instincts take over. No matter what lower instinct it will be. I'm starting to worry. What if something goes wrong and we can't fix it?"

"Nothing will happen to them. The angels will be near, only they will leave some space for the ones from the dark side. How terrible it sounds."

Nolachiel flew to Chasariel, who agreed to the request and along with other guardian angels quieted down his soft voice of the heart. The wild party could start.

Rick, Will, Andy, and Peter dressed in Bavarian costumes and masked with fake beards and mustaches sat in a famous inn in Munich, and their mood rose with the amount of the golden fluid that the Germans could prepare really well.

Under normal circumstances, they were really decent and reliable guys, but tonight somehow, they stopped to control themselves. Occasionally they ordered liquor and the disaster was imminent.

In addition, Will's worry that with wearing this terrible mask, he won't be able to hit it with somebody better than a granny disappeared as quickly as the speed of light. It didn't take long and there was a large group of women gathered around them. From the age of a child to real grandmothers. No matter how hard they tried to hide their pretty faces, it wouldn't help. Their charisma attracted women as light attracted flies in the dark. Will was happy that he would not go to bed with some grandmother and so the rest of the group. Of course, if they would drink less golden fluid and less strong spirits. As typical guys, they wanted to show themselves off in front of their female catches before they take them to their hotel rooms. And how better to impress them than with a fast and furious ride. The cars, although luxurious, were rented, but their hot chicks didn't mind. Chasariel watched for a moment, as seven people approached two cars with crazy laughter and with uncertain steps. He told Avariel, the guardian angel who was supposed to protect Peter: "The situation is getting more complicated. More than we wanted. We need to do something,"

Avariel asked: "Where is Apollo? He promised he will interfere if things would start to take a bad turn. So, where is he?"

Mechiel, Will's guardian angel told him: "I guess you don't think Apollo has time to wander somewhere in Germany along a street full of beery human beings. He has other duties."

Ameliel, Andy's guardian angel pried: "So where are the executors of his orders? I don't see anyone yet. If they get into those damn cars, they can endanger themselves."

Avariel sighed: "What should we do then?"

Chasariel replied: "Nothing, Apollo has promised to take care of it. We have to believe he has a plan."

Chasariel, Rick's angel was right. Although with great difficulties, the group of beautiful, human beings managed to take off. But they moved for a few meters only before they were stopped by cops. That saved them all. Chasariel smiled. "I told you that Apollo had planned something. He has executors for his plans. Though that will cause troubles anyway."

Mechiel, Will's angel said: "How long do we have to be silent, and let the hideous dark creatures drag them into even greater difficulties?"

Ameliel, Andy's angel replied: "Apollo said until morning, until the effects of the poison that they have in their bodies will evaporate. Now they would not hear us anyway. Don't you see how they look now?"

"We have to wait. Just observe the situation. The life-threatening situation is over, so the worst-case scenario is over."

The angels watched from a distance what was going to happen. Two police officers saw the state of the passengers in the cars. Unfortunately, the inexorable pedantry and incorruptibility of the German nation, for a few exceptions perhaps, prevailed.

The taller of the two policemen greeted the driver: "Good evening, gentlemen. So, I see you are slightly overwhelmed by alcohol, right? And still driving."

At this point, the policeman didn't know that half of the passengers didn't speak German until Peter tried to explain that they were foreigners. The male part of the group still had this terrible camouflage on their faces. Their beautiful companions obviously didn't mind. They didn't care who their temporary partners for a short adventure were. The important was that they had charisma, sexy bodies and, of course, paid them their drinks. For the German cop, it was not enough though. The other cop, a little shorter, looked closely at the strange-looking man and urged him: "Sir, your driver license, please."

Andy, the soberest from the group cursed in English: "Fuck! We are in big shit."

The taller policeman didn't like that. "If you want to curse please do it in German, otherwise please be quiet."

Will, whose alcohol level was the worst, couldn't control himself. He shouted in English: "You better learn English! German asshole."

Rick's head was spinning. The combination of beer and spirits was acting like a poison. Nevertheless, he realized that Will has screwed up the situation.

"Shut up, asshole!" he chided him.

The shorter policeman scolded them in English: "So, let's all calm down now. Once again, please show me your driving licenses and identity cards."

The beautiful companions in the car realized that the situation is more than bad. The boys, with their impaired motor skills, tried to take out their identification documents and they realized, that what is about to come will end up badly. The taller cop was examining the documents than he started to look confused. He alternately looked at them and at the documents. Finally, he asked them, this time in English: "What does this mean? Are you trying to make fool of us, or what? You don't look like in these photographs. Can you give some reasonable explanation for this? Hellooo... Gentlemen...are you still with me?"

Peter, who had this idea of getting disguised, tried to explain the best he could: "Excuse me, Sir. We wanted to be incognito, so we won't be recognized because we do not have bodyguards here. So, we got the masks...the beards...the hair...different hair..."

The shorter policeman smirked: "Well, I've already begun to think that you are here as an actor in the entertainment program."

The other policeman looked at them silently, then looked again at their names. The names seemed familiar; he just couldn't tell from where.

"Okay, now show me your faces without your masks. And quickly!" he ordered them.

All the guys put down those terrible wigs. Their hair was completely wet because they were hot, and their faces were red and sweaty from those fake beards and mustaches. Nevertheless, when they showed their faces, their companions began to scream. One of them fainted. At that moment no one knew whether from astonishment or from a high dose of alcohol in the blood.

The taller cop shook his head: "I knew I know you from somewhere. My children love you. We have almost all your movies at home. But today, you aren't acting like heroes, are you?"

Everybody was silent, only Will couldn't stop himself from a comment: "So, what? You have never screwed up in your life, or what? Look, you know now who we are. Tell us how much we put in your pocket to be silent and we all forget about this. So, cop, do we have a deal?"

Rick, pale as a wall desperately shouted: "Oh, my God! I told you to shut up. So, shut up!"

Andy tried to rescue the situation and began to apologize with the humblest voice: "I apologize. He didn't mean that. He is drunk."

The shorter policeman was no longer very pleasant: "You are all drunk. But, that doesn't justify the arrogance of some of you and the fact that you have just tried to bribe a public official. I haven't mentioned driving under the influence of alcohol. For that, you can end up in prison. Now we'll take you to the police station. You will get sober and, in the morning, we will write a report."

Peter was terrified and whispered: "Prison? Report? We drove only a few meters. No one got hurt."

The taller cop was merciless and overly correct: "Nothing happened, but it could have. You have endangered your lives and the lives of other passengers. Not to mention other possible consequences. In view of the unusual circumstances, we will send your companions home, they didn't sit behind the steering wheel, and you all will go with us."

So, this was how it was decided about their next day celebration with fake beards and wigs. Surely, there was no party taking place tomorrow. All four of them ended up at the police station. Their guardian angels were close to them, but they could not get closer yet. They could only watch the dark angels with the dark wings with a nasty smile celebrating the results of their work. Andy, who always tried to keep his cool head said to desperate Peter: "We have to call home. We need a lawyer to let us out of this shit."

Rick, who was starting to get sick to his stomach, said with a concern: "He won't. Andy. He won't. Don't you see that the Germans can't be bribed so easily."

Will furious as a wild dog huffed: "I didn't know they were such assholes and cold fishes. Who do they think they are?"

Peter scolded him: "Can't you just be silent for a moment? This is all your fault! You wanted to bribe him, and you told him he was an asshole."

Will was furious.

"My fault? It was your stupid idea to fly across the ocean just to get drunk. We should have stayed home. There the lawyer would get us out of this shit. And that stupid idea with wigs! Only someone like you can come up with such stupidity!"

Peter felt offended.

"What do you have against me? I didn't force you. You got a choice. There are always two options."

Andy looked at Rick, whose color began to change from red to greenish, with anxiety. He wasn't used to drinking so much and certainly not used to mix beer with brandy.

"You don't look good."

Instead of answering Rick vomited into the horrible toilet at the police station, and Will said in a quieter voice: "None of us look good."

Then a policeman came, Andy asked him: "Can I make a call? I know I have the right to that."

The cop brought him his cell phone. Andy sighed and dialed the lawyer who boarded the first plane available to get to the four of them, normally, reliable and decent guys. He didn't understand how they could get into such a mess. Little did he know that they could thank Apollo for that. He was very precise and had thoroughly planned every step of the plan.

Meanwhile, the group of four handsome men have slept in their temporary custody. The dark angels have departed satisfied with how well they have done their job. In the morning when they woke up, after a roaring night, they were surprised by the unpleasant discovery that the bad night they had, was unfortunately not a dream. Andy woke up first and waited for the lawyer to arrive. Will, now much quieter, asked: "Just what happened yesterday? I remember bits and pieces only. We sat in cars with some chicks and then…"

Andy continued: "Then you fucked it all up. As usual, you didn't keep your mouth shut and it made everything worse. You have to learn to control yourself more."

Peter rubbed his eyes and his conscience woke up. He felt guilty that he had invented this whole crazy idea. "Jesus. My head is just splitting. What do the Germans add to that beer? God… I feel like shit."

As soon as he uttered these words, his guardian angel Avariel could approach him. Rick, who felt better but his stomach was still like on a swing objected: "It's not your fault, we all had a choice…Well, this is what we choose, and this is what we get."

At that moment, his guardian angel, Chasariel, could come close to him. Andy's angel was already there because he was the soberest and the most sensible of all of them.

Will grabbed his head. "God! What a trip! Now to whom I should pray so we won't end up in jail?"

At that moment, his guardian Angel, Mechiel, flew close to him.

Andy replied: "To whom you want. You have a choice, but I'm afraid that won't help you. Not even our lawyer can get us out from this shit. We were unlucky we came across loyal cops. We will pay dearly for the attempt to corrupt them."

Peter tried to come up with something, but it was difficult with the banging in his head: "There must be some possibility. We have never committed a crime before. Maybe it will help us."

Rick said: "So far. But yesterday we did. I'm waiting for journalists to get in here and write about us everywhere. How irresponsible we are that we were driving under the influence."

Peter smirked ironically: "Do you call these few meters before the German nerds stopped us a ride? We just had a stroke of terrible bad luck! I don't understand how yesterday could turn up so wrong."

Their guard disturbed them and brought something that looked like breakfast. He couldn't help himself but to make a remark: "Well, American beauties are probably used to some other breakfast and service, right?"

Will wanted to say something, but Andy gestured him to be silent. Peter tried to be polite. "No, no, we are not very demanding. Thank you for taking care of us so well here."

Will laughed ironically and everyone except Rick tried to eat at least something. Then they just kept silent and waited how things will turn up.

The lawyer arrived the next day. When he saw the state they were in, he asked: "What the hell are you doing here? Couldn't you take a cab? I can't believe this! How did that happen?"

Andy explained to the lawyer as thoroughly as possible what had happened that night. He wasn't excited about what he heard.

"You are bind by contracts; you have duties. What about your image? The Germans are terribly fair and relentless. I tried to defend you. I said that you are a reliable citizen. However, I failed. I will have to defend you in court."

Will shook his head in disagreement. "Jesus, as if we were some criminals! Nothing terrible happened!"

The lawyer objected: "Even those few meters that you have passed counts. For those few meters, your stupid remarks, and the idea of bribing a cop you will have to be sentenced. I'll try at least to make it as gentle as possible."

The guys were silent, and they looked like they didn't care anymore for what will happen. The price of one bad day and one bad night will be high. The lawyer was right. Negotiating with the German judge was more than complicated. Little did he know that Apollo stepped in again.

Nolachiel, my guardian angel flew to Apollo, who was busy working. "Apollo, I can see that your coincidences work more than well. What is going to happen next? Maybe those poor people don't deserve what's happening to them? Now I feel sorry for what we've done to them."

"Nolachiel, a little humbleness wouldn't hurt anyone."

"Humbleness? What's your next plan?"

"I had to manipulate another guardian angel, the angel of the loyal judge, to make him mitigate his sentence. Moreover, he will introduce to him the idea of how to make up for their small escapade and where they will serve their sentence. That will be especially difficult. Their lawyer wants to avoid bad publicity, and that will play in our favor. He will want them to be sent and hidden in some remote place. A place that you might call boondocks."

"Hidden? Place? What do you mean, Apollo?"

"Well, Nolachiel, the judge knows a director of the nursing house where your protégé works. All I have to do is to make the guardian angel of the judge make him sentence them to a few hours of public work and they will be out of this mess. That tiny dot on the map will provide the discretion, and they will experience a reality that they have never seen before."

"And my protégé will gain some time. Apollo, that's a great idea! Actually, they are all good men and have their hearts in the right place."

"Then the time for Eros and love potion will come. I still have not decided how much of that weird beverage we shall give him. We didn't verify its effects."

"Apollo, is that drink really necessary? Can't we try to go on without it?"

"No, we can't! Didn't you see how hard it was to get the finest of the Earthly Olympus to the other end of the planet? And made them end up where I needed to have them? Shall I risk no spark if I don't use the potion?"

"Apollo, I know, you have not had too much luck with love yet, but what if we just tried to believe?"

"Nolachiel, unfortunately, the world has changed. People become more focused on their bodies and looks than what they carry in their hearts and souls. I want to be sure that she will at least get the time she needs to bring him the unusual gifts. That potion will guarantee that."

"I know, but you saw how it all can get complicated. People have free will. Often as you see, they don't decide according to plan."

"Exactly for this reason we need that love potion. When its effects are gone, it will all be just up to them."

"All right, Apollo. It's up to you, but you know that the potion is not quite as it should be."

Apollo knew that love was not to be played with and could not be manipulated. No one knows how love is born or when. It is like the source of the invisible, purest, living water that flows out of hidden invisible corners of human hearts and devours the whole human being so much that as from that moment he or she sees the world as it should be. Beautiful and colorful. Full of joy. Such is the greatest and most beautiful gift that mankind has received from the Creator. Only he knew how it was created and how it works. Scientists call it a chemical reaction and attribute it to the hormones. Love is the most powerful magic and cannot be explained scientifically. Soon, four near-perfect men who accidentally got into trouble, are to be convinced of this. They will see and eventually show themselves how the higher levels of love that have not been among the human beings so popular look like.

Then the day, when the judge had to decide how they would render their unhappy evening full of troubles, came. The judge was sitting in the courtroom, watching all four of them. Then he started with a sly smile: "Well, you got me in a very peculiar situation. So far honest, impeccable citizens, good guys. Nevertheless, the law does not allow me to leave your actions without punishment. Your lawyer came up with an interesting proposal that could be a solution that will make both parties happy. Usually, we use this solution as an educational method for adolescents who commit some minor offenses. Although you are grown up, I think this solution will let you think even more about the fact, that there are places where people who aren't famous or movie heroes, live. But they are heroes of their ordinary lives. I have decided to send you to an unusual place where you will be hidden from publicity. There you will perform 180 hours of community service."

The lawyer was excited that he had managed to save them from an even bigger problem and asked: "Where will you send them?"

The judge corrected his glasses and replied: "My acquaintance is the director of a small nursing house in a tiny village here in Bavaria. It's a perfect place for you. There you will have a lot to do."

Will was petrified and couldn't control himself. "I hope you don't expect us to change diapers for old people! I'd rather go to jail!"

The judge looked up at him and began to explain: "No, you don't have to do this. People who do this had to learn how to do it in schools and practice it.

Same as you had to learn how to act whether in movies or theater. There's a lot of other types of work for you to do. But it's not going to be easy for you even without those diapers."

Later, they sat in the hotel's room, the lawyer told them: "I know you're not over the moon over this, but 180 hours is not that much. You will be safe there. I have arranged that almost none, except for your loved ones, of course, will know why you are there. The director of the nursing house has arranged appropriate accommodation for you in the nearby village."

Andy objected: "We won't be able to hide it for a long time. If only we go out for lunch or for shopping, the next day, everybody will know."

"Well, I don't know how this problem can be solved."

Rick looked at Peter and remarked: "Peter knows. With fake hair and beards. Let's not forget the sunglasses."

Will scolded him: "Please, can't you just shut up? Hadn't you had enough of all that? Look where your brilliant idea of getting disguised got us! As for me, I won't put on any mask or costume no matter what!"

Rick turned to Will: "Oh, but you will. You will. At the end of the day you are an actor, aren't you? So, get used to it. We act all our lives. Maybe we should not think about it at all and let it go. If we will be recognized, then yeah, bad luck."

Peter sighed: "Well, then the journalists will be staying in front of the nursing house all night. It probably won't be a very pleasant stay when I imagine where we're going."

Will nodded, and added: "We are going to a godforsaken place."

The lawyer didn't have any further advice for them, and they had to rely on the idea that the less they think about it, the better. He agreed with the head of the nursing house on the date when they will start their community work. The guys got used to the idea. Except Will. There are worse things in life than working a few hours in a nursing house. They just didn't know where they were actually going. Many people have no idea how the last stage of human life will unfold. How they will again turn into defenseless beings entirely dependent on the mercy and compassion of other human beings, who must have a heart somewhat larger than others to endure such a job.

It was the last morning of my two weeks' working period. I was awakened by the awful sound of the alarm clock; it was 5 am. I rubbed my eyes, woke up, and did my morning ritual. Around 8 am my boss came to see me; she took me aside. I was washing Mr. D and realized that I didn't put on my plastic apron. *What the hell,* I thought. However, she didn't come because of the apron.

"Tina, I have a special task for you. After two weeks, when you come back, four people who must serve some community work, will be here. Unfortunately, they don't speak German... If I'm not mistaken you've been giving English classes to Tim."

"What? Have you heard me speaking English? It's a disaster!!! Yes, I used to take English classes years ago, but as you see, I can't do all I want to do in life. So, I had to stop. I had different priorities. Dance and theater. I communicated with Tim, but he is from Macedonia, and I didn't care about the quality of my English and the words that will burst out from my mouth. But to communicate with native English-speaking people? Please, don't ask that from me!"

The boss explained: "They are Americans. In addition, they are VIP. One of my old acquaintances asked me for friendly service and I agreed. He needs to hide them."

"Hide? How important VIPs they are? Why it's always me who must deal with all the criminal teenagers?"

"Because you are our cleansing devil. They're not teenagers. They're all men in their best years, and they'll definitely look great since they're actors, don't you think?"

"What they look like comparing to our demented grannies won't help them. How will I manage my department along with a bunch of male creatures who probably didn't hold a rag or a cleaning mop for years? How will I speak with them?"

"Oh, I'm sure you'll manage somehow! You're smart. You're going to communicate in a non-verbal way."

"Shall I play pantomime, or what?"

"You will use your smartphones and you'll be communicating through a translator. Many people do it this way."

I couldn't help myself and made a remark: "You have forbidden mobile phones at work."

"Yes, but in this exceptional case, I'll allow it. Look, there will be four of them. Two will be down here on the first floor and the other two will go upstairs. You will give them work tasks. What will do the two of them here will do the other two upstairs."

"You can't be serious!"

"I am! You are allowed to be strict. The judge said that despite being good men, it won't hurt if they learn something about humility. Do you remember that recalcitrant girl? You got her for a few hours when she had to serve community work? She didn't show up after one day. Apparently, it was the first time in her life to hold a rag in her hand. You've done it brilliantly."

"For god's sake, this can't be compared! Educating a wild teenager is something else than giving orders to four adult men! That's terrible!"

"Men are a bit of a teenager all their life. They are not able to manage without us."

"Neither can we without them. Who would protect us? Who will build houses, bridges, highways? We need each other. God, why I wasn't born a man? My life would be much easier."

The boss ordered me something and I must do it. I remembered a colleague from the second floor who, at the time when Tim was my trainee as a new caretaker, saluted me as if we were in the war and called me general. That's going to be my problem. I can't be bossy. I can't be bossy. I repeat it in my mind. But I have inherited from my father, who was a lieutenant in the army, some of his stupid military genes. I can't be bossy. I have some time to repeat this affirmation in my mind until the cleaning hell with four alpha-males starts. Oh my god, how am I supposed to achieve that? I remembered one spiritual leader who had a channel on YouTube and who claimed that leaders should be men. Yes, but the leaders can only be men who deserve it. Men who can take care of a woman and protect her. While many men just whimper and blame the misfortune, the circumstances, women must take over the command in the house, and then disaster is born. I wasn't alone in that. For years, when I traveled for work in Austria and Germany, I have realized that there are many other women in a situation like mine. Who is, however, making the life of the families more and more difficult? Politicians? Governments? Hard to say. I had to leave my children because my husband supposedly wouldn't manage it. Hmmm. I had to if I didn't want to live like a beggar. I didn't want to.

Chapter 3

Two weeks passed and I came back to work to start the first of the two craziest weeks of my work assignments. I was unpacking in my tiny room that previously served as storage. Little did I know that at the same time four handsome men came to check the nursing house where they were supposed to serve their sentence. Rick wandered around. "This is a shithole. Where the hell are we? Shit, there is nothing here. Where are we going to eat?"

Andy smiled.

"Look here! Opposite the nursing house, there is a German pub, The Rabbit."

Will was disgusted. "The Rabbit? Thank you very much. Don't they have some luxury restaurants here?"

Peter was wondering aloud: "Not here, but five km away is a bigger town. You can go there. Or we'll cook something ourselves."

Rick laughed. "After the community service, we'll be glad to sit on our butts on the couch. Who would still have a mood for cooking?"

Andy reminded them: "If you want to stay unnoticed as long as possible, you should be satisfied even with the Rabbit pub. Or do you want to show up on the very first night at a luxury restaurant? Maybe it won't be so bad. This Rabbit."

The guys sighed. They knew that during those few days when they will have to work as ordinary people they will have to improvise.

Meanwhile, Apollo was impatiently waiting for Eros. His most important role in this crazy plan was supposed to unfold in a few hours. Unfortunately, things have fallen out of Apollo's hands from the very beginning and he had to improvise.

Nolachiel, along with Rick's guardian angel Chasariel, watched him nervously walking in the room and murmuring: "Where is this winged loser? He was supposed to be here a long time ago! He is completely unreliable!"

Chasariel warned him with concern: "Maybe it's a sign that we should let everything go. Apollo, you can't play with love."

Apollo objected: "You have no idea what I had to do to arrange this meeting tomorrow! I don't want to risk anything."

Nolachiel whispered: "We risked so much that we can't afford to risk more. Chasariel is right. Let's leave it up to them."

Apollo objected: "You wanted help for your protégé, so I'm helping you. I have already violated so many rules. So, don't tell me to give up now!"

The angels kept silent. Then Eros entered the room in a great mood, as always. This was caused by the fact that he had caused both joy and worry of love to many people.

"Where the hell have you been? You're late!"

Eros answered: "I was busy. Why do you mention hell? Oh, okay, I know. It's probably going to be related to the fact that these guys from down under are up to something, right?"

Apollo asked eagerly: "Do you have that potion?"

Eros pulled a vessel from beneath his wings in which Petal fairy love potion was stored.

Apollo took Eros's vessel and ordered him: "Tomorrow, precisely at 10 am Central European Time you will be where you should be with your arrow. To be on the safe side I'm taking the vessel. Don't dare to be late, are we clear?"

"Why are you so grouchy? Everything is wonderful. We are going to try to create love, aren't we?"

Apollo objected: "Love? I wish! Is there any love at all? We don't create it. It's created by human beings. We just give them a chance. Then it's up to them."

The angels returned to their protégés to fulfill their duties, so did Apollo. Eros returned home to Psyche and told her: "We're getting closer to our aim. I hope things will go well after the effects of the potion fade away. I believe in the time they got, and I believe in the ability of human beings to do good deeds."

Psyche hugged Eros and didn't say anything. Words have power. But unless people transform them into deeds, they remain only words. If someone says, "I love you," but won't confirm his or her love with deeds, love will die.

I woke up a little later that morning. On the first day of my two weeks working period, I worked from 10 am till 9 pm. I was worried about how I will manage it all. How are we going to communicate? Just like the first people in the caves? With gestures? Oh, my god! It will be terrible! I went down the stairs and through the glass wall I suddenly saw those poor people who had to serve their time in our nursing house. I almost killed myself on those stairs. My goodness! Not this!!! What have I done? Unfortunately, I didn't have a choice. My boss was smiling. She could speak some English and she welcomed me. When I entered the room, I froze. I didn't realize what was going on in the invisible sphere near us. Eros and Apollo were hovering near us and were stressed out. The problem was that Eros's arrow, which was ready to be used, got stacked in the bag. Apollo was furious.

"What are you doing?"

Eros finally managed to pull the arrow and apologized: "Sorry, I don't know what is happening with me today."

Apollo opened the vessel with a love potion and ordered to Eros: "Just use a quarter of it. I'm not sure if even that is not too much."

"A quarter? How did you find out that it must be a quarter? Did you saw it in the tarot cards or used your intuition?"

"Shut up and pay attention! Is it clear? Not a drop more!"

They were nervous about constantly breaking one Olympus rule after another. Eros didn't pay enough attention, and the drink that was in the vessel spilled out all over the arrow. Apollo was terrified. "I said a quarter, not three quarters! You don't listen to me!"

Eros was suddenly angry and without a single word fired the arrow covered with three-quarters of the mysterious, imperfect love potion straight into the heart of poor Rick.

Apollo shouted in despair: "Are you crazy? Why did you do it?!"

"I won't let you give me orders! I asked for your help, but I'd better help myself."

"Yes, you did it yourself!!! We have no idea how a small drop of our great potion will work! How about three quarters?!! I'm resigning immediately! I will let Zeus form human reality from now on if he thinks it is easy to fulfill people's stupid wishes! I don't like you, Eros. You destroyed my divine life. You have never sent me a decent love! Only scrap!!! You send to all people in the world imperfect scraps!"

Eros calmly smiled and defended himself: "The Creator created people to his image. But sometimes, the free will turned them to scrap. That's why they sometimes attract imperfect love into their life. I just shoot."

Chasariel and Nolachiel observed the quarrel between Apollo and Eros unfolding on the cloud. They were arguing about old issues and they knew that the situation would become even more complicated. Well, nothing in human life is perfect, not even love. Perhaps this is what the Creator wanted. For people to at least try to reach perfection even with making some mistakes. It will be now mainly up to them, the guardian angels, to whisper the right decisions.

Poor Rick's head was spinning in a strange way and heat spread all over his body. He didn't know how to explain it. I didn't even look at him. Just for a moment, I dared to look into his eyes. Suddenly my stomach turned into one big rock and I couldn't breathe. God. Why are you doing this?

The boss introduced us with a big smile. Hmm introduced. She really didn't have to. Only if she knew that my foolish fantasies just materialized in a disaster. It's a completely different story to have someone's picture hanging on a wall imagining everything that a person would like to. But even these men are just human beings with mistakes. She explained something to them in English, but I wasn't paying any attention. My head was spinning from stress and nervousness. I felt like I was starting to blush. Oh, no, please!! I tried to forbid my body to reveal that I was uncertain. I didn't have a choice. Maybe they won't be cocky pricks and they will understand that I can't do anything else than execute the orders of my boss. And they will have to execute my orders because the boss will check on them. I decided that the whole terrible situation would be a bit easier with a bit of humor.

I introduced myself in my weak English: "Hi, my name is Tina. Unfortunately, due to my work, all my life I was only learning the German language. My English is terrible, and my Slavic accent is terrible. Well, maybe we'll be able to communicate somehow. If nothing else, we will use gestures."

The guys looked at me as if I just fell from Venus, but they also took it with humor. Well, what to do. We will probably manage somehow. I guess I will really be forced to play that pantomime and they will think I'm a fool. I didn't have a choice. I told them: "Please, follow me."

The guys obediently followed me to the room that once served as a bathroom. Now it was storage full of various things. With difficulty, I started to explain everything. I had no choice but to spill out random words the same way I did when I was teaching my colleague Tim how to take care of the residents of the nursing house.

I was helping myself with gestures, so I looked like some failed actress who was trying to get a part in a third-class movie. After a while, I had to laugh at myself and they did too. It couldn't get any worst. Smile and humor really help to cope with stressful situations.

"First of all, you will disinfect wheelchairs and rollators. I will show you how."

The guys watched as I picked up a wheelchair and mimicked the washing process. When words are not available, deeds often save our lives. Thanks, god for that.

"I'll show you the whole department. Some wheelchairs are in the rooms, you'll clean those first."

When they walked through the dining hall, only then they realized where they actually were. A couple of patients sat in the dining hall, some in wheelchairs. Some of them had rollators. They were mostly women and, sadly, most of them no longer noticed the world around them. They lost their memory, orientation in time and space, mobility. It was due to a disease for which scientists have not yet found a cure. Dementia. While this place was called the nursing house, in fact, it was a geriatric-psychiatric department. One of those that wasn't very popular among healthcare professionals.

I showed them all the departments and all the rooms. Thus, they got to know what is awaiting them during the next few days. In some rooms they saw human beings shriveled, curled into a ball, oblivious to nothing, just emotions. They were in the last stage of their lives and were totally dependent on the help of other human beings. When we are born, we wear diapers and when we die we wear them as well. I saw on their faces that they were affected by what they saw. And how not? Seldom do people know how it actually looks like in such facilities.

I started to further explain in my terrible English: "You take a wheelchair or a rollator from each person and clean it. The gloves are on the nurse's cart. The disinfecting towels are in this bucket. Please always use gloves, the cleansing solution is aggressive."

Andy asked first and tried to speak slowly so I can understand at least the core meaning of his question: "What about the wheelchairs that are occupied?"

I understood the meaning and responded with words as they came to me. It was such a terrible situation that I had to laugh at myself aloud: "Sorry, I'm sorry."

The atmosphere was lighter a bit and Peter said: "It's okay. We can't speak German well either. Everyone knows what he or she needs."

I explained to Andy: "When patients get their lunch, we put them in bed, then you will clean the rest of the wheelchairs."

Rick only looked at me. I tried to ignore him as if he wasn't there. What else I could do. Mortal woman, an ordinary nurse, and such a handsome man. I'd rather not look, it'll be better. I didn't know that by unfortunate coincidence Eros had poisoned his heart and awakened his darker self.

Normally, he wouldn't do that, but the magic has its price. "You like to boss people around, right? You're good at that."

When he said that it was as if he stabbed into a hornet's nest and my blood was boiling. At that moment, all my illusions disappeared. Is this supposed to be my favorite hero? Oh, actually, it's just his representative. The hero that he played the role of does not exist. That was the main problem. I pierced him with the iciest look I could at that moment, and I didn't care that I didn't speak good English. I was combining the words as they came to my mind: "You too, or not? It's not my fault that you ended up here. I'm executing my boss's orders."

"Really?"

"Does it hurt your ego that unfortunately for a short time, a woman will be your boss? This is a place where not many men survive... Women fight and survive here. You will understand later."

Rick didn't understand what was happening. Unfortunately, he went on: "You want to give us orders? Who said we must obey you?"

"You don't have to. You can do what you want. I'm just doing my job. You can watch your friends as they wash and clean."

"I will. I won't take orders from some woman."

He didn't understand why taking orders from this particular woman was bothering him so much.

I told him: "Clearly, you men, are the managers of the whole planet and this is how your management ended."

Rick stared at me with eyes wide open and asked contemptuously: "What does that have to do with it?"

"Everything. For these ego moments that often win over people, our planet looks this way."

"Are you from some other planet, or what?"

"I'm from Venus and you are from Mars."

Rick laughed. "Listen, you're really different. Men should be leaders. That's how it should be."

"Leaders? You are used to be a leader, right?"

"Not always."

"Okay, you can stay here. I have to go to work. I understand; you have another job. To take care of your body, smile at fans, look like a beautiful Sugarman. I know your work is very, very difficult, but here you are not fighting fictional monsters. Here are real monsters. We'll see how you will deal with them."

Rick was angry that I called him Sugarman. Once again, I managed to hurt his male ego, thanks to this unfortunate potion that effected all his instincts, except his heart and soul.

"Who do you think you are? What can you know about my job? I'm no Sugarman!"

"You're right, I don't know much about your hard work. Just what a few VIP people told me about that. You are not the first VIP person I know. I took care of one man in Austria who was VIP as well."

Rick was quiet for a while. He didn't understand why this unpretentious woman was irritating him so much. He could have ignored her, but it wasn't possible due to this bloody potion. What does this ordinary nurse think about herself? He can still have any women in the world if he wants to. Yes, he can.

I was destroyed inside when I realized what type of person I'm actually talking to. I thought he was different. He behaved like a typical superstar who can do anything he wants. I didn't understand. Oh, how naive I was. Oh, Aphrodite! Please, help me to forget about him. Aphrodite didn't hear me.

Rick asked after a while: "Do you think it's easy to be perfect?"

"You must be perfect in your earthly Olympus. I think."

"It's not up to us do decide. We have contracts and obligations."

"Ah. Me too. I'm going to my job that feeds me. I don't have time to discuss with you whose work is worst. I'm too tired of the language barrier."

"You were supposed to learn English. It's a world language."

"You know nothing about my life. I was studying it years ago. I didn't need it. I needed to learn German. It saved my life."

Rick was intrigued, but I was already gone.

The other guys were cleaning their wheelchairs. Rick sat on a weird-looking cart in the bathroom. Will was angry at him and grumbled: "Why the hell are you sitting there like a king and doing nothing? Do you think that the punishment doesn't concern you?"

Rick was really like he was replaced with somebody else. He could not recognize himself. "Give me a break. I don't want to do anything."

Andy shook his head and wondered what was happening with him. He couldn't but make a remark: "By the way, lord Mr. King, you are sitting on a movable toilet."

The guys looked at that strange chair on wheels. Rick stood up, lifted the cover covered with artificial leather. Inside they saw a hole for a plastic bucket. They burst into hilarious laughter and Rick closed the cover. He sat back on that weird looking chair and remarked ironically: "So what? Throne like a throne. It's comfortable."

Peter was surprised by Rick's behavior. "What's wrong with you today? Did you drink a spoiled protein drink, or what? You are loitering around while we are working our asses off."

Andy added: "Listen, we are all in this. You have been driving one of those damn cars. So please, get up from your throne and start working. I can see that you are quite weird. It's not like you."

"It's me. Yes, this is me too. I'm tired of being always good and perfect. Kind and helpful. I just discovered my dark side. I'm starting to like it."

Peter couldn't stand it anymore: "Lift up your ass and start to work, Mr. Dark side. If you don't want to have problems."

"And who will know? That little nurse? She means nothing to me."

Andy smirked: "Really? So why did you mention her?"

The guys laughed ironically. All women are the same. Men respond to the opposite sex quickly. They have 20 times more testosterone than women. They were created to conquer and hunt women. For that, they often don't need love. In the first place is the initial satisfaction of their natural instincts, which sometimes complicates their lives. Women are different. Women can't separate sexual instincts from love. They have a rare hormone, estrogen. Its tenderness and affection mitigate and guide male aggression and all other instincts. Unfortunately, in the begging, the sexual instinct in men always prevails and often urges hunters to go to places where they do not always want to be. Many times, it's not even their fault.

Rick growled angrily: "I'm not going to let any women give me orders."

Will couldn't help himself, but he had to tease Rick again: "By the way, she looked at you like at a holy picture. But you didn't notice."

The guys started to laugh again. Rick was so upset that he threw the gloves he had in his hand on the floor. "She is all yours! I don't care."

Andy shrugged his shoulders: "I find her very nice. I have seen her talking to patients and other colleagues. If you wouldn't stubbornly just sit around and didn't act like a macho man, you might change your mind. I know, we're all used to other types of women. Perfect as we are because we are different. We are famous… Stars. One day we will look like these patients. When we are ill, we suddenly become equal."

Rick shook his head.

"I don't need to change my mind."

Peter sadly asked: "Are we all going to end up like this? With dementia? Wearing diapers and getting washed by women?"

Will sighed: "I don't want to live this long. It's a frightening idea."

Andy explained to him: "Not everyone will end up like this. She told me that we should not think about it and be afraid of it. We just need to be thankful for our health."

Will wouldn't give up. "You mean these people haven't been thankful enough, or what?"

Peter wondered aloud: "These are people who survived the war. A real war not some fictional in a movie. The pain and misery they have suffered may have been the reason why they simply wanted to forget the past."

Everybody went back to work. They had to work eight hours a day. Will and Peter, who were assigned to the upper floor, suggested to Rick that they could swap with him if he was so annoyed with this ordinary nurse, but he objected: "No, I'm staying here. No matter where I go, I won't work anyway."

Peter caught his forehead and didn't understand. "Let's see how long you will be rebelling. Suit yourself. Sit down on your temporary throne. Now it really suits you. I hope tomorrow you change your mind."

Rick was angry although he didn't know why. Was it because he agreed to this unplanned trip, or because Tina called him Sugarman? Why the hell she said that? What does she think of herself? Yeah, she was not even an actress or a model. Normal, unobtrusive woman. Sugarman? The worst nickname he could imagine. So far, he has been reliable and nice. And yet not all things in his life went the way he wanted. Sometimes he felt that it was because he gave more than he should. He was still disappointed as many people who try to give and give. Until one day, something may break in them. *Did that happen to him now, a few hours ago? He could not explain it. So, what? He is going to survive this somehow,* he thought. He has always been the first to help and manage things. Why should he do that again? Let others worry about that now. He'll try to be the man of the dark side now.

He opened the glass door and saw the annoying nurse, who would want to boss him around again, as she sat at one of the tables and ate a strange-looking lunch. He observed her from behind an aquarium that was empty. The fishes had died because no one cleaned the aquarium. Only sand was in it. As if it symbolized the terrible disease that left emptiness instead of a mind. Thoughts were gone. He watched her for a moment, then came closer. Tina was a little bit curvier type of a woman comparing to women he had before. Therefore, he couldn't help himself but say a remark when he saw what she had on the plate. Vegetables and colorless something that looked like pieces of meat. Once again, his remark was like a bee sting: "Are you on a Hollywood diet?" I was surprised, I didn't expect him to show up, let alone say something. I was wondering how to put words in English. God, that's terrible.

"It's not a Hollywood diet. It's a pancreatic diet. Believe me, it's worse than yours. You need yours to look perfect, I need mine because the doctors have kind of ruined my possibility of eating like others."

Rick contemplated and asked: "Again you think yours is worse?"

"Well, I don't know. My diet allows me to eat some sinful food. I hope that yours also sometimes allows you to eat a few forbidden things. I mean, sometimes."

Rick looked at me: "Maybe... Sometimes..."

I was loading the dishwasher and told Rick, who was sitting on the chair: "Did you change your mind and want to help? Or will you hide in that bathroom again?"

Rick was still angry for the Sugarman, but at the same time, the word 'help' had some sort of special strength. As if for a while it had weakened the effect of that terribly powerful love potion that had worked exactly the opposite way as it was supposed to. It awakened in him the curiosity to explore how the department looked like behind the door of the bathroom where he was rebelling. I tried to look neutral and not show any sign of disappointment at how cold and strange Rick acted at that moment.

"This is a dishwasher as you can see."

Rick laughed.

"I can see."

I didn't respond to his remark; it would not be meaningful. I had trouble with composing English sentences so that they will make sense.

"We load and unload it many times a day. That takes a lot of time. You didn't want to clean the wheelchairs, so I'll show you where the dishes are and where you will spill the leftovers. You have a dishwasher at home, don't you?"

All I said irritated Rick. "No, I don't! Do you think I live in Antarctica or what?"

"I don't know where exactly you live, sorry. I saw nice cupboards and a beautiful dog. The dishwasher wasn't visible."

My answer gave me away. Rick looked at me with a smile. I was horrified. I shouldn't have said this. Somehow it slipped out despite my bad English.

"Cupboards? You were looking at the cupboards? No way!"

"Why not? You have good taste. Anyhow, let me show you our cupboards, where we put the dishes and the bucket for leftovers."

Rick was a little less angry and was wondering who would notice cupboards in his post. That was funny.

"In a few moments, the patients will come for coffee. Now you will just observe and tomorrow you'll work."

Rick's ego was awakened again.

"Yes, Mr. General."

I didn't give up. "I'm a woman. If you haven't noticed."

"I noticed. Your ass and legs."

It offended me, but I couldn't show it, I just said through my teeth: "Priorities at your earthly Olympus are different. For me, I am grateful to my body that it allows me to work."

"Olympus?" Rick laughed. "You really must be from Venus. You have a body little like a Venus as well."

He added ironically. He couldn't understand how he could be so tactile, but he couldn't control it. I swallowed and tried to shout out the embarrassment. I was looking for an appropriate answer.

"Would you prefer a world where only perfect, flawless people exist? You are such a person. I believe you are perfect inside too. Maybe I have a body little like my favorite goddess."

"Do you think I have such a high opinion of myself? And self-confidence?"

"I don't know. I don't know you yet. I only know the hero you played. I believe there's something in your heart out there."

Rick was disarmed. I explained to him his work tasks with gestures and confused English and I laughed at myself how terrible it was. But I had to explain it to him somehow. I was forced to give him orders again, but I had no choice. My affirmation that I must not be a leader completely failed because of our strict boss. I didn't want him to get in trouble. But men are competitive creatures, and when Peter, who just came out of the bathroom with a clean wheelchair, saw what kind of work Rick was assigned he got mad: "Shit! So, our Lord the King ended up in such a luxury job, and we're working our assess off with wheelchairs here. I also want to go to the kitchen! That's unfair!"

Rick shouted with a wide smile: "Tough luck men! I'm lucky. That little annoying thing is having a crush on me."

"You've probably become a damn macho, haven't you? I'm going to complain to her and don't think you're getting yourself out of this."

"Complain. I'm staying in the kitchen and you continue cleaning the wheelchairs."

Peter angrily pushed the wheelchair into the patient's room. Then Mrs. H entered the dining room. She was our only patient who didn't have dementia. She was with us because her body didn't obey her. She listened to their debate and wondered who they were. She had never seen such beautiful men in her life. A few moments later, I pushed another patient, Mrs. K, into the dining room. We could still communicate with her a bit.

Mrs. H asked me: "Tina, who are these new faces? And so handsome on top of that?"

I answered with humor in German because I knew they couldn't understand: "The Olympus gods, Mrs. H, have come down to us."

Mrs. H laughed. "As nurses?"

I objected: "First I have to teach them how to disinfect and clean everything then we'll see what happens."

Mrs. K who was once an attractive woman laughed. "I hope I'll live long enough that I would be washed by such a divinely beautiful man at least once before I die."

I blushed a little. Peter and Rick glared at what the three women were talking about and laughing at.

Mrs. H told to Mrs. K: "These guys aren't interested in old grannies like us," and shouted at me: "Tina, what about you? You are still young! You told me that you would like to meet someone because you and your husband no longer live like a married couple."

I was red like a crayfish.

"I'm just a nurse, Mrs. H and they're used to a completely different standard. They're famous actors."

Mrs. K didn't give up and continued with her typical nipping humor.

"Men don't need a standard. When they are horny, they see nothing but darkness. Black darkness down there."

Mrs. H shook her head. "Tina when a man's heart is in its right place, he won't look at your imperfections, believe me. I lived with one man all my life."

I looked her in the eyes. "That didn't help me so far. Men just like to hunt elsewhere."

Rick and Peter didn't understand what was going on. Those patients liked me and I liked them. They were women who had a hard life. They taught me a lot and liked to talk to me when there was an opportunity. Mrs. H watched Rick in the kitchen, and I served coffee with a dessert alongside bringing patients from the rooms. Peter thought about what those women had so passionately debated about. Rick leaned against the glass door and tried to catch at least a bit of the German conversation that was going on between us. German was for god's sake a Germanic language after all, but he only caught snatches. A moment later the dining room was filled with female patients and two male patients. Almost everyone was seriously sick. At that time, they realized that fame and money and the perfection of the human body were so insignificant and so relentlessly fast-passing. Was this place a reason why people around the world, especially in earth's Olympus, Hollywood, are struggling with wrinkles and aging? These people with different fates found themselves in a place they hated. A place where death meant hope and liberation from their terrible affliction. Different rules applied here. Mercy and compassion and higher levels of love showed on daily basis the way to those who nurtured those decrepit human beings. Without that, it will be impossible to work here. Four men were about to be convinced about that. As if they had indeed descended from earthly Olympus among ordinary mortals just to remember that the body was just a box. After some time, it begins to crumble. Emotions and love remain until the last second of human life.

Meanwhile, Peter finished cleaning the wheelchairs. I didn't want him to think I favored Rick, so I told him: "If you want you can sit with Mrs. P. You can occasionally stroke her hand and face. You can speak to her in English. Sometimes she doesn't understand what you want from her even if you speak German."

"Stroke her? Why?"

"Human being reacts to touch, especially the one whose mind no longer functions properly and very intensely. They have very little touch here. We wash them, feed them, take care of them. There is no much time to calm patients in this way."

Peter was taken aback, and Rick was collecting used cups and plates, putting them in the dishwasher, pretending he wasn't interested in what was going on. However, when he saw Peter sitting beside Mrs. P, who smiled at him as if she had a revelation, he felt a strange prick in his heart. So little is needed to create a smile on human face. Mrs. P didn't care what he said in English. She could only sense the tone of his voice, his smile, and his touch. This is how love can look like. Pure, endless magic, that although only for a while, brings back everything that was already dead.

Rick picked and loaded the dishes into the dishwasher, and it seemed like an endless story to him. Emotions, even though they were rather negative so far, shook his soul. He felt an inexplicable rage. Rage towards his lawyer for him sending them to this place. Rage towards this little pain in the ass that allowed herself to call him Sugarman. He felt angry that he will go to bed alone tonight. Anger and fear that we can all end up like those poor people. Where did all this come from?

The end of their duty was approaching, and I thanked them all for their help. I always do that, although many people don't. Even if everyone gets money for the work they do, we all forget to thank each other. Well done work is not common.

"Thank you for your effort and excuse the language barrier. We will continue tomorrow."

Andy asked me: "And what about you? We thought it's the end of your shift as well."

"I work here only 15 days, so I have to work 80 percent of my working hours in two weeks. That means working from morning until evening."

Rick pretended he didn't care, but it wasn't true. Why does that asshole ask her when she finishes her shift? He didn't know why he was upset with that as well. Actually, he was angry at everything all day. We said goodbye and I continued my work until evening. They went back to their temporary male nest and rolled into their bed for a while. It wasn't that they weren't used to physical hard work. For men it's just difficult to witness suffering. The whole world thinks they are strong, and they have to handle everything. That's a mistake. Their hearts are more fragile.

In the evening they went to the Rabbit pub for diner. They were unusually quiet.

Peter broke the silence first: "I've never seen so much misery in one place. It's terrible."

Will shouted: "Oh, tell me that! Upstairs they were changing the diapers for the old ladies. I thought I won't survive that. Not even disinfection helped. I'd rather go to jail. I can't do this! Old men and woman in diapers that's really too much for me!!!"

Rick had not finished eating yet and throw his fork angrily on the plate.

"Can't you shut up? I'm still eating!"

Will sneered: "Just wait, you are the next on the line. You'll have to get used to that. Mr. King who was sitting instead of working."

Peter defended him: "He was working in the afternoon. Loading and unloading the dishwasher."

Poor Peter shouldn't have said this, Will and Andy were upset. "Dishes?? So, we clean, and he stands at the dishwasher? It's not fair!! We also want to operate the dishwasher. That's the easiest job!"

Peter told in a desperate voice: "You have to ask Tina tomorrow. It's not my decision."

Rick shrugged his shoulders. "So what? The little nurse with Aphrodite's ass has a crush on me."

Andy told him: "You are really weird. By the way, do you know who Aphrodite is?"

"Of course, I know! I'm not stupid. Goddess of love, beauty, and..."

Peter sighed: "Fertility."

Will added: "And sex. Which means passion...or something like that."

The guys burst into laughter but at the same time, they realized that they will go to bed alone. They weren't used to live like teenagers, sharing a flat. At that very moment, they realized what kind of existence is awaiting them here. They were good guys, but guys. Machos who needed their testosterone code to be fulfilled at any circumstances otherwise a disaster was waiting around the corner. The name of this code was my idea. In my mind it had four main points: point 1. clean house, point 2. clean clothes, point 3. full belly with worm food, and point 4. empty...you know what I mean... Unfortunately, the last point was very important in their lives, but that wasn't their fault. Only after these main points were fulfilled, came the other points like love, respect, tenderness, faithfulness. Men needed much more time than us, women, to come to these points. That's why there was so much trouble with love in our world these days. Because each one of us thought he can eat any fruit and moreover we thought that we can eat it under any circumstances. Love? That's only causing a headache. Friendship with benefits is a much better idea.

The guys went back to their miserable existence, the consequences of which began to manifest a little bit later. They had no desire to even contact their loved ones. The first day was difficult for them, even though they went through it quite well.

I finished my duty at 9 pm and hurried to my little room where I was staying. Actually, I just went to sleep there and just occasionally to relax. Since my working day was very long and I had very little time for all the activities that I wanted to fulfill, I had my day timed by minutes. That was because I wanted to save another of the gifts that humanity has. Time. I had everything prepared in baskets in advance. A laundry basket, a cooking basket, a bag for dancing and exercise. After the duty, I tossed my nurse's uniform into the laundry basket, put on the clothes I had prepared in advance. I grabbed my dance props, my bag, and ran down to the laundry and then to my paradise. The patient's entertainment hall served as my dance and exercise room in the evening. Here, after a hard day, I filled my body with endorphins in order to be able to go to work hell the next day. Although I liked my job, because of the stress, bad system, and the desperate lack of staff, it became hell. There was less time left for me to dance, because of my long working hours. I remembered Rick. What do we women have to do to make men notice us? What is sexy for men? I still couldn't understand them. From every side, I hear that men care about character and kindness, and so on. The exercise didn't bother me. I was doing it mainly for myself. I was just wondering about men in general. What about Rick? How is he really like? Oh, whatever! He's a famous man, I'm a nurse. I'm not from his world.

Rick also thought for a moment about this annoying bossy nurse with legs and ass like Aphrodite. It occurred to him that her having a crush on him can give him some advantages. *Why wouldn't he take advantage of that?* Woman as a woman. She is good enough for a flirt. Besides, it's annoying to sleep alone. His male strength echoed. Moreover, it would be a great risk to just go out and have fun and try to pick someone. They already had one spoiled evening and that was more than enough.

Finally, everyone in their male nest fell asleep and their guardian angels were guarding them. My guardian angel Nolachiel flew back to them. "We were right, Chasariel. Love is not to be manipulated with. The potion works with Rick as poison!!! It was supposed to allow her to get closer to him but look what it is doing to him?"

Chasariel told her: "Well, it wasn't tested, and the high dose of dill seeds did its job. We just have to wait until it evaporates."

Mechiel, Will's angel objected: "Don't forget, Chasariel, that Eros shot him an arrow with three-quarters of that poison. It will take a while to evaporate. It is up to me to try to alleviate its effects and to whisper to him the right decisions."

But Ameliel, Andy's angel said: "Human beings rarely hear our voice when their hearts are fine. How do you want to drown out his ego's voice, which unfortunately now has such wonderful conditions?"

Avariel, Peter's guardian angel remarked: "Recently, the ego has favorable conditions everywhere on Earth."

The angels fell silent and Nolachiel flew back to me.

The next morning, our new adult trainees came back to work and were waiting for me. Although the wheelchairs were clean, the work in the nursing house never ends. We greeted each other and I explain to them new tasks:

"Today you will clean the cabinets in the patients' bathrooms. We have a lack of staff, not enough time to do all the work."

The men nodded, only Rick made a mocking remark: "Cabinets? You are obsessed with your cabinets, aren't you?"

For a moment I thought of how to express what I want to say with my weak English. "You men have a lot of cabinets in your head. Divided. Women have only one where everything is connected."

Peter laughed, he understood what I was talking about, Andy too. Will and Rick looked at me blankly. I continued: "You have a lot of cabinets, and sometimes there is a need to make some order in them. There are also a lot of cabinets here, so you will have a lot of work to do."

"Why are you always teasing her? You said you aren't interested in her," Peter whispered to Rick.

Rick shrugged his shoulders. "It's true. I'm not. Not even in her stupid cabinets."

I called all four of them into one of the bathrooms and showed them how to do it. *Terrible,* I thought. Well, I wasn't responsible for them being in such a situation. I also obeyed orders. I gave them everything they needed for the task and Andy and Will went to the second floor where they started cleaning. Peter, too. Only Rick sat on the couch and thought to himself that no way he is going to clean some stupid bathroom cabinets. What has this nurse again came up with for them? He didn't even clean his own bathroom cabinets at home! Yeah, he always had somebody to do this job.

I came to him and asked: "What about you? Don't you like to clean bathroom cabinets?"

"No, I don't. Can you believe that?"

"I have this feeling that you don't like anything here. I haven't seen your smile since you are here. Well, that's a pity. But do as you wish. I don't want to give you orders. We are in need and we do really need help. You saw yesterday, there's a lot of work to do and you saw nothing yet."

Rick wanted to resist, but her humble words and the word 'help' again drowned out the cold voice of his ego and he said: "Give me a minute, I'll go…"

Meanwhile, while he sat there, I unloaded the dishes from the dishwasher and then cleaned and disinfected the whole kitchen after breakfast. four times a day there was always a mess that we always had to clean up. Four meals a day meant four times a mess in the kitchen. Suddenly while Rick was watching me with a corner of his eyes, Mrs. S sat next to him and wanted to show him her photo album. There were pictures of her youth. Rick was stunned because he didn't know what to say to the old lady.

I came to him: "You can show him photos, but he won't understand you, he is a foreigner."

I told Rick: "Just look at it and say the photos are nice."

"I can't speak German."

I laughed. "See? The world's most important language won't help you here."

I told him the sentence he needed to tell, and Mrs. S was happy to show someone her album. Rick was finally starting to melt a little. When he finished with the album, he joined Peter and started to clean those unfortunate cabinets. What does this Venusian woman have with these cabinets? Peter had already finished cleaning some of them and Rick watched him for a moment. Peter saw him and welcomed him with ironic enthusiasm: "Ooo Lord the King has risen from his new throne, the couch! Well, today you advanced a level higher than you were yesterday on that portable toilet."

"Just shut up and give me that stupid rag! Most importantly don't be so keen. The faster we have finished, the more work this little pain in the ass will give us. Have you seen how much furniture they have here?? Fuck!"

Peter shook his head blankly. "Man, since you are here you are like you have fallen from Mars. Normally you are working your ass off and now?"

"I'm telling you; I like my dark side. I feel less vulnerable."

Peter begged him: "For god's sake Rick, have you looked around? Let's be glad we have feelings, we have our head in the right place, even though it hurts sometimes."

Rick defended himself coldly: "Love always hurts. It's better this way. Without emotions. Without fear."

Peter objected: "Fearless? I rather feel like you're afraid to open your eyes now. Anyway, yeah, work slowly rather than quickly since there is so much furniture here. We have 180 working hours to work here. So, we will be working and cleaning here till we get crazy. Whether slowly or quickly. Who knows if the jail wouldn't be better?"

"It wouldn't! And what about our image?"

Peter spitted: "Well, now your fans should see you. You are a great example for them… Now you have an image of a hero."

Suddenly Rick didn't care. So what? Being a symbol of perfection could honestly get on your nerves. Now he could be a bad boy for a while. He quite liked it. So, he started cleaning the bathroom cabinets with Peter. He thought about how there can be such different worlds on one planet. The Venusian woman is an ordinary nurse; he is an extraordinary famous actor. However, she is from Venus. Maybe she's right that they're like the Olympus gods on Earth.

While they were cleaning, they heard lively noises. Rick didn't realize that he was cleaning the bathroom cabinets in the double room, where we had two of the most difficult patients on that floor. He peeked into the room and stayed frozen. He saw two women who were in the terminal stage of their lives. They laid motionlessly twisted into the shape of an embryo and didn't respond to any stimulations. Their mind was already empty as the aquarium in the dining room. Then I entered the room with washing and bathing aids.

"You're surprised, right? You won't see such scenes in the TV shows from the hospital environment. People would be horrified."

Rick asked: "So, this is how we will all end up?"

"No, scientists don't know the cause of this disease. Maybe we'll all end up with diapers. Probably."

Rick was once again upset about how the Venusian woman talked to him. He was confused, he didn't feel well at this terrible place. And that bossy woman on top of all this. He just wanted to go home and forget about the whole horror around him. He was putting up a hell of a fight and resisting to open the gate of his heart because emotions could sometimes hurt. I went on the best I could, and I helped myself with my cell phone. I didn't care anymore that I looked crazy. I felt it was important to try to communicate with him. But I was running out of words and time. So, I just told him: "If you want, you can have a look. I don't have time to explain everything to you. You have everything on the Internet."

Suddenly, Rick smiled a little: "You are right. The cabinets are on the Internet as well."

I smiled. "Sorry. It's not my fault. I was searching the net to find something about you and your movie, and I found your cabinets."

We laughed and Rick decided to sneak peek at the unpleasant reality. It was a terrible sight for him. He didn't show it, but at that moment his heart shuddered, and he understood why women were working mainly in this area of nursing. It was their tender estrogen hormone that symbolized softness, kindness. That was more than necessary for this kind of job. He watched a petit nurse trying to wash a patient with a difficult health condition and therefore it was a challenge. Rick asked: "Is it always so hard?"

"Always. It gets worse. I call the technique of washing such patients *Wash what you can reach*."

Rick smiled a little again, but he didn't feel good inside. Where did that rage in him just come from? Until now, he was nice, romantic. I finished one patient and tried to get the porridge and liquids into her. Rick watched what was happening and asked: "Is this a technique called *pour in the mouth what's possible*?"

"Probably yes. We have to try. Our bosses are checking everything. Weight, how we care. How we write. All the rules."

"We also have difficult rules."

"Perhaps more difficult than us here. Well, wait when we give them laxatives tomorrow. I feel sorry for you from now."

Rick was quiet and I begged him: "Stay here a minute, I'm going to bring Zeus or Thor."

Rick stared at me and didn't understand. *She probably is really crazy*, he thought. I came back to the room with our medical device, without which we could not work with immobile patients. It was a lifter. I called it Zeus or Thor.

"This is our real God in the department. Without him, we couldn't work, you'll see why in a moment."

I took a bathing net and packed another patient into the net using my nursing techniques. Rick wanted to help, but he still didn't have the courage to approach that destroyed human being. He felt angry again. Why is this actually happening? Why do people have to suffer like that? Why is it necessary? So, he just watched as Thor lifted the patient up. She was slightly spinning in the net. That created a big smile on his face. He didn't realize how dear it was to my heart that the cold had melted a bit. Although only for a short while but oh that smile. Rick couldn't continue to clean the bathroom cabinets at that moment, because I was washing the patient in that net. He watched as I struggled but he still didn't dare to come closer He remarked only: "*Wash what you can reach* technique."

I smiled.

Rick continued working, but he was slow. Emotions made him uncomfortable. He no longer recognized what he felt and why. When the temporary adult trainee-beauties finished with the cabinets, they had to wait for me for a while until I finished my shift. It has always been stressful when I got someone else in charge in addition to my tasks and I had to show them around, give orders, and delegate work. I noticed that not all people have organizational skills. I inherited them along with my sister from our strict father, a lieutenant colonel. He was as strict at home as he was in the army. He always knew everything about us, even when me and my sister lied in puberty like snakes, just to fool around and he would let us do it. We were afraid of him as the forest was afraid of fire. Life was sometimes unbearable with him. He loved us, he just wanted sons who would also be soldiers, but that didn't happen. His sisters, our aunts often blamed him for being too strict on us as he was strict on his soldiers. They reminded him that we were girls. He didn't care. The order had to be maintained. My sister's closet, although still a child, was so tidy that it couldn't be tidier. The soldiers in the barracks were also afraid of him. When they drank or did something wrong, he didn't put them in jail. Instead, he made them clean anything possible, especially oil spots in the garages. When I studied at nursing school, I often went to his work for him to take me home. If some young soldier saw him, he either ran off the road or started marching like on a show just to make my father happy. When we walked by the car park, I saw these poor people cleaning the cars and the hideous stains that didn't go away down the path, I asked my father: "Why are you torturing them? Look how they're trying! What did they do?"

"They run away from the barracks to meet women. Got drank while wearing a uniform. So, they must be grateful that I didn't put them in jail. They must be turned to men; at the moment they are just boys."

"Dad, for god's sake! You can't blame them! They're young men! Can't you show some mercy?"

"Mercy? They can forget! They must learn how to clean and put things in order. This will help them in the future. You also have to learn it. You will also need it. Remember, sloppy work does not stand. What you don't do well will return to you in worse condition than it was."

I watched those poor men who didn't even dare to look at me. When my father wasn't looking at them, they gazed at him. But at the end of their compulsory military service, they were thankful for his sternness.

I was wondering if I might be better off in a man's body. My strong nature complicated my life. Since the second year of elementary school, I have been unwittingly always the leader. This continued all my life, though I didn't want it at all. I was an inconspicuous kid, but apparently smart. Mom taught me to read when I was in kindergarten, and I read one book after another. There were infinite beautiful realities that influenced my life. All this swirled inside my head. I know that superficial beauty vanishes. We need to take care of ourselves, but our body just ages. I had to smile at the memory of my father and his soldier because I often felt like him. In my life. Usually, nobody wanted to organize things or delegate tasks, because it meant more responsibility. For me, it always happened somehow smoothly. Without organized work, chaos and stress arose everywhere. At the end of the day, every trainee will always end up with me because I have the patience to teach and show. That's a gift. Poor handsome guys from Olympus. No one else would bear the responsibility of managing them. Not even in German language.

"Sorry, you had to wait."

Andy smiled.

"Now two of you will be in the kitchen during lunch. One on the first floor, the other on the second floor. You will operate the dishwasher."

Rick smirked and thought he would avoid working again. I disappointed him. "To be always fair, I invented a system. You will rotate. Each of you will be in the kitchen every other day. Additional tasks will be added. Cleaning and setting up tables, giving fluids to patients. And smile at them. If you want, you can sometimes sit with them and make them company like Peter did yesterday."

Rick was surprised because he expected to be in the kitchen. Peter asked: "What are the others going to do?"

Rick couldn't stop himself and shouted with sarcasm: "Clean more cabinets. I told you…"

Will glared: "I'm going to the kitchen today. Andy will clean."

I looked at Rick: "Some of you don't like cleaning furniture, so I have more special tasks for you."

Will knew that it doesn't matter which day he will be in the kitchen. The petit nurse created a system for them. I was very upset with myself. I didn't like to delegate tasks, teach, and explain all the time. But then you need patience for that as well.

"Rick and Andy, please come with me."

I took them to the dining room and the corridors. I showed them space under the big windows and the railing that stretched along the corridor.

"When you finish, you will continue with the railing on the stairs. There are many other things besides furniture that desperately need to be cleaned."

Rick lost control. "And where are your housekeepers? Isn't it their job?"

"It is but you're here because you have to do community service, aren't you? Housekeepers are doing what they can. That's why we are happy when someone breaks the rules."

Andy tried to ease the situation: "Guys, we're glad that we can help, right? Get to know a little different reality, right?"

Will cast a sour smile and Peter humbly agreed: "Yeah, before we'll leave, all the furniture, the cabinets, and everything else will be pretty clean."

I added mysteriously: "Your hearts will be a little cleaner as well. Good deeds count both in Heaven and Earth."

Rick was irritated. "Good deeds? Isn't it enough that we give a lot of money for charity? What else should we do? We are not the saviors of the whole world. We can't do more."

Oh, that was a challenge, but I remained calm. I wondered how I should answer such a difficult question with my poor English. So, I helped myself with my cell phone. I wrote my answer on a piece of paper and tried to read it. I really felt like a teacher trying to explain something to a disobedient pupil. I knew that these pupils had good hearts.

"Right, you are not saviors. But maybe you are. The characters of your heroes try to save the world and they are supposed to inspire everyone else. Money is fine. It can help. Except with the money you send to charity people can't buy everything. They can't buy a touch, a kind word, a smile but especially they can't buy love. These sick people need these invisible gifts as well. Not just to be fed or washed. Nobody listens to us, ordinary people. Maybe they will listen to the heroes, or to those who play their roles. I'm sorry that my answer is maybe confusing. I hope you understand what I want to tell at least a bit."

Rick didn't give up. "Do you think a couple of men can save the whole world? This is different than what we do in movies."

"It's different you are right. I told you, you are going to face real monsters here. In movies, you are facing the fictional ones, but they are symbols. Symbols of the biggest problems that humanity has and can't solve itself. Thinking and feeling positive is important. We need more deeds. Deeds of love. First, we try to define the problem. That's what you do in your difficult work all the time. You are messengers. That's how you pass these messages to mankind. All artists do."

Rick stayed frozen, Andy nodded, Peter looked at me with a strange look. Will said on their behalf: "It's true. Money can't solve everything."

I added: "Food is also a gift. I am grateful that we still have food for us and for the patients. Well, so let's go and try to do the ordinary things."

The guys smiled, only Rick continued to frown, though he knew that Venusian woman might be right in something. Only in something, but she was still giving orders. Even to him. Until today he used to manage things. But here everything was upside down because of one stupid, unlucky evening. None of the four earthly Olympians could explain why that happened. They had no idea that those at the heavenly Olympus, knew why.

Chapter 4

Zeus stood on the Fields of Pearls with one of the angels and watched as the other angels collected light from white and pink pearls. They gathered them on snow-white meadows. Every time someone did something good down on Earth, whether be it a word or a deed, a beautiful sound was created, and one white pearl was added to the Fields of Pearls. Pink pearls and their light were even rarer. They symbolized the deeds of goodness in the level of love that brought joy to mankind. Sometimes the most torment. It had the name of the god of love. Eros. Love that created pairs on Earth. Couples. Zeus asked the angel: "How does it look?"

The angel replied quietly: "It's not getting much better. Though the number of pearls is growing, we have never had so little before a fight. Something is going very wrong in the world."

Zeus agreed. "Their technology and intelligence are spoiling them the most. Sometimes, these gifts are used with malicious intent. On one hand, it allows them to push the boundaries of reason, on the other the hearts of people are shrinking. They need evidence for everything. The scientists are constantly searching for evidence even about the existence of the Creator. Their pride and ego won't allow them to admit that the universe is infinite and that they are merely an insignificant drop in it."

The angel continued: "They're not insignificant to him, otherwise he wouldn't try to save them all the time. Nothing in the universe is insignificant for him, Zeus. There must be hierarchy and synchronicity throughout the universe, otherwise, everything would collapse."

"But back there everything is already collapsing. Soon, even those human worms will have no place to live, because they are delightfully destroying the resources of the planet."

"Zeus, they have free will. There are only two religions on Earth, but they don't want to admit it. Their pride won't let them. They think they are fighting for the Creator, but they are actually fighting for power and for superficial pride. Only two religions, Zeus. One of them is the religion of fear and the other of love. People, even atheists, are unconsciously believing in him, with every decision they make. No one has ever seen or measured emotions, fear, or love. Yet everyone believes they exist. No one has ever seen the Creator or the ruler of the dark side, yet they constantly need to find evidence of their existence. It does not matter what religion people on Earth believe in. There are only these two options in each one."

Zeus sighed: "They are still afraid to believe that the Creator is endless love. Therefore, He will save everything He has created, and we will fulfill His will."

The angel asked: "How do we save them this time when the number of pearls and their light is diminishing?"

Zeus contemplated: "We'll believe in a miracle. There is nothing else we can do. This time we really need a miracle."

"This time it will have to be a huge miracle," the angel added.

Zeus thought: "Perhaps the angel of mercy and compassion, should call all the guardian angels. They are the closest to human beings, aren't they? Many people believe in guardian angels."

Angel agreed: "Everything needs to be tried. The more options we try, the better. Well, I believe it will all end well."

Zeus stroked his chin. "You angels always believe in good and love. Why people don't always believe in good and love?"

The angel smiled mysteriously and replied: "You know, the angels have given up their free will. They gave what people received as a gift, for their love to the Creator."

Zeus kept silent. Free will was a gift. For human beings to have an option to choose from, evil must be present. The question was why more and more of them chose the wrong way?

At the same time, down on Earth, in one place, in the middle of nowhere, four male human beings continued to do unusual good deeds, and some of them didn't like it that much. Peter stood by the dishwasher and smiled at Rick, who was angry. Angry because this annoying nurse wanted to humiliate him this way. With her fairness. Well, wait, bitch, I'll pay you back one day. Sure, an opportunity will come. Don't think you will get out of this. At that moment he didn't realize that it isn't her fault. She as well had to perform the tasks that were given to her from above. That's how the world works.

I felt sorry for him, but I thought a little humility won't hurt anyone. Many of the high society people think they are superior to us, ordinary people. They think that they are something more. They often call the very necessary jobs on Earth as inferior. No job is inferior. If the garbage men wouldn't come to work, we will be buried in trash. If the cleaners won't come to work mess will be everywhere. If the nurses didn't come to work, we will be buried in... Well, you know in what.

Rick stud by the railing and held a disinfectant wipe. He watched Peter serving coffee to the patients. They were excited because they haven't been served by such a handsome man before. Right next to the kitchen two gorgeous grannies were sitting. They looked really like fairies. One of them thanked for every little thing. Peter melted like ice in the sun because he was beginning to realize that one smile and touch, that didn't cost a dime, was like a cure. Rick was pretending that he didn't notice what was going on around him. Nevertheless, he couldn't hide his beauty and charisma. Not even behind his bad mood. When Mrs. H came to her place, she saw how he was acting. She was very observant and when I brought her coffee, she was curious. "That handsome man is gazing at you. He looks pretty angry at you. What did you do to him?"

I explained to her: "Well, I must distribute work fairly and he doesn't like the result. Oh, Mrs. H, I'm just not good with men. I don't know how to treat them. I know they're amazing beings and that we need them but... Well, look what's happening!"

Mrs. H explained: "A negative emotion is still an emotion. Believe me. Everything will be good. May I ask you something? Do you know him?"

I smiled sadly. "Not really. I never met him in person before. I don't know who he really is, but I believe he has a good heart."

Mrs. H told me: "Time will solve everything, and he will smile."

Yeah, I thought. Unfortunately, the circumstances again destroyed the chance of his smile. Moreover, I don't have any special abilities. If you won't consider me unintentionally ruling over other human beings with my service as a special ability. This ability I had all my life.

The paradox was that I didn't want that. It was always circumstantial. Is he a leader in his own way? I contemplated. Oh, why I'm dealing with this? It doesn't make any sense. The relentless boundaries between our worlds have divided us even more than his current strange coldness. I believed he had a big heart inside. Oh, god. If naivety would bloom, I would be like a rose.

I ordered myself: *Stop dreaming and go back to reality. They are from earthly Olympus; you are an ordinary mortal.*

I looked into the corner where Rick gazed at all his surroundings in disagreement. He was frustrated from this terrible place. He had this military general woman over his back. How terrible. He would have to endure that for a few more days. He watched the grannies whose mind didn't work like it should and so their actions looked the same. Suddenly an old lady entered the dining room, almost naked, pushing a cart filled with various things in front of her. She didn't mind at all that the dining room was full of people. As always, she has been on her way home. For months. Peter froze. Rick as well. Well, they haven't seen such a woman's body a long time ago. There was not even a trace of beauty and sensuality in it. Mrs. M approached me and asked: "Nurse, where is the exit? I have to go home! My husband is waiting for me."

I came to her quickly and was trying to be very patient, though it wasn't always easy. "Mrs. M, come with me, we will get dressed, okay?"

Mrs. M was very stubborn. "I'm hot. I don't want to dress."

"But we have two men here, look."

I pointed at Peter and Rick.

Ms. M had a pungent sense of humor in the past and she objected with a smirk: "Oh, really? Are you sure they are men?"

I was shocked. With such notes, she would occasionally bring the staff to the boiling point. They tried to keep their head cool.

"Well, they look like men. They look like your husband."

Mrs. M looked at them with a scornful look: "Hmm. My husband was more handsome and better."

I remembered what she told me when she had a bright moment about her husband. How a good man he was and how she loved him. Strange. People from her generation withstood with their partners through all. They often suffered, starved, didn't always have everything they needed. We, though, we didn't succeed in many cases. Nor did I succeed. The work that forced me to be away from my family along with my disappointment that only words as proof of love are not enough destroyed my relationship. Only two beautiful children remained. All that remains is to learn from the mistakes. I said to the granny: "Look, I'll put some clothes on you, unpack your cart, bring you some coffee, something sweet, and then the assistant will take you down to the living room and you will do something nice there, okay?"

"Oh, really? You're so good to me. Will I get some coffee? But I don't have money."

I convinced her: "Everything is arranged for you. Your daughter took care of it."

So, they all watched as I took Mrs. M into her room.

Peter asked me later in the kitchen: "What did you say to her? I didn't understand well."

"Unfortunately, I don't understand you well, too. Here it doesn't matter what you tell. Every granny has her own reality where she lives. She doesn't care about real life. She wanted to go home to her husband who died a long time ago. For these people time is irrelevant."

Peter was a little bit sad. So ruthless is the time. We can't bring it back. We are helpless against it, no matter how hard we try. These women no longer cared about how many wrinkles they had, how much belly or thighs fat they had, or whether they had perfect outfit or makeup. They were left only with food, sweet word, attention, and those unfortunate diapers. On Earth, time ruthlessly smashed all to dust.

Rick worked very slowly. He was not indifferent about what he saw. Deep inside he was a very good and sensitive man. Unfortunately, that didn't always bring him luck. Anger and negative emotions began to mix with compassion. It started to hurt. Since he was here, he has seen some terrible things. A reality he might not even want to see. For all his life, he tried to be a good person. So why the hell he has to be here?

Later I said goodbye to all of them and the guys went to their male nest. None of them was very much talkative. Certainly, they had big problems even in their shiny reality, but they no longer knew which one was worse. So far, they have not realized that both realities have both good and dark side. Their silence was proof that they were in one of the worst places they may have seen so far. These patients were not afraid of death. For them, death was the liberation of the soul from their miserable bodies and minds that had long since failed to function. While the body and head obey us, we don't realize that we are healthy. We take it as a fact and enjoy life with full sips. Once we get sick, we no longer have any other desire just to heal. That our body, head, and mind work well again. In the evening, the guys just threw their clothes on the floor and fell asleep like babies.

Rick was thinking about her words. With terrible English and with even worse Slavic accent, she explained symbols and points used in their movies. Of course, those fights with the monsters were really cool. Today he saw what kind of monsters this woman from Venus and her colleagues, only two of them males, are fighting with. Real, scary monsters that could not always be defeated. Even in their movies, it was not always possible to win. And later he found out that Venusian woman and her colleagues didn't always manage their reality with a smile and a positive attitude. Mercy and compassion have sometimes lost the fight because people are imperfect.

The next day was the 'D' day. I called it ironically the Celebration of Macrogol. I tried with humor to mitigate the effects of one pharmaceutical preparation that every nurse actually hated. But they couldn't manage without it. Four strong and handsome men were about to witness that in a moment. Dementia is a disease that kills the nervous system of the body, not only the mind. Orders that are normally given by the head of the human body, the brain, must travel through neural connections, synapses, but the disease systematically destroys them. The result is terrible. All humankind lacks humility in recent times. Only when we get into situations where another human being has to clean our exclusions and everything else that is so unpleasant to all the people, we understand our mortality. In families where people love each other, it's easier. Husband, wife, children, family. If someone else has to do it, the highest level of love, mercy, and compassion is needed. Without it, it would be impossible.

"Good morning. Today we will continue where we stopped yesterday. You will just swap your places. Rick and Andy in the kitchen, Peter and Will cleaning. Please prepare for today. For people from outside, it can be very annoying. For sure, I have something for you to protect you from the effects of our favorite medicine."

Will seemed to know what was coming and sighed desperately: "Oh, god."

I smiled and pulled out four surgical masks. I gave each one of them one and continued: "You won't enter certain rooms without warning. You can breathe through your mouth, but it doesn't help much."

They all laughed, they realized what was coming. Andy tried to show his power. "You think we can't take it? We all know it."

They all laughed again, and I was a little afraid. "Maybe. Well, but is different than here. Believe me. You are strong guys, some of you might be able to do my job. These miraculous estrogens work better against these monsters. Testosterone prefers to operate or prescribes medicines. The less popular jobs are often left for the estrogens."

The guys understood that, and Peter asked: "When we should prepare for the fight?"

I explained: "Do you mean if we have a defense schedule? No. These monsters attack unexpectedly."

Rick stared at me with his eyes. "I prefer to go to jail."

I ordered: "We don't have time for discussion. Everyone please to their work."

Guys put their surgical masks in their pockets, and we all went to work.

Rick was in his luxury post of loading and unloading the dishes, and he was satisfied that he won't be in the rooms or other places where the monsters can attack unexpectedly. He forgot that most patients wore diapers instead of black lace panties. That was a betrayal. I was washing the patients one by one and in addition, I was gradually distributing medications. Strange bags were prepared on the counter and there were a lot of them there.

Rick asked: "What is inside of these bags?"

"Something that will awake the monsters."

"Couldn't you drop them in a sink, for example? Why are you giving it to them when it causes a catastrophe?"

"I can't. It's an order from the doctors. We also have to execute orders, Rick. Sorry, this language barrier is terrible for me."

"I don't know your language or German."

For a moment he didn't feel angry at the nurse who was forced to give them unpleasant tasks. She too had to obey. This time he looked at her for a long time and realized she was actually a female being. She wasn't some sexy actress, but he had little choice. In this tricky situation, it was risky to show his famous face.

All got worse when Mrs. K pushed her cart to her place at the table. From the very beginning, she was fascinated by my kind of little curvy figure. She always said that when she looks at me from behind, even though she was a woman, she had a desire to spank my ass. With the help of not only my girlfriends whom I danced with, I understood that each of us was unique and original. Human external beauty is a subjective thing. Chemistry always decides. That was something people wanted to decipher, but so far nobody could do it or find out how it worked.

Mrs. K was sitting and telling everyone, as always, everything she experienced. A fairy-tale looking granny sitting opposite her just listened to her, sometimes answered her question. Rick collected the dishes and I brought another patient to the dining room. Mrs. K welcomed me with her wide smile. "Good morning, Tina. Do you have those flowers in your hair again? Oh, and your ass. Too bad I'm not a man."

I blushed and thanked god Rick didn't understand German. Except Mrs. K did something she sometimes did to me when she wanted to make me a little angry. When I crossed the aisle to give her medication, she gently slapped my ass. I was horrified. "Mrs. K! Please! Now it's not appropriate!"

"I've always liked only men, but sometimes I can't resist this."

Rick was shocked and stared at what was happening and I blushed. "She doesn't have bad intentions. If it makes her happy?"

So little is needed to ignite the testosterone flame in the male body. Well, that's life. It's not easy for them. We women sometimes don't understand it and are angry with their hormone, which at certain moments absorbs them regardless of what kind of female unknowingly irritates them. They lose their head and their hunting instinct takes control. Woman as a woman, right? One ordinary nurse who has a crush on him. That won't be difficult at all. The language barrier? It will be somehow solved with hands, legs…

And so, Rick, who was overwhelmed not only with his natural male hunting instinct but also by the third quarter of a failed love potion with a double dose of dill seeds, decided to show his interest in his male way. He did it just like Mrs. K. He waited until I came to that tiny kitchen where three people could barely fit in and gently slapped my ass. He thought maybe it would work on me. I asked him: "What are you doing?" Rick pretended he didn't understand. He smiled and shrugged his shoulders.

Then he confidently replied: "Don't pretend you didn't like that. Look, you're a woman, I'm a man. You said it yourself that you like me. So where is the problem?"

I answered: "I like the hero you played. I don't know you; I don't know who you are."

Blood was bubbling in Rick's veins because this woman ignited rather negative emotions in him. He continued: "That doesn't matter, does it?"

"It matters to me. I just don't want it that way."

Rick didn't believe his own ears: "What you mean *This way*? What does that mean?"

"Is this your new male way how to charm a woman? Don't you even try to use some sweet words? Just because you are a man and I'm a woman, that should be enough?"

"It is for me. Romance is useless anyway. Everything ends the same way."

"You know nothing about me."

"What for?! I don't want to."

"Well, I want to know you. I don't know you. The face is one thing, I believe you have a good heart, but I don't know what kind of person you are."

"Why do you need to know? We want to have some fun."

"I'm not for one night."

"Does it all matter? Don't tell me you want to deny yourself pleasure because of that?"

"Pleasure? In one night, you can't decipher the estrogen code. Everything you will take will remain at the lowest level."

"What? What level? Do you think I don't know about women or what?"

"No, of course not. On the contrary. You're just kind of odd since you are here. I'm a nurse, I'm neither a model nor an actress, I even think I'm not your type at all."

"What are you saying? How can you know what type of women I like?" I laughed.

"Well, I'm sure the beautiful and famous ones."

Rick tried to handle the rush of negative emotions because he realized the price of fame at that moment. Even the most ordinary person in a remote village knows some of his privacy. Despite everything that the media and fans demanded, this was the worst thing in the life of celebrities. Everyone knew even what they shouldn't know.

"You are all women. That's what you have in common. No matter what type you are when it comes to…"

He couldn't find the right word, I added it: "You mean sex? Exactly. Come with me. I'll show you something."

Rick was delighted, he thought I had changed my mind. It occurred to him that the Venusian can't be so stupid that she will miss the opportunity that he was offering. That was his ego whispering and his male instinct that was huge. I brought him to the empty staff room. "Sit down, please."

Rick sat on the bench and I started: "Do you see this?" I pointed to the large cabinets where we kept the medicaments and many other aids we used. Rick started to smile.

"Oh, my god! Those cabinets again. I see. So what?"

"These big cabinets are your sexual area."

Rick frowned. I pulled a little yellow box out of my bag where I kept my USB stick and dropped it on the table and handed it to him.

"This is your area of emotions. I know you're a good guy, but you men are different when it comes to love than us women. The box is tiny at first and is far from the big cabinet. So, men need a longer time to make a connection between the large cabinet and that small box."

Rick held the little yellow box in his hand and looked at the big cabinet... He wanted to be angry, but somehow, he couldn't. He knew part of what I was saying was true. He kept silent. I continued: "We women have everything in one box. That's why we can't understand how you can separate sex from love."

Rick was still silent for a moment, then said: "Do you really think this is true?"

"Isn't it?" Rick didn't know what to say. He knew that nothing was perfect not even love. We are looking for it, but we are often unable to handle it.

"So, you think men are heartless?"

"Oh, no. Not at all. Only you have all things divided into your boxes and we have everything stored in one."

The situation was a little bit of light. I continued: "I'm trying to protect our hearts. It is unfortunately a woman who must do it all the time. A woman is a decision-maker in these situations. That is often very difficult for us, women."

Rick remained silent. So, she's not oblivious and is tempted. He asked: "Our hearts? My heart is none of your concern. You don't know me."

"And you don't know me. I think we both have holes and scars in our hearts, don't you think?"

Rick's eyes widened. He probably didn't understand what I said, so I took a paper and drew two hearts and marked holes and scars on them. Then he understood.

"So, you would like romance first? All the stupid things like dating, and so on?"

"No, I don't. That wouldn't be enough for me. I'd like something special, but you are not ready yet."

Rick got angry again. Not only did this beast rejected him but she wanted so much more.

"I'm not ready? Man is always ready for such things. I don't get it. What do you mean?"

"What kind of things? Do you mean those intimate activities? Oh, yes, I believe you are ready immediately. I just don't want it that way. In addition, it is difficult for us to communicate. I have to finish my work and you too. We'll talk some other time."

Rick remained curious. "So, we can continue tonight. If you want that date so much."

"I don't want a date. I want something special."

"Oh, you have such high demands. You're just a nurse."

"You're right. Just a nurse. The differences between our worlds are one thing and the size of our hearts and souls is another. I'm sorry, I have to."

Rick said nothing because he was disgusted. One ordinary nurse and so many imaginary obstacles. Why did she actually rejected him? Maybe she is shy? Or just playing it like most women do? That is what all women do at the beginning. He took the paper with those drawn hearts and looked at it again. Normally he would laugh at it, but now he was just angry and frustrated. He didn't know why. She is just an ordinary woman. He is a famous personality. What does it actually mean? What is the difference between a nurse who works with sick people and receives a certain reward and him, a famous man who has a job and got a certain reward for it? The difference in the size of their rewards was great. What was the difference between the size of their hearts?

Rick went back to the kitchen and tried not to think about what happened a while ago. Okay, what to do. She must be romantic. All women are. Men don't need romance. Only some of them. So far, he was one of them. But how many holes can one human heart take? Date… Adventure… Love… Sex… Do women keep all those things in one box? Do men keep them separately? How does it work in the world then?

The conversation with Rick took a long time so I had to catch up with missed work very quickly. Lunch was coming, and a lot of work with it.

Meanwhile, Peter ended up cleaning the railing and I told him: "I don't have time to give you another task now, you can stay here and help Rick with the dishes."

Peter wasn't thrilled to be helping him with that luxury job. While working they watched as the patients ate, and I fed a seriously sick woman who could no longer talk and made strange noises. She was like a box that perceived emotions. In order to calm her down a bit while eating, I used to hold her hand. Sometimes it helped. These were different kinds of touches from those exchanged at one of the levels of love by partners. Not only when having an intimate connection, but often at other times.

Touch was an important part of all levels of love. The touch was what people on Earth were most eager for because it was made possible with their physical body. Although it was fragile it was able to show love with touch. I remembered one interesting study where scientists found the most common cause of infidelity. It wasn't just the desire for sex, but for touch as well. Many couples slip into a routine due to difficult circumstances and sex becomes a duty in order to keep the relationship going. When difficult situations come, and the communication gets difficult both parties or one of them loses interest in romance, and touch becomes rare. Then all you need is a little temptation, and everything will collapse. Human beings have already become accustomed to artificial passive entertainment. Many of them have ceased to be creative and entertaining in their relationships. Humor and laughter are the best cure for trouble. But they must both want to do that and be kind of soul mates. It's even harder for famous people. Thanks to their work, men and women are particularly tempted and not always able to resist. Touch is important not only for couples. No small child or old human being can live without a touch.

Feeding patients required a lot of time and patience. Here too, we often had to be very creative to make it all happen. We have always been grateful for every helping hand. Guys tried and worked as best as they could. They started to realize that the world was actually full of heroes. Though the world didn't talk about them so loudly. They've already forgotten that they have surgical masks in their pockets in case the monsters will attack. That usually happened in the afternoon or in the evening after we distributed the most important pill. Gradually, my colleague and I started to put our patients to bed when, unfortunately, our favorite medicine started to work.

Peter had just taken a dirty plate from one of the patients when he realized that one of them had a very unpleasant smell: "Oh, Jesus, Rick! It seems that the crap that Tina gave them in the morning is beginning to work. Go and get her."

Rick rolled his eyes. "No way! I'm not moving from the kitchen."

"Okay then. I will go to look for her if you're afraid."

Rick told him: "Are you crazy? I'm not afraid, I just don't want to."

Peter shook his head in disbelief.

"Yeah sure. You can't avoid it anyway."

Peter went to look for me and found me in the room changing the diaper of one of the patients. He stopped by the door and I told him with laughter: "Don't come in. You got to get used to it first. You know, it's hard to believe, but you need a lot of skill and talent to change diapers for adults."

Peter sighed: "How can you do that? I never thought how scary it might be."

I objected: "It will be scary if we don't change the system and, in the future, no one will want to change diapers to powerless human beings."

Peter held his breath and I spoke with laughter: "As I say, not all of us are created for this kind of job. Well, I think any job if it is done properly is very difficult. Put the mask, but it won't help that much anyway. Well, we all have different talents."

Peter took out the mask and then told me: "I don't want to scare you, but I want to report another attack in the dining room."

I was not surprised. "That's just the beginning."

Peter was shocked because I stayed calm. "How can you smile? How on earth can all the nurses handle this?"

I answered mysteriously: "Humility. Fourth, the highest level of love teaches people humility. This is a gift that can purify the human heart from the filth that is often carried by the human ego."

Although my English was confusing Peter understood.

Rick still stood in the kitchen, thinking he was hiding from the monster attacks, but the consequences of one attack had already approached him. *Damn!* He thought. *What should he do? After all, he has always tried to be helpful and good to other people. So why must he stick around and endure this?* In short, those diapers were a tough level for many men. Suddenly his heart trembled, and he realized that no matter how hard we tried to reach physical perfection, we would lose our fight with time once and we will be forced to go back to where we came from. We will become fragile helpless beings. Only then, at the end of life, we will have the chance to understand human futility and pride. The gift of humility will help enlarge the human heart so that other parts of the highest level of love can enter it. Mercy and compassion. Yet it was difficult not only for him but also for other earthly Olympus who were forced to experience another reality.

I finished with the patient in the room and took another one out of the dining room to groom her. I was wondering how the four handsome involuntary trainees might feel. I assumed that, like most people who don't come into such close contact with so much suffering, they didn't feel good. Well, every job has a dark and bright side. Now they will get to know the darker side.

Peter came to the kitchen. "I don't know if there is anything worse in the world than these diapers. I don't want to get old anymore."

Rick was silent and then agreed in a humbler voice: "Probably not even me. We haven't been very concerned about this yet, because we're still young, aren't we?"

"It seems that there are still challenges waiting for us. Well, let's just go back to work at least we won't think about that."

Rick grunted: "All this is happening because of your damn idea to get drunk on the other end of the planet! Even in some of our movies, the shit was always happening on the other side of the Earth."

Peter laughed mockingly: "Yeah and you guys went to clean it. So, what the hell are you complaining about? Now we have the chance to see real shit. Take it easy and don't be so angry."

Rick was still angry. "Hmm. Sure, it's way too real. We've been here only a short time and I feel like it's been weeks. Fuck such an existence. I can't even blow a fuse here! We don't have women here, too. Damn it!"

Peter shrugged his shoulders. "Then ask her. She is head over heels about you. It shouldn't be hard, or?"

With a sour smile, Rick stroked his hair and admitted: "I already asked, but somehow, she didn't like the way. I don't know what she thinks of herself. She wants something special. Special."

Peter closed the dishwasher and looked incredulously at him.

"I can't believe she refused a date with you."

Rick looked at Peter, shrugged his shoulders, and then Peter understood. "What did you do? Don't tell me you harassed her instead of inviting her out!"

"Well. Nothing terrible happened. If a patient could do it, why couldn't I?"

Peter laughed. "I assume that your way was really successful with the mother of an adult son. Oh, my god, what's wrong with you?! As if it wasn't you. Where did your nice, romantic side of nature disappear?"

Rick was irritated. "Nowhere. You know what? It's better this way. I'm tired of being always the good guy. I can be different once, can't I?"

"Of course, you can be what you want. Only I'm not sure if this is the right place to show your worse side."

"After all, no catastrophe happened, so what? I guess her ass won't get damaged because I spanked it a little bit."

Peter caught his forehead. "Oh, god! You really showed your interest in the best way! If you continue like this, I'm sure you will be successful one day."

"What do you care if it works or not? Eventually, every woman will give up. She wants to play impregnable. Fine, we'll see how long it will last."

"Why don't you go look elsewhere? You said you didn't care about her."

Rick looked indifferent. "Yes, yes. I don't. Who could stand to be with such a woman? But the feeling that I would win over her would make my heart warmer."

Peter burst into laughter. "Your heart? Yeah sure. Your heart. Something else I would say. I'm afraid that with mothers who know the male world from infantry to adulthood it won't be that easy."

Peter didn't realize that these words had woken up the hunting instinct in Rick even more. In addition, he had no idea that the spoiled love potion had worked the opposite way and awakened Rick's hidden darker side. A side that every man had and fought with all life. Ego versus heart.

Rick didn't care who this undistinguished nurse actually was. This was not important at all at this point. He must get her at any cost. The reason was not clear to him yet, except for his initial satisfaction. And he didn't even want to know.

"She will break eventually, you'll see! Everybody breaks at one point. We know all those women's games, don't we?"

Peter nodded and asked uncertainly: "What will you actually gain when you get her?"

"Nothing. I'm going to have fun with her. That's all. She's crazy about me."

"About you? I'd rather say she is crazy about the hero to whom you borrowed your heart."

"Give me a break with him."

"She still sees only your worst side."

"Well, she wants higher levels of love, so I wonder how long it will last. Love. It always ends up the same."

Peter did not give up. "Little did we see here? Open your eyes! A higher level of love is present and soaked everywhere here."

"Yeah, it is. We smelt it just a moment ago."

Peter burst into laughter. "I mean, man, I'm shocked. Well, finish your work and then we'll go to have lunch at the Rabbit. That if we will be able to eat something."

Rick agreed: "Yeah. You see? This is the result of Tina's higher level of love. Shit, everywhere you look."

"Well, this is a tough reality. It's not like when you run around fighting the bad guys and monsters that you must imagine until they are drawn. Even though I get it, that isn't easy as well."

Rick contemplated. Peter was right. It wasn't easy. The path to playing the role of hero is even harder. People see the result only. Only snippets, if the actors want to share how it all worked out. One must learn to love his work. If he does what he wants, it's easier. What can we love about the work that Tina and her colleagues all around the world did? Is there anything you can love about cleaning other human beings? Or to clean the dirt of other people? Is this why people want to be millionaires so others will do the less popular jobs instead of them? When everyone in the world has finally become a millionaire, who will be willing to do those jobs? Tina's right. There's no functioning system in the world. Justice is disappearing and that's why everyone wants to quit these less attractive jobs. If that happens, who will harvest the corn? Who will take care of the animals so that we have something to eat? We are not all vegans yet. Sci-fi movies artificial intelligence solutions haven't been successful as well. So how will the world deal with inferior, unpopular jobs? In all motivation videos, successful people shake hands with laptops in backgrounds, have coffee talks, or they work out like crazy to achieve something. To succeed. Being a nurse is not the right type of success. Nor to be a baker. Or it is? Does success mean to have millions in the account? Increasingly, his heart began to tremble, though he didn't want it at all. Perhaps because of this chaos, people have been spending more time on social networks so that they don't think about how the world is shaking. We pretend that everything is fine. Until an illness or other misfortune touches us. Only then we wake up.

Meanwhile, I brought back into the dining room a patient, whom I had to shower. I sent Peter and Rick to take a break. "You can go to lunch. It was hard today, wasn't it? One will get used to everything."

Peter did not believe. "Are you serious about getting used to this?"

I confirmed. "One has to get used to all types of work. Even being successful is challenging. If love is present, it can be done."

Rick couldn't stay silent. "The savior of the world spoke! Love."

I replied: "Oh, no! I don't look like a savior. You guys look like saviors. You sometimes say: 'God... God, when the situation getting worse...' The only missing sentence was 'Why did you leave me?'"

Peter laughed and Rick stared as if I had showered him with cold water.

"What do you mean by this bullshit?"

"Bullshit? Yes, bullshit. Do you know when a true savior said these words? The day before he was crucified. He was afraid, and his faith in the Creator, the God, faded for a while. He was ready to die; he knew it was his destiny. Yet he was afraid of death, for he had an ordinary man's body to take this burden with humility. Humility is important for real kings. Only the person who serves humankind with humility is a true ruler. Pride reigns only for some time. Humility forever."

They both fell silent. Though I couldn't say it right, they understood. Rick asked: "You have all this in your head? Oh, my god!"

I objected: "No. The head is not big enough for such things. The heart is. What do you think, why heroes are so important to the world? Because they are ready to take on humbly the burden of all humanity on themselves. I think that religious literature is not very popular with young people these days. Although exactly there one can find many archetypes of saviors. Movies about heroes try to show what's important. Humility. Sacrifice. Love. Don't be angry, I didn't mean to offend you."

Peter said nothing and Rick couldn't come around the fact that he is been seen like this. Like a hero he played and all the other heroes. So far, they thought their movies were for teenagers and dreaming women. But many of those dreaming women were also looking for a deeper sense, not only how amazing they look in those movies. Though physical perfection may be part of it.

Rick was irritated. "I'm a little shocked, you just compared heroes to the savior."

"What's the difference? In clothing? When real human beings, for example, deploy their lives in wars, they wear uniforms. Doctors fighting for a patient's life are saviors in different clothes. Fortunately, the savior's legacy is still alive in many human hearts. We just don't realize it sometimes. Uniforms or plain clothes. It doesn't matter. A piece of the savior and his legacy lives in every human being. This is part of that higher level of love. Humility. Sacrifice. Mercy, Compassion. Gratitude. Hope."

Rick wanted to get angry because this little creature had compared him to the savior. Somehow, he couldn't. Actors always lend a portion of their hearts to the fictional characters they played. It was as if they were attracted by certain roles. Sometimes something from that fictional character passes into their real life.

"Okay, we're going for a break. We must clear our heads a bit from all those saviors and the consequences of your higher level of love."

Peter came closer to me when Rick was down the stairs to get some fresh air and whispered to me: "Honestly? You shocked me. I like it."

"I hope I didn't offend him. I didn't want to. I just wanted him to know that even movies for teenagers have a rare punch line."

"He knows that. He is just different. Weird."

"None of us is perfect. Sometimes we try to hide our weaknesses by trying to look perfect, but our imperfect, dark side sometimes wins."

"I think this whole failed trip is starting to make some sense to me."

"Maybe I am to blame."

Peter thought: *Maybe we needed to experience another reality for some special reason.*

"All of you are good guys. I believe that. What you will learn and understand here will stay in your hearts forever. Now go for the lunch."

Peter left to catch up with Rick and they waited for Andy and Will. They walked silently those few meters to Rabbit pub to fill in some material energy, for the intangible one has made their heads spinning and their hearts trembling a bit.

Andy asked with a little irony in his voice: "So, how did it go on your first floor today?"

Peter laughed, adding: "You want to know if any monsters have been attacking? Yeah, yeah. That's just the beginning."

Will was nervous: "I mean, guys. Never in my life, I was so eager to go home like now. Everything here is so depressing, annoying. As I can see, Rick is still not himself, is he?"

Peter rebuked him. "Leave him alone. He just found out that someone has compared him to a savior. Actually, all of you. He is now trying to come around that."

Andy said: "Well, we're all really kind of saviors on the movie screen at least."

"Make fun of someone else, okay?" grunted Rick with anger.

"Tell me, are you so angry because she sees a perfect savior in you, or because she refused to go on date with you?"

"She didn't refuse. She just wants something special."

Peter laughed at him: "Don't make excuses!"

"Well. Somehow your second dark side isn't working well with picking chicks. Don't you want to try the old way? Maybe it will work better."

Rick pretended it didn't get to him what the guys were saying and replied: "Just shut up and mind your business. I know what I'm doing."

Andy shook his head in disbelief.

"I wouldn't be so sure. Since you are here, I feel like you don't know what you're doing. Believe me. Flowers, candy, gifts, and sweet talk always work. Women are naive."

Peter objected: "How so? If you do it the right way, they'll all take the bait. Or not?"

Andy agreed. "Yeah, yeah. Tina probably also knows how to make a guy take her bait. Right, Rick? Such women can be foxy. Today she patted your enlarging ego and you are already thinking about how you could win over her."

The word 'win' irritated Rick. Clearly, he wants to win. All men want to in such situations. He didn't care about the reason why anymore. Yes. He must win. He can't make fool out of himself in front of his friends. Because men are hunters and women are catches. He only needs to find her weak point.

Meanwhile, Will complained: "Where can we get some chicks here? There must be some pretty young chicks here too!"

Andy ironically laughed. "You can disguise yourself. Put your sunglasses on and start from where we left off on our great trip, which made us end up here. Maybe this time you won't end up at the police station. Or you can try Tina's colleagues, maybe there you will find something that suits you."

Peter added: "You have two departments full of different kinds of women. Ah, I forgot all are over 80. They don't have sexy bodies anymore."

Will shouted angrily: "Just shut up and don't mention grannies to me. I've had enough of them!"

Peter continued: "You called it upon yourself when you said that because of that stupid costume you won't be able to pick up even a grandma. You see? Law of attraction works. You shouldn't have mentioned the grannies at all."

Will rolled his eyes. "Well, I wasn't supposed to mention grandma and you shouldn't even have organized such an idiotic trip!"

Peter didn't give up. "So, go on the net and order some. And give me a break. You didn't have to go; I didn't force you. Or invite your girlfriends here. Maybe they would come—"

Andy interrupted them: "Come on, men! You behave like kids! We are adult men, hell, we'll have to endure it somehow. We've been doing all sorts of things. We must improvise a little. There is nothing we can do about it."

The guys returned to work after a break and tried to bravely manage other attacks of monsters and their consequences. They had surgical masks, and some employees laughed a little behind their backs because they knew they were useless. On top of that they had to wash and clean.

Rick silently watched ordinary nurse Tina at work and wondered where her weak spot might be so he can prepare his strategic battle plan. In order to win. Well, the language barrier complicated the communication. He could see many deeds and non-verbal communication. Why do businessmen learn to understand nonverbal communication? Because it never deceives. Neither do deeds. We can say many words, but deeds, our deeds, either confirm or disprove them.

The next few days had passed, and it was the seventh day since four perfectly handsome and even good guys started their inferior jobs to make up for one unfortunate evening. A clutter had accumulated in their male nest, and testosterone level was rising at a dangerous speed.

Although they were always grateful and willing to pay for performing ordinary inferior work in their private life, they found themselves in an unenviable situation here. Somehow everything stopped working. Those times when their moms ran behind them and asked them to tidy up their things were long gone. Since they became famous actors, they didn't have time for things like that. Here in their temporary prison flat, there was no cleaner or cook who would fulfill the three points of testosterone code. Clean house, clean clothes, full stomach with warm food. Although they had their meals in Rabbit pub, it wasn't the same. Not to mention that their situation was getting worst because of the fourth, most important point of the testosterone code. Sex also didn't work as they hoped it would. All the luxury they have taken for granted has been taken away and the result came quickly.

Although Andy tried to ease the situation, he underestimated the strength of the male testosterone hormone that was responsible, from the worse side, for their male aggressiveness, which began to show its face with each passing day. They were all tired of the endless fulfillment of inferior work. Dirty clothes were scattered everywhere. Dirty dishes were piled up in the kitchen, in addition to plastic containers from take away. The apartment looked just exactly like these poor guys felt. It was horrifying.

One day Andy couldn't stand it anymore. "Listen. it can't go like this any further. We must tidy up the place. We are running out of both civilian and working clothes."

While lying on the couch and playing with his smartphone Rick said: "If you don't like it, you can get start. The others won't mind, right?"

Andy didn't give up. "Don't you mind pushing bullshits into Tina's head wearing a dirty T-shirt?"

Rick replied indifferently: "She also has stains on her uniform. I think she won't mind a few of mine."

Peter was horrified. "So far, you have been so clean and tasteful, what happened to you? She washes her uniform every night if you haven't noticed. And shortly you won't have any clean white shirts."

Will joined. "He's noticing other things. Not the stains on her uniform. So, what? Grannies can be dirty, and we can't? Besides, we are clean. Not only do we wash ourselves every day but also this damn nursing house, so what do you want?"

Andy said in a tighter voice: "Grannies have bibs, so they won't get dirty. If you didn't notice. I'm not your butler. Come on everybody! Clean your mess, pick up your clothes, and load them into the washing machine. I guess we can do it."

Will proposed: "Look, we'll borrow the bibs and we'll protect our last shirts from stains."

Peter shook his head. "Well, we've been in this amazing reality for a long time. The hormones have properly brainwashed us. Andy's right. Let's forget the bibs and get the work done."

Will was angry. "Yeah, that was a joke. But I'm fed up with cleaning in the nursing house. I don't want to see a rug anymore. If the mess is bothering you, you can start. It doesn't bother me that much. Clean clothes can be bought or even better ordered. See, that's an idea! We have enough money. Then we just throw away the dirty clothes and all will be fine."

Andy asked him: "Are you serious? Do you want to waste money just because you don't want to turn on a dumb knob on your washing machine?"

"Well, you can do turn the button if you want it so much."

Andy didn't give up. "Stop talking and kindly start working! Unfortunately, no tricks or spells will help us."

Will asked in disgust: "Can't we pay a cleaner to do that for us? We have enough money!"

Peter considered uncertainly. "We can, but the fewer people know we're here, the better. Do you want to read about yourself tomorrow? That you clean lockers as punishment in the nursing house?"

"I don't care anymore. Let everyone know. We're not the first nor the last. Besides, we haven't done anything that bad."

Rick finally objected: "No, you should've shut up and everything would be fine. You wanted to bribe a German cop. So, it's your fault."

"Excuse me? My fault? It was Peter's idea. This stupid trip. Oktoberfest! There is nothing worse than that."

Peter defended himself: "Oh, my god, you went with me! If I knew I wouldn't ask you to join me so stop blaming me!"

And so, a fight between the decent, good guys, started. It was the consequence of the stress from unwanted work, their male ego, and the high level of testosterone. Peter and Andy wouldn't mind eliminating the consequences of their miserable existence in their temporary home, but they couldn't see the reason why they should do it on behalf of Will and Rick as well.

After the fight, where the failed trip was mentioned in addition to all the old sins, their male nest looked like a war zone. Each of them then drew back to their male caves and searched for the answers to why their fate made them end up here.

Yes, overall, they were good men. So why? Andy thought that maybe what they see here every day was supposed to be used in the future. Tina said that these issues need to be pointed out. No one listens to the staff. While someone still comes to work to take care of those people, nothing changes. Words. All the powerful people use words, but until their words turn into deeds, it is often too late. Why is it so? Of course, we need to be grateful even for the small things that we have. Why then the conditions of ordinary working people who don't desire luxury, just to live in dignity, is deteriorating? No wonder everyone wants to escape their existence. It would take so little and everything would be a little better.

Peter watched Rick, who seemed to be completely oblivious. Only some time ago it would have been him who would become the leader in this situation, and with his natural respect, it would probably work. He started to miss old Rick. He didn't dare to ask him what he was thinking about. All of them were struggling. Every human being struggles with some problems. Money gives certain freedom, but it does not guarantee happiness. That is why many famous people have taken upon themselves the responsibility to mitigate the consequences for at least part of humanity's burning problems. They couldn't save everyone. It just is not yet possible.

Then Peter got an idea. Crazy, but worth trying. He looked at his watch, it was half-past seven. He knew that Tina would still be at work. He decided to do something that none of his three friends would do. Because he had a little more of kind energy in him, he did it. Humility. He had to use a little humility. When he came to the first floor, I was in the staff room. I was surprised to see him.

"What are you doing here? Aren't you fed up with the cleaning?" I asked with a laugh.

As if I suspected it and hit a nail on the head. Peter fidgeted and started: "I'd like to ask you something. I just don't know how."

Then I understood what he wanted, and I started to laugh. Peter didn't understand what was going on, so I explained to make it easier for him: "You can't fulfill the testosterone code, right? There is no housekeeper in your apartment. And you don't know if a stranger will be discreet. You quarreled because none of you knew how and where to start cleaning up your mess, right?"

"How do you know?! What does that testosterone code mean?"

"Wait, I need my cell phone to put together what I want to say. Look, you're good, brave guys. But guys. I live in a house with three. For years I have been working abroad and when I would come back home, I would find the apartment in a dilapidated state. There are exceptions, but a woman is a woman. Have you ever seen a housekeeper in your millionaires' houses to be a man? My sons often argued about who was going to the market or clean the house. Until recently my older son surprised me when I returned to a clean house. He lives with his girlfriend and I teach him all the time that he must help her. Share with her the house chores. Acting deeds of love. I cherish this the most. This is how my son showed me how much he loves me because he knows I have a tough job."

Peter looked at me and didn't know what to say. He knew that no job in the world was inferior or less important. It was only the human ego that whispers to people to be ashamed to admit if someone is working in the restaurant or washing dishes. But why? Clearly, it's not a brilliant career, but if nobody did that, in a while, customers will have to eat from the pots. Oh, human pride and vanity. How strange is the world?

All successful people, when they talk about their path to success, they recall their thorny beginnings in various unattractive jobs. Did it occur to someone that it is precisely in these works that one must learn humility so that when he or she becomes a millionaire he or she never forgets and continues to help those who are not rich but want to live with dignity? Human beings who fulfill their dreams, intuitively and for a higher level of love, begin to correct the injustices in the world caused by pride, ego, and vanity.

After a while, he begged: "You wouldn't mind help us to clean the greatest chaos? After that will we try to keep the order."

I laughed. "No, I don't mind. I was never ashamed to admit, that I was 24 hours nurse for geriatric patients in German-speaking countries for years. Which meant full service including home management, cooking, shopping. It was an excellent but very hard school of humility and higher levels of love. Everyone should try it. There I learned everything. Detached from children and alone. I have no problem with it. I have my only day off tomorrow, so I'll try to help you."

Peter asked: "You haven't explained to me the code yet."

I explained: "We made it up in Austria with one colleague. She always said that a man needs four basic things: 1. a clean house, 2. a clean dress, 3. a full belly of warm food…and how to say this…empty…you know what…"

Peter laughed. "You mean sex?"

"Yes. This point is crucial. Otherwise, it is not good."

Peter nodded: "It's not good for us now as well. I'm glad you'll help us. Even though I feel a little stupid. Of course, we'll pay you how much you want."

I mysteriously rejected. "Deed for a deed. Maybe I'll need something that can't be paid for with money. Some acts of love cannot be paid for with money. You know that some have a very high price."

Peter was surprised. "You don't want money? Why?"

"I'm not making millions here, but I've always tried to take care of myself and my family in some way. That's one of the reasons why my marriage is over. For me, the deeds are important They have to come at the right time. If they come late, they're sometimes useless."

Peter told to me: "You're a very strange woman. Do you know that?"

I laughed sadly: "I know. My strength has caused me a lot of trouble in your man's world. If I wanted to survive with my father, lieutenant colonel in a real army, I had no choice."

"Really? Your father is a soldier?"

"He was. He died. Perhaps that's why I've been looking for someone to protect me all my life. Unfortunately, it didn't go well. I can tell you all this. You're different. You know. I mean. That's why I can say such things."

"Oh. That's okay. Sometimes some people have a problem with it."

"I don't. The heart is essential. Come with me, I'm late. I must turn over two more patients and then we'll arrange for tomorrow. Don't tell your friends yet."

"Why? Let them be glad I found a solution."

"It's not important who will help. Trust me. I'll do it gladly. Maybe I'll really need something from you."

Peter was surprised. "Oh. That sounded strange. Thanks god, those egomaniacs didn't hear that."

"It's very difficult for you. Well, it has a deeper sense of why you're here. God has sent you here just because you have a big heart. Believe me. He wants to remind you of something."

"Why us?"

"You don't know that? Your friends have become symbols of perfect male human beings. Good and nice men ready to save the world. People listen to you. Nobody listens to us, ordinary people. I'm just a nurse. No hero."

"Well, there are many problems in the world."

"Amazing things as well. By making decisions we create the world and our reality."

"That diaper reality is a pretty brutal level."

"It purifies human hearts faster and makes it larger."

Peter watched as I swapped diapers for one of the patients, he didn't mind and helped me to turn her over. I told him: "Leave the keys in the staff room. Say nothing."

"Thank you. You can't imagine how glad I am!"

"Every guy would be glad, trust me. Well, I guess you always had a housekeeper back home to fulfill your testosterone code. And for the fourth point, you have your loved ones. It should be easy for you. Yet, somehow, even there, the relationships don't always work as they sometimes don't work for us ordinary mortals."

Peter smiled mysteriously. "That's true they don't."

We looked at each other for a moment, and then he left. When he came back to their apartment, he didn't say anything. He was just thinking about our conversation. She actually told him more than she did to Rick. Her weak point was easy to guess. She had strong leadership character in order to survive difficult situations. Men didn't like it. The deeds worked with her. Deeds of love. He wondered if he should tell Rick. In his current mood, when for the last few days, he was so strange, it probably wouldn't make much sense. Maybe she'll tell him once herself. Maybe. He didn't recognize his friend and didn't even know what was going on inside of him.

Men didn't like to discuss what they felt in certain situations. They didn't like to admit it, but they suffered more from breakups and disappointments. They couldn't endure any kind of suffering. They even suffered more due to physical pain. That is why women bring children to life and can endure it. Women could bear the breakups and divorces a little easier. When men lost their love, the easiest solution was to replace it with someone new to make the pain more bearable. Silly phrases that men don't cry don't work. They too are sensitive and have emotions. Even negative ones.

The next day, that was the eighth day of their stay at the nursing house my colleague was in charge of delegating tasks to the guys. Rick asked Peter: "Where is our commander sister with Venusian's ass?"

Peter shook his head and splashed into his face: "She's off. And leave her ass alone. You don't know anything about her."

Andy looked at Peter. "Wow, and I guess you know something?"

Will added: "Well. Our Peter can be confided in. He isn't dangerous for her."

Peter had enough: "It's clear you're without women! Testosterone beats you in your heads."

Andy commented: "For god sake guys! Let's be adults."

Will sighed: "That is the thing. We are adults and yet we are forced to live like some kind of stupid teenagers! Even the punishment we got is the same teenagers get! What a miserable life!"

Andy couldn't help himself but tease Will: "What to do. We don't have any luxurious beauties here. Only nurses. Two male caretakers and Internet."

Will scornfully added: "Maybe we can have a walk around this shit hole. There must be some women here."

Rick smiled ironically. "Women are everywhere. Men as well. You have to ask Tina, maybe she'll know where you should go for a walk."

Andy objected: "Yeah sure because she has time to walk around the village and look at men and women! She is trapped with demented grannies and grandpas from morning to evening!"

"And diapers. Talking about diapers. Do you have your surgical masks? Today I saw in the kitchen those bags with that nasty poison." Peter informed them.

Will grumbled: "The surgical masks won't help shit."

Rick agreed. "Exactly. Nothing will protect us from this shit."

Peter gave an order: "So, let's go to work!"

Rick added: "Work slowly and precisely. The longer we do one thing, the fewer tasks we will get."

"You really returned to teen life. But from the worse side." Andy said to him.

Rick just shrugged his shoulders. This life had many advantages. He didn't feel so much pain and fear. That was just fine for him.

I was preparing for my big cleaning challenge and since Andy and Will were working on the second floor where my little room was, we met.

Andy asked me: "What are you going to do today when you're off?"

I mysteriously replied: "The same what you do. Good deeds of love, just somewhere else."

Andy was surprised and I continued: "I have to go. I don't know what awaits me there and I have just a few hours for that."

"Okay, then bye. Have a nice day."

"You too. Good luck with the attacks. You're very brave. I admire you how you are handling it all."

If you just knew how we couldn't handle it and how everything started to fall on our heads, Andy said to himself. *We have a mess in our apartment, in our souls, in our bodies, and in our hearts. We have to endure it. Like soldiers in the army.*

Meanwhile, I went down to the first floor to get the key and the address of their male nest. Of course, when I came out of the staff room, Rick was hiding in the kitchen by the dishwasher. He was waiting for the dirty dishes while the patients had breakfast. When he saw me, he shouted all over the dining room, because there was almost no one who could understand English: "Where does a general nurse go when she is not bossing around in work?"

"Why do you need to know?"

"I don't need to. I'm just asking, I'm curious."

"Well. I'm going to help to another place today."

Rick paused.

"… Isn't helping here enough for you?"

"Here I have to, and I want to help. If I want to survive. Where I go now, I'll do it because I want to. Have a nice day."

Rick shouted: "Wait a minute!"

I stopped, and he asked: "What about the date?"

"What date?"

"You said you wanted something special. Today you have a day off, you won't work, so you can tell me about that at the Rabbit."

I laughed. "Which Rabbit do you want an explanation in?"

"What you mean which Rabbit? Here, in this nearby pub. Is there any other rabbit?"

"It's standing in front of you. I am a rabbit in the Chinese horoscope. I mean, doe rabbit bunny."

Rick started laughing, and the potion started somehow to work the other way around again, and he said: "Ah, rabbit. Now it's clear to me why you also have. Well…little curvier…legs…and Venusian's ass."

I wasn't disgusted and added: "Does my plus Venusian's ass irritate you again? Well, I know. You aren't used to that. There in Hollywood, you prefer perfect bodies. Well, what to do? You have bosses too. We have to change diapers and clean up. You must lose weight and exercise like jerks to look great. It's not easy as well. I know. I'm a little curvier doe bunny. You are a beauty with a trained body. I am what I am. I am happy with my body. We have overweight patients here."

Rick paused, then asked: "… So, little curvier bunny, will you tell me about that *special thing* you want in the other Rabbit?"

I smiled.

"I want something from you? I think you want something from me. In need, little curvier bunny is good enough. If you don't want more trouble."

What was this bunny thinking about herself? Rick was annoyed, but he didn't show that this time. Still, curiosity was stronger than his ego, so he tried to lighten the situation: "Look. We can at least talk, can't we? Just talk."

I sighed: "It's very difficult for me. That language barrier."

Rick shrugged his shoulders.

"We can communicate non-verbally. How would a bunny communicate?"

I laughed.

"Bunny sits quietly in the cage, or silently eats the grass."

Rick's sense of humor was awakened a little: "Well, I don't think you're such a silent bunny."

"Be glad there is a barrier between us. Sometimes I tell crazy things and people get angry. Sometimes the words slip away. Sorry."

Rick said: "It's all right. We all say things that we later regret."

For a little while, he felt that he could be himself with this bunny. Because this bunny sees day-to-day suffering so close.

I contemplated.

"I'll think about it. If I come to the other Rabbit, it will be in the evening."
Rick paused.

"… How do I know if you will come?"

I looked at him and replied: "You won't. You'll just wait."

Rick shook his head in disbelief. "What? Wait? Don't know if you're coming?"

"Why not? Sometimes we have to be patient and we don't know the result."

Rick had no idea that I told Peter to keep them away from the house for as long as possible. We agreed that I'll send him a message when I was done and leave the key in the post box. I didn't know how long my work would last there.

Rick did not give up. "Tell me at least the hour."

"Maybe at seven. I'm warning you. It's not going to be a date. I don't have any nice clothes here. The kind women wear on a date. I wear a uniform all the time."

Rick smirked: "Sure. No date. Just non-verbal communication between a curvy bunny and trained man."

"Go to work. The dishwasher needs to be filled," I ordered him.

"Aye… General!" shouted Rick.

"I am a woman. I think, looking at my ass and legs, it's clear, isn't it?"

Rick remembered his first male attack when he told me exactly the same. It seemed that with humor, the poison Eros had poisoned him with will begin to melt a little. He had no idea that Eros' faithful love Psyche, didn't approve his action. They both sat in their fairy-tale garden and Psyche blamed Eros: "How could you do that, Eros? You wanted to help her get the time and show him higher levels of love and she should bring him invisible gifts. Instead, you poisoned his heart! Now everything is going exactly in the opposite direction than it should. Why?"

Eros looked at Psyche and answered her: "I didn't want to. Apollo made me so angry that I didn't think, and I shoot…"

Psyche was thinking aloud: "Every magic has a high price. She wanted something special, so the unfortunate accident makes life difficult for her now. That we somehow forgot about. I should have destroyed the potion if I knew what it was going to cause."

Eros contemplated: "Nothing's happening on Earth or up here without a reason. Believe me, everything is exactly as it should be. Maybe it will eventually turn out better than we expect. After all, what is perfect on Earth? Nothing."

Psyche disagreed. "You and Petal fairy have cooked a botched poison. That's a lesson for you to really obey what Zeus commands. Even Zeus must obey those from above."

Eros wouldn't give up. "And who do people obey? They do what they want. They destroy love as they want. They also take from love what they want and often hurt each other. They all want my level of love the most."

Psyche sighed: "By shooting your arrows as you want, you really don't make it easy for them, do you? Look how many unfulfilled love and broken hearts are in the world. No wonder people are fed up and unhappy, and they don't want higher levels of love anymore. They don't want to feel the pain anymore."

Eros contemplated: "You're right... They have free will. Their souls and hearts must learn something. I shoot as they feel and think. You know the polarity must be preserved. Human beings have to learn to accept the dark side of their lives. In everything, even in love."

Psyche objected: "They're focusing on their bodies. Somehow, they ceased being interested in their heart. Because of that endless pain."

Eros didn't give up. "Because of the joy, Psyche! If they have free will, they have to feel both, joy and pain. Otherwise, they wouldn't be able to choose. Their whole existence would be meaningless. If they make mistakes, but they can humble themselves and ask for forgiveness, many things can be corrected. The mistakes are made in order to be rectified by good deeds."

Psyche considered quietly: "Some of the evil deeds are no longer correctable, not even with love. That will probably be the reason why more and more people reject love. There's a mistake somewhere, Eros."

Eros continued with a passion: "It's not like that in all love relationships. You know that, despite the difficulties, many people can still handle it."

"Yes, Eros. Well, according to the number of pink pearls, they are becoming less and less."

Eros resignedly asked: "So, I should stop shooting my arrows? Will we leave them completely without love?"

Psyche replied: "I don't know, Eros. There are still a lot of happy people. They didn't lose faith. New and new couples arise. I don't know."

Eros and Psyche sat in silence in the garden and both thought of love. How it is with love in the world. It hurts and gives endless joy at the same time. In the beginning, people want love very much, then they reject it. Out of misery, they give their hearts short adventures to feel at least for a moment what it is like to be loved. Then they no longer want each other. They hide themselves from one another, they don't answer messages, they don't pick up the phone. They make holes in their hearts and try to close those holes with patches made of passion. When the passion fades away, the patch breaks up and there is an even bigger hole in the heart than it was before. Nevertheless, it all had meaning. Maybe the Creator did this, who hitherto has not revealed to anyone how the most precious chemistry works between two people. After some time, a mysterious spark bursts into the human heart. It either gets bigger or disappears after a while. What is this miraculous moment that makes the sparkle, this tiny miracle, to even ignite? So far nobody knew exactly. This secret, like many others, was left by the Creator for himself. So that people don't decipher his code and don't try to exploit it. As they do with all the discoveries. Almost all the discoveries that humanity had in order to improve were abused by humans and used for destruction. Not only Earth but themselves as well. Still, the end of the world has not yet come. While Earth is shaking, it still works. Temporary, but it works. With such infinite love, the Creator endows both Earth and Universe. Unconditional, eternal, and the only perfect. He is trying to keep his creation alive.

Chapter 5

I arrived at the house where four handsome and famous men lived. When I looked around the apartment, I couldn't hold myself and I burst into laughter. It does not matter whether Slovaks, Americans, Germans, Hungarians. Men were born for a different type of work. The household chores don't suit them well. The apartment didn't look like there were mature men living in but unscrupulous teenagers who rebel and leave a mess behind. And why not? Eventually, someone will come in and cleans it up, right? The apartment reflected what they now felt inside. A housekeeper lady wasn't probably part of that. While cleaning I couldn't but sometimes laugh loudly because I remembered that I was the perfect Cinderella. During my life, instead of ashes, I swept, well, anything one can imagine. Even ashes.

During the long years of nursing work, I cleaned up so much dirt, put into order so many houses, so many weeded gardens, and raked so many leaves. I hated deciduous trees. Fall came and I was in tears because they all had subsided, and I had to rake them. That if I wanted new dance props and costumes for I could not take money from my family budget. Not for my 'stupid' thing. I had to earn the money for that somewhere else. Because there were no good guys in those gardens who wanted to support my love for dance. All the families were very thankful. I clean the dirt and everything else, and every day I try to thank God for being able to work. God, I thank you, that I can get up in the morning and serve others. It wasn't that bad. Sometimes I felt that it wasn't what I wanted as a child. 90 percent of people in the world do jobs just to survive, pay the bills, and feed their families. Everyone is trying to feel and think positively and be thankful for their health. Because without it we can do no work.

I laughed at myself when I remembered all my dance costumes and props. Even the ones I made for the girls in my dance group. How much hard work was behind them? Real hard work! That's why rich actors must indulge in luxury because what they do is actually hard work. They basically deserve it. They must pay the price for glory by sharing some of their privacy with ordinary people. Otherwise, we, the fans, wouldn't buy tickets for their movie or their DVD or merch. While recalling these memories I tried to fix the chaos that was in the flat. When I finished, I send a message to Peter that I was leaving.

Meanwhile, the guys were having a walk in the village looking for chicks to pick up. Suitable chicks that would help them lower their alarmingly high level of testosterone. They would have most probably found them, but then they remembered how one unfortunate evening had gone bad in this damned country. That's why they changed their mind. Well, they're grown up. They must improvise. Luxury was not yet in sight. The only female beings that made them company over the last days were women from 80 to 100 years old and nurses. Nurses preferred other qualities than sexy dresses, jewelry, and perfect outfits. Oh, of course, sometimes they turned into princesses for a few days a year as well. Is it true that a dress makes a man? Probably yes but at work, nurses wore uniforms and their sexy outfit was endless patience and love. At first glance, perhaps not very attractive for men. They weren't Barbie dolls for sure, but they radiated another kind of beauty. One that can withstand some wrinkles and a few character imperfections. But how do these famous men actually see them? That was a mystery to me.

The guys walked towards Rabbit pub silently. Rick smiled inconspicuously as he remembered the curved Bunny in her uniform. For some special reason, he wanted her to come. *Was it just curiosity or something else?*

Peter disturbed him from his thoughts: "Wait here, I just forgot something."

"We're so overworked from the cleaning that we are starting to lose our memory," said Will.

Peter took the key and wished that the guys won't be upset when they realize that he has found a solution to deal with the mess in their flat. To make it easier afterward for them to keep it in their male kind of order. When they returned to their male nest, they knew what had happened.

Rick got it immediately and was upset: "Peter, tell me it's not true what I think had happened here! Tell me it's not true that the general-nurse was here to clean the flat!"

Peter answered in a calm voice: "She was. I asked her to. To make it a little easier for us to handle this chaotic existence from now on. Why does it bother you so much?"

Andy teased Rick: "Well, this might ruin his reputation. He'd like to get her to the bedroom first and not make her a cleaner."

Rick splashed into his face. "Shut up and stay out of this! What can you possibly know about where I want to get her?"

Will poured some more oil into the fire. "Sure because you don't care about her nor she is your type, right? So, it probably won't be to the bedroom."

Rick was getting angrier. "That's none of your business! It's my business! And you," he turned to Peter, "next time you want to come up with some stupid plan, kindly share it with others."

"You still haven't answered what's bothering you? That she helped us? And she took care of our clothes? When our female staff do it, is that all right?"

Rick was annoyed because he felt stupid. A strange woman got a sneak peek into his privacy, without his permission.

"But that's the problem! She's not our employee, you idiot!" Andy defended Peter: "Well okay, she is not. And so, what? When our female employees do it, is it okay for us?"

Will started ironically laughing. "But we probably don't have any affairs with our employees, do we? The affair between Rick and that nurse general started somehow from the wrong end. First, she comes to clean up the mess. That bothers him."

Andy told him: "Jesus! How horrible it sounds. Employees. Okay, so we have no affairs with female employees, but we have affairs with female colleagues. What is the difference? Oh, god. Don't make this a tragedy."

Peter agreed with Andy. "Andy's right. Look. We're her colleagues now. Everything looks the same as in a regular workplace. It's absolutely okay to have an affair at work. Our punishment is to work as cleaners at a nursing house. She's not our employee but a temporary colleague. That's an interesting career, isn't it? We have more than enough challenges in our new job."

Then the guys got it and started to laugh like crazy. Humor is truly a brilliant means to cope with difficult situations. Moreover, they reminded themselves that all human beings are important because we all need each other in this world. No matter who does what kind of job currently.

Rick then asked Peter: "I hope our temporary colleague got paid for her work."

"That was just strange. She refused the money."

Rick shook his head in disbelief. "This can't be true! You mean she did it for free? And you agreed? Oh man, you're driving me crazy!"

Peter continued: "She said one day she might need something from us. That not everything can be paid with money."

Andy noted: "See? She wants something from you. You have the road prepared. She is so crazy about you that she didn't mind coming here and neutralize our chaos!"

Rick told him: "Who said I wanted her? I said nothing like that!"

Andy added: "Oh, this song you've been singing since the first day. So why you're so angry about her cleaning the flat?"

"Mind your own business," grumbled Rick and Peter grinned:

"If I did, you'd go out tonight wearing our temporary uniform today. In white trousers and a white T-shirt with a few stains."

Andy told Peter: "We are so grateful to you. To her as well. Just wondering what she wants from us."

Will scratched his head and wondered: *What she wants from Rick is clear, but what does that have to do with us?*

Peter looked at Will. "Do you really have nothing but sex in your head?"

Will agreed: "Well. Currently not. The hungry dreams of bread."

Rick told him: "It's not a date and I don't intend to share with you what I want from her."

Andy objected: "You don't have to. We know that already. Yeah, you're not interested. She's not your type. And you're not going on a date with her. She's just an ordinary nurse and you are a famous actor."

Rick turned to Andy: "What does that have to do with her being a nurse?"

Andy explained: "Her reality is different than ours, Rick. Too high boundaries separate your worlds, don't you think?"

Peter objected: "Do you mean we are superstars from birth?"

Andy thought: *No, I didn't mean that. But...*

Rick continued: "The reality is that we are always described as if we are above ordinary people. Hahaha. Civilians. That's the right word. Better and higher reality. Hierarchy. That's how it works in the world. Those who are up and the ones who are down. Just a few of the chosen ones can make it up. For a huge price, what few people realize."

Something shivered in Rick. He could not explain it, but he suddenly felt that the high boundary behind which they lived on Earth's Olympus was ruled by harsh rules. There was nothing for free there. He could no longer distinguish which of the realities he is living in is more complicated. The one who unwittingly forced him to do unusual inferior work, or the other, in which he served as a beautiful idol to his admirers. Did Tina also consider him a perfect idol? Why did she dare to compare him and other heroes to the savior? Why from all the heroes in the world she like his the most? He wanted to know, or rather not. Negative and positive emotions began to mix in his heart with the questions he was afraid to get the answers for.

She perceived beauty somehow differently in her own way. This terrible endless suffering with which nurses must cope all their life really pushes their love higher. But higher where? Suddenly he wanted to know the answer. Except he was scared. Everyone would be scared. Especially men. They don't like to talk about any kind of emotions, especially when they are exposed to pressure and stress. In such cases, they prefer to remain silent and to wait until the worst passes away. Only then they can reveal a little. A strong male world without emotions? Is it a solution to avoid occasional suffering and pain? Or must men also be brave when they have to fight for themselves? Their own emotional battle for positive emotions? Even more than women? Is it strength to hide their pain and fear in the most hidden corners of their hearts so that no one can see? He didn't know yet that for the strong nurse general, male tears had a huge price. A man who shows a tear will show his unbeatable power. A power that can truly defeat many evils. Everyone else was silent and knew it was true. The world, to be able to function at least temporarily, made borders everywhere. Since people invented money and wealth and destroyed the barter trade, they have been fighting for those borders and for wealth endlessly. There has been a real endless war for people's desperate survival since the birth of mankind. Powerful people tried to destroy those virtual borders, like the ones in the European Union. The truth is that they still exist. Human beings from economically weaker countries have been grateful and happy to work in economically stronger ones. They did less attractive jobs and maintained the temporary operation of human existence. In short, human beings really need each other. The human instinct of self-preservation and the desire to leave some legacy has ensured that human beings are bringing more and more people into the world without considering where their descendants will live in a few years. Human beings seemed to stop loving not only themselves but also the planet they live on. They post family photos on social networks; they search for the latest fashion trends and diets in magazines. Just to get closer to human perfection. They compete for a spot in the light and want children at all costs to leave something behind. This is all great. Family is a very rare thing. Children need to be taken care of. Children need time. Rich people are getting help from nannies and babysitters with raising their children. Those less wealthy have difficulty in providing children with the most basic things like food and clothes. Dads or mothers are often forced to work two jobs to handle it. In some cases, children don't get the most precious thing they need. Mother and father who give them their time. To answer their questions and play with them. Not only feed them. When adults become parents then will they understand that raising a child does not mean giving him a roof over his head and basic needs only. Parents feel responsible for their children even when they grow up and fear whether their children will be happy in life. What future can we give our children when humans have been fighting each other for centuries? Yes, fighting. For survival. For everything. Is this right? Is this how it should be? What kind of legacy will we leave for our children? Our kids go to the movies to watch heroes and admire them. Villains too. Childish movies? Are we adults really so blind and deaf and one ordinary mother crazy, when she says these are not movies for kids? Even on Earth's Olympus, they are trying to suggest that there is something wrong with the world and that something needs to be done. Of course, no one can say that loud. Earth Olympus has become a messenger of a true deity and is trying to pass on the news of how it is with humans and Earth. Mankind does not want to wake up. On one hand, our technology has helped us tremendously. Life is much easier now than it was in the Middle Ages. But there are still the poor, whose only dream is to drink, eat and have a roof over their heads. They also try to feel positive and imagine their stomach is full…How awesome and terrible. Polarity must exist. Good and evil must be preserved. We must not give up and believe that we all are doing much better. We must be grateful for the things we already have because someone in the world doesn't even have that.

Such heavy thoughts whirled through their heads, for their momentary existence made them think deeper. Because to suffer in a movie and to suffer in real life these are two completely different things.

Rick stood under the shower and was no longer angry at this madhouse, which included all four of them. They have been without luxury, without women, without their loved ones. In an unenviable situation that was supposed to teach them something. What was that? They have tried to fix the world before. Whether on screen or in reality. So why did God put them in such a terrible place? He dressed up and went to the Rabbit pub to meet this strange, somewhat curvy Bunny who admired the hero he really lent his heart to.

I was terrified when I imagined how weak and terrible my English language skills are. My older son writes a bachelor's degree in English, the other communicates on-line in English with everybody, and their mother English is just horrible. With an appalling Slavic accent on top of that. They both can't understand how I could handle the German language because German grammar is even worse than English. Not the mention the Slovak grammar. Even Slovaks can't manage it properly.

Well, God has punished mankind for their pride in the Babylon Tower, and they have forgotten their languages forever. We deserve that. The languages remained forgotten, but he couldn't eliminate pride. That still lives on.

My older son, who is going to be an English language teacher for Slovak children, warned me that Google translator translates bullshit in most cases. So, what am I going to do? Then I remembered what he had told me if I ever went on a date with a man.

He told me: "Mom. Promise me that you will just stay silent, smile, and do nothing."

I already broke the promise. Unfortunately. I still have to give orders to a real man in his temporary job. It can't get any worse. Now I'm going to fix it and do exactly what my son asked me to do.

To be on the safe side, I decided to relay on an outdated method, but more reliable than a modern Google translator. English-Slovak Dictionary. Christ in heaven! That's going to be a catastrophic date. To be even safer I packed a notebook and a pen. I knew what was coming. An embarrassment of gigantic proportions. I didn't want to change my decision, because I just wanted to go. It had its advantage. At least I will see a real person, not only a picture on a wall. I have just the dictionary that would try to alleviate the consequences of God's punishment from the Babylon time.

Rick sat at the Rabbit's with a hood on his head and he was wearing his sunglasses. He reminded himself that the unfortunate sunglasses had gotten him into this mess along with his friends. Myself, I was standing in front of the entrance breathing heavily thinking that maybe it wasn't a good idea to agree with this date after all. Oh, God, help me. I just went in with a beating heart. Now I was not a nurse general. I was just a frightened woman. I looked around and then I saw Rick sitting in the hideaway corner of the pub. Wearing his sunglass. In the dark.

I said hello and sat down opposite of him. I tried to make a sour smile, but I couldn't. I wanted to run away. Though I was forced to organize many things around me throughout my life, I wasn't that good with men. They think differently than women and I was just shy and fragile. But I couldn't always afford to show that.

Rick looked at me. I wore no luxurious clothes that should seduce him, just plain jeans and a black-laced T-shirt. But I didn't realize that this average outfit emphasized my curves, even more, that my uniform. For Rick that was more than enough. Spoiled love potion with a double dose of dill seeds affected his heart, which I had no idea about. Still, in our reality, love potions don't work.

Rick didn't bother to hide the astonishment at the look of my curves. I noticed it and got some courage. I said with laughter: "Yes, I know, I have a little Aphrodite body."

Rick laughed. "Do you think we only have perfect people with perfect bodies in our place?"

I looked at him smiling. "It depends on what is perfect for you."

"We all have imperfections, don't we?"

"You mean, on the body? I can't see one on yours."

Rick laughed louder and shook his head. "What do you mean, you can't see?"

My hands began to sweat, and tiny red spots of stress appeared on my neck. I felt that the situation was bad, and in stressful situations my body always betrayed me. Not even regular breathing helped. The adrenaline worked perfectly. God, what am I doing here? I was supposed to be quiet. I took a deep breath and answered: "Oh. Sorry... I just...what I see with my eyes...is perfect...actually...what am I saying...even what I don't see...definitely.

Your soul... and your heart...although you're acting a little strange...now... these days..."

Rick took me out of my misery even though he hadn't even thought of his heart or soul at that moment. Guys are interested in other things at the beginning.

"Oh. You thought of the heart and soul. They are also invisible now. And you know what I'm like when I'm not weird?"

"No. Just. I think so. It's just a feeling. I can't explain it reasonably."

"Did you watch YouTube again?"

"No. What for? Now you're here in person. Really, I haven't seen that much. Just that you are good with your fans. Nothing more."

Rick laughed again. "Nothing more. Just cabinets, dog, fans, and my girlfriends. Something else?"

I was already red not only on my neck but also on my face: "Well... I don't know. Do you understand now how we are? Your female fans? All we have to do is find one post and the universe will send us another one... And another one. I'm sorry."

"Universe? What universe? I thought it was the YouTube."

Rick laughed again at how I was trying to explain to him in my horrible English that we, the female fans of him, were looking at information about him on YouTube.

"Yes. I know. Wait, I'll take something to help."

I picked the dictionary from my purse and shivered like an aspen leaf in the breeze.

Rick was amused. "For god's sake what do you need this for? We have a translator."

I tried to explain. "My son says it's not doing a good job."

Rick didn't stop laughing at all this situation and started to feel a bit sorry for me. "Doesn't do its job well?"

"Oh. I can't think of the word...how do you say it... Translate..."

"Have you tried it?"

"What? Do you mean Google or the dictionary?"

"Google."

"Yeah, I tried. I can't work well with this. I don't have the talent for technology."

"Oh, so you prefer old ways of communication."

"Yeah. My sons are desperate because of me. I don't have a memory for technology. Communication with you is complicated for the Bunny. Bunnies are actually a little shy. When they arc close to the danger."

Rick looked at me with interest: "Danger? Why?"

"For a common Bunny, you pose a danger."

"Are you afraid of me? I'm just a living man."

"Yeah. You're just a man. With the beard, you look a bit like. I can't even say it...better no. Without it, you look like a beautiful god. Apollo. It's bad I have to be your boss at work. At the same time, I feel a great deal of respect. Not just because of the body. It's all your being. I feel like you're good."

Rick was silent for a moment, then asked: "How can you feel it when you don't know it? Believe me, it's not always so great when everyone considers you to be a symbol of perfection. I don't feel that way. So, how can you?"

"I have a strong intuition. It never deceives, but we don't listen to it."

"What would you like to know about me?"

I was surprised by his question because men don't like to talk about certain things. "I don't know. Just what you want, and can say. It's not good that we know so much about you. About you, famous people."

"We don't tell everything to the public."

"It's so hard to speak for me with you. You talk. I try to listen. We can write something. On paper."

Rick confirmed: "On paper. The old way. No cell phone?"

"It doesn't matter. Paper is a little bit romantic for me."

"A little? Romantic? Are you romantic?"

"I'd rather not say. Everyone's laughing at me. Do you know that I learned the German language from romantic soap operas? The same words, then you remember quickly."

Rick was still curious. "Watching soap operas is not proof that someone is romantic."

"You have to talk about yourself first. Since you've been here, you've been everything, but no romantic. I mean in the nursing house."

"Shall I be romantic while loading a dishwasher? Or when I disinfect?"

"Why not? I see romance almost everywhere. Except for some things."

Rick knew where I was heading.

"Ah, your work is not romantic."

"Depends. Sometimes it is."

Rick's eyes widened in disbelief.

"Washing people and changing diapers is romantic?"

I continued: "I'll try to tell you one real story from my work. It'll be hard, but I'll try. Once there was a married couple who lived to a very high age. Although grandpa had a permanent catheter and grandmother had to use diapers, they stayed together in good and bad for all their lives. They loved each other very much. Even though their bodies were no longer obeying them, every Saturday they spent their night together in grandfather's bedroom. The nurse had to prepare them for this special night. It was a whole complicated procedure. The nurse put both in a double bed and wondered what they did there as the grandfather, unfortunately, could not function as a man. Touches. They needed to touch each other. That was the last thing they had. Every week, the nurse had to do this complicated procedure just for the touch. This is the romance that lasts forever. We, our generation, have no idea. Not even I. Sorry, my language. I hope you understand a bit of what I wanted."

Rick was speechless. Romance can have many forms. All women love flowers, candles, candy... to be able to live and experience this kind of romance is the most precious romance in the world. Love and touch accompany human beings from cradle to grave. Thanks to our, though fragile, but in a special way, most well-arranged box, we feel precious touches on our skin without which we cannot exist.

Rick asked: "What went wrong with you?"

"Rick. Not now. Please. I answered you a question. Now it's your turn."

"You like all the romantic things, right?"

"All women do, but I like more how you are loading and unloading dishes into the dishwasher. I see romance there too. Now you."

I was adamant. I asked him with caution about his work because the reality of Earth Olympus was more than interesting to us mortals. I left to him to decide how much he was willing to reveal. It was funny when I couldn't express myself. I was straggling with a paper dictionary or with the g-translator that didn't always work properly. Although the words didn't come easy the laughter saved a lot. It was very comical, it seemed to me that I came from the Stone Age. When people communicated really more with gestures. I was glad to finally be quiet and I tried to understand what Rick was saying. So, I was doing exactly what my older son told me to do.

Suddenly we realized the Rabbit pub was about to close. I looked at my watch. "God, is it so late? I have to get up at 5 am!"

Rick was surprised. "Why so early? You said you start at seven-thirty."

I explained: "You, men… You are beautiful as soon as you open your eyes. You wash and that's it. You don't have to do anything more. We, women, need to put so many things on our face before we can go out. Higher the age, more is the time."

"Do you think men want that?"

"I guess yes. I'm not sure."

Rick looked at me. "I guess not always. Sometimes there is no need for a mask."

"Women feel more vulnerable without a mask. I can't explain that."

"You're doing it for us. To look more beautiful."

"And…does it help you? Do you see us more beautiful?"

Rick contemplated: "Grandmothers in the nursing house no longer have masks. They don't need them."

"No. They need something else."

Rick laughed. "Diapers!" We both laughed and realized that as the years went by, a human being actually becomes more modest. Priorities change. Grannies no longer need an anti-cellulite gel; they just need a gel for sore joints. Well, women want to attract men. They use different techniques to do it.

External beauty was a priority for men. Or is it really just about chemistry? About a mysterious code that nobody in the world could explain? No one knew when and how the miraculous spark was set in the human heart and then human beings fell in love. Scientists stubbornly claim that only hormones play a role when males and females fall in love and totally blind, they start to reproduce. Then how can they explain that people can fall in love at any age when reproduction is no longer possible? Just the hormones again? The whole human body is one giant magic. Miracle. Though not quite perfect because it ages, but a miracle. When we stopped laughing, I asked: "How is the kitchen here?"

Rick wanted to answer, but we had to leave because the waitress wanted to close the pub.

Rick replied outside: "Why do you care?"

"You definitely keep your low-fat and low-carb diets. Don't you?"

Rick answered: "Since we're here everything is upside down."

"Even you. As if you were turned. Upside down."

I teased him. Rick waved his hand. "It has its benefits. To be this way now…turned around…with the dark side on the surface."

"I understand you. More than you think."

Rick asked me: "How is the kitchen at the curvy Bunny?"

"In our country, some people die unfortunately at a young age. In Slovakia, food is paramount. We cook a lot and some Slovaks eat a lot. For example, at Christmas and Easter the worst combinations that you can imagine. Some of us, don't bake dry turkey. Some Slovaks bake greasy duck or goose and fish. With that, they will eat high-calories mayonnaise potato salad or red cabbage with homemade dumplings. On top of that bunch of homemade baked Christmas cookies and homemade pralines. Then it happens. After this feast, many of them will end up in the hospital emergency with gall bladders problems or other stomach problems. They continue to eat all the harmful, greasy, and good things. Food is sacred to us. Nothing dietary has good taste. Nothing."

Rick laughed like crazy and me too. Then Rick continued: "What about you? You eat all that as well?"

I sighed: "I can only cook it. I can't eat most of it. It's a very sad story. I have my special pancreatic-chocolate diet."

Rick's eyes widened. "For god's sake! What is that?"

"You don't want to know, trust me. Chocolate saves me. You've seen my work. Sometimes I have to have some sugar. Sometimes grannies drive us crazy. Shit everywhere. Sometimes you just can't go on without sugar. That's why I'm a little curvier Bunny. Carrots and broccoli don't taste good. No vegetables taste good. Egg whites are tasteless. I know chocolate is sinful. But it tastes great. Almost like…"

Rick added with interest: "You mean like sex?" Thank god, it was dark outside. My face was on fire. I covered my mouth: "I wasn't supposed to tell you this. Sorry… It's late… I've got to go…" I literally ran toward the nursing house entrance. But I didn't realize that the entrance was closed, and I had to ring.

Rick followed me. "Why are you running?"

"Danger. I always say what I don't want to. Then I always have problems. Please let it be. Good night."

Rick didn't understand. "Nothing happened."

"It always starts this way. It ends in a disaster. I... I'm glad we're friends."

"Friends? Are you serious?"

"I know. I have to give you different jobs. I don't like it. Believe me. I'm a nurse. And you... Man from a higher reality."

Rick frowned: "We can continue talking tomorrow."

"It's not a good idea."

"Why are you afraid? Do you think I want to bake a bunny?"

"You men always want it. I have to. Good night."

Rick stood in front of the doorway, staring through the glass door as I ran up the stairs quickly. He didn't understand. The commander-general changed that evening into a shy bunny who just ran away because she considered him a danger. How is that possible when she's crazy about the hero he has lent a part of his existence to?

I ran into my room and then I laughed at myself. It couldn't get any worse than that I thought. I can't speak good English, yet those inappropriate words that ignite the disasters always get out of my mouth. I never knew too much about flirting with men. My only gift, that occasionally allowed me to make miracles was my pen. I had a gift of word. With words, I fought where other women fought with their usual weapons like their face or body. An inconspicuous nurse had to use her inner qualities and imagination to try to show the male being an unusual way of female seduction. But so far no one suitable was to be found. Endless fantasy was saving my life. Because sometimes I couldn't survive my reality without dreams. While cleaning the dirt of other people I was creating stories, fairy tales, choreographies. When I was little, my sister and mom were getting desperate because of me. I was doing horrible things from my early childhood. I regularly sewed costumes for theater from my mom's new fabrics and curtains. I changed the children's room to either a hospital, a dental clinic, or a theater. And it all had to stay the way I arranged it otherwise I would cry like an elephant. My sister used to shout at me, my mom was desperate. Why can't I play like all the other normal kids, she wandered. But what was normal? I didn't get it. For me, it was normal even when I was creating games for other kids from the neighborhood. I organized them. Even then I believed life was easier for the boys.

When Rick arrived home, his buddies were sleeping like babies. He could not fall asleep. What does that mean? One ordinary woman, a nurse, makes him strangely angry and at the same time is entertaining him. While in bed, he smiled at this vocabulary meeting that wasn't even a date. And above all, this crazy nurse, despite the language barrier, speak words that she doesn't want at all... Chocolate... Forbidden... Sinful... Sweet... That comparison to sex fits.

I was thinking about the comparison as well. Chocolate and sex complicate the life of women the most. Chocolate makes them more fat in all the wrong places. On the ass, thighs, belly. Sex often creates scars in their hearts. Because men have a micro box of emotions. Oh, my god, why did you make it this way?

While still in bed, Rick recalled the little, yellow box the nurse had given him when she was handling the cabinets. He got out of bed and was looking for it. He couldn't remember where he'd put it. He lit the light and opened the box placed on the chest. It was there. He took it in his hands and opened it. It was empty.

The light awakened Peter who was sleeping in the next room. He knocked at Rick's door.

Rick grunted: "Why the hell are you knocking? You know I'm alone here."

Peter laughed mockingly. "It doesn't matter whether you're alone or not. I don't want to disturb your private sphere."

Rick ironically exploded: "Private sphere? Thank you very much for such a private sphere. You can't even bring a woman here. You can hear everything. That's terrible."

Peter watched him with interest. "Wow. Did you change your mind about that nurse? That you don't care about her and she isn't your type?"

"She's funny. You should have seen her. Using this old fashion dictionary."

Peter burst into laughter. "That suits you. You... savior. Or how did she call you? Oh, my god. At least you see what your effect is on dreaming mothers. Not a sex symbol but the savior of the world. Not only you but all of you who play the roles of heroes. God. See? The older the women, the higher the level of love. You should be happy."

They looked at each other and laughed quietly. Rick told him: "Be so kind and stop teasing me, okay? It's the worst comparison I've ever heard. Worse than the god Apollo."

"Apollo? Oh, god! Did she compare you to that? I can't believe that!!! That's crazy!"

Rick explained to him: "To make it clear, I look like Apollo without the beard. Terrible."

Peter laughed at him. "That's logical. Beard is less sexy for some women. Apollo is a Greek god."

"And the other? The savior? Where does that one belong to? It seems that this little nurse head is not okay."

Peter contemplated: "Maybe it is. Who knows for sure how things are arranged up there?"

Rick replied: "What does Greek mythology have in common with Christianity?"

"Well, at first sight, nothing."

Rick defended himself: "I am no perfect being, for God's sake. I am a human. A simple man. With mistakes. With doubts about myself. She can't see me this way!"

"You have chosen a role that turned you into the perfect being. Maybe these male archetypes have similar energy. They save the world. Yeah. That must be it!"

"It can't be."

Rick was desperate. Peter contemplated: "It's not so bad. You are a good man."

"Yes! A man! Only a man but nothing more. I'm tired of people seeing me this way."

"I don't think it's too bad. Ask her tomorrow."

"What is this?"

Peter grabbed the small box and Rick replied: "Man's box of emotions."

Then he went to the big closet where he had his clothes. "And this... is my box of sex."

Peter looked into the big closet, and because there wasn't much in it, he laughed. "You don't have that much in there now."

Rick shrugged his shoulders. "When in need a curvier bunny is good enough."

In need? Peter wondered.

Rick continued: "If she was on the other side of the ocean, she would be on the other side of me. My employee. Taking care of my clothes and my house. I wouldn't even notice her."

"Are you sure?"

"I don't know… I don't know…" They both remained silent. Huge, almost insurmountable boundaries between the world of ordinary mortals and Earth Olympus didn't allow to enter Olympus without permission. So, it had to be arranged. The rules had to be obeyed.

Peter yawned. "Let's sleep. Tomorrow is another day. With a higher level of love. We're going to do good deeds."

Rick added: "Unfortunately, we have to forget the lower levels. That's really awful. I'm fed up with the higher level of love."

Then Peter remembered the testosterone code: "Higher love cleans the heart and fills it with. yeah… You know what I mean. Good deeds."

"Are you insane? What the hell you are talking about?"

"That's not me. Ask Tina to explain how the filling of the testosterone code works."

"Jesus Christ! What code? What does she carry in her head?"

"When I asked her for help, she explained to me that she and her colleague come up with such a weird code for guys. They say that when it doesn't work, guys are angry. Very angry. That's exactly how you are now."

"What's this code about?"

"1. clean house, 2. clean dress, 3. belly full of warm food, 4. empty… Well, you know…"

"Really? And that's it?"

"In our luxury reality, we have people who take care of the first three points. For the fourth, we have…"

Rick finished it: "Other people. Yeah. That's right. Yet the relationships are not always successful in our world. Now, it looks as if no relationships are successful in the ordinary world. It's all the same shit. Virtual. Oh, tomorrow we are going to deal with the real shit. Anything positive about this disastrous situation that we have found ourselves in?"

On the ninth day of their punishment stay, I had to assign new tasks again. This time the guys had to clean up the small, ordinary, real mess instead of the movie mess, and they did it really well. I tried to avoid Rick. I didn't know how to communicate with him after yesterday. But he was curious, he wanted to ask so many things. It was difficult during work because we were understaffed and the load of work was huge. I just smiled at him when I passed by.

Only when I finished the morning washing of our patients could we talk for a while. That is, if my Stone Age communication could be called communication. Rick saw me in the laundry room. "I still haven't figured out what is it that 'special' thing that you want. And I have many other questions."

I asked him: "Don't you have enough? Why do you really want to know?"

"I'm a curious man... Man..." He laughed and emphasized the word man.

"Do you want to blame me for the savior or the god Apollo? Forgive me. I didn't mean to insult you."

"I know. I just don't see the connection. You mix all the religions together."

"You think that? How many religious books have you read?"

"And you?"

"Not so many but I have found that religions have very similar patterns. By the way, you in Hollywood mix everything together too. I don't mind. About the religion and the world up there. I believe everything is connected up there. People are still trying to tear it up. It doesn't work."

"Wait. Connected? How connected? I don't understand."

"Did you realize that pagan religions are basically the same? Thor, Zeus, Jupiter, Aphrodite, Venus, Isis. And so on."

"What about the savior? And Apollo?"

"They both have strong charisma. Each in his own way. Doesn't matter."

"Doesn't matter? How so?"

"Rick. Do you think it's a good idea to talk about religions next to a dirty laundry?"

Rick thought: *Of course, it's a good idea. Chaos needs to be cleaned.*

"Look. It doesn't matter what people believe in, what kind of religion... God... Some people would kill me for these words. I feel what's important is that there are saviors in all of them. Some good etheric beings that help human beings. On top of them is the highest Creator. And its negative opposition, which is also trying to create, but bad things. I believe it is arranged like on Earth. In levels. Let's not talk about it today you are kind of...different..."

"Well, that's because of the savior and Apollo."

"Yet it has caressed your self-esteem. Or your soul?"

"You are a very strange person. So, will we meet again at the Rabbit?"

"I don't know. It's not a good idea."

Rick didn't give up. "Of course, I've heard that."

I was desperate. "Look at me. You are complicating my life. While you were just a picture, everything was easy. Now you're real. I am a nurse."

"I'm an actor... A man... A human being..."

"With strong radiation. I think... Charisma ... Yes... Apollo, the god of light, prophecy, art, music. His prophecies tried to warn people. They never obey. The savior also tried to save the world. Even his prophecies were not obeyed by people."

"Just tried? What do you mean, just tried?"

"Do you think our world looks like it was a saved world? And all we have to do is to ignore the problems and imagine that life on Earth is only beautiful? Wait for our dreams to be fulfilled?"

Rick said: "A dream come true. Do you think my dream came true? Many say that dreams can come true, all you need to do is to believe. Maybe the world looks like this because people stopped believing. In themselves. In humanity. Nobody can save the whole world or all people. That is impossible."

"He can save at least a few. Even though it will cost something. We can't save all the nurses in the world, but one can at least draw attention to a particular problem."

Rick looked at me for a while. This conversation was absolutely unsuitable to seduce somebody. Yet he was trying to perceive one ordinary bunny from a lower reality, or a social status, who sees in him two at first glance incompatible male archetypes. And on top of that was his role of hero, who also saved the world. For god's sake! It was just his role. Nothing more. He was beginning to be a little bit afraid of that unobtrusive bunny. When that bunny cares for living people, has children, and lives her normal life in normal reality, it should be okay. His reality was far more dangerous and harder. Bunny had no idea. He didn't tell her that much yet. The price that had to be paid for success in higher reality was often too high.

I started laughing. "I've ruined everything. Instead of being silent and smiling, I'm tormenting you with stupid things like how miserable the condition of our planet is. Or gods...and we haven't come to angels and fairies yet. Exactly what my son told me not to do. Oh, god. Go to work. I can't take it anymore."

Rick also laughed.

"This is a really very good topic do discuss on a second date, that takes place next to a dirty laundry cart filled with grandma's consequences of higher love. Sorry, not a date."

"It really suits me. Dreaming saves my life. When the consequences of higher love are waiting for me in the third room. I'm trying to imagine anything."

Rick was surprised. "Does it work?"

"Not always. There are times when I hate old ladies and grandpas. Sometimes. You'll see. How the days pass by the fatigue and stress grows. By the end of the two weeks term, my negative thoughts will attract various disasters. You'll see. How's it with you? Do you ever feel that way? I mean in your work?"

"So, this is where all the motivational speakers in the videos are right. Thoughts make a reality. What you see all day is not very positive. Day after day the positive attitude fades away."

"Yes, we also feel gratitude. Though it's a different kind of gratitude. We are thankful for having less dirty diapers to change, fewer tiles and toilets to clean…painted with you know what."

"Yes, I know, with shit."

"Yes, our imagination helps us to continue."

"The result is positive. So today at the Rabbit?"

I sighed: "What else do you want to know? I've already told you so many stupid things. Your head will explode."

Rick shouted unintentionally: "Not just my head!"

I looked at him and pretended I didn't understand. "Even your heart and soul. From the higher levels of love, I mean."

"Exactly…that's it! Higher levels complicate everything."

I objected: "That's only in the beginning. Believe me. Those who will start from the end will understand."

"From the end? How from the end?"

I smiled at him. "First, I came to clean up your mess. Look, we're standing here for twenty minutes. We're using cell phones, though it's not allowed. For the sake of translating. My break is gone."

"Oh, and by the way, why didn't you want to be paid for the job?"

"Why? I do it all my life. It doesn't matter who is the client, does it?"

"It matters to me."

"Okay. I'll finish earlier today. We can finish this conversation at the Rabbit."

Rick was hit by the testosterone in his head again, and he really didn't care that Bunny was a little curvier anymore.

"We'll finish the Bunny today."

I warned him: "Do you want me to come? So, don't say that."

"Why not? I can say shit, but I can't talk about finishing the Bunny?"

"I'm not deaf. No bunny will be finished today, is that clear?"

"When?"

"Never. Do you want answers to questions or not?"

"Answers... Answers..."

"Oh, god. I've already told you I don't want it like that. You ended up there again."

"It's not men's fault. They'll always end up where they start. In the lower levels. I mean the levels of love. By the way, Peter told me about your code. Look, I'm getting angry again and you don't care."

"No, I don't. You're not angry. The first days you were. It's not quite my code. I created this code. But it works."

"Unfortunately. So, what do I do?"

"Patience. Your stay here will come to an end and you will return to your reality. There will be no problem with filling the testosterone code."

"How can you know?"

"I don't know. I just think so."

"So, what time?"

"I have training today. Let's make it at 5 pm."

Thanks to a malfunctioning code, a spoiled love potion, and chaos, which Bunny had caused with her strange ideas, the major male hormone stumbled into his head. He imagined a different type of training, but he didn't say it out loud. The shy Bunny was so scared that she would try to escape again. He didn't know why but he wanted those answers. She wanted them from him too. Communication was more than difficult but this nurse was full of secrets. He was in awe of her mind. What she had in her heart he only started to suspect, but he wouldn't admit it. How to be grateful despite not very kind reality. Yet, one can't be grateful for such a reality, can he? Then what about her soul? Not mentioning the body. Oh, Bunny was right. When in need even a little curvier Bunny is good enough. Any Bunny is good enough. Brown bunny. White bunny. Black bunny… Splashy bunny… In short, men know how to separate their feeling and that's it. To hell with feelings. They only cause pain. Sometimes Tina was for sure the splashy bunny. In the morning she came wearing a clean ironed uniform. By evening it was full of stains. Not only from the patients. When she was stressed things would start to fall from her hands and would end up on her white uniform. Stains from the juice. Stains from the mash. From chocolate. Chocolate. Rick banned himself from thinking more about the sinful chocolate because splashy Bunny likened it to sex. That was what the four handsome men currently were lacking. They were forced to use plan B in their unenviable situation. Will was bitching and cursing the damned Germans and this terrible trip. Andy humbly reconciled with fate. Peter was a bit different and he dealt with it internally. And Rick? In spite of fate and the lack of lower levels of love, he also tried to accept the unexpected reality. Splashy Bunny is so close and yet so far away from him.

Meanwhile, on the second floor, desperate Will was observing other nurses while working by the dishwasher. He was looking for a suitable candidate for a friendship with benefits at least. But their age category was worse than Tina's and all of them were married and virtuous women. Meanwhile, Andy sat down on a couch. He was wearing gloves and holding a disinfectant rag in his hands. Will came to him grumbling: "I'm really fed up! Here in this damn nursing house, they don't have but older nurses. Nobody to hit on. They all act like nuns. They don't even notice us."

Andy laughed. "I doubt any of them have seen our hero movies. Probably just their kids. They have their husbands and partners. They don't care about us. Oh, by the way, why aren't any young nurses working here?"

Though he didn't realize it, Will hit the nail on this head with his answer: "They would be crazy if they wanted to do this job with such salary. Cleaning shit, washing, feeding grannies and grandpas? Who would do that for this money?"

"Tina is right. Nobody from the young generation wants to work in this department. It's supposedly one of the worst ones. They say there are few young pretty chicks in the hospital."

"See! We will make a problem here, then they will transfer us to the surgery department, and we will hit on somebody there."

Andy objected: "Is this nursing house not enough for you? Do you want to clean the surgery department instead? Give it a break! Or hire a professional.

Anyways, soon you'll be back home to your luxury lifestyle and luxurious women."

As he looked at the two nurses and assistants who were doing their work, Will was wondering. *Luxurious women, actresses, models, and then… Nurses with virtuous expression and humility in deeds.* Luxury was on both sides though it looked differently. Andy interrupted his thoughts.

"Maybe we should realize that everything we have including our women is a gift. Our luxury is a gift and we should try to fix the world with it."

"Women. Women. Luxurious women. I'm sure at night clubs there would be few hot chicks."

"Get over it! Don't be a teenager and act like an adult man."

Will laughed mockingly. "We live like teenagers. I've said it before. Oh…it's a punishment."

Andy was already fed up with Will grumbling about not having sex and told him: "You know what? If you're not satisfied you can go to that jail, maybe there will be a better choice of luxury."

Will laughed desperately. "You're disgusting. Do you know that?"

"We all are disgusting and frustrated. Let's go to work. We won't think about it."

Later, Andy wondered about what their temporary colleagues were thinking. These ordinary women with whom, for various reasons, it was impossible to have even a flirt. Dignified walking creatures in white uniforms, often without makeup. Who would wake up an hour earlier to take care of patients over 80 years old? Just because they had different priorities in their work. Values and some working partnerships. What about Tina? He wondered how far Rick has progressed in his attempt to seduce her. How would that benefit Rick? And Tina? A woman living in such a reality might not be too much into jewelry and expensive gifts. Strange. Here the material values have narrowed down to the most basic things. To be clean, dry, fed. Stroked. They didn't need more. What about us? We want to have a lot of things that we really don't need and on top of that we're showing off. What for? To make ordinary people from lower reality envy us? Or does it meant to somehow motivate them to no longer want to be nurses, for example? Luxury and money meant freedom too. But it was also necessary to handle it properly.

The longer these four strong, male archetypes who had millions of fans, stayed in this hidden place in Germany, the more they thought about how the world works. They were starting to understand that it wasn't a punishment for them. It is a gift that they could see with their own eyes how gifts of the highest level of love work. Mercy, compassion, humility, gratitude.

Later that day the guys met in their favorite, right now the only available pub, the Rabbit, for lunch. Andy asked curiously: "So how did it go with seducing the ordinary, little older than you, nurse yesterday?"

Rick looked at him with a bad look. "Why do you care about her age? She is not that old."

Will asked: "What does that mean to you? Not that old?"

Peter defended Rick: "Give him a break!" Rick didn't even realize that the anger was slowly really going away from his heart.

He said quietly: "Life is not all about young or beautiful chicks."

Andy burst into laughter. "Look who's talking! Look at your collection!"

"You better look at your collection," Rick retorted.

For a moment, Will found himself inside his strange, unreadable, once-positive, once-negative character and said viciously: "No blaming, man. Some of us, have got too big collections."

He wasn't supposed to say that. Inside the men, worried about the lack of women, who were now cleaning up some stupid nursing house, the emotions flickered like torches. That was the prize of fame. Although it was often done by ordinary mortals as well, they didn't have nasty paparazzi breathing on their necks and making their lives difficult. Unfortunately, even the paparazzi had to feed themselves and sometimes their families. Peter was horrified. He didn't want them to draw unnecessary attention.

"Guys! Come on! Calm down! Everything is fine! After all, even ordinary mortals are doing it, aren't they? So, why does it bother you? You are good looking, sex symbols, so what? This is no tragedy. That you're enjoying life, is it? The collections are far, you can only call them."

Andy and Rick looked at each other and Peter turned to Will: "Next time you take care of your collection. Kindly let the others be."

Andy approved. "Well, I'm wondering when you're going to add that plain Bunny in your collection."

Rick also laughed and replied: "Actually, I don't know what I want from the Bunny. She's a strange kind of woman. She's carrying all the dangerous things in her head."

Andy warned him: "Watch out for ordinary women. Fantasy is dangerous. A woman who has it is even more dangerous."

Will thought: *Why? She's not an actress. Or something like that.*

Peter said, "The actresses and models portray what they are told to portray. Someone must create a reality for the actress or actor to be portrayed. For models, dresses must be sewn. Coaches must make icons out of them. But the initial ideas and thoughts must come from fantasy, without it, it's not possible."

Rick was silent for a moment, then said: "Do you mean that such an ordinary Bunny can be dangerous? She told me that I was dangerous for her. The rabbits never hurt in the wild."

Andy looked at Rick and nodded. "That's it! Shy Bunny with a dose of imagination can be a very dangerous mixture. Better get your hands off her."

Will teased him again: "You think he should put his hands away so that Bunny will end up added in another collection?"

Rick warned him: "Shut up! Take care of your collection and leave ours alone."

Peter laughed mockingly. "He would do that, but all your collections are at the other end of the planet."

The men laughed at each other. This is how people are. Everyone in the world has his or her collections. Secret ones. Beautiful and famous people have a huge disadvantage. These poor people can't enjoy life without everyone knowing about it. Modern technologies make sure that the world is well informed. In a speed of light. Not only about collections. So, what? We all have our past and present. The future is uncertain. That is what human beings are making, decisions and deeds.

And so, the guys calmed down a bit and after their eight-hour shift, they reached their male nest.

Andy ordered them: "Don't you dare to make a mess here again! Put your dirty stuff in the laundry basket, please. Not on the floor."

Will muttered: "So said our new housekeeper."

"No one will come to clean up our mess anymore. I'm sure we are able to maintain order."

Rick laughed. "We have a female general in work, and here we have you. What a life!" Rick and everyone else obeyed because they no longer wanted to create such a terrible mess. Rick was in a hurry because he wanted to go to the, still not a date, with the allegedly dangerous Bunny.

I myself was pretty scared when I imagined the horrible communication that consisted of putting words together randomly. My Slavic accent? That was even more terrible in English than my accent in German. *Why am I going there?* It's all terrible. I looked desperately at my uniform full of all sorts of stains and was crying and laughing at the same time. What's the point of changing my clothes? Rick sees this uniform every day. He sees how it starts to change quickly depending on the state of our grandma's department. The time, that we never had, actually destroyed our lives, because by half-past ten o'clock all grannies and grandpas had to be washed and fed. Yeah. Until the unpredictable things happened. When we were entering the rooms in the morning, we never knew what awaits us there. There was a difference whether we cleaned the old lady alone, or we had to add the time to clean up everything else that she encountered the night before. Especially those who could still walk. Even the guys have figured out that theory, regulations, and standards are one thing, but practice was another. So, I washed myself and wondered what to wear. Oh, god. I don't have a sexy dress. I have to be okay with the clothes that I have.

I was afraid that someone would recognize Rick. With beard or without. Even if he looked like a homeless man, his strong charisma was dangerous.

Rick started the conversation immediately: "So… first, I want to ask about the code. Do you really think man only needs these four things? Clean house. Clean clothes. Full belly with warm food and—"

I interrupted him: "No, please. Don't say the fourth point. Please."

Rick smiled.

"Why not? Men like the fourth point the most."

"I know. It complicates the life of people the most."

"It's easier for the animals. They fight for the female; they get her and that's it."

"How do you fight for females in your reality? Me, you spanked my ass…and there? What you do there? In your country?"

Rick remembered the debate about the collections. "Let's not discuss this."

"You don't even have to. Never mind. It's okay. I just want to know if it's easier for you to fight for women when you have that. Financial freedom. Ordinary guys buy fake jewelry instead of emeralds and real pearls. Stones like stones, aren't they?"

"Everybody can afford flowers, can't they?"

"If they can't, they can tear off one in the garden. Or in the meadow."

"That doesn't satisfy all women. How about you? What would make you happy?"

"And you?"

"I asked first."

"Rick. We've already talked about it. I'm not flirty and adventurous. It's not for me anymore. My heart has already had enough of it."

"I'm just asking."

"I'm just asking too."

"It is really difficult to communicate with the Bunny."

"Why do you need to know? I said that I don't want to do it like that."

"Exactly because of that! I want to know how you want it."

"We know each other for a few days. We don't know anything about each other."

Rick thought, *I have seen enough.*

"You mean work? I've seen yours too. A little bit of the behind the scenes."

"On YouTube."

"Oh, be quiet."

"The fans will attract them with their thoughts, right?"

"My son tells me about it."

"Yeah sure. He also tells for example, what the savior has in common with Apollo."

"It's not on YouTube only. Pieces of information are everywhere. You'll find only bits and pieces, fragments. Nothing is complete. It's very difficult to put it all together."

"Do you really believe what you said?"

"Human beings have fragile hearts. They need to believe in something good above us. I believe."

"Ah… So, you believe there is both Apollo and the savior, but you don't know how they are related?"

"I don't know whether it is true. We people need evidence. If we can't see and catch something, we don't believe."

Rick looked at me and remembered Andy's words. Hands away from the Bunny. However, the curiosity and competition took over. "We don't see love and yet we know it exists."

"The scientists don't believe in it. They say it's just hormones."

Rick continued: "We see its deeds."

"Deeds of love. I believe there is a hierarchy in love. Everybody knows that Universe and Earth are created from four basic elements, I think, that love is formed from four levels. Fire... Water... Earth... Air too."

Rick was getting a little worried, but it didn't matter to me. If he wanted to understand, he needed to try at least.

"Sounds interesting. Keep going."

"Fire is the first spark. It rules our actions. Water represents emotions. It rules our hearts. Earth is passion. It rules our bodies. Air is mercy and compassion. It rules our minds and what is above the mind. The highest level."

"Is that the special thing you want? All four levels?"

"That's complicated. It takes time. We people want to have everything instantly. Immediately. We're not patient. If you plant a seed, you can't see the result right away either."

Rick was getting more interested. The danger that both felt was big, but the curiosity was bigger.

"What happens then? When a man passes through all four levels?"

I couldn't answer. Then I tried: "I... I don't know. I was just trying to put together experiences, good and bad, and ideas of many people from multiple countries. I was looking for answers in books. I know one thing. I couldn't make it...at least up till now... I tried to find where I made mistakes. Some I could find, some couldn't."

Rick didn't know what to say. Men didn't like such deep words or deep conversations about the state of the world or human love. Maybe it really was all oddly connected. Because of love, people were the happiest and miserable at the same time. Emotions formed the world around us. Out of eagerness people often created failures instead of true love. Eros tormented them with unhappy, unrequited love because he shot arrows where he shouldn't. However, no one saw him. He was just a myth. A naughty god who could really trouble people.

Rick asked: "What do you think, how much time does love need to pass through all levels?"

"Sometimes a few days. Sometimes a lifetime."

Rick paused.

"... I don't understand. What do you mean?"

"Please, Rick. Don't you see how difficult is this for me? Is that important?"

"You started, so finish it."

"Nowadays all people are obsessed with searching for a soul mate. But even that won't give you a guaranty that the love will last."

"And what will?"

"Our ability to forgive ourselves. Not to make mistakes that are too painful. Some can destroy love. Maybe. I don't know. It's difficult. There is no guarantee that relationships will work forever. Today they fall apart fast. Very fast. Maybe we want everything. We can't give up anything."

Rick looked at his glass, then at me. "You mean sacrifice?"

"Yes. Sacrifice. Everything has a price. We don't want to pay anything. We want to have everything. We think we must have everything. Maybe it's not entirely true. What do you think? Do you think sacrifice is needed in love?"

Rick thought for a moment. He thought about people he knew, and how it was with them and love. Nothing was perfect.

"I think yes. I guess it can't be done without it. It is quite difficult for us. We are exposed to temptation much more."

"Yes, you are. You have beautiful people around you. We admire you, but we don't know how much sacrifices in love you have to bring."

"What about you? You probably understand sacrifice. Your job."

"My job cost me everything. All I have left are my children. The rest is in ruins. I didn't have a choice. It doesn't matter."

"So, if we had the time, how would it go? I mean the levels?"

"Rick. I'm an ordinary nurse. Look at our communication. It's a disaster. How am I suppose to show you?"

Rick shook his shoulders. "You should know how. To which level belongs the clean house and clean clothes?"

"Perhaps the fourth. Mercy. Compassion. Humility… Helping another human being is the higher level. Like our mind."

Rick exploded in laughter and me too.

"Well… We're starting from the end. What's next?"

"Nothing. I have no more strength. I've done all the wrong things. I am your boss at work that is your punishment. I'm just saying stupid things, instead of being silent. With horrible English. I can't flirt. I don't want to. I don't have the appropriate weapons."

Rick looked at me. "You're using the worst weapons. Trust me."

Then I got the idea. "Worst weapons? Weapons?"

"You're a dangerous Bunny."

"You're dangerous, I'm not. You don't have to do anything and you're already dangerous."

Rick smiled again and saw me blush again. Crazy situation. The nurse admired the hero he was playing and feared him.

"Why am I dangerous?"

"Let me be. Now you speak. I will think of how I will answer you the question and explain the levels of love."

Rick, a combative male, suggested: "You can explain the low, the physical, right now."

"No way! You will return home and you will have everything you are used to. You'll forget about the bossy nurse. In other circumstances, you wouldn't even notice me."

Rick was silent. She was right. Flirt meant nothing to men. Or did it mean something? Men had separate boxes.

"These are not normal circumstances. Even that crappy evening wasn't normal. We can't explain it till today."

"Are you sorry about that crappy evening?" Rick was surprised.

The anger that was shaking his soul at the beginning was slowly fading away. He stared at the shy, splashy Bunny who was afraid of him and was afraid to flirt. Why did he want to know all that?

"Everything is as it should be. It makes sense. We got to know another reality and came back for a while to the point from where we came."

I smiled. "It's good to remember sometimes where we were at the beginning."

I looked at my cellphone.

"Rick. I must go. I've already said too many stupid things. Sorry. These are not the proper things to talk about on a date. This is me. I don't know otherwise."

Rick wondered himself: *Do you think it bothers me? Maybe it's interesting for me to know how the Bunny who claims she doesn't know how to flirt, flirts.*

I blushed again: "We both have a past."

"Are you always flirting like that?"

"I'm not flirting. I told you I don't know how."

"What weapons do you use?"

Rick remained silent for a moment, and I continued: "Actually. You don't have to bother too much, do you? All you have to do is to be yourself. Nothing more."

Rick listened carefully and then said: "You think so?"

"It looks so. At first glance."

"At first. I guess not at the second. Why are you rushing?"

"I have to go. I want to dance and practice. I need to be alone now. It's not good. The whole situation is not good for me."

"You think it's good for me?"

"Stop torturing us, please. I'm a woman from a lower reality. That's the truth. We say, that we are equal, but we know, that is not the truth."

"Did you say dance? Are you a dancer?"

"Only amateur. I have a group. Theater and dance group."

"Theater? With dances?"

I started laughing. "We're just pretending to be actors. We're acting that we're acting. It's not the type of performance you're used to."

Rick asked with interest: "Do you think I'm a good actor?"

I answered sophisticatedly: "Is it necessary for a handsome man to be a great actor? All you and your colleagues need to do is to be yourselves. Just be, and half the planet will stubbornly claim that you are the best actors in the world. I mean, mainly the female part."

Rick did not give up. "You didn't answer the question."

"You are a very good actor. Indeed you are Not because of your looks. I would like you no matter how you look."

"Oh, yeah. Of course. With beard or without."

"You still have the same heart. I feel it. Otherwise, I wouldn't compare you to the two male archetypes that have nothing in common. I'm sorry that you are in such a difficult situation."

Rick was silent. We came out of the pub, which for a transitional period became our place for the worst communication in the world.

"So, I'll see you tomorrow."

Rick wanted to come with me to the entrance and I said: "I'll take those few steps myself."

"What type of dances are you dancing?" he asked.

"Different types. Now it's your turn to search the net and social networks. Everything is there… That's where currently people are living. In virtual reality. To forget about their own. We have dancers of different ages. Even beautiful ones. You'll see."

"You don't consider yourself beautiful?"

"Everybody is beautiful because everybody is unique. Thanks to me the group is performing for thirteen years. My fantasy keeps it alive. I'm one of the groups' leaders. The leaders don't have to be the most beautiful. I'm just creating, embroidering costumes, teaching. At an amateur level. You're a professional."

"What's the difference?"

"I don't have the opportunity or the time to be a professional. I already have a certain age. Well, I don't mind. Not everybody has to be professional. We give joy to ourselves. To the audience. We don't do it for money. That is mostly a joke."

"Can I find something on YouTube? If I wanted to see?"

"Not much. I don't allow it. I feel like my group has something unique thanks to our crazy fantasy. We have combined oriental, fantasy, and historical dances with stories. Mine and our stories. With words. While sometimes our acting is awful, people are excited. They are surprised when they see belly dancing mixed with fantasy. I teach. Children and mature women. I don't have to be a professional with them … we are surviving."

Rick wondered how many amateur groups are working in the world and are happy to spread invisible values further. Professionals learned to act in schools. Amateurs are learning only in their free time from different coaches. We said goodbye and I was still blushing. I could feel how everything was beginning to crumble on my head. *Get over it* I said to myself. I was looking forward to exercising and dancing to wash away the stress hormone.

Rick went home and started looking for my social media profile.

Every time I showed photos of our performances to strangers; people were surprised. Belly dancing groups appeared and disappeared quickly. Ours still lived with our ideas and flexibility although the number of young dancers was decreasing. We, mothers, were getting old. The situation with men was even worst. They were ashamed to dance ballroom dancing, let alone historical ones. The few we had were trying their best but there was different energy with them on the dance floor.

Rick stared at the images and didn't understand, as many others throughout my amateur dancer career, where those mothers got the free time for all this. He must ask Tina. He saw few, young, beautiful dancers as well. In few pictures, he saw the Bunny sitting on a throne made especially for her own first story…

Chapter 6

Rick came to their temporary living room. The guys were resting there. They were silent and tired. Peter interrupted the silence: "The first half of our sentence will end soon. We'll be back home in two weeks."

Andy was cheerful. "Back to our luxury for a while. We will gain power."

Rick added: "The testosterone code will be luxuriously filled again."

Will was surprised. "What code? What testosterone? What are you talking about? You only have sex in your mind."

"Wrong, guys. My head is full of higher levels of love."

Andy nodded. "We've got everything full. By the way, today, on the second floor, the grannies had a singing class. It was better than a casting show in America got talent."

Will said with a scornful look: "Oh, yeah. I haven't heard worse songs in my life. When the out of tune singing of grannies was added to that. For Christ's sake!"

Andy defended the grannies: "What kind of traditional songs do you like in America? You have such a great choice. German grannies can sing only German folk songs. It's still an old generation. Younger ones might be able to sing some American songs."

"Will, they still must do something besides eating and sleeping."

Rick burst into laughter. "And many other things! Oh, god. Where did you send us!"

Will asked Rick: "You haven't explained the code yet."

Rick smiled. "Tina and her colleague have somehow made it up. It's supposed to be a helping tool for women about what we men actually need from women. First a clean house, second clean clothes, third point full belly of warm food. The fourth point, the most important. Empty... You know what... They say that if these points aren't fulfilled, we become angry."

The guys burst into laughter. Andy warned him again: "I told you, put your hands off this Bunny. Don't underestimate ordinary women."

Rick objected: "She's not an ordinary Bunny. She's a nurse. Nurses are dangerous… Very dangerous."

Peter teased Rick: "And how is the hunt for the Bunny going on? Any progress?"

Rick spoke uncertainly: "We've made little progress. Bunny is still somewhere in the clouds at her higher levels of love and she doesn't want to go down."

"So, you can start baking her."

Rick shouted angrily: "Don't worry! Bunny must come down once! For sure. I just don't know why it's taking so long."

"Long? You know her for a few days. You said you aren't interested in her and suddenly you want to bake her? What will you get from it?"

Rick replied without hesitation: "What? I want to know how she cares about everything. In the lower levels of love. I have seen the higher ones already."

Peter disagreed: "Let her be! You will get back come home and then what?"

Rick contemplated: "Yeah well. Her dangerous words, which she puts together as they come up to her. I want her to show me the remaining three levels of love."

Andy mumbled: "Levels of love. We're only interested in that particular one, aren't we?"

Peter considered: "Not always. Now we have reached the highest one. How would the other three looks like according to Tina?"

Rick admitted: "I'm trying to make her show me the others."

Will asked him: "Will she? What are the others good for? Love creates only problems. You are better without it. Bake the bunny and that's it."

The guys laughed; Rick didn't say anything. The natural competitiveness of men, hunters was stronger than reason. Stronger than Bunny's awkward way of trying to explain to him the difficult thoughts. Despite the language barrier, Bunny tried hard to tell him something, and it was kind of oddly exciting. She even admitted that it wasn't supposed to be like that but that was her. She didn't pretend to be different. As the days went on, and his anger was diminishing, Tina, the Bunny, became even shyer.

The next day, guys got their tasks. Some were the same because in such a nursing house dirt was produced very quickly. There was always something to do. Even the little help with taking care of grannies sitting in the dining room was a huge help. In addition to washing and endless cleaning, the guys spend some time with the old ladies, smiled at them, stroked them. The grannies that could still appreciate their external beauty melted away from the happiness that they could look at such handsome guys. Not knowing what the female half of our planet would give for such a smile. The half that was 50-60 years younger than these grannies. Well, we would probably have more work with such patients. They would fate from the excitement and the guys would have to hide in that same bathroom, where they were cleaning the wheelchairs. They didn't have to hide from those grannies who were happy that someone had given them such special attention.

I tried to avoid Rick because I didn't want to speak to him. I was upset because of the language barrier and the whole situation. I couldn't find free time to learn another language in my busy schedule. Years ago, I have chosen dance and theater. I had to make magic to find the time for that as well.

However, Rick still didn't have enough of my endless tormenting words, the red spots on my neck from stress, and the stains on my uniform. He just started looking for me in the rooms. I was accompanying one of our two male patients to the bathroom. Poor Mr. D always sat in the dining room and silently observed the madhouse that was happening occasionally because of the grannies. The one who was sitting on one side of him was shouting constantly and refused to eat. As soon as we took her plate away, she started to eat the virtual food that wasn't there. The other one who sat on the other side, Mrs. K, wouldn't stop talking all day, the third one would shout 'Haloooo' and 'Bite' constantly. On top of that occasionally the other grannies, who could still walk but had dementia would quarrel. They would constantly ask Mrs. H the same things all over again. Until she would tell them to shut up. Only then they would stop. Other ladies would sing or play. Every Friday they would bake. The guys wondered how the staff can endure this chaos. Ladies who were responsible for cleanliness often did their job in vain. After five minutes some rooms looked, and unfortunately smelled as well, like the worst toilets.

Let's be honest, many people would use a different name for our department. They would call it by its real name. Madhouse. Regardless that the boss blamed the nurses and caretakers for using regular expression for human feces. That they sometimes cursed out of frustration. Shit remained a shit even when the nurses called it professionally or by its Latin name. It had to be cleaned whether it had a Latin name or expressive one. The same was with the name "nursing house."

The nice name didn't change anything on the cruel reality that it was…yes…a madhouse. By all means. Earth's Olympus observed all this up close and personal. Loving such no longer functioning beings was sometimes very difficult. That is why all employees had to have hearts of XXL size. I took the quiet, most obeying male patient to the bathroom to give him a bath.

Rick was getting curious: "Can I look?"

"Why? You have seen me washing one of my lying grannies. From a distance."

"Yeah but I haven't seen you wash somebody from a close distance yet."

I shrugged my shoulders.

"Why do you want it? You don't need to know how to wash patients. You wash yourself, don't you?"

Rick smiled. I underestimated the man's sophistication when they wanted to triumph.

"Is it the same?"

"What do you mean?"

"Washing. When you wash yourself or someone else?"

My breath stopped, but I told myself that I had to remain a professional at all costs and not show how scared I was.

"It's a big difference. We have to follow…the exact… How is the word… I mean where do you start and where do you end up. Because of the bacteria."

Rick laughed.

"That's ridiculous! Really?"

"Don't laugh. I recently did a washing exam. It's complicated nursing procedure."

"More complicated than diaper procedure?"

"Oh… You have to follow the rules very precisely. Disinfect your hands a thousand times. You can't throw anything on the floor. Here it's difficult to follow all these rules. But you at least adhere to the point where you should start."

Rick was having fun. "Where do you end up? That's easy, isn't it?"

"Easy? So, look. I'm not sure. When you have to wash so many people and you have so little time. You must not break the rules."

So, Rick sat on the shower stool in the bathroom and watched what I was going to do with the patient. I knew I was making a big mistake. Huge mistake. I was blushing again, and my neck was as spotted as it was when I was doing my nursing test in Germany. Or when I had my graduation exam in Slovakia. I had the same nursing procedure, washing a patient.

Rick was the worst spectator. I had no idea at first. I communicated with the patient in German with my Slavic accent and the obedient grandfather did all I asked him to do.

"So, Mr. D, we're going to wash. We'll take off the pajamas."

Rick watched with astonishment the checkered pajamas and wondered if it was sexy. He watched as I undressed my patient, took him to the sink, and told him what to do.

"Now wash your face and ears. I will wash your back…and…" I stopped. Now the worst part was coming. It was only at this point that I realized what I have done by not throwing Rick out of the room immediately. If I did that now, he would win. I must not show weakness. I'm a professional nurse. I'm an amateur dancer but I'm a professional nurse. I washed my patient's back and hands.

I put his T-shirt on and quietly said, "I will wash your private parts now."

Rick understood that one word and enjoyed me trying to hide the shame and embarrassment.

"Don't you want to go out? You know, you're stranger. He knows me."

"No. I want to see it till the end. I'm a man. If he lets you wash him sure he lets me stay here."

My hands shook gently, and Rick was merciless and didn't move. He saw that Bunny was embarrassed, and that suited him. So, I slowly pulled down my patient's underwear and pretended that nothing was happening. I tried to imagine that Rick was a nursing school professor and I was doing my exams. I started to clean my patient's private parts as slowly as possible. His head didn't mind but down there it was quite a different situation. That was the hardest moment for every nurse. Old men, though they couldn't function that way, the tiny traces of their masculine power persisted. Until the end. The end. Rick wanted to see the end. Oh, I underestimated him. He watched how the old man, whose mind didn't care but the body did, responded to my gentle touch, though unobtrusively. It was a little bit visible. I already knew I couldn't hide or run away, and then I started to laugh. "You see? How dangerous nurses can be? Sometimes we make miracles, and we'll wake up such old men. Just a little. But still. That complicates our lives."

Rick laughed with me and remarked: "This is how you wake your old man. What about the younger men?"

I wiped my patient with a towel. He didn't understand why we were laughing.

"Look what we did to him! That's awful! See how he feels bad now?"

Rick sighed: "And how do I feel now?"

"You feel nothing right now. Everything you have is down here at this moment. Even your head."

Rick fired back at me: "You have everything too much up there."

"You're a man. You're not giving me a choice."

I sat my grandfather on the special chair for bath, I disinfected the sink, prepared clean water washed his legs while I was on my knees. The position of humility, but also because of my problems with the spine. He understood the danger of ordinary nurses. They can take care of a human being from a newborn to an old person. He continued with a smile on his face. He knew he pushed the shy Bunny into the corner for a moment.

"Do you always work like that?"

I didn't give up and tried to be a professional, but it went a lot worse.

"I work exactly by the book."

"According to what kind of books do nurses work? According to Kamasutra?"

"Be quiet. Be quiet. According to… Nurses Books."

"Are you sure?"

"Leave me. The theory for practical…nurses. Well… God, how am I to call it?"

Rick added: "Procedures. Why are you angry? It's funny."

"It's not funny. Washing is an important thing! For patients as well. because of…how they feel…to keep them…dignified…oh, god!"

Rick tried to comfort me. At the same time, a little bit of that bad love potion slipped out of his heart. The higher level of love and Tina's humility that he saw every day caused the poison to disappear faster. But we didn't know that yet. Love is the greatest magician.

"Don't be angry. It's beautiful to see it with own eyes. How a nurse wakes up an old man… And funny."

"You think so? Not always."

I dressed the poor old man and Rick moved and leaned on the door: "I'm interested. You can explain this at the Rabbit."

"I won't…explain anything. All is messed up…"

"What is? What is messed up?"

"Please. Go away."

Rick watched as things started to fell from Bunny's hands. The bucket with used towels and grandpa's pajamas rolled over. Even the order she gave him didn't work. Everything inside that petite nurse was shaking and this is how it was externally manifested. Desperate, Tina sat down on the shower stool and said with her head down: "Please. Leave me. Look how am I working because of you."

"I see. I see. Is throwing things around you part of the nursing book?"

I laughed but I was about to cry. *God, what am I doing?*

"No, this is not the way the nurse is supposed to work. She's not supposed to leave… Damage behind."

"Damage? Damage? What damage?"

"Please. Go, work now."

Rick laughed and didn't forgive himself a remark because at that moment he felt he had won. I underestimated the man's sophistication, and he enjoyed his small victory.

"Okay, I'm going to work. I'm going to try not to leave any damage behind."

Well, wait, I thought. You can laugh at me as much as you want, but *you haven't won yet. Not this time…*

So, after a lost battle, I slowly took the dirty laundry. I didn't care whether I could wash everyone on time. When I held the man's pajama in my hands, it occurred to me that if someone really loved someone, he didn't mind such pajamas.

Rick and Peter watched one sad Bunny who worked much worse than at the beginning of her two weeks term. It was not only that she was tired, but also because she was horrified by the current situation. From what was happening around her and inside of her.

Rick had no idea what was happening inside her. She had never understood that strange male hunting logic and she couldn't see inside their hearts or souls either. She just felt kindness. Her friend, a therapist, often blamed her for wanting to see only the good sides in everyone. This complicated her whole life.

Peter was in the kitchen helping with the dishwasher and watching the grannies doing yet another interesting activity. Baking. The assistant who had been with them was grateful for his help that day.

When I came to the kitchen Peter asked: "What's wrong with you? Are you upset?"

"I'm tired, stressed out."

"What did he do?"

"You mean Rick? Nothing. I am to blame myself. I shouldn't allow him."

"Allow him to do what?"

"Let him tell you. You'll have something to laugh about. It doesn't matter."

Peter thought of something else and wanted to know what had happened. He went to look for Rick. He found him in one of the rooms cleaning cabinets. He was working very slowly and precisely in order not to get any more tasks.

"What did you do to her?"

Rick replied with laughter: "Nothing. Nothing at all. I just watched."

"Watched? Watched what?"

"How nurses work at lower levels. It was very funny."

"What? Have you progressed so far?"

"Not really. I just watched the nurse washing an old gentleman. That made her quite uncertain. I made her feel a little bit embarrassed. You should have seen her!"

"I see. Oh, god! How did it come to your mind?"

"It didn't. I entered the room just when she was about to wash one of the male patients. I thought I couldn't miss that. It was worth it. Watch out for nurses. They are dangerous."

"You better watch out. Quite Bunnies are too dangerous. If you irritate them too much, they will bite you."

"So, what? Let her bite! It won't take long, and the bunny will nicely roast on the spit."

"I don't recognize you man! She's just a nurse! Leave her alone! She looks like a good person."

"I'm a good man as well."

"Yeah. You just act like one. Oh, whatever! Do what you want!"

"I will. We'll see how the little one gets out of it. I just can't decide what will work better. Which male archetype. What do you think, boring rescuer, or Apollo?"

"What? I don't understand what you mean."

"Little Tina is still in the higher levels. I have to fight with her weapons when the usual ones don't work."

"Really? Have you tried? I mean a flower or something like that?"

"What for? She sees romance differently."

Then Rick paused and remembered the story of the old couple and his heart trembled a little. *Maybe he could try the flower. Part of his dark side still roared inside of him. But if he wants to get her, he has to be a little bit humble. Yes. Men could be so humble when they want something from the lower levels from women. But often as soon as they get what they want; the humility vanishes because of the size of their boxes. The difference was too big.*

Peter disturbed him from his thoughts. "How differently? Don't tell me she's not interested in the usual ways of seducing!"

"That's exactly what I want I say. She wants something special. She refuses to tell me what it is."

"You can't go wrong with flowers and all the rest of the bullshits, can you?"

"Yeah, Yeah. I can't, but it probably won't help. Look at those women here and how they are. You can really feel the higher level of love shining from them."

Peter thought: "And humility. Yet you have beaten her today in the battle."

"Today. But for how long?"

"You have to think of another battle."

"Or a game. Nurse Tina lives in the clouds. That's her weakness. She says she doesn't know me, just feels I'm good."

"Well, I don't think she still believes that after the disaster in the bathroom. Such a dirty trick."

"What trick? I just wanted to see how she works."

"With grandpa? For god's sake Rick!"

They both laughed.

Meanwhile, I came back to the kitchen to take the medication and saw the assistant melting chocolate on the stove. When she saw me, she already knew what I wanted: "Yes, I'll leave you the rest in the bowl."

They've all known me. Every time they baked and made chocolate icing; they gave me the leftovers. It didn't matter that my stomach didn't like it. It was just like with people and sex. In some situations, we can't resist the temptation, although we know that we will have pain after that. Not stomachache but heartache and soul ache. Especially human males have a much harder situation. Their little box of emotions, a huge box of sex, 20 times higher testosterone level, and hunting instinct often led them off the right track and they went hunting elsewhere. They had their official female and they were sure of that. So why would they bother? She was responsible for the perfect fulfillment of all testosterone code points. However, the fourth point has often gone wrong due to a variety of problems. If they were not trying to maintain the spark of passion with fantasy and new experiences the stereotype and routine brought a disaster. So, the unhappy human male, who tried hard to resist, could not resist any longer. The fool one would confess to his official alpha female because he wants to fix it. But he wouldn't fix anything. Offended pride and a broken heart that could no longer be sewn or glued would not let him fix it. No matter how hard he tries to explain. Or to say that it meant nothing, and it was just sex. Like the female would understand. Just sex? Because females have both love and sex in their one and only box. Unlike males. The female threw all male's things, sometimes out of the window, and threw him out of the nest. She sent him to the other female not only for the fourth point of code. Let the other one take care of the less popular first three points of testosterone code, which for sure belonged to higher levels of love. Sometimes the exact same thing happened the other way around. When the female decided to go and try another human male, a competitor, to see if he would be a little better. Because he was able to revive the routine of the dried-up romance that the female began to miss so much. Some human beings have become lazy. They don't want to fight for love all their life. Not all of them but many of them. Even adults need romance, imagination, and playfulness. That we are forgetting about. Sometimes we don't want to be creative. So, let's leave it altogether. Let the other partner try. However, both must give and take. There must be a balance. Otherwise one of them will leave forever. Whether with heart or with the body. Sometimes ruins can't be fixed. Love turns into hatred and despair. Circumstances like lack of financial freedom force many couples to live together. And that's not good either.

I returned the medicaments to the shelf in the cupboard and took the sinful chocolate bowl. The most beautiful part of Christmas for me was when I was baking cookies and truffles. No one blamed me that I eat it because it is harmful. I had to taste it at regular intervals, right? Everything smelled so good. Chocolate. At low levels, it saved my existence along with other dangerous, bad types of sugars. Chocolate contains dangerous hormones of falling in love. That was why women loved it and hated it at the same time. I leaned against the wall and started to eat it with a small spoon. Oh, god. All fats and sugar. Just the right thing for my estrogenic figure. No problem, in the evening, I'll dance it out. Yes, but it was very difficult. I totally forgot about the world around me. I have forgotten that there is one extra dangerous alpha male somewhere nearby, who didn't care if Bunny had a little Aphrodite figure. He wanted to win. Perhaps it is precisely because of this, Bunny was tirelessly blabbering about the unpopular higher levels of love. Rick wanted to pull Bunny down at any cost. He had seen her weak point when she was washing the old man. Very soon he will see another one.

He saw her when he wanted to tell her that he was finished with cleaning the lockers in the rooms of the patients. Bunny was stuffing herself with that chocolate as if it was the last one in the world. She got scared when she saw him. Since she was sometimes clumsy, she poured the chocolate all over her uniform.

"So that is why Bunny is a little curvier."

I was embarrassed. "What do you want from me? You have to look perfect; your bodies are worth millions. My body is just fine for this work. For 1,500 dollars a month."

Rick had a sense of humor, and at the same time he couldn't take his eyes off the stain Bunny had caused by her appetite. She had several of them on the uniform, but the only one that was irritating Rick was the one from chocolate. It reminded Rick, that Tina linked sex to chocolate: "I see you're willing to do anything for chocolate."

"Not only for chocolate. For everything I love. Even though often after such acts there is damage."

Rick repeated: "Damage. That chocolate leaves damage. On million-dollar bodies."

I explained: "Look. Every night I try to eliminate those chocolate damages from my body. After 10 hours of work, it's complicated. Yes, you see my failure. At this moment."

Rick laughed at the voracious, chocolate Bunny who was ashamed but had no strength to hide anything anymore. He felt somewhat sorry for her. He saw that it wasn't easy for the staff in this madhouse. The stressed-out nurse solved the stress like this. Badly.

I try to defend myself: "You know. After all I experience here, sometimes I can no longer resist. I know sugar is poison."

Rick was silent for a moment, then asked: "What if you came to the Rabbit again this evening and explain to me more about how you eliminate the chocolate damage?" Different kinds of damage control were in Rick's mind.

"Not today... I... look at me... I have nothing special you could want from me. You are really like Apollo."

Rick disagreed: "I'm a man. You said you didn't know me. So, let's try to continue with the dictionary."

"We women are afraid of male beauty. It means danger to us."

"I still don't know the answer to the question of how an ordinary nurse would show the remaining three levels."

"I can't. I don't want any more damages. Now I have to work."

Rick continued: "How do you want to know me when you don't want to communicate?"

"Exactly! Look how we communicate? It's terrible!"

Rick was startled because he realized that curvier Bunny was not used to be so close to the good-looking alpha males. She took a rug and began to clean the chocolate stain from her uniform. How she used to do it every day. When she was with her colleagues, who also often laughed at the stains. Bunny was always splashy. At work and at home. She wasn't paying attention; her energy was sometimes unstoppable. Rick didn't move and watched the voracious Bunny eliminating the damages made by the chocolate. She was soaking hard the rag and didn't even realize how scary her movements in certain parts of her body were. Especially when she was wearing the snow-white uniform that was white only for the first minutes of work. Only then she realized what was going on and she turned away.

Rick poured oil into the fire and suggested her: "I can help you."

She almost screamed: "No! I can do it myself!" Rick felt amused by what the nurse was blabbering about. He saw, even though she was turned away, that the chocolate spot had not disappeared.

"I see. You still haven't been able to eliminate the damage from the chocolate anyway."

"The chocolate spots are difficult to clean. Even the other spots… on the soul…very difficult…often damage remains."

Rick sighed: "They stay. So what? What time will you come?"

"I'm not coming. I'm back here tonight. You saw how much sugar I ate. I have to go in the evening to fix it."

Rick couldn't stop laughing. "Then why are you eating it when you know what's going to happen?"

"Why? Because people often can't resist the temptation. They know what's going to happen. Damage."

Rick remarked: "Not always."

"No? Almost always. Because you have a small box of feelings. In the beginning. I've got to."

Rick was thinking. Although Tina was shy and was afraid of him, he knew that it wouldn't be so easy to triumph quickly. *Why? Age? More experience? Fear? Even men were afraid. They were afraid of emotions. Sometimes more than women and they wouldn't admit it for a long time. Their broken hearts hurt perhaps more than women's. Was it so?*

He wondered how he would convince her to come. He didn't know why, but he wanted to know some answers. She did too. Despite the very high wall that separated their worlds. So high that ordinary mortals turned the Earthly Olympus to unreal beings. However, every human being has a heart and soul. Only someone wanted it that way. They wanted for the ordinary mortals not to be able to come close to the beautiful, perfect Olympus. The price of fame and wealth. Olympus needed more protection. Some are down, the others up. Nothing in between. That was always the case. That's the way it is now. The patterns of human functioning have not changed much for centuries. We say we are getting better thanks to progress. Are we? What are we doing? In many places on Earth, there is still evil and injustice. Yes, we make good realities. Beautiful. Perfect. Shiny. Noble. For every human being, these realities meant something else. Depending on the size of their hearts and souls. Depending on how they imagined their shiny and noble realities. Everyone had a specific idea of how this shiny reality should look like. Ordinary mortals were raging around the world. They didn't need luxury. They wanted to live in dignity. What does it mean to live in dignity? For every human being, something else.

Rick had no new assignments, so he waited on the couch in the dining room until confused Tina will come back to decide what he should do. Everything was mixed in his head. His success, fame, wealth, wonderful friends, family, feelings. Thrown by an unfortunate coincidence into, for men, one of the worst realities. Where he saw women and men on the end, from the other unpopular side. Men were created to manage another kind of suffering than women. Both needed each other very much. Otherwise, they could not exist. Since the beginning of time, woman was more vulnerable because of her physical fragility. Man was supposed to protect her. She was supposed to abrade the male brute force. Because men have forgotten their original mission, women had to defend themselves and had to come equal to them in order to survive. Is this what we want? Is it correct? Woman is the light of the family and the bearer of life. If a woman gives up the family, the family falls apart. The original spark of passion, the spark that was supposed to create love fades away. Without man's protection and love, that spark will cease to exist. Man and woman should complement each other. They are on the same level but have a different role in life.

Meanwhile, I hid in one of the rooms to recover. God, everything's falling apart. I was losing ground. I was wondering how to regain my power to give orders to the four beauties. Their stay with us was a punishment, but as the days went by, they began to understand many things differently than they have done so far.

I must keep my head calm. Hmmm. Just how? Rick won't leave me alone until he knows the answer to the question about the other three levels of love. How the hell am I suppose to show him? How? Here? In the nursing house? Besides, I didn't want to get into any more trouble. Today two situations caused me to show my weaknesses. I am a Bunny, which is currently hunted by a hunter. I didn't even know why. At the beginning he was just angry with her and rebellious, but now?

First of all, I must regain a little bit of my strength. Oh, god. I should have thrown him out of the bathroom! How could I think he just wanted to look? Look? Then I looked at the huge, wardrobe closet in the room and thought. *Wait. You won the battle, but not the war*, I said to myself.

I took a deep breath and came out of the room. Rick was waiting on the couch in the dining room. If he just knew what he was sitting on. I was thinking wickedly, how many grannies had peed on that couch. Sure, we cleaned it every time, but I was pleased at that moment. I lost the battle and that woke up the worse side in me. With a chocolate stain on my uniform, I walked to him and I gave him a new task. "Small cabinets are done, aren't they?" with a mischievous smile, Rick watched me try my best to regain my commander force at any cost. It went very badly.

He was enjoying it. "Yes, General! All is done!"

"Come with me." Rick followed me to the room. With a bitter smile, I opened the door of the huge wardrobe where patients' clothes were stored. The mess that was inside was far from any kind of military order.

"See how it looks?"

Rick immediately realized my plan. He pierced me with as bad look as he could create.

"I see. So what?"

"This wardrobe needs to be disinfected and the clothes tide up nicely."

"What am I? Some kind of cleaner? I'm fed up with cleaning."

"Yes, you're still cleaners. You're just in the middle of your sentence."

Rick was furious. This little nurse whom he managed to shake up for a while, caught a second breath. *Wait,* he thought, *I'll get back to you. Yeah, but how?*

I showed him exactly what he should do. I saw his despair that he tried to hide with anger. "How many of those wardrobes should I clean?"

"All of them but don't worry, you won't do it alone. Peter will help you. It's a lot of work. You still have one day before your first part of the sentence is over. When you come back two weeks later. You'll continue."

Rick frowned: "And what about those two upstairs? Are they going to clean those wardrobes too?"

"They will. What you won't finish, will wait for you and everything else. People make a lot of mess."

Rick didn't say anything and started in that same room, where he embarrassed a professional nurse in the morning. When he began to remove the clothes from the closet, he spoke to himself: "*It looks it won't be so easy with her.*" Bunny returned from the defensive and attacked. Not maliciously, just to defend herself. Because she was really scared. People usually attack when they're scared.

I returned to the kitchen and told Peter: "When you're done in the kitchen, you can help Rick."

"What is he doing?"

I said wickedly: "Cleaning big, very big, huge wardrobes."

Peter waited for me to go to the other side of the department to call Mrs. K for lunch and went looking for Rick. When he saw him cleaning the huge wardrobe, he remembered their nightly conversation about man's big sex box and a tiny box of feelings and started to laugh.

Rick mumbled: "Why are you laughing? You're going to join me in a while. Damn her! I underestimated her."

"Still not your type?"

"No… She's not. I want to know at all costs how this lousy, bossy, nurse will look when she comes down to the lower levels of love."

"Where we men feel the best, right?"

"Don't tell me you feel great here. Where nurses work and look like nuns. I am fed up with the higher levels of love! I want to be down and see beautiful women again!"

Peter smiled. "In the Middle Ages, this work was mainly done by nuns. They served God and people. They had bigger hearts I guess. That's why you see those nurses look so humble like nuns."

"This damn Bunny is not a nun! She has two children! She must have done something to have them, right?"

"And what does it have to do with it?"

"Because she's pretending to be impregnable. She started playing some wicked game."

"Andy warned you. Hands off the Bunny!"

"No way! I have to get the answers from her about those other levels of love."

"Really? Why? Why are those answers so important when she's still not your type?"

"You don't have to know everything. I'm going to deal with it somehow."

"Hmm. This I see. Did you forget that she is in charge of us? We are still employed as nursing house cleaners."

"Exactly! I hate to be a cleaner! I'm fed up with everything here!"

"This is unfulfilled testosterone code speaking."

Rick threw the disinfectant wiping on the floor, put down his rubber gloves, and mumbled: "We are famous actors! What a miserable existence we have here. Give me a break with that stupid code."

Peter said while walking out of the room: "How I look at you and this big closet, I'm starting to believe that the code is true."

Rick took one of Mr. D's pants and threw them on Peter. Peter managed to escape and shut the door. After a while he opened them again: "We're going for lunch in a while."

"I'm not hungry."

"Look, when the fourth code point is not filled, at least fill the third one," suggested Peter with a laugh.

Rick yelled at him: "Get out!" Peter disappeared and Rick remained alone. Anger roused inside him again. *What kind of game is this Bunny playing with him? How dare she? He is a famous, good-looking man. He is not dependent on a nurse. Screw her!* He stayed in the room startling for quite some time.

The guys went out for lunch that day alone. Andy was surprised: "Where's Rick? He's not eating today?"

"He's rebelling again. He thought he was starting to win over the nurse but she somehow managed to get over the lost battle. She is getting even, and he is furious. Unfortunately, everything rages in him. I don't know why. He was never like that before. Of course, anger, we all know that. Now it is as if his ego has woken up even more."

"Don't talk about him when he's not here," said Will.

Andy was surprised. "Since when does it bother you?"

"It doesn't. It's just not fair. He can't defend himself."

Andy noted: "Well, those higher levels of love are beginning to bear fruit. Somehow, we're beginning to see some things differently. Humble. By the way, I was right. This Bunny is somewhat dangerous. All those nurses who look like nuns are dangerous in their own way."

Will looked at him in surprise. "Are you kidding me? Dangerous, why?"

Peter added: "They know how to care for people. How to serve them with humility. They don't mind looking at the most imperfect bodies. They respectfully try to perceive beauty where others feel that it's no longer there. They probably can find it everywhere. Even in such a frightening reality."

Then all three of them fell silent and remembered the innocent, clean smiles of the grannies. When they patted them, poured drinks, brought food, or took away the dishes. Their brain and bodies didn't work anymore. But the heart, the emotion, the soul still worked. They were like children who showed emotions without restraints. They returned to the beginning. No order from their ego or brain prevented them from loving or hating with the whole force. Without limits. The guys will always remember their smiles. Even the employees consider this smile a gift. Of course, there were many not very pleasant works and realities. In order to survive, human beings were able to believe until the last second of their short life that everything around them would improve once.

Me and my colleague were putting patients to bed for the afternoon nap. Rick was thinking hard and didn't want to work at all. When the anger passed a bit, he thought again about his crazy decision to go to this damn trip that brought him here. At the end of the day, he knew they had to work, though this time Tina really enjoyed this special task. Suddenly he remembered the chocolate stain on her uniform and smiled a little. Nurse general was not a nun, even though she sometimes got on his nerves. Slowly his anger faded away and he began to put the clothes in the clean cabinet. *At least we do good deeds,* he thought. It was a punishment, but that didn't matter. Help was appreciated anyway.

The guys returned from lunch and I gave Andy and Will their new task. They didn't mind. Poor things, they didn't work during the weekend so that they won't get too much tired. They were looking forward to their last working day after the weekend. After that, they would go back home for a while. My two weeks working term was coming to an end as well. My boss didn't want to let someone else to be in charge of them. Of course, because no one else could think of so many unnecessary tasks as I could. Me, the bossy nurse. Others never wanted to share their time with some trainees or those who served their sentences in the nursing house.

My boss decided that they could finish the other half of their sentence when I come back. The guys didn't mind. They were eager to finally go back to their beautiful, shiny, luxurious reality. Rick was without lunch, but somehow, he didn't think about that. Not only because he was angry at me. Most importantly because he was happy to be finally going back to his beautiful life where everything he wanted was waiting for him. There won't be any woman to command him.

When the guys left Rick hardly looked at me. I felt sorry for him, but at the same time, I was glad. Everything was more than complicated anyway. Him leaving back home and me too was the best solution. He'll forget me right away anyway. I can take good care of patients and all human beings around me. But is it enough? For men? Especially for men like him?

Of course, I tried to do good deeds all my life. Acts of mercy and compassion. Even they have a dark side because people can abuse them. I have paid dearly for my good deeds. My silly and naive decisions to do good for love ruined many things. However, that didn't change me. My stupid, naive, and romantic nature along with my belief in human good didn't deter me from believing that there is such a human male being who understands the word sacrifice. Not only in real battles in war, but also in the ordinary little battles of our day-to-day reality. Is that the unfortunate reason why Rick's hero disrupted my peace of mind and my heart? *My goodness,* I said to myself. *We are from incompatible worlds! Let it be! Yes, it will be the best.* I tried not to think about Rick. I was looking forward to my evening workout and a few minutes of dance to wash away the stress. To eliminate at least a bit of the damage made by the chocolate.

When he got back to his temporary residence Rick was quiet. Actually, all of them were quiet. The difficult challenge they faced was really unpleasant reminiscent of human misery and suffering not only in movies or real war. But in the everyday life of ordinary mortals who have always worked with their hands and cleaned all sorts of dirt of others. Or cooked, baked, built.

The young generation was less and less inclined to dirty their hands. No, it wasn't an exaggerated statement. An article has recently been published in the German newspaper that a new, young generation of plumbers, tile makers, bricklayers, electricians is missing. Not mentioning the shortage of staff in the health system. Why, despite the human technological advancement, some young people don't want to work in jobs where they need to use their hands? Humans should work and they deserve their dreams to be fulfilled. If someone wants to follow his or her dream, it's fine. We are supposed to fight for our dreams. That's right. We must not forget that we don't yet have robots to do ordinary jobs for us. It may take a while until we will have such technology. Managers and businessmen are currently managing ordinary mortals, not robots. Good businessmen know that. They try to appreciate those without whom their big million-dollar business wouldn't work. They do it in many ways, such as by giving good pay for the job done. For someone to integrate and adapt to a foreign country, time is needed. Humanity is losing time. Everything needs time. The running of the world and the fact that every human being is desperately needed would only be discovered at that moment when all people on Earth will stop working. The consequences would be fatal. Our modern technologies are fine, but the world has become dependent on them. Progress made by mankind is beginning slowly but surely to have a heavy tall on Earth. The half-destroyed planet was rebelling.

When the guys thought about the age of the nurses, they questioned who would take care of them when those nurses will get old. When they won't have the strength. They hoped that robots will take over this responsibility by then. In movies, they played the roles of world's saviors but in the real world, they could help only a few individuals. Even that was appreciated greatly.

Will entered their temporary living room and tried to persuade his friends to get out somewhere in the evening.

"Listen, guys. We could at least try to go out and have some fun. Decently, without alcohol."

Andy laughed at him. "And without women, right? Can't you wait? After all, we'll be back home shortly. There you'll have everything you are used to. Especially luxuriously filled Tina's testosterone code."

They all laughed only Rick was silent. When Andy mentioned the code, he reminded him of Tina. He looked at the cell phone. It was only six o'clock in the evening. She was still at work. Actually, she was there every day from morning till evening. Except for that one day off she had when she tried to tide up their mess. Will looked at Rick and tried to tease him, for he saw that he was not in a good mood. Since they were in their miserable existence and improving their nursing house cleaners' careers Rick almost never had a good mood.

"What about you? Aren't you going to the Rabbits today? To fool the Bunny?"

"What you want?"

Will continued: "I thought the nurse was an easy prey since she is so crazy about you. She even compared you to a savior."

Peter objected: "Not only him. Basically, all of you."

Rick objected: "She's crazy about the hero I played. Not about me."

Andy wondered: "Are you sure? Where is the difference? You have the same hearts, aren't you? So where is the problem? Ah, maybe in this new way of charming women that you started to use since you are so weird…"

Rick murmured: "Can't you tease someone else?"

Peter told him: "I don't get it. You are so weird all this time."

"I can be different for once, can't I?"

Will grinned: "That's probably why you're not winning over that naive, romantic nurse. We told you to try it the old fashioned, proven way."

Rick thought: "Maybe the old way isn't good enough. Maybe it needs to be improved."

"Improved? How?"

Rick smiled mysteriously.

"This must be exactly what the little one wants. Just how I'll make her finally say it?"

The guys didn't understand what he meant. Rick got up, put on his clothes, and left without a word. The guys looked at each other and Peter remarked: "He went to find out if he had already deciphered. That special thing."

Andy, who was sitting on the couch, laid out his legs: "If Tina has a testosterone code, then there must be the other one, right?"

"Oh, yeah! Estrogen code! Why we didn't think about that before? Tina hasn't talked about it yet."

Will said: "That little nurse has weird stuff in her head. Who knows if she has the answers to this code as well."

Peter added: "She said that this version of the testosterone code is incomplete. It's missing some other points." Will shook his head in disapproval.

"God, I wouldn't want such a complicated woman! Codes, levels… Jesus!" Andy laughed.

"Sure. You prefer it without codes… Without complications."

Peter finished it: "Sometimes without love."

The guys went silent. In those few days, they met both women and men who were on the dark side. In the end. Looking at the final stage of human being reminded them of what people are trying to find. And they are less and less successful in that. A higher level of love is closely related to humility. Level that is neither shiny nor noble. This level was too common for them because they belonged to the handsome and famous men on Earth. Only when they became one of them it was as if their hearts were growing slightly larger. It's not a shame to serve others. On the contrary. Was the reason for the relationships to fall apart after ever shorter time intervals, lack of humility? Or because mankind didn't care about inner values despite saying otherwise? We were concentrating on our appearance, our bodies, our possessions but we don't care about our hearts. Maybe because humility meant pain. Pain is the dark side of love. The person who loves for real and wants to rise to higher, lasting levels of love must be prepared for the pain that unfortunately accompanies these levels. The gift of free will meant polarity. The human being had to accept that. With the heart's decision, he or she had to try to alleviate the pain that could leave scars and sometimes holes in the heart. The pain also taught human beings what we often refused to learn. Humility. Its counterpart was pride. In pride, humanity didn't need to improve.

Rick didn't know why he wanted to know the answers to the questions that were bothering him. Despite Tina's task of cleaning the huge closets. That was her small revenge for the old patient washing incident. He knew that the entrance to the nursing house was open until 8 pm. He reached the first floor and there was hardly anyone in the dining room. Only two grannies sat at the table, waiting to be nursed and put in bed.

He didn't see anyone from the staff. Through the kitchen's open door, he could see the dishwasher that had just finished its job and was waiting for someone to unload it. Rick smiled and without hesitation, unloaded it, loaded the remaining dirty dishes, and turned it on. No one had to order him. He just did it. Grandma, who regularly loaded different things on the cart and was looking for a way home observed him with attentive eyes. Rick smiled at her and she smiled back. The second grandma was sitting in a comfortable chair and was thirsty. She didn't realize that Rick didn't understand German well and simply shouted: *"Bringen sie mir bitte etwas zum trinken!"* and pointed at the empty mug. Rick poured her tea. She was always very thankful and very polite. As long as she didn't have to wash herself.

"Danke," she said with a smile. Those were the smiles of two women from the dark side, who no longer had such high demands. They didn't need much to be happy. They needed deeds of love. Deeds of a higher level of love. At this moment Rick didn't have to fight imaginary monsters and yet he felt that he was saving the world. It was then when he realized and knew exactly what

would work with Tina. The curvier Bunny who humbly served others all her life. This is what she meant when she said that even unloading the dishes is romantic for her. She said that flowers are fine, gifts...candles...all those things that women supposedly want so much were important in the relationship. However, that was just one part of the other code. The female estrogen code that Andy unintentionally mentioned. But Rick wasn't home anymore, so he didn't hear that. He started looking for Tina, he knew she was in one of the patient rooms. He heard her voice and the voice of a male trainee. He walked quietly to the door, not wanting the two of them to see him.

He peeked cautiously through the door and saw the dark side of one severely ill patient. He saw what theoreticians and all those who invented different rules to protect patients refused or could not talk about. It was one giant taboo. The rules and theory in these cases differed with practice. No one had the exact recipe of how to follow the rules when there is not enough time or personnel to solve such a precarious situation. Rick saw a giant man who had the power of a horse fighting two desperate persons who wanted to help him. Of course, he pooped into his diaper and wouldn't let the staff clean him. He was shouting and fighting. Tina, a petite woman, was trying to talk some sense to him. She stared into his eyes while holding his huge hands softly. The male hormone testosterone and the adrenaline put huge power into these hands. Young Tim, Tina's trainee, tried to help her. Only tried. He was too slim.

"Common. Please. Look at me. Mr. Z. You're an adult man. You can't act like a little boy." Tina released one of his hands and stroked his cheek. The furious grandfather looked at her eyes for a moment, puffing his mouth to send her flying kisses. Tina also sent him flying kisses. That calmed him down for a while. A small part of his male power turned into the better male side. Then, after a short while, he continued his aggression, which was a taboo. Nurses were not allowed to mention it in the patients' reports. Recently, the world has often wanted all unpleasant truths to be replaced by noble names. Nurses were not allowed to use the word 'aggressive'.

They could use the word 'restless' but they had to describe exactly what the patient was doing. This was how we closed our eyes in front of a very unpleasant reality. That in the human world things were often not called by their true names. Although some names were rude. Psychiatrists desperately tried to adjust the levels of calming medications for the patients and find the right levels that will work. They were not allowed to make the patients completely sleepy. However, if the level of these medications in the blood was low the result was what Rick saw happening in that room.

Now Rick saw with his own eyes that Tina's little bit curvier body was useful for this kind of situation. Handsome, tiny Tim with a body that was far away from a hero, was trying to clean that terrible mess in the patient's bed. Tina tried to calm the old man with some nice flattering words. She was sending him flying kisses that turned him into a calm lamb. But only for a few seconds then he turned into an invincible animal again. Rick couldn't hold himself and went in.

We were in shock. Rick, who's physical power was much bigger than ours said: "I'll try to calm him, and you finish the cleaning." Rick probably didn't mind the very unpleasant smell anymore. The old man felt instinctivly that a much stronger male came in and didn't resist that much. Natural respect caused by the tone of Rick's voice calmed him down. Tim and I cleaned the mess that he made. Indeed, for these reasons, men also had their place in such workplaces. They were able to intervene when a woman's tenderness was no longer helping.

Rick held his hands softly. The old man, who was unmanageable just a few moments ago, was laying quietly and was waiting to be cleaned. When we finished, Tim, who spoke a little English, thanked Rick: "Thank you for your help. You came at the right moment:"

Rick laughed. "The saviors always come at the right moment."

I smiled at Rick and approved: "Yes. Sometimes, it's good to have Aphrodite figure."

Tim watched us closely with a sneaky smile. We forgot he was there, and he quietly disappeared from the room. Rick responded to my words exactly as any man would have done.

"Well. It seemed to me that the flying kisses, the stroking, and the words you repeated to him worked better. How did you say it in German? *Wunderschoen? Wunderbar?* Or how was it?"

I laughed. "It means beautiful and amazing in English. I repeat those words to him every time I clean him. I send him kisses. As you could see, it works. For a few seconds."

That's when Rick started to laugh even more and chuckled through the laughter: "A few seconds? A few seconds?" I tried to be serious and tried to explain with my terrible English.

"Yes. A couple of seconds. We women, we have no choice when we want something special from men. We have to give them those few seconds and say those words. Amazing. The most beautiful in the world. When we combine those words, and strokes and kisses…real kisses…they turn to lambs. For a few seconds. Then women can control not only powerful men. This is their only weapon that can destroy your male aggressive weapons for a few seconds."

Rick was already crying out of laughter. He was looking at me and my chocolate-stained uniform. An ordinary, inconspicuous Bunny spewed all the dangerous words in random order. But Rick understood the point. Bunny looked at him truly as an idol, but at the same time, she was afraid of him. Rick stopped laughing and asked: "When will you answer the other questions?"

"Oh, god. Don't you have enough?"

"No. I want to know."

"What exactly do you want to know?"

"How could Bunny make me calm for these few…seconds."

"Are you kidding me?" At that moment my strength returned to me.

"Are you hitting on me now or are you just curious?"

We stared at each other and after a while, he said: "I just don't know."

"But I know. I'm not a one-night stand type. That didn't change. Even if you know how I admire your hero."

"I didn't say I wanted to flirt. You said you didn't know how, but you're flirting all the time."

"Me? I'm not doing anything. Except the stains anmy words with a terrible accent."

Rick objected seriously: "That's exactly it! Each of your stains and words is kind of a special way of flirting."

"You haven't seen anything yet. Just stains."

"Will I see what's under them?"

"No! Why would you?"

"I won't know until I try."

"Yeah, just try."

Rick continued: "Are you playing games or are you always like that?"

"We won't talk about our past. It's not necessary yet. At the beginning of love people always play some kind of game. To get what they want. Women want something else than men."

"Here we're...talking about boxes again. I have cleaned some large wardrobes today."

"You were angry with me. On the other hand, I showed you how I wash an old man."

"I wasn't angry then."

"Rick. What exactly do you want from me?"

"I just don't know. I want to know the answers to the other three levels of love. All of them. Even the lower one."

"Do you want more wardrobes to clean?"

Rick shrugged his shoulders. "I still must finish my sentence, so it doesn't matter."

"Oh I'm late. I have to clean the floor in the dining room and unload the dishwasher."

Rick said sneaky: "That's already done. I can clean the floor." I stared at him.

"You didn't have to. Your shift is over. Why did you do that?" At that moment my heart trembled.

"You helped us so much and without being ordered to. It's such a help for me. Thank you."

Rick was looking at me and was already beginning to understand what the splashy Bunny might want. He was happy that she thanked him for his help again. At that moment he remembered that she thanked everyone around. Although her colleagues just did their job.

"You love doing good deeds, don't you?"

"Emeralds or genuine pearls shine. They're beautiful. When you put real jewelry next to the fake one you can't recognize one from the other. At first glance both necklaces glitter."

Rick was silent and I released words: "One of them has tremendous value. The other one is fake. It's worthless. Just glass. Nothing more. We people often just want the shine. That glow."

"Why emeralds and pearls?"

"Emerald is a stone of true love. It belongs to Aphrodite or to Venus. If you want. I heard about the hidden meaning of pearls. They are the symbol of deeds. Good deeds."

Rick was quiet. Romantic, naive Bunny. She believes in the power of good deeds.

"Will you explain it to me? Is it related to your four levels?"

"Oh. I have no power to think now…and talk…with you… English…"

"Then come to the Rabbit! We can continue there."

"Continue? In the disaster? In a few days, you will go home. Deeds of pearls won't matter anymore. Besides, I thought men don't like this kind of conversation. About deeds. Emotions. Sorry I have to go."

I quickly left the room and ran off to finish my work. Rick stayed in the room where the window was wide open and contemplated. Bunny had a full head of dangerous ideas. But even men could sometimes be romantic, especially if they wanted to get something. He walked out of the room. Rick found me in the kitchen as I was preparing the dishes for tomorrow's breakfast.

"So? Shall we continue at the Rabbit?"

I didn't answer his question. "Do you want…to clean the floor?"

"Never before I had to fight so hard just to get somebody to go with me on a…oh…not a date. Just a meeting."

"See? Every woman wants something else."

"You want those deeds, right?"

"Come on. I'll give you a broom and a mop, for that floor."

"Sure. General!"

We both laughed and I handed him a broom and a mop. "Thank you. It seems that my intuition wasn't wrong. You have a big heart."

"Because of the floor?"

"Not just because of that floor."

Rick helped me though he didn't have to. His actions meant more to me than his words. When words turned into good deeds, only then they gained immense value. Together with Tim, we finished our work. We wrote the patients' reports. Tim's German was about the same level as my English. Therefore, I dictated to him the sentences and words in German. We watched Rick cleaning the floor. Suddenly I laughed when I realized how human beings try to maintain their national pride. Yes, it's very important. How does it look like in reality? In the staff room sat one Macedonian man with one Slovak woman. In her veins circulated both Slovak and German blood, in addition to the blood of Hungarian's earls. But our Hungarian ancestor lost all his fortune in gambling long ago. What a pity. In the dining room, an American man was cleaning the floor. Who knows what kind of blood, in addition to the American, circulated in his veins? All three were stuck in this godforsaken village in Germany, doing the good deeds.

Thanks to extraordinary coincidences, sometimes unexpected things happen. The reality of Earthly Olympus meets the reality of ordinary mortals somewhere in the middle. To make human beings aware of the immortality of invisible gifts of heart and soul. We need each other. We have a different mentality, different roots and we come from different corners of the world. If we have big hearts, we look for what we have in common, not what divides us.

Rick finished the floor. "Where does it belong?" pointing at the broom and the mop.

"Leave it at that door," Tim answered, pointing to the room opposite the staff room.

"Can I join you?" asked Rick and Tim told him:

"Sure, you can! Today you came at the right moment. Perfect timing!"

Rick, who had a sense of humor, confirmed: "I said that the savior always comes at the right moment."

Tim continued: "The poor, old man is sometimes restless. It's not his fault. He doesn't want to fight for life anymore. Maybe that's why he fights with us."

I explained: "It's very, very difficult. We want to save everything at any cost. Sometimes it's not possible. To save all."

Rick thought, and after a moment agreed.

"There are always some sacrifices. Always. People are afraid of death."

I continued: "Well, for these human beings, death is their best friend. Because it means redemption. They put their dysfunctional body aside. Then the soul can go where it belongs."

Rick asked: "Where do you think it belongs?"

"No one knows. No one has evidence. There are only pieces of information. There is no evidence of what's up there."

"Or down there," Tim added. Suddenly I stood up.

"I'm going to give out the evening medication. Tim, your shift is about to finish. You can go now."

I left the room and Rick asked Tim: "Does she give you orders as well?"

Tim replied with laughter: "Of course! It took me four months to learn to work independently. I'm grateful to her!"

Tim told him what he said to me when he learned how to handle the whole department by himself. Without help. Thank you for your help. He used to tell me several times a day that I was just…a good woman… But what does it mean to be just good? That he didn't explain.

Rick asked further: "What kind of person is she? I mean, how was she before we came?"

Tim didn't quite understand Rick's question.

"She's a good woman. I said to her too."

Rick did not understand. "Good?"

Tim shrugged his shoulders. "Good. She's good to me too. Sometimes she warns me when I don't do something and sometimes, she gives me orders. She must."

Rick fell silent because I was coming back. Tim picked himself up and walked toward me into the kitchen: "Listen. This guy, you like him, don't you?"

"Oh, Tim. He can have all the women in the world he just wants. You know how things go on Earth. You men have an advantage. You look good even with the wrinkles, tummy and extra weight." Tim laughed and left. We were alone and I was beginning to feel scared. Really afraid. It was the fear of the damage but not the one that happens to our bodies after eating some chocolate.

"Thank you again. For help. You can go now." Rick looked at me with a smile and felt my uncertainty.

"Where should I go?"

"Well… Home…"

"Where *Home*?"

"Well, first into your male apartment. Then back to your country."

"Are you still scared of me?"

"No. I'm just scared of the damage."

Rick asked: "What kind of damage this time?"

"Oh, please. All kinds of damages. I better not go anywhere today. It was a hard day for you. Today. All days."

"They were. Maybe they're not that hard anymore."

"Sorry. I still have to write a few words." Rick was having fun because my shyness betrayed me again. My voice was shaking. I was really scared of the whole situation. I tried to write, but Rick started again: "We don't have a lot of time. For those answers. Levels of love… All four levels of love."

I lifted my eyes from the reports. "You already have one. The fourth. Today you helped us. It's enough for friendship. That is the fourth level."

Rick stared at the splashy Bunny that looked important because she was supposed to write important things. In reality, she was desperate.

"Please, be silent for a moment. Look. I am a Slovak woman. You speak English. I have to write in the German language. I have a mix of three languages in my head. I'm writing English stupid words, because of you. Now I must correct it."

Rick was curious. "Correct it? Why? What delusions did you write there? Can I see them?"

"Same delusions, that I analyze with you all the days. I should be quiet. I did everything wrongly. I opened the Pandora box and I'm tattling stupidities all the time."

Rick shrugged his shoulders. "Well, you seem to like your boxes. Stupidities? Why do you say that?"

"And you like yours, don't you? Look. You've cleaned up a few big boxes today. Another one awaits you on Monday. When you get back, there's going to be a mess in them again."

"Okay, I will. What about your box? Is it clean?"

He got me into the corner. Foxy guy. He fights with my own weapons. *Wait, I'll show you what kind of box I have* I said to myself.

"No. Women have a heap of junk in one box. It can never be completely cleaned. Everything is in one...in one..."

I didn't know how to explain it to Rick, so I took a piece of paper and I drew one box with scribbles inside of it. Same that kids draw and show their parents and tell them that is an elephant.

Rick stared at the box and at the scribbles in it.

We both burst into laughter and I explained: "I saw it somewhere. The chaotic female box. Full of junk."

Rick stared at the splashy Bunny, and he wanted the answers even more. Bunny didn't want to give it to him. Why? Then he said cheerfully: "That's why you women have to clean up all the time! Because there's a mess in this one and only box of yours. See? At least we have all the boxes separated. In our heads."

"That doesn't mean that when they're separated, there's order."

Rick became serious, and I continued: "Sometimes we have to wait for the answers. For the right time. Saviors also come at the right time as well as the answers. They come at the right time. We need to fight for some of the answers."

Rick wondered: "Am I not fighting enough?"

"Depends on what you consider to be enough."

"We are here. We clean, we wash everything again and again. And then all over again. That testosterone code of yours it's not even filled. That's hard. We fight every day."

"You're starting to win."

"These answers are a reward. For the good fight."

"It wasn't good at the beginning. Your fight. Something happened. Good Rick is coming back."

"You said you didn't know me."

"I only know you a little. You're good. I can feel it." I stopped talking. I was trying to correct some of the stupid things I wrote in the report. Rick was thinking. He was curious. There were still remnants of negative emotions in him.

When I finished, I explained: "For some answers, a human being must be ready. I don't know. Are you ready for more difficult words and challenges? Not just related to the body?"

Rick laughed. "You mean eliminating the damage from the body?"

"Not only from the body. It's much more difficult to eliminate the damage from the heart and soul. I don't really belong to your luxurious world."

"Where do you belong? You have a great deal of imagination."

"You haven't seen anything yet from my imagination. Okay than. I'll come to the Rabbit. In an hour. I want some answers as well if it's possible. I don't just want me tattling stupidities."

"About saviors, gods, Apollo. What else? What else is in your head?"

I laughed. "Box full of junk. What's still in your head?"

Rick asked again: "So, what time?"

"Half-past nine."

Rick said goodbye and I stayed alone. Everything was terribly absurd and unfortunate. Although the wall between the two incompatible worlds was diminishing, it was still there. Maybe I really shouldn't discuss and analyze anything anymore. I'll let it go. Today I will remain silent and just smile. I handed over my work to a colleague. I tried to make myself look at least a bit presentable for the date, but after 10 hours shift, it was really difficult.

When I came to the Rabbit with my dictionary, Rick remarked: "Do you still trust the old fashion ways of communication?"

"Sometimes those old fashion ways are better. Sometimes some of them."

"Which ones for example?"

I thought: "In the past men really, really had to fight for women. For example, with swords. They would even die. Today, the rivals scold each other on social networks and send a devil emoticon."

Rick listened with wonder.

"You don't like that? Would you rather if we were really fighting?"

"You're fighting…in the movies…it looks like it's real… You really have to fall, don't you?"

Rick talked about how the actors shoot battle scenes and how sometimes they fight invisible monsters, which are created after the shooting is over. It was more than interesting to an ordinary mortal. It is not easy at all to act and create emotions when half of the movie must be created after the shooting. All this was created with state-of-the-art technology, which in this case had a very positive purpose. To enchant the audience, who sometimes watched the movie breathless.

When he finished, I noted: "Maybe even your noble reality isn't that easy."

"It's not. Trust me."

I thought about how I was trying to eliminate the damage in the German reports just a little while ago. Because few English words ended up there. The head nurse will be raging. We were not allowed to erase the mistakes in a way that the original text wouldn't be visible. The obsolete paper method didn't allow lying. In the computer, the original words could be deleted. Not on paper. Therefore, thanks to a few English words, the head nurse will know that splashy Bunny's mind was elsewhere. Not in work.

We sat quietly on a table tucked in the corner of the pub. I had my dictionary, paper, and pen on it and Rick had his cell phone. The situation seemed exactly what Americans often thought of residents of the other side of the ocean. That we are backward people. Although it wasn't true everywhere, the eastern part of Europe was often depicted this way in some American movies. That sometimes annoyed me. Yes, there are regions around the world that are still backward. On every continent. Not only in Europe. Rick asked after a moment of silence: "Where is your cell phone?"

"In my purse. Paper is paper. What is written on it will remain."

"You said you aren't good with modern technology, right?"

"I can make phone calls and write messages. Even a few other things. When it's something more complicated my sons help me. They keep explaining to me how it's done but I can't remember it and they become furious and desperate."

"Why don't you remember that?"

"I don't have the talent for logic mathematics, physics. Probably because the right hemisphere of my brain works better the art the creativity. The fantasy."

"Oh."

"Look, you have a relationship with art, and I believe you have no problem with modern technology."

"No, I don't. Maybe my translator is doing a better job."

I said humbly to him: "I want to apologize to you for the Sugarman. I didn't mean to offend you. At that time, you were so weird. Like a typical snotty superstar."

"Yeah, you compared me to so many things. Sugarman. Savior. God Apollo. I'm just a man. An actor."

"Hmmm. Just a man. All the world is celebrating you. You are celebrities."

Rick sighed: "Celebrities? It's all about business. Because of advertising. People have to have information about us to go to the movies."

"Yeah to buy DVDs, T-shirts, toys, costumes for children."

"Nobody knows about you though. I feel like it's unfair."

"Why? It has been so for centuries. The world has been divided into the rich, those in the middle, and the poor. Do you think it is different today? It is not. The functioning of the world has not changed too much throughout human history. Only technology advances. Trying to conceal the fact that we didn't learn from the greatest mistakes of mankind. Wise people say that history is repeating itself. The difference is only in technology. Human wealth and misery remain. When we invented money, we lost our freedom. Today, having money means having freedom. I think that's an illusion. We are not completely free, despite the material wealth. Every one of us has a boss."

Rick agreed: "That is true. Where the big money goes, very strict rules also apply. We as well must do things that are sometimes difficult. We don't like to do them. Despite all of this, everything is better than living in complete poverty. Material wealth means being free at least partially."

I agreed: "You are right. Everything is better than poverty and feeling of powerlessness in dealing with it."

I was glad Rick was talking and I was trying to capture as much as possible. When I didn't understand, he wrote it to me on a piece of paper or on the phone. Once again, the time ran away very quickly. It was almost midnight. I looked at my cellphone.

"I have to go. I have to get up in the morning."

Rick glanced at me. "You still got to get up early? Because of the mask?"

"Yes, because of the mask." We went out and I didn't even look at him. Inside of me, everything went down where I didn't want to. I haven't seen inside of him.

I just said quickly: "Good night. See you at work Monday."

Rick agreed with humor: "Yes, colleague nurse."

"Colleague. Mr. Cleaner. Oh, my god, how horrible it sounds. For sure you are handsome cleaner."

We both laughed and I looked into his eyes for a while.

"I really have to." Rick walked in the opposite direction but looked back as I climbed the stairs. When he reached his temporary accommodation, the guys were sleeping. Since he still didn't have the answers, he wondered how he could get them out of Tina. After a while, he fell asleep.

I fell asleep in my little dark room very quickly. I was tired. The next day was Sunday, and in the morning, when the men had breakfast, Will said: "Hey guys it's time to start packing. Half of our sentence is finished. Never before I looked forward eagerly for my big bathroom."

"Yeah and standing in line to use this shabby bathroom will stop. For a few days," Will grinned.

"Even the provisional operation of other things ends for a few days."

Peter watched Will, who was as happy as a little boy waiting to open his Christmas presents. Rick was silent. Thoughtful. The guys didn't know if he was angry or silent for another reason.

Will teased him: "What about you? Are you leaving the unbaked Bunny here, or are you taking her with you?"

The guys burst into laughter and Rick replied with no interest: "Why are you teasing me again? Mind your own females."

"Well, soon I'll be doing just that. But what about you? You're leaving, and you couldn't get the Bunny to be all into you. We told you. The old-fashioned ways work with all women. You wouldn't listen."

Andy defended him: "Leave him alone. He has two more weeks to figure out how he can get her—"

Peter interrupted them: "Oh, come on, guys! Why are you so nosy? Soon you'll be home with your women so enjoy yourself and leave him alone."

Rick remained relentlessly silent. He didn't want to go into such discussions, and he didn't really know what he wanted. Splashy Bunny was running away from him. He didn't understand why. What was surprising, he didn't know why he started thinking about it. Sure, maybe she is shy but still… He didn't have much time left. Andy and Will went on with the conversation and Peter quietly asked him: "Do you want to talk about it?"

"I don't know if it'll help. I'm confused. I don't know what to think. I don't even know what I want from her."

"I thought you were clear about it. Just a few days ago, all you wanted was to catch her and that's it."

Rick sighed: "Is woman like her the right prey for some affair?"

"Why not? You will both enjoy your time and that's all."

"She just doesn't want that. She didn't tell what she wants. Something special…special… She's pretty complicated."

"There are always some complications. We can't avoid them. It depends on whether we want to fight for something we want despite some complications. Nothing is perfect. Same is with you, although you look like perfect men, you're not."

"I know that. She knows that as well. She compared me to Apollo and all of us to the saviors. That's crazy! She can even justify it."

"In the beginning, you didn't act like a savior. Are you still angry?"

"I don't know what's in me right now. As if the days spent in this frightening reality cleaned some part of my heart and made a place in my heart that is clean and empty. I feel this strange sadness for those people."

"Where were you yesterday?"

"First, at her work. Then you know."

Peter patted him on his back and said: "At the Rabbit."

Rick continued: "Yesterday I helped a patient who was aggressive and was like an animal. If you don't see something like this with your own eyes you won't believe it. They must handle it. If I wouldn't have come, he would have surely hurt them."

"Did you ask? I mean, did he really hurt them?"

"What for? It's clear. He was strong as a bull. Who would have thought that they had to handle this and still pretend all can be solved with a stroke and a nice word?"

"And the fact that you saved them didn't help you?"

Rick disagreed: "How would that help me? I did what anybody would do at that moment."

"Maybe yes. She will take that as a special deed done by you."

Rick looked at Peter: "Special?"

"Because it was done at the right moment and by you."

"That won't help me get closer to her."

"You're wrong. You'll see. Exactly that will get you not only closer to her, but maybe even closer to the answers. You still don't know why you care about those answers."

Rick thought: *Yes, I don't. It doesn't matter.*

"Look, maybe when you come back you won't even remember. We'll be in our reality again. You won't have to clean any lockers, or cabinets, or closets or whatever size of boxes."

Rick nodded. "Sly Bunny."

Peter told him: "Don't see her today. Maybe she will miss you. Maybe she'll say something on Monday."

Rick was silent for a moment, then added with a laugh: "What difference would that make? One day? Who knows how long she has me in her head?"

"She doesn't have you in her mind. She is just getting to know you. Your role as a hero. That are two different things."

Rick looked at Peter. "Different? Do you see our influence on women? For half of them we are sex symbols and for the other half... I better say nothing more. Saviors. Terrible." Peter laughed at him.

"You forgot god Apollo."

"Oh, go to hell with him!" Peter looked at him with interest: "Go and shave! The savior look is probably too prudish for Bunny. Maybe she needs more of that sex symbol."

Rick got a bit angry again: "Sure! Great idea! It will be best if I shave only half of my face so splashy Bunny will have an All-in-One pack! Crazy woman. Apollo!"

"Okay, you better not shave than. Forget it. It was just a joke."

Rick began to pack and thought about the ordinary nurse who was giving them orders with the worst English language he ever heard in his life. Then, when they would talk, she would use random words. However, those words were strange and even dangerous. Maybe Andy is right. Hands away from the Bunny, but male competitiveness and human curiosity were stronger. Rick obeyed Peter and didn't go to see Tina on Sunday.

The penultimate day of my two weeks' term was always catastrophic. I was running out of power, I was irritated, patients felt my nervousness and they were also nervous. Grannies who had lost track of time and space were all packed to go home that day as well. Each in her own way. One had her things packed and loaded on the cart, the other one in the wheelchair. They walked from one side of the department to the other and from room to room.

One of the lying patients had a seizure. She hallucinated and I had an experience that I wouldn't forget till the end of my life. Poor old woman, who almost never moved, was crouching and screaming like an animal. She was trying to scramble on the wall. She looked like she was obsessed with the devil. Her roommate was probably afraid of her. She was in bed and was praying the holy rosary loudly.

This was how the exorcism looked up close and personal. Even in Hollywood, they wouldn't have been able to arrange it more realistically. At that moment, my girlfriend, a Slovak colleague who had a room next door, came in. She started to swear with her east Slovak dialect: "Jesus Christ! Nuts old crazy women! For god's sake, how can you stand working in this department on the first floor? It's a madhouse!!!"

I didn't know how I could get the granny down from the wall. I had to sedate her. Now I could use some help from the savior again. Unfortunately, today Rick wasn't there. My colleague helped me, and I managed somehow to pour the drug inside the old woman. She spilled the drug out and continued shouting. The other nodded with her head like a stick figure on the rubber band and continued to pray. We were both desperate and I got an idea. "Someone should make a movie of this once. That would be a success! Such scenarios that our patients play to us every day can't be made so easy."

My girlfriend agreed: "If we put it on YouTube, we'll have a billion views! We'd call it 'Exorcism live'."

I objected: "Are you crazy? We will be laid off right away. You know the German laws. It's strictly forbidden because of the personal data protection! We need the job."

"Laws? Okay, but then let the priest come here regularly. Let him souse them with holy water."

I exploded in laughter: "Priest? He comes here often."

"Really? It seems that he can't help these nuts anyway."

I added with laughter: "Maybe we could use some help now…some savior… We don't have any here."

"That's right. We don't."

So, we looked desperately at this image of human misery and tried to ease it with humor. "I'll wait until the few drops of medicine will work."

"Nothing's going to work. Wait until the crazy one finishes her prayers; the other nut stops shouting and fuck them all. Tina, will you please shoot me if I'm like that?"

"It won't matter anymore. You're not going to feel anything… Oh, god…" I sighed sitting on the bed next to the praying granny and begged God for help. In such moments I felt helpless. I thought that was the worst thing in my shift. But it wasn't. Unpleasant surprises waited for me in every room I entered. A different scene in each room. This is how the patients have said goodbye to me regularly on the last day. When I entered the fourth room, I was so desperate that I began to cry. The old woman, whom the most popular medicine wouldn't help, probably got the worse poison in the morning. Drops. Since I was distracted and constantly thinking about the handsome savior in the world, I forgot that I have to cut this grandma's panties. Otherwise, everything will spill in the bed. Of course, I forgot.

My granny was in a bad mood that day, so she blow a fuse on me: "Nurse! Let me go home immediately! Do you hear? I have to take care of my parents."

I tried to be patient, and started to clean the mess that I worsened with my inattention: "How old are you?"

The granny who was almost 80, shouted without hesitation: "Thirty-eight!"

"Ah, less than me."

"Of course! I look better than you!" When she said that I realized all the obstacles and the reasons why I should just forget about Rick. I left the battlefield for a while like I used to do when I was too tired. I sat on the shower stool and cried like a little baby. At these moments no positive affirmations or gratitude for great work helped me. God. All nurses around the world are actually Cinderellas. Not really. They are Shitrellas. I was wondering how this word would sound in English.

Granny heard my silent cry, and something happened that I didn't expect. "Nurse, are you crying? Do you hear me? Nurse! Come here!" I wiped my tears and went back to my granny to finish my job.

"No. I'm not crying. All is fine."

Granny looked at me and said in a different voice: "Has anyone ever told you that you are an angel?" When I couldn't take it anymore and wanted to give up those were the moments that made me continue. The answers to my affirmations and the words of gratitude. In these bad moments patients' words of gratitude always came. The Law of Attraction worked. In the worst moments, God would send his answers. This is how he spoke to human beings. But we still didn't understand.

I sighed: "I'm not an angel. We all make mistakes."

As if it wasn't her at that moment the granny added: "Mistakes are a sign of humanity." I stood shocked at the bed. I no longer cursed at my work. These tiny moments of human gratitude kept all people believing that their existence had a deeper meaning. However, we didn't want to understand that because we had no evidence.

When I finished my shift, I hurried to my temporary dance room. On my way, I run into a colleague who worked until 9 pm.

"Oh, Martina! Every day you go down there to dance. Do you still have the energy for that?"

"This is the brightest moment of the day. Without that, I wouldn't have survived those two weeks."

I realized how many days I had left out. But the endorphins created by the dance and the workout were not a threat. The other endorphins created each time we tried to communicate with Rick were a threat. A huge threat.

The next morning was Monday, the last day of the working career of handsome cleaners. I've divided the work tasks and tried to avoid Rick. I felt I couldn't avoid the trouble anymore. Guys worked like bees. After all, they'll finally get on the plane tomorrow and get rid of this miserable existence. First for a few days and then forever.

As always on Monday morning the head nurse was checking patients' records from the previous days. When I walked past the glass door, she nodded at me and asked me to go inside: "Tina. I wanted to talk to you about something for a while."

I already knew what was coming. The head nurse continued with a strict voice: "Don't think I'm blind. I see what's going on and I want to warn you. Don't get into trouble. Huge trouble. This isn't a man for you."

I was silent for a moment and felt how these words stuck into my heart like needles. I didn't know how to react properly. Reason reminded me mercilessly of all the logical arguments that the human heart has always tried to push away. The nurse voiced my concerns and fear aloud. I felt helpless. She continued: "You have to come back to Earth, down to reality and stop dreaming. You have to live here and now. You are a nurse. They don't belong here. They are famous people. Such men are very unreliable. You need a real man who stands firmly on the ground."

These words irritated me. "Just because they're famous people, does it mean they're not standing on the ground with their feet?"

The nurse sighed: "You know what I mean. They are perfect, handsome, rich. They can have and they do have everything they wish for. That includes women."

I took a deep breath. "Of course, I can understand exactly what you mean. One ordinary nurse who is taking care of sick people is not good enough for a famous man."

"I didn't mean to hurt you."

"No? And how did you mean it? You know, I was wondering if those beautiful women who live in the better, higher reality than we do, look in the morning the same way they look in the movies and magazines. With perfect makeup, beautiful gowns, and jewelry."

The head nurse said strictly: "It's their job, isn't it? To look perfect. They have to earn their money in this way. We earn it in a different way. The difference in the size of nurse's and actress's pay is probably big enough, don't you think?"

"Yes, yes. You are absolutely right. We don't need perfect figures or beautiful clothes for our demented patients. Our cotton uniforms are good enough. They are destroyed by the evening anyway. I understand. Please don't be angry about the messed-up reports. I'll try to focus more and ignore our Earthly Olympus, who don't stand firmly on the ground."

"What actually happened on Saturday night? Tim said you, that had a problem with our complicated patient again."

I almost had tears in my eyes, but I swallowed them. "One of those perfect, famous men who can have everything in the world helped us with him. Though he didn't have to. Maybe they can save people from the lower reality as well. With ordinary deeds. So, I'm going back to my ordinary work."

"Trust me; I just want you to avoid unnecessary problems."

"I'm used to the problems. Everybody has them. By the way, it doesn't matter from which reality human beings are coming from. The truth is that we are dust and we will turn to dust. In the end, we will all end up the same way. And perhaps as sadly as our patients. Helpless and dependent on the help of others. I will be cruel now. What will be the difference between you and a model after years? Besides being slim, she will have a luxurious nightgown and you or me a cotton one. Beneath the nightgowns, our bodies will be wrinkled and devastated the same. I don't know how many plastic operations one human body can take to stay as beautiful and perfect as possible. Every human being is beautiful to me."

"Stop it! I know you think all human beings are the same, but they are not! This is how the world works! Either you will reconcile with it, or…"

"Or what? Oh. I'm sorry, I know. I'm terrible that I'm saying this. I'm just tired of the empty clichés that the world has internal values. People usually just want the shine. The glitter. Nothing more. Nobody really cares about what's inside. Look around. Good people are really stupid and naive. They pay for their goodness."

"Wait, Tina. You know it's not true."

"But it is. It is."

I tried not to think about what the head nurse reminded me of, but it wasn't possible. As in trance, I tried to complete the work. I was just with Mrs. K, who kept talking to me. When I didn't respond, she asked: "Tina, are you sad? Is that because you still haven't found a new man?"

I looked at her with a sad smile. "Excuse me. I don't have a good day today. What did you say?"

"I asked if you finally found a man."

I replied bitterly: "First, my sons must finish their education. I can't give up my job, and that unfortunately only means half a month with my kids. Oh, it's all so complicated. I don't want to talk about it."

"Oh, Tina. I didn't have a good man. Sometimes he would hit me, but I had a lover. He was good to me. In my days, divorce was something inadmissible. So, I had to solve it this way."

I told her: "This is not for me. I don't want incomplete and failed relationships. They only bring trouble."

"Tina, there are always some problems. Nothing is perfect. With love you can overcome everything."

"Love. Love. I don't know if it exists anymore."

Mrs. K looked me in the eyes. "It does! Without love, life is sad. I know how you feel. We all love you. Look. We can't give you what you want and need, but whenever you're here it's like the sun came out. We know you love us. Every employee here like us. We feel it. Even those demented grannies and grandfathers feel it."

Mrs. K showed me with these words, as she always did when I lost my strength, that love has really many faces. The only disadvantage of her confession was that I felt really like a nun. That was the less popular face of a higher level of love. The level that delighted, but also hurt at the same time. I helped Mrs. K to get dressed and as I pushed her in the wheelchair, Rick came out of one of the rooms.

We looked at each other and I started: "I can't really talk to you right now. The head nurse is in the staff room and is checking the reports. My conversation with her wasn't very pleasant. Sorry."

Rick thought: *Because of the English stupid things that you wrote there?*

"That's not my biggest problem. You are."

Rick smiled with his eyes and said seriously: "You see problems even where they aren't. Why am I your problem? I'm trying to execute orders. Look, I've cleaned so many things."

"Rick, please."

"Then tell me what happened."

"Not now. I can't."

"So, when? Evening?"

"I'll be sitting in the car on my way home tonight… Tomorrow you'll be sitting in the plane There's no time."

"There is always time if we want."

"Rick, it doesn't make sense. I don't belong to your world. The head nurse reminded me today."

"I don't understand. What's she got to do with it? Why is she interfering?"

"I don't know. She's right. Nurses belong to another reality. I have to."

"Wait a minute! What about those answers?"

"Which answers?"

"About the other levels of love for example."

"I told you some answers. For the rest, patience is needed. Human beings must be ready for them."

"I'm not ready? What else should I do?"

"You've done a lot. You're a good man. Simply a good man. See you in two weeks."

"Aren't we going to say goodbye?"

"We'll see each other later, won't we?"

Mrs. K didn't understand our conversation, but she sensed the tension. When I met her in the dining room, she asked me: "What about this handsome man? Isn't he good for you?"

I replied sadly: "He's neither a nurse nor a cleaner. He is a famous man, Mrs. K. That's true. He's an actor."

"So what? I told you. A guy is a guy. Whether handsome or not handsome."

"The fairy tales in our world don't exist. Just a hard reality."

Mrs. K didn't say anything anymore and I worked as a robot with no mood. Rick was curious, so he came to the room where I was working and asked: "Will you tell me what your boss told you?"

"Why? Is it important for you?"

"And for you?"

"She just said what I already know. That you're handsome, famous man and I'm a nurse. Two worlds. Two realities. They're very…distant."

"Are you giving up so fast?"

"I never give up, but she's right. Tomorrow you will return home. Maybe the answers won't be so important to you."

"Can you see what's in my head? You can't know how I'm thinking, how I'm feeling."

"You're right. I can't. I don't know how. I'm just trying to avoid more damages."

"What are you afraid of? You said that man must be ready for some answers. Do you think I'm not?"

"I don't know. You're right. I can't see what's in your head or in your heart. I only know that you are a good person. I thank you again for everything. For help and all. You worked great."

"Your reality is hard, but ours is too."

I noted: "I think yours is harder. Though you seem to have everything."

"So maybe in two weeks, I will be ready for the answers to my questions about other levels of love?"

"Maybe. I don't know why you want to know. I don't think you need it."

"As you said, you can't see inside my head or heart. You can't know what I need and what I don't."

"Well. I don't know, but I'm glad we're friends now."

Rick laughed ironically. "Friends. Friends."

"You men are in a hurry. Remember the box. The little yellow box. I must go now. You might have time to think."

I left the room. Although Rick's initial anger had disappeared, it didn't leave him completely. Now he was angry, and he didn't know why. Sure, she's just a nurse. We both thought about how problematic relationships can be. How fragile, and yet we can't exist without them. After work, I was packing and was on my way home and the temporary cleaners too. They were quiet and thoughtful. They had no idea how many pearls were added to the Fields of Pearls thanks to their help. Other people on Earth had no idea either. They just tried to act according to their hearts. Therefore, they unconsciously settled the disturbed balance between good and evil. Nor did they know that Zeus had asked the angel of mercy and compassion, to summon the guardian angels.

Zeus sat on his beautiful throne made of diamonds, and, the angel of compassion, stood in the middle of the main hall. Zeus got up and came to the angel, who knew why he did call him: "Zeus, do you think that if I summon the guardian angels, human beings will start to listen to their hearts or intuition?"

"I'm surprised you doubt it. You are an angel of mercy and compassion. Your faith in goodness is unshakable."

"That's true, but human's faith is shaking."

"That's why we have to do something. The condition of the pearls on the Fields of Pearls is alarming. Earth is falling even lower. We've been trying to hold it, but this time I don't know if we can do it."

Angel of mercy and compassion spoke quietly: "Earth is littered with rubbish. The real rubbish that is rotting in landfills, seas, oceans, but also the invisible one. It's rotting in human hearts and souls. Darkness succeeded in destroying human beings from within. It distorted their essence. Unless they believe they are good enough to be loved, they will hardly be able to love those around them as well. It's a vicious circle."

"You are responsible for the highest level of love. White pearls grow from the deeds of mercy and compassion. Something must be done! Otherwise, it will end badly."

Angel of mercy and compassion continued: "I'll try, but what exactly should I do? Look Zeus what values rule on Earth. Power. Glory. Superficiality. Pride. Money. These things are responsible for most problems on Earth. People live in the illusion that money gives them the freedom to do the job they want. But in fact, even rich people are not quite free."

"You know that many of those rich people are helping those in need. I just don't understand why it's not enough."

"Zeus, every act of pure love count, yet the world order is as it is. You know we can't interfere with what's happening on Earth."

"Yes, I know. Because of free will. The only thing we can do is wait for each pearl. The more the pearls the less is the chance that Earth will fall down to those who have been striving for it throughout the ages. We have to find a way to awaken even more humans' hearts. This is the only option."

Angel of mercy and compassion remarked with a mysterious smile: "That is one option, but not the only one."

"What do you mean?" Zeus asked.

"If we lose our faith, how can we expect the human beings find their lost faith? They must believe that they are beings capable of making decisions based on love. These decisions can often really reverse the catastrophe. But if they are to love the other human beings more, they have to start to love themselves even more. However, this is getting very hard these days when they are told that they are not pretty enough, not good enough, or not talented enough. The journey to fulfill their dreams is more difficult lately. That is why they sometimes lose faith."

"Unfortunately, Earth is losing perfection because mankind is losing faith in itself. But it is still worth fighting for them and for their planet."

"Maybe they should start working even more on their hearts and souls, Zeus. More deeds of love equal more pearls. More faith, more love."

"Sounds so simple. So why is there always something wrong on Earth? Now even the planet itself is in very bad shape."

"Earth has not yet been destroyed. There is still love on Earth. Beauty. Tenderness. Kindness and so on... These gifts must be protected and preserved. The balance must be in order."

"Yes, you're right. Go! Call the guardian angels!"

Angel of compassion and mercy disappeared to summon the guardian angels. Among them was also my guardian angel Nolachiel and the guardian angels of the four famous male beings who were thrown by accident into one of the really hardest realities. In that reality, they saw little snippets of the highest level of love up close and personal. Chasariel, Rick's guardian angel asked Nolachiel, my guardian angel: "What happened to your protégé? Why she backed off? Because of her crazy desire, you and Apollo caused that Eros poisoned my protégé's heart with your stupid love potion. Thank you very much for that!"

Nolachiel shrugged her shoulders. "We didn't want it that way. Eros was impulsive."

Chasariel continued: "Impulsive? He acts impulsively for ages and does whatever he wants! Then we, the guardian angels, need to comfort all the unhappy human beings whose hearts have been broken by his stupid arrows. Nothing ever happens to him."

"Chasariel, I'm sorry."

"Look what you caused."

Ameliel, Andy's guardian angel defended Nolachiel: "Chasariel, the potion has done its job. We are convinced that the higher level of love can remove any poison from the heart. I think it was not in vain. On the contrary."

"Ameliel is right! At the end of the day, nothing happened to Rick."

Chasariel objected: "We don't know yet. Nolachiel. I hope that your protégé's crazy ideas won't cause any more problems. Look where they've brought them."

Mechiel, Will's guardian angel told him: "I don't think it was useless for the four of them to get to know such a reality. Seeing the agony and doing humble little deeds of love has not harmed any human being yet."

Nolachiel agreed: "That's true. Little humility helps to enlarge and purify human hearts."

Chasariel said more quietly: "Look, the angel of mercy and compassion is coming."

All five guardian angels went silent and turned toward the angel of compassion and mercy. He appeared in front of a vast array of beautiful, kind beings whose only task was to protect and help human beings.

For a moment they heard beautiful music coming from their pure angel hearts. The angelic hearts were pure because, for their love of the Creator, they completely gave up their free will to serve the good forever. Angel of compassion and mercy spoke to the angels in a serious voice: "You all know why we are here. Human beings are losing faith and thus the right direction. Few of them follow their hearts—"

One of the guardian angels who belonged to a male human being interrupted him: "We've been whispering to human beings for centuries to follow the voice of their heart. They have free will. We can't force them. It's amazing to follow their technological progress. But as if thanks to that they need evidence for anything that they should believe in. As if our voice was because of that ever quieter."

Another guardian angel continued: "They don't have to believe in us or in the invisible world that they can't capture with their human senses. It is enough if they believe in the power of love. That is the greatest miracle."

Angel of compassion and mercy contemplated: "It is all about love and all its levels. We must try harder. Many human beings do deeds of love, but evil deeds are increasing as well. Everything happens because of a lack of love and too much fear. Nevertheless, we have to try to communicate with human beings in every possible way."

One of the guardian angels protecting a female human being was worried: "What else can we do, and how? People don't believe in themselves, let alone in the power of love. We all know why this is happening and why it's getting worse. Someone from below is gradually, for centuries, trying to disrupt and destroy the essence of human beings. By destroying their faith in themselves. Only the strongest human beings can humbly accept the toughest tests. On

Earth, time moves differently than here, above. Their Earthly journey is only temporary. They should fill it with love and good deeds, but to maintain balance, evil must also be present, we all know that."

Another guardian angel added: "However, the balance is constantly being disrupted over the ages and we constantly have to fight for Earth. Even the flame of faith gushing on Earth is often used by human beings badly. The energy of such evil deeds can't, as we know, go back to the vessel. It goes down to the dark rulers. As if human beings were repeating the same mistakes all over. They are learning history, but they are still fighting each other. They denounce war and violence in words, yet innocent people die every day of the aftermath of war and violence."

Angel of compassion and mercy agreed. "Yes, that is all true. But for the sake of polarity and the balance between good and evil, everything has to be repeated for centuries. Despite their wisdom and technological progress. Well, we must try to communicate more with human beings and show them the direction of love. We need more pearls."

Angel of compassion and mercy fell silent, and the guardian angels who could only whisper in human hearts knew that despite their efforts, faith was quickly fading away from the human world. The evil system of functioning of the planet has forced human beings to constantly fight with each other for survival. The belief that the world is a beautiful place full of love has disappeared in many places on the planet. Human beings who tried to fight evil in those places felt the higher level of love, mercy, and compassion but also infinite grief and emptiness because there were always sacrifices. It was impossible to save everybody.

Nolachiel, Chasariel, Ameliel, Avariel and Mechiel, all returned to their proteges, to whisper in their hearts, and to protect them.

Chapter 7

In the evening, my girlfriend and I sat in my colleague's car and we took off for the two-week well-deserved holiday. Fifteen days of service was over, and we were eager to go home. I was thinking about this weird term until I fell asleep. There were a lot of responsibilities waiting for me at home. As if everyone was waiting for me to come and clean everything around.

The next day, four handsome, famous men flew home to get rid of their temporary miserable existence for a while, looking forward to finally having their better existence back.

After getting over the jet lag, Will decided to party as a famous star should. Safe in his own country he didn't need any silly camouflage. They all enjoyed their luxury bathrooms and beautiful homes. Moreover, strangely enough, they noticed their employees who were doing the most ordinary jobs in their homes and gardens. Because they were increasingly aware of how precious and necessary every human being in the world is. Even an ordinary cleaner. It no longer seemed obvious to them that someone would come and do for a wage all those unpopular jobs. They were more grateful that there are still ordinary people and employees in the world who are contributing to the functioning of the world with their small actions.

Rick occasionally remembered the splashy Bunny and her crazy, dangerous random words that she would speak with a horrible Slavic accent. How by using her female weapons she could overcome a furious old man who had the power of a horse. Although only for a few seconds. For a few seconds, the whole world was getting crazy. Those who read history books knew that even the history of the world was sometimes changed in a few seconds. During those few seconds, even the most powerful monarch could be turned into an obedient lamb. At least briefly. And wise women knew that too. Which of these weapons were stronger? Male weapons that used brute force? Mighty weapons that over the ages have evolved into menacing and destructive means of killing? Or female weapons that used femininity, kindness, tenderness? In order to disarm men at least for a while.

I've often wondered how men have been fighting for ages. Using wooden kayaks, swords, revolvers, and nowadays modern fighters and dangerous weapons that can destroy so many lives at once. We fight in real wars but also in our everyday lives.

At home, time always ran very quickly. I didn't even notice, and I was already on my way back to work. I have not talked to anyone about the four temporary cleaners. They didn't talk about what they saw either. They came a few hours earlier because of the time difference. When they entered their temporary accommodation Andy immediately ordered: "So, gentlemen. From now on, everyone has to wipe their tracks. It can't be as the last time."

Will was still in a good mood and delighted. During the last two weeks, he had filled luxuriously his testosterone code. He said with a smile: "So, what? We can survive for two weeks, right? We have more clothes with us this time."

Peter looked at Will. "That's the solution! As I see, some people didn't change even after staying in this cleaning jail. Right, Will?"

Will continued indifferently: "I will survive here for the next two weeks, and then I will avoid any other madhouse till the end of my life. What about you? You have left the unbaked Bunny here. I'm wondering if those two weeks will be enough to blow her away. Maybe you should try it in your shiny reality and not here. In the madhouse between the mad old men and women. Christ, when I think what awaits us there."

Rick told him: "I already told you to take care of your females, and leave mine alone."

Peter laughed. "Moreover, this time we have prepared a little better for our punishment. Rick wasn't dependent on some ordinary Bunny, was he?"

Andy shook his head. "We are just a few days away from our luxury reality and you are already returning to your old ways. You're talking about women again. Can't you talk about something else? About sport for example?"

"Sex is also a sport, isn't it? The best in the world. Maybe for some, it's probably better to keep lifting dumbbells to be sexier."

Rick retorted Will: "Better lifting weights than talking nonsense."

Rick went to his room and Andy asked: "Well, Peter, I'm afraid it's going to be very exciting two weeks. I want to ask you though. Do you know anything about Tina? Was Rick in touch with her, over those two weeks?"

"We didn't talk about it. Why do you want to know?"

"Just curious."

Peter responded: "I don't know anything, ask him."

"I won't ask him; you see how irritated he is lately."

I myself had mixed emotions. On one hand, I was reminding myself of all the logical reasons for staying away from Rick. On the other hand, my heart was pulling me closer to him. I wanted to know him better. I couldn't identify whether I felt positive or negative emotions. I felt one negative emotion for sure. Fear.

The next morning, I greeted our temporary helpers: "Fortunately, you already know the system, so we'll start again from scratch. The mess is created very quickly."

The men laughed. Rick watched me hand out the tools and disinfectant wipes and then, with a mischievous smile, announced: "According to the just system can I go to the kitchen today? To the dishwasher?"

Peter replied instead of me: "Of course, that was expected. But tomorrow the cleaning will be awaiting you anyway." I looked at them.

"Sure... You can start again the same as the first time."

Rick remarked: "I hope I'll do better than before."

I looked at him thoughtfully.

"Please go to work."

Will asked: "We're going to go to the second floor again?"

I answered mysteriously: "Certainly yes. There is one small change on the second floor."

Andy was curious. "What change?"

"Go on. There is not much time."

The guys left and left me and Rick alone in the bathroom. The same bathroom where they were will be cleaning the wheelchairs. Rick didn't waste time.

"What about us? Are we going to continue where we left off?"

"What do you want, Rick? You just came from home."

"You owe me some answers."

"I told you that one has to fight for some answers. Be prepared for them."

"I'm fighting."

"Sure. You're fighting."

"Isn't that enough for you? What should I do?"

"Do what you want."

"I don't know what you want!"

"And you? Do you know what you want?"

"What should I know?"

"The reason why you want the answers. I don't understand why you want them. Those answers are not suitable for flirting."

"Do you think I'm flirting?"

"I don't know, Rick. I don't know anything. Please not now. We both have to start working. Your punishment is not over yet."

"How do we move forward and get to know each other?"

"That's the problem. We're friends. That's enough for friendship."

Rick looked at me. "I thought you believed me a little bit."

"I believe you. Sometimes it's better to keep quiet."

Rick noted: "It's not possible. You opened Pandora's box."

"Pandora's box in my head yes. Not the other one, the dark one. It's too early for that. It's hard to open this dark box with such a man like you."

Rick asked with interest: "So, women still have more than one box? You haven't mentioned that before. What do you mean, hard? I'm human."

"You're very high."

"I thought you were higher. Still at the higher levels. Of love."

"They're safe."

"Safe? Really? What about that grandpa and the few seconds? Was that safe?"

"You saved us."

"If I am not here, who will save you?"

"Nobody. We must improvise. Use plan B."

Rick nodded. "I saw. Air kisses. Well, they worked for a while."

"Yeah. How long do the real ones work for you?"

Rick smiled. "So, you can flirt."

"I'm just defending myself. You're attacking."

"Attacking? How?"

"Just because you are. I have to go. We can continue later."

"At the Rabbit?"

I looked at him. "All right, but you won't ask for answers. You're not ready yet."

"We men are always ready to flirt."

"If the chemistry works."

"Do you think it's not working?"

"I can't judge."

"You can't?"

"I can't. We'll meet as friends."

"As friends."

So, Rick hid in the kitchen by the dishwasher. Peter started cleaning his wheelchairs again. When Will and Andy went up to the second floor, they saw something that seemed like a miracle. A trainee started working on the second floor. First-year pupil at school for future nurses. She decided to care for geriatric psychiatric patients. She was young and beautiful. Her long blond hair entangled in braids reached her waist. She had a beautiful smile and was very nice. Will's eyes shone and Andy laughed.

"Well, at least you can show how hard you work to somebody. This one may know some of our movies."

Will was joyful. "Wow! Does such a girl want to do a nun job? That's incredible! I will finally have something to look forward to! Not just austere, strict nurses' faces, and wrinkled grandmothers and grandfathers. Life is beautiful!"

Andy agreed: "Well, yeah. You see? The universe rewarded you. You worked hard and it sent you at least one young, beautiful woman. Of course, just to look at. You'll behave, okay?"

"I'm always behaving. Rick can bake a bunny and I can't?"

"Oh, god! Not all fruits are for eating. Some are just to look at."

"All right, all right. I'll just watch."

And so, while working Will could sometimes look at this beautiful young girl. Andy was watching over him should he try to do some stupidity. On the first floor, Peter was cleaning the wheelchairs and Rick was helping in the kitchen. I came to the kitchen to warm up the tea and opened a microwave that looked terrible after two weeks. I looked around the kitchen and murmured: "Why is every mess always waiting for me? Everywhere?"

Rick asked: "Did you say anything?"

"Yeah, look around you."

Rick looked around and saw a couple of dried stains on the wall and kitchen counter: "Well. I see. Stains…"

"They always wait for me."

Rick smiled. "Even the ones on your uniform? I'm curious what's under them."

"Nothing. And work."

I left the kitchen and Rick said to himself: *It doesn't look like nothing.*

He wondered how he could speed up Bunny's decision to explain and finally show him the other levels of love. But for that, she would have to descent. He was observing Tina's colleagues at work and he began to realize that if all human beings will fulfill their dreams there would be nobody to do the ordinary human labor, which was also very necessary.

So far, mankind has not progressed so much that all these unpopular minor jobs will be done by robots. We are not yet there. Moreover, there were countries where it was not possible to find any job for any wage. Maybe not everyone was longing for the luxurious and lavish live of millionaires. Maybe somewhat higher wages and decent living conditions would be enough for some. The whole world was on the move because of the terribly disturbing balance on our planet. It was actually always like that. We have the technology; we are doing better in some countries. Just some of them. Maybe my son was right. He said the system should work in a way so that people could still dream to be doctors, nurses, builders, gardeners. Who knows.

When we put our patients to beds in the afternoon, Rick had just finished unloading the dishwasher. I silently helped him load another lot of dirty dishes. After a while a told him: "You can go to lunch to Rabbit."

Rick had a sense of humor, and the remnants of the unsuccessful love potion were still circulating in his blood. "Baked bunny thighs wouldn't be a bad choice. They say it's a diet meal."

I looked at him for a moment, then said with a wide smile: "Mine are not diet, as you can see. Enjoy your meal! See you in an hour."

Rick laughed. "So, what. They don't look that bad."

"Thank you for your compliment. Leave, please … go for lunch." Rick left.

I was raging. My thighs are not slim, but they don't look so bad either. Guys are sometimes terrible. Their heads are always full of nonsense. At least I could blow a fuse in the kitchen for the damage that always waited for me. No one else wanted to clean it. I wanted to have it clean, but I wasn't so clean inside. There was chaos right now. Damn, what am I suppose to do? Yeah, it's better if we stay friends and avoid the damage. Hmmm. But how to do it? Rick's been here for few hours only, and he's already attacking me with his man's weapons. Why wasn't I born as a man? Maybe my life will be better.

Meanwhile, the guys finished their lunch and Will started: "So, how's your Bunny? She looked a little uncertain, this morning. It seems like things are going in the right direction for you."

Rick was silent and Peter rolled his eyes. "We're here only two days and you're starting again."

Andy remarked: "Starting? He never stopped! He is in a good mood. We have a young, good-looking girl on the second floor."

"Wow, so maybe someone will take care of us. That's positive."

Rick thought: "By the time we're old, she'll be like nun nurse. You must pray that some young chicks will decide to do this job when we're grandfathers. Maybe we won't be as attractive as today."

They laughed and Andy approved: "Well, if we take care of ourselves, maybe we'll be still a little bit good looking by then."

Rick wondered himself: *A little? What does it mean a little?*

Peter added: "If we work out, maybe we will have some muscles left. God! Fortunately, we are not yet there. We are on the other side and we can help. It's not that bad."

Rick contemplated and realized that they will stay in this reality for just a few days, but Tina and her colleagues would remain on the other side. To continue helping with small deeds.

When four famous and good-looking male beings came back from lunch, I tried to finish cleaning the mess in the kitchen. It could never be done in an hour and a half. I was on the ladder putting the cups in the cupboard. The second trainee, who was assigned to the first floor, was disinfecting the carts. Peter came to the kitchen, and I got off the ladder to give them new tasks.

"So, as you can see almost nothing remained after your cleaning. The cabinets are waiting. Start with the bathroom." The guys went to work except Rick who stayed with me in the kitchen. He leaned on the door and said: "What about your box?"

"Which one? The Pandora's that I have in my head or the dark one that controls some of you men and therefore the whole world?"

Rick was silent for a moment, then said: "With both."

"Big wardrobes are waiting for you."

Rick, as a true combative male, did not give up. "Yours are waiting for you too?"

"Please. You're complicating things. I told you we were friends. I don't want more problems. Go to work."

However, Rick saw my trembling hands and knew I was fighting with myself. He told me confidently: "I'd like those few seconds."

"I want something special. I don't want any flirting. For a few seconds of pleasure, you can have any woman you want."

Rick agreed sneaky: "Maybe, but I want to know how nurses do it."

"So, find one. There are millions of them in the world."

"That's true. But I don't know how many of them would give me such comparisons as you."

"Certainly, there are some. Now start."

"I already started."

"Work! I'll check you out."

I tried to be strict, but it wasn't working anymore. Nothing was working well. What will I do? Rick smiled and I felt terrible. A nurse who was always flying up in the clouds was beginning to break. Who could resist such a handsome man? Moreover, it turned out that I was right. He was a good man.

Fear was not a pleasant emotion, but sometimes it served its purpose, but for how long? Being friends is the best option in this situation. The words of the head nurse still resonated in my mind. They reminded me mercilessly of the height of the boundary between my and Rick's reality. Doubts have persecuted every human being in some situations. Why not? The whole world wanted to achieve perfection and it was increasingly difficult to get close to it. We humans have sometimes lost the faith in ourselves because we all wanted to get closer to that perfection. Why we wanted that? So that the others will admire us? Or love us more?

I had to interrupt cleaning the kitchen and hand it over to the next shift. My thoughts remained in work. Since I was a qualified nurse, I had to concentrate more. In order to remember everything, I made notes not only on papers but on my hands as well. Because my mind was full of unnecessary stuff. Like Olympus gods. Those who were above me and, at the same time, the ones who were here on Earth. They have improved day by day in their irresistible cleaning career.

While working Will was observing the young trainee who occasionally smiled at him, though she had a boyfriend. When Andy saw that he came to him and ordered him: "Not every fruit can be torn. Tina said she had a relationship. So, don't flirt. And most importantly, don't go into someone else's garden."

"Since when did you become such a moralist? I'm not doing anything. I can watch, can't I? What about you?"

Andy replied: "I think this monastic environment influences me. I don't know."

"Ah, the environment. Old grannies aren't interested in sex, are they?"

At that moment a grandpa came to the dining room with a rollator. He couldn't hear well. A granny was walking beside him. She also couldn't hear well. They were having a heated debate. Granny was holding a banana in her hand and was giving it to the old man.

"Look what I have for you... You can keep it; I still have one." Grandpa stared at her and shook his head in disapproval.

"I don't want to. I've already had one... You keep it."

Obviously, granny was angry that he didn't want to take that banana from her. "Just take it, it's good."

Grandpa didn't have a chance or desire to resist so he took the banana. Both sat at the table to wait for coffee and pastry. They continued with their loud, passionate conversation. Andy and Will looked at each other and smiled. Andy patted Will on the shoulder: "So, you see, you were wrong. Erotica is important in every age. Only it has minor changes over time."

Will was disappointed. "Minor? Hmmm. Okay, depends for whom. Minor."

Andy went back to cleaning the bathroom cabinets and Will sheepishly observed the banana grandpa as he communicated with the granny who later offered him her dessert. With such small things, she tried to get grandpa's attention. Will smiled. Well, for grandpa, fruit and pastry were enough to feel that grandma was interested in him. What an irony that much younger human beings must do much more if they want to win their love. Yet they are not always successful.

When the shift change was over, we were giving out coffee and pastry. Peter walked between grandmothers and grandfathers who were happy for every little attention they were given. The punishment for that unfortunate evening began to change into one mission of a higher level of love. All four of them began to understand that only when they became a direct part of it. Peter realized how important it was to pursue charity. Not only for the royal families who visit various institutions and places where a higher level of love, mercy, and compassion is a common thing. Many other people are trying to do good deeds as well. Tina was right. If someone is directly involved in doing such small acts of love, his or her heart will be for sure enlarged and cleansed from dirt. This empty space will be filled with love faster.

Rick was cleaning the closets and was beginning to hate them. Since his last visit, they looked like they have never been cleaned. When their shift was over, Rick was in the kitchen with Peter. He asked him: "We're finished, who are you waiting for? Oh, why I'm asking. Really, have you moved somewhere? Or is Bunny still somewhere in the clouds?"

Rick replied: "Don't worry, she'll come down. She just needs more time."

"Maybe she's waiting for you to get higher."

"Higher? I'm high enough, don't you think?"

"You are high, that's true. Only this particular height seems to be an obstacle for her."

"She compared me to Apollo. I can't really go any higher, can I? I don't understand what she wants. Special. What can it be?"

"Good deeds ... depth not just the surface." In Rick's head, depth had just different meaning. That's man's main problem. They felt the most secure and safe when they stayed low.

Rick grinned: "Depth... Height... God!"

Peter patted him on the shoulder. "It seems like you are beginning to understand. I mean different depth. Inside."

Rick sighed: "Dark box."

Peter's eyes widened. "What did you say?"

"Nothing. You're right. It's necessary to go inside."

Then Peter got it and said: "Inside the soul and the heart."

"Yeah, Yeah. Sure." At that moment I came to the dining room with a tray.

Rick asked: "So, what time will we meet at the Rabbit?"

"Rather not today. Now your words are dangerous."

With an innocent look on his face, Rick defended himself: "Mine? I thought spewing dangerous words was your specialty. Look, I've cleaned up almost all the bathroom cabinets. I work much faster than before. I do good deeds. What else should I do?"

"Nothing, for friendship it's enough. I already told you."

"Friendship between man and woman? Is there such a thing?"

"Yes, there is. It is a clean, uncomplicated relationship. Sex won't destroy it."

"Sex destroys relationships?"

"I want to believe that not always. But it's hard. Fighting men. Very hard."

"Are we fighting?"

"All mankind continually fights. Unfortunately, men and women sometimes fight as well. I will come if we won't analyze the answers to other levels of love for a while. We will chat as friends."

"As friends? Friends usually don't analyze the sizes of various boxes."

"They're analyzing. Those furniture ones. Others are banned. For now." Rick smiled.

"All of them? Even the little emotional box?"

"It's irrelevant now. It's too early."

"Early?"

"Yeah, pretty much."

"So tonight. Friendly meeting. Without analyzing boxes."

"Yes, without." Rick looked at me and I looked away. When he finally left with Peter, I was relieved. I didn't really know what to do anymore. Everything was all so complicated.

In the evening I came to our pub. I sat down and was nervous. Once again, I took out my aids that helped me mitigate the Babylonian punishment of confused languages. I looked like some crazy teacher who entered the wrong class by mistake. God, it's going to be a disaster again.

"I see you are still faithful to the old fashion way of communication."

I explained: "Some old fashion weapons work better than the modern ones."

"What do you mean?"

"We talked about men and women fighting occasionally. Each with his or her own weapons. You are pretty sharp from the beginning."

Rick watched as I stroked the dictionary tenderly: "Be grateful! I haven't even started yet. I haven't used the strongest yet."

"You are one big, dangerous weapon yourself. Unfortunately. You don't have to do anything. It's enough that you exist."

Rick laughed loudly and objected: "Yet it's not enough for you."

"You're right. It's not enough."

"You have high demands."

I approved: "That's why I said that you look like the Apollo. You shine like the light. Your heart."

"That you can't know when you are distant, and our communication is complicated."

"Therefore, deeds are important. Sometimes we say a lot of words and yet don't understand each other."

Rick looked at me for few seconds then he said: "Words are true only if they become deeds."

"Sometimes it is better to use fewer words. And rather act. We people talk a lot."

"Sometimes circumstances don't allow it. To act as we would like to."

"That's right. Tell me something more about yourself, if you can. Please talk slowly. Your language is complicated. You write one way and pronounce another way."

Rick talked slowly, and when I didn't understand something, he wrote it to me or used his translating application hoping it did its job well. He corrected me and we were having fun. The language barrier complicated our communication. The huge wall between our worlds complicated the situation. I thought it would be less complicated if Rick was a real colleague. In a few days his cleaning career will end and we will no longer be temporary colleagues. We said goodbye because we both had to get up early to the same job in the morning. The work that was for Rick just temporary. For a few days we communicated in a friendly way, and he tried not to speak dangerous words. He didn't want me to be more afraid than I already was. Even so, I was scared enough. The weekend came and all four of them had two days to rest. Rick was trying to avoid speaking about me. He didn't want to hear the same advice all over again. He was confused. He didn't know why he wanted answers to what other levels of love would look like with an ordinary nurse. This nurse, who during her two weeks stay at home, floated in the clouds of fantasy with her entire theater-dance group. Where all the actors and dancers just pretended to be actors and dancers. Nevertheless, she has been doing it for years. Why didn't she give up when they never moved to a professional level?

Tina told him she is not coming to the Rabbit that day. She said she was losing her concentration in work because of their nights. And how not? What about him? There was chaos in him as well. He couldn't identify it but the heavy diaper reality, grannies and grandpas with destroyed bodies and minds turned his inner self upside down. Yes, there is a difference between reading about it, seeing a few pictures on TV and being part of it. The later was much worse. Much worse. And maybe better. In their hearts, human beings still had enough empty space that they could fill with love. If they can clean their hearts regularly. That was very, very difficult. No one wanted to endure the physical not alone the mental pain. Modern medicine can handle the physical one with painkillers. Meanwhile, humanity didn't invent anything effective for mental pain. Many desperate people have resorted to drugs and alcohol to suppress the pain of the soul for a while. Lately, psychotherapists have been busy all over the world because the enormous pressure and stress on people have taken their toll. In the past, we had friends to hear us out and comfort us. Now we have to pay the therapist for this service. Our friends are busy, they are in hurry and don't have time.

For some reason, Rick felt good in the company of the splashy Bunny. She was really just a nurse, no woman with hidden special abilities. She could take care of people. Suddenly Rick decided to go back to work to see what she was doing. He remembered the situation with the grandpa who was almost unmanageable. He saved them then. What if they need help now?

Andy was sitting in their temporary living room and furtively watched Rick for some time. He couldn't stand it anymore: "Can't you stand without the Bunny for one evening?"

Will explained with a smirk: "Leave him, his time is running out. He must use every free moment. Have you bought her at least a flower?"

Peter defended Rick: "Do you have to tease him all the time?"

"We're friends. That's all," said Rick.

Will exploded in laughter. "Friends? Is that supposed to be your excuse that you haven't been successful until now? So far, we had no problem with speed."

Rick looked at Will and he was a little angry: "Take care of yourself and your friendly relationships."

Will didn't stop: "I care. You are my friend."

Andy asked: "Did she told you what she would want for that friendly service? When she helped us then?"

Rick answered: "Not yet. Now we are trying friendly communication, without allusions to…" Will did not understand.

"Sex. I don't understand why she is making such a fuzz out of it. You are both adults, aren't you? What does that friendly service have to do with it?"

"Patience. You'll learn everything. Don't worry, she would not want from you the same thing she wants from Rick."

Peter patted his shoulder and he looked at Rick with a smile. Andy sat down on the couch. "Then go. Before her shift ends. Nicely develop your friendly relationship for a few more days."

Rick put on his jacket and told him: "Not every relationship has to end in bed, right?"

The guys burst into laughter and Will noted: "Everything starts and ends in bed. Only circumstances change."

Rick slammed the door and went straight to the first floor to look for Bunny. There were just a couple of grannies in the dining room waiting to be put in their beds. He decided to wait until Bunny comes for the next granny. Tina's colleague came to the dining room and smiled while pointing to the side where she was. "Tina's somewhere there."

Rick hoped Tim will be working. Women were dangerous, he knew that now there would be gossips. But they were really running out of time. Why did he want to know the answers? Tina assigned one element for every level of love. Fire. Water. Earth. Air. She said that all four were important, otherwise love wouldn't survive. Was it true that people were just enjoying more the earth element that ruled the body? And men enjoyed just those few seconds so that emotions won't make their life more complicated? He found her in the room with two paralyzed patients.

She saw him at the door. "I'm not going to The Rabbit today."

Rick asked straight away: "What else do I have to do for you to show me the remaining three levels?"

"Rick, you're doing enough. There are reasons that are complicating our situation. It's not possible here. The conditions are not suitable."

Rick was surprised. "There are always some reasons. What conditions? Tell me here and now."

I started to explain: "It's not possible. Answers for a man like you must be exceptional."

"Exceptional? Why? Look, I know you compared me to Apollo, and I don't remember those other saviors, but I'm a man. So, tell me what you want me to do so you will show me. You are very complicated."

"Maybe. Those answers are for brave human beings."

Rick watched as I tried to get one patient that had problems with breathing to take some medicine and asked: "What's wrong with her? Why does she reject everything?"

"The process started. Dying." Rick paused.

"… How do you know?"

"Experience. Every human being probably feels when his or her time comes."

"Time for death?"

"Yes. She'll stop eating. She'll stop drinking. Refuses medication. We respect it. We try to give only painkillers."

Rick was silent for a moment, then asked: "Do they feel pain?"

"Sometimes."

"How long will it take to die?"

"Nobody knows exactly. Some human beings will die in their sleep. Some suddenly. When they are conscious. They don't feel it. I asked the doctor. It happened to me before. One patient died in my arms. Suddenly. It looked awful, but the doctor said he didn't feel it. They'd fall into a coma right away. When they die in their sleep that's the most beautiful."

Rick sighed: "That's sad."

"Not for very old people. Let's not talk about others. Please."

"Okay, let's go back to the answers. What do I need to do and what are the right conditions?"

"You have a good heart. The whole world knows you're a strong man. Physically."

Rick agreed: "Maybe yes. It's obvious."

"Yes. I see. Different kind of strength is needed for such answers. The one that is in your heart and in your soul. Such strength is greater than the physical."

"Oh my god! Well, now the unpleasant part will come." I smiled.

"You're young, good-looking man. Actually, you men are younger and beautiful for much longer. For us, women, it's harder. For us, time is a curse. Sometimes. Here you met women from the other side."

Rick agreed: "From the end. We both are going from the end."

"Maybe. We'll see. We don't know what's coming. So, for a man, this diaper reality is very difficult. You're created for another kind of suffering. For example, on the battlefield. It's easy to love a perfect, young body, and take care of it."

Rick knew where I was heading and got scared. "What a foxy Bunny you are. Isn't it enough that I'm serving coffee to them? I still have to do the cleaning of all sorts of boxes and the effects of the bag poison you are giving out three times a week?"

"It's not enough for my answers."

"I had right, you have high demands! Wouldn't jewelry be enough for you? An emerald necklace with pearls, for example?"

"It wouldn't fit with my uniform. Now you see how high you are? You're angry that I compared you to Apollo."

Rick was curious. "How do you know what your Apollo looks like?"

"I don't know. I've never seen him. As a child I imagined him, and he looked like you. Then I saw you."

Rick stared at me. "So, you didn't see him."

"I've never seen anyone from above or from below. I just imagined them. I believe they exist."

"All of them? All the gods? Oh, Jesus!"

"Yes, all of them. Gods, angels, fairies. All ethereal beings. They are beautiful. So, if you want the answers you have to wash one of the patients. Don't worry. I will take care of the private parts and diapers."

Rick rolled his eyes. "Are you kidding??"

"I am not."

"Look, if you want, I'll wash you... But grandma?"

"Fortunately, I still can manage myself."

"Why do you have to invent such crazy tasks?"

"I want to know how your heart looks from inside. A little. I care about deeds. I know what I'm doing."

"Well, I'm not sure you know."

"Look, I've been serving other people my whole life. Love is also about humility. We forgot that."

Rick noted: "Well, you're still going from the end."

"All right. The bottom line is, you will wash one old granny, you will humbly serve her body, which is no longer sexy."

"We're still in the higher levels. Shit."

"Still. If you want to go to the lower levels, you need to show me how the inside of your heart looks. This will mean that there is a small chance of igniting the first spark."

"How do you know?"

"I know. You men have only been responding to the body for a very long time. It's not your fault. You have been created this way. Remember the box of sex and emotions?"

"Oh my god. Can we analyze it? Ban is lifted?"

"You started."

"You're such a demanding person!"

"Maybe...do you remember our conversation about sacrifices?"

"Sacrifices?"

"My whole life is full of sacrifices. One sacrifice cost me half my time with my children. Because I didn't want to be poor anymore, but every magic has its price. We have to pay it."

"Pay... Price... Sacrifice..."

"When you play the role of hero you are ready to sacrifice yourself instantly and for all humanity. In real life even a small sacrifice count."

"I hope your answers will be worth it since I have to wash the old lady."

"I think you probably haven't fought this way yet. Look, I believe you're special inside your heart. Not just outside."

"What about the necklace?"

"Do you think I need it? If you can wash the granny, you'll need money for other things. The answers will be difficult and expensive."

Rick kept silent for a long time, then sighed: "Well I hope it will be worth it."

"I can't promise you that. We'll try it. If the spark does not light, we can't go down."

"I'm starting to be scared, myself."

"I believe you."

"Why do you make it so difficult?"

"Because a divine man needs divine answers."

"Have you done anything like that before?"

"No, I haven't. No one was good enough for the answers. Maybe strong enough. Inside. I can recognize cowards. The strength of a man is not just in his muscles. Look, I'm late again. My colleague will be angry. We didn't finish cleaning the kitchen."

"I can do it."

"No, not in front of her. She saw you, that's enough for rumors."

"Rumors? So, which granny should I wash?"

I thought for a moment, and then I remembered Ms. K. When she saw Rick, she said that for one time in her life she would like to be touched by such a handsome man.

"Mrs. K. She can still walk to the bathroom by herself. So, don't worry, no big disaster. I will take care of the private parts."

Rick grabbed his head. "Why?"

"I don't want to cause you a trauma."

Rick did not understand. "Trauma? The other parts of the body are not traumatic?"

"Mrs. K. weighs a lot. So, I guess yes. I don't know."

"You're really a strange person."

"I'm. I see and feel things differently. You don't have to do anything. You have free will."

"Hmmm. I don't have to. I'll think about it."

"Before you do it you have to ask our boss for permission."

"Just a second! Do I have to ask for permission? Isn't it enough to wash her?"

"You can tell her you want to try it. You've done a great job as a cleaner." Rick stared at me. He was angry. Why this splashy Bunny wants such crazy things?

After a while, he said: "Okay. I will think about it. Are you really not coming to the Rabbit?"

"No, really not today. I'm tired. Those evenings are hard when I must get up at five in the morning. I won't rehearse today."

"Why you eat sugar? Sugar is poison."

"That's true...you're right."

Rick said nothing. He saw enough to understand that sometimes human beings had to improvise and break the rules.: "You don't have a chocolate stain today."

"Grannies didn't bake today. It's Saturday. They don't always bake with chocolate."

"That's a pity."

"Yes. That's a waste of chocolate and its endorphin."

Rick was definitely thinking about other kinds of endorphins. *What was more dangerous for women? Sex or chocolate?* he asked himself.

"How about tomorrow?"

"I don't know what will happen tomorrow. You'll have time to decide. You have free will."

"Well, free will…"

"Now go. I have a lot of unfinished work."

Rick noted: "Me too."

"Good night. See you on Monday."

Rick watched for a moment as I was turning the dying patient on the other side and said: "Good night."

When I was alone, I quickly tried to finish my work tasks. I was happy that the head nurse was off, otherwise, she would give me that speech again. My colleague, who was working with me fortunately said nothing. If she would ask, I had an excuse that Rick had forgotten something. I was forgetting too. I was distracted and everything fell out of my hands. That's why everything lasted longer. When I was leaving, one of my colleagues surprised me with a question: "What did our temporary trainee want? Isn't it enough for him to be here during the day so he comes in the evening as well?"

"He just forgot something."

"Ah… Recently both of you are forgetting."

I said with ease: "Yes. You know that sometimes my hands and paper notes are not enough."

"Yes, I know. By the way he really looks like a true superstar."

"They all look like that. It's part of their job. To look perfect. I think it's not easy."

"All right, you can go now. See you tomorrow."

"See you tomorrow. By the way, Mrs. G is not doing well, it probably won't take long."

"It must have come once. She waited long enough for that."

"Yes, that's true."

I wished her good night and left.

The next morning, when four beautiful guys finally rolled out of their beds, Andy asked Rick: "Well, how did yesterday's date go? You came somewhere early. You didn't go to the Rabbit, did you?"

Rick mumbled: "What do you want? You have nothing else to do?"

"No, fortunately, we have nothing to do."

Rick looked at the kitchen where the dishes began to pile up. Their temporary apartment was slowly but surely starting to get messy again.

"Can you start tiding things up instead of asking stupid questions?"

"I'm not anybody's maid. I warned you at the beginning that everybody should get rid of his own mess."

Rick added: "This time Bunny won't come here anymore, okay?"

"None of my business. I have extra clothes."

Peter asked him: "Did you also bring extra clean dishes?"

"There is enough of the clean ones." Andy entered in the kitchen: "Hmmm. But not for a long time. So, it's time to use our free day to replenish our clean dishes, clothes, and so on."

Will mumbled: "How the hell can one take all this? We clean like idiots in some stupid nursing house, we bear those horrible smells, crazy grannies and grandpas, diapers... That is crazy!!!Women are really better at cleaning. We are good at other types of work."

Andy asked him with interest: "What kind of work do you have in mind?"

Will replied immediately: "For example, build buildings, roads, and so on."

Andy teased him: "And have you ever built something?"

Rick laughed ironically. "He demolishes more than he builds. But you can call the blondie from the second floor for a change. Maybe she would come. You'll pay her, of course. Maybe she'll be okay if she gets you instead of money."

The guys burst into laughter.

Will shouted: "Shut up! I can see that so far you haven't been successful with the nurse with bunny's thighs. Not with your money nor with your appearance."

Peter defended Rick: "He is successful but only partially, right Rick? Did she tell you what she wants?"

Rick sighed: "Yes. I won't tell you anything, because you would have stupid remarks again. She revealed part of it."

Will ironically grinned: "She's all special."

Peter said more quietly: "Maybe that's why her answers to love levels will be very special."

Rick nodded. "I'm already very pleasantly afraid. But she wants me to do something for her before she gives me the answers."

Andy laughed. "Well, it's not going to be difficult, to do something for her."

Rick objected: "It's not like you think."

Will looked at Rick and shook his head. "What she thinks of herself? She is not some movie star."

"That's true, she is not. So, tell us what is that you have to do?" Peter was eager to know the answer.

They were expecting all sorts of things, but not what Rick replied with a sigh: "I have to bath one granny." The guys were silent for a moment, then started to laugh loudly. Tears of laughter were running down Will's cheeks.

In between the laughter, he asked: "Granny? Oh, god. No, no!"

Peter stopped laughing. "Is she serious? What's the purpose of that?"

Andy replied to him: "What we're experiencing in the nursing house all the time. Humility."

They remained quiet for a while then Peter continued: "Did she give you a reason?"

"Yes, it's related to humility. I don't have to tell you all." Will shook his head in disbelief. "This nurse of yours is a tough woman. Screw her! Let her wash her grandma herself. What she needs this nonsense for?"

Rick explained: "I'm surprised myself that I'm even considering doing it. If I don't do it, she won't say anything."

"Is it so awful to wash a granny?" Andy asked.

Peter replied instead of Rick: "Not awful, but hard."

Will teased Rick: "I wouldn't do that. For god's sake which woman would ask a guy to do such a thing?"

"Maybe the one who sees beauty everywhere. Even where others don't see it. All those nurses and employees like their crazy grannies. Although they sometimes are getting crazy because of them. Sometimes they curse and are desperate, but still, they see the remains of beauty in them. Those old people were once young as we are. We saw the photos. What we see now is the result of the ruthless time. The time that flows only forward in human reality." Peter commented.

Andy approved: "The time from which everybody is so afraid. Especially in our Earthly Olympus."

They were all quiet, but Will wouldn't give up. "Whatever. If she wants someone to wash her granny let her find some staff to do it."

Then, Rick got it. "That wouldn't be special. The staff does it because it's their job. I'm supposed to do it for other reasons." Peter looked at Rick with a thoughtful look.

"What will she do in return?" They laughed again.

Rick continued: "I know what you mean. It's not so sure. I haven't decided if I was going to do it. Anways it's none of your business." Andy seemed to know what was going to come.

"Well don't be surprised if you will need us later. Now start working! We have a small mess here again."

Rick looked at the kitchen. "A small mess? It doesn't seem to be smaller."

Will muttered confidently: "We are good in doing other jobs. . By that, I don't mean building houses or roads." And so, the guys started making order in their temporary male nest. Special male type of order. Hiding order. Which meant to hide as many things as possible from visible places.

Rick was thinking about the strange Bunny and her crazy request. *It can't be that difficult*, he thought. *There are worse things. If I don't have to deal with dirty diapers, I can definitely manage it. Well, wait, you curvy Bunny. You'll pay me back. Big time. You'll never get away with this.* He had no idea what great truth he was saying.

Men and women fought with their own weapons. Sometimes there were moments when both tried to put down their weapons. Thanks to these wonderful moments, they endured until the next battle in the most exciting war that took place between men and women from the beginning of creation. The fight of intimacy.

The god of love, Eros, his faithful companion Psyche, and the goddess of love, Aphrodite, really had more work than the god of war, Ares. The poor thing was sometimes so overwhelmed because men had been fighting in real wars for ages. The aim was to conquere cities and borders and in wars of intimacy, they conquered women. Their male testosterone hormone roared in all directions… And women? Their weaponry looked tender. But that was an illusion. They were often invisible and therefore more dangerous. All men were afraid of them. Feelings and love complicated their efforts to conquer cities and borders, but also other women. Therefore, it took them a very long time to be willing to open their hearts at least a bit.

They came to work on Monday morning, but I didn't see Rick. They smiled wryly, knowing what was coming. I asked them: "Has something happened? Why are you looking so strange?"

Peter shrugged his shoulders. "Nothing. Everything is fine."

"Okay. So, there is still a lot of work to do. Let's divide the tasks."

Suddenly my boss and Rick came to the bathroom. I already knew what was coming. I understood that the other three beautiful cleaners knew it as well. That's why their smiles. The boss told me: "Tina, I have one task for you. This young gentleman would like to try to bath one of the patients."

The guys couldn't control themselves anymore and the corners of their mouth started to bounce.

They didn't want to laugh in front of her, so she won't think they had no respect for patients. She didn't know the motivation of the young gentleman who wanted so much to do this task. Will couldn't control himself. "He is tired of building a cleaning career, so he wants to move up a level at any cost. He wants to try being a nurse."

The boss understood him and Since she was a great diplomat she replayed: "Anyone on this planet should try it once. Maybe we'd better understand what really matters in life. Serving people and helping each other."

No one said anything, and the boss continued: "He can try to bath Mr. D. He is easy going."

Andy remarked in a low voice: "It has to be a granny. Not a grandpa."

"Did you say something?" asked my boss.

Peter answered quickly: "No. He didn't say anything."

Rick sighed: "I can try to wash Mr. D and one granny."

I tried to object in my weak English: "That is not a good idea. We know how the toilet looks when Mr. D goes there. On his own. Everything is dirty from…"

"Shit…" Rick added.

The boss said sternly: "Oh, come on, gentlemen. Please don't use such expressions. We are adults."

She turned to me: "And it also applies to you. If Mr. D does it again, you will clean it up. A strong stomach is needed for such disasters."

I sighed: "Sure, testosterone will take the better part. Estrogen the worse part and shi… Oh, I'm sorry."

She looked at me strictly: "Tina! Again? We don't use such indecent expressions! So, you show him how to bath Mr. D and one female patient. If there are any disasters…with…"

"Shi… Sure, we will share the work. Fairly."

The guys burst into laughter. Rick also started laughing. Never in his life, he would have thought that because of some inconspicuous splashy Bunny he would do such foolishness. Men would do many foolish things for women for ages. In the past, they would even kill each other. Thank god there are social networks and mobiles now. They no longer have to kill each other. They just scold each other. Maybe some of them sometimes get killed. The boss sighed. What to do? They were men of another reality, not used for such kind of work and suffering. She thought it wouldn't be a bad idea to give each one of them the same task. So, they'll see firsthand how difficult that is. After a while, she gave me an order: "All right, take your trainee and show him everything according to the rules. He'll try it tomorrow."

At least I don't have to clean furniture, beds, and wheelchairs, Rick thought.

"In addition he can give them their pills and other stuff as needed. So have a nice day, gentlemen. By the way, job well done. I'm pleasantly surprised."

She left. When we were alone, I reminded them: "You three, you know what to do."

Andy cheerfully agreed: "Well, we're still just cleaners, in the lower level, so we're going to clean the furniture. We wish Rick good luck."

They all laughed and went to work. When we were alone with Rick, I remarked surprisingly: "You decided quickly."

"We don't have time."

"We don't. So, come. Mr. D is already washed today. Let's go to Mrs. K first."

Rick thought: "I don't understand what I'm doing here and why."

"Nothing special. You are going to do good deeds. You will fight with real monsters and you will use humility. That's awesome. Don't worry. I will do the unpleasant part of it."

Rick shook his head. "Yeah I'll be thankful for that. I hope the answers will be worth it. All of them."

"Answers. I told you we'd try to. We need to light a spark. Without it, we won't have all the answers."

Rick objected: "How do you know it's not burning yet?"

"It's burning. Down there. In you guys almost always everything burns down there. Women need another kind of spark. Let's go to work."

Rick said nothing and obediently followed me. The other colleague was in the room with two lovely fairy-tale grannies. We came in when she was washing one of them. Rick observed it from a distance because of the familiar smell spread from the bathroom, but fortunately not the worse one. I saw his facial expression and explained with laughter: "Instead of toilet they often go to the shower. Welcome to my world."

"He is not cleaning today?" asked my colleague.

"He wants to advance higher. He'll try to give a bath to two patients."

"The boss allowed it?"

"Why wouldn't she? We've had so many trainees here. Let him try it. It won't hurt anyone. Actually, I wanted to tell you that from now on we will take care of Mrs. K and Mr. D. You take care of Mrs. L and Mrs. B, please. As for their mobility, they have a similar condition. So, it's fair."

My colleague agreed: "Mrs. K is not done you. You can go to her."

Rick was glad to come out of that room and I said: "It's horrible, but someone has to do it."

Rick didn't say anything, and maybe he already regretted that he agreed to do this task. He wanted to get the answers about the four elements of love; fire, water, earth, and air. Nevertheless, it was more than crazy that he decided to try this kind of fight. A fight with real monsters with whom the employees of such institutions fought daily using the best weapons against evil and pride. With humility, mercy, compassion, gratitude, hope and forgiveness. These weapons belonged to the highest level of love, which, according to all religions in the world, were closest to the Creator. These weapons awakened in human beings the most precious piece they had in themselves. The image of God. The Creator. Nothing in the world could overcome evil as strongly as sincere, pure love with all its levels linked by the basic elements of creation. Fire. Water. Earth. Air.

We entered Mrs. K's room and she greeted us with a wide, sincere smile: "Oh, Tina. Who did you bring to me? Oh my god, this is such a handsome guy!"

"Mrs. K, I brought him in because he would like to give you a bath. Since he's a man, I have to ask for your permission. I will take care of your private parts."

Mrs. K. asked with an impish smile: "Why? I wouldn't mind. Oh, yes. I see. I'm already an old woman."

"I don't want to cause him a trauma. You know, young men have a little problem with that. They're probably used to other types of bodies."

"Other types of bodies??? Just wait how he will look like when he is 90. Then he'll remember."

I objected: "He will surely be a beautiful grandfather. The grannies will fight for a sitting place next to him in the nursing house."

Mrs. K laughed loudly. "Sitting? You think they'll be satisfied with that?"

"Well, I don't know. Maybe by that time medicine will advance so much that other things will be possible as well."

"You're a monster, Tina! Thank god he doesn't understand you. He looks a little scared. I think it's because of my figure. Oh, Tina, I have to lose weight. Look at my belly. What about him? Does he have any imperfections?"

"Maybe not."

Mrs. K asked with an impish voice: "What you mean 'maybe?' You haven't seen his body yet? What are you waiting for?"

My face turned red like a tomato. Mrs. K was a monster, she didn't care, and she often embarrassed me with her crazy remarks.

I warned her: "Mrs. K! For god's sake. No, I didn't. I doubt we will ever get there. It's very complicated. He's a movie star."

"And so, what? Star? He is a man as well, isn't he? My lover was a man too. Above all. This one is too."

"Well let's get to work. He doesn't speak German. So maybe he'll be silent. I'll write him a few words so he can give you the basic instructions."

Mrs. K laughed. "Don't worry, we'll be fine. I will be blabbering like a fool in German as always and he can blabber in English. We'll manage somehow, eh?" She looked at Rick.

I told him: "You can tell her yes, even in English. Don't worry. She is a great woman and has a sense of humor. She knows what to do, she'll help you." Rick smiled at Mrs. K.

"Yes." We both laughed.

Then I send him out of the room. "Sit in the bathroom. I'll call you."

Rick obediently did what I told him. When we were done, I started putting up her special net pants that held the diaper. Then we found that they had a hole in the middle. Mrs. K burst into laughter. "Oh, Tina, look! They're *Schnellfickerhosen*. You can borrow them."

"Well, that lace and the shape of those panties would kill the last remnants of passion in every man."

Mrs. K shouted in German: "Hey, beautiful man, come over here!"

I put my head in the bathroom door where he sat on the shower stool and called him in. Rick obediently came into the room. Mrs. K explained in German while holding those terrible panties with a hole in the middle: "Look! Apparently, they're not sexy enough, but practical." I translated that to Rick. All three of us laughed at it.

Mrs. K interrupted us: "You see? He has a sense of humor. That's a good sign. He's a good guy."

Rick tried to catch something from that conversation and I objected: "He's unreachable for me, Mrs. K."

I went to replace those netted panties and Mrs. K was watching Rick, who was just smiling at her. I came back with new panties and put them on Mrs. K along with a diaper. I continued: "Now look, I'll show you." First, I thoroughly disinfected the washbasin and the plastic container in which the water was used. Mrs. K sat on the shower stool and I started to show him the procedure. I dipped the washcloth under the running water. I didn't touch the prepared water in the basin, where there was also a little wash emulsion.

I explained: "Always use clean water on the face. From the faucet. You start with the face." Rick watched as I began to clean her eyes, continued on with the face, and washed her ears.

I asked her: "Mrs. K would you mind if I take off your top?"

"Of course, I won't. I just hope this beauty won't faint."

she said with a smile.

Rick looked at Mrs. K with dog eyes and didn't say anything. I took off Mrs. K's top and soaked the washcloth. I washed her face and started to wash her hands. Rick watched my every move. I washed Mrs. K's upper body and back. I told him: "You must follow the skin. Especially under the breasts."

We couldn't stand it anymore and we all laughed again. Mrs. K. was very gifted and ate a lot. She had that type of body that in Hollywood she wouldn't earn a dime with it. It didn't bother her anymore. I showed him how to dry her, put the body lotion, and dress her up.

We placed her in the wheelchair, and she cleaned her teeth. One of many activities that every human being performs automatically as soon as he learns them as a child. Until he begins to lose strength due to merciless time. Then he must humbly accept the help of another human being. The other human being must also humble himself to gain the power of the highest level of love for such a service. Rick began to understand that I had not asked him to do this task to humiliate him. On the contrary. Serving such a body required a great deal of inner strength and, above all, humility. From both sides. The whole world is talking nonsense about the inner qualities, the values that are most important. Supposedly. Unfortunately, the rules of our planet have often been set exactly the opposite way. Superficial glitter. Wealth. Luxury. Yes, it was wonderful to use these gifts. They could help other human beings. There was enough for everyone in the world, but we couldn't set up the system to feed everyone. Mankind still needs money. To feed our bodies. Money is unsatisfactory and not enough to feed the hunger of the soul and heart, which, like the real hunger in some countries, has destroyed and crushed the unhappy human beings. We are fighting for recognition, success. Success was the most important goal nowadays. What did it really mean? Few people went to the depths because we were terribly afraid of pain. The pain was the nightmare of humanity. Yet it has been chasing us from the beginning of the world. Everything rare is born of great pain. For example, children. Even true love. There is also pain in love. We don't want it. We just want that glitter. Tina tried to show him human beings from the other end. From the other side where the superficial glitter had no value. From a side where one could pay only with the most precious invisible gifts. Gifts with a glitter that was visible only to those human beings who regularly cleaned their hearts with deeds of love and, in particular, with humility. Sometimes people have become slaves because of the superficial glitter. The constant struggle with time and fear of death forced us to do mad and meaningless things. Only to slow it down. It didn't work though. Time, the most powerful ruler on our planet will catch every human being. Whether rich or poor. While searching for evidence of the existence of other dimensions that have remained invisible to human eyes so far, faith has disappeared from human hearts. Humanity was not fighting for love and values. It fought more for power, money, and superficial glitter. Our existence, where the word poverty was partly covered with technological advances, began to take its toll. We are still sleeping and waiting for someone to come from above and save us. How can somebody save us if we still didn't understand why we are on our planet? That the reflection of the Creator in us does not mean hatred, but love? Deep, true love, that teaches human beings to forgive their mistakes and be generous. Such type of love sometimes doesn't give us everything we want but for which we are willing to sacrifice something. The sacrifice may not only mean caring for the disabled and the sick. The sacrifice is also when I help a friend, or I throw a coin to a beggar. Every sacrifice will be rewarded. People deserve a reward. However, it was necessary to deal with love even with the reward.

Later Rick took Mrs. K's wheelchair and brought her to the dining room. Grannies were a bit jealous. How not? Mrs. K. felt like a real movie star at that moment. Because one handsome man she was in the center of everybody's attention. Peter, who was in the kitchen, gave her breakfast and watched as Rick went with me. He was observing and helping me when I washed the patients. He didn't feel humiliated at all, on the contrary. It seemed to him that those real monsters in the nursing house were as hard to handle as the fictional ones in the movie. The world can be saved in various ways. With a high and noble way such as in his Earthly Olympus or in the ordinary reality operated by all human beings on Earth. When we finished, the assistants, responsible for the patient's entertainment took them to the living room. Only a few grannies stayed in the dining room waiting for lunch and to be taken to bed again. We sat with Rick on the couch, which in the meantime had been replaced with a new one and covered with a special rubber sheet to protect it from various attacks from our grannies.

I asked him: "Are you afraid? I mean of washing? Is it worse than your falls and battles in the movie?"

"I don't know yet. I'll tell you tomorrow."

I praised him: "You are doing a good job. I mean cleaning cabinets, changing bedding and so. You're a bit different than at the beginning."

"What do you mean? Different?"

"Your glow is stronger. I told you. You are shining more."

Rick shook his head. "You won't stop with that?"

"I see and feel a bit differently because of our grannies and grandpas. All staff see and feel differently. They see in depth."

Rick remembered his conversation with Peter about the depth and height. "May I ask what happened? I mean with your relationship."

"Now it's not a good time. Acts must be done at the right time from both sides of the partnership. If they come late, love dies. Not everything can be saved. My case. Some acts came late."

Rick remained silent for a moment, then continued: "Why isn't it a good time?"

"It's too early. The right moment didn't come yet. Maybe once it will come. Now it's not important."

Rick didn't ask anymore, and I told him: "Tomorrow I'll show you, Mr. D, without the private parts."

Rick disagreed: "Why? I've seen it before."

"Yeah. Just once. You don't have to see again. You're going to sit in the room. Then I'll call you."

"It is not fair!"

"It's not? You didn't hurry to Mrs. K. Ah sure, you had enough when you saw other parts of her body. Even those scared you."

"I'm not scared."

"No? You looked scared. Although you can take a lot, this battle will be harder. Trust me."

"I'm wondering what I'll get from you when I will do your task."

"You'll get invisible gifts. How many I don't know yet. It depends on the spark."

"Why does it have to be so complicated?"

"Because we want to go deep, right? We want to know what's under the surface."

"Deep. Thank you so much. That dark box of yours is really deep."

"It's as deep as it is. No, it's too early. Let's go to work."

I got up from the couch and Rick followed me. "Wait, you didn't finish it."

"The right time. Rick. The right time. Step by step."

"You're stubborn."

"I'm. I must be. Sometimes. Because of the circumstances. Go to help Peter now. Set up the tables."

"Sure, boss."

Rick went to the kitchen where Peter was cleaning the cupboards. He asked him impatiently: "Well? How's did it go?"

"What do you want to know? I just observed and changed beding."

Peter stared at him: "Wow. Well, better than scrubbing furniture cabinets, right?"

"Yeah, I just have to bath one granny tomorrow. She speaks constantly. Shame I don't understand what she and Tina are talking about. She's a beast. She weighs a lot."

Peter quietly added with laughter: "Yeah, a lot. The wheelchair is full of her. She's a cheerful granny."

"Cheerful? How does it help me with washing her?"

"Is it so bad?"

Rick replied: "I don't know. Fortunately, Tina will do the worse part."

Peter laughed louder: "Worse?"

Rick laughed as well and answered through laughter: "Worse. Her Dark box."

"Jesus. Dark box? Doesn't your head burn from this Bunny of yours?"

"Head? If only my head! I'm already worried about what those answers will."

They put dirty dishes in the dishwasher and Peter continued: "Women sometimes use very dangerous weapons. Even she does."

"Why do you think so?"

"They are invisible. She's using them in small doses. You never know what's coming. What will be her next step? You have to dust off your weapons as soon as possible."

"Hmmm... Dust off. It seems that with this splashy Bunny dust is going to be gathering on them for a while."

Peter looked at Rick. "Did you use at least one of them?"

"What for? Tina told me that I was one big weapon. My existence was."

"All right then. Do as you wish."

"Damn it! Tomorrow I have to wash one granny whose ass and breasts are XXL size! Isn't that enough for her? This crazy nurse!"

"Probably some of her invisible weapons are working a little bit since you're going to do what she wants from you."

"I'm just curious. As I said, I want to know how the splashy Bunny cares at the lower levels of love. If we ever get there. So far, we are still in the higher level full of all kinds of shit and nasty things. What is this good for?"

"For humility. For humility."

"Okay, be my guest. You can wash one granny as well. Look, you have plenty to choose from. One better than the other."

Peter looked around the dining room and his eyes rested at one of the lovely, fairy tale looking old ladies.

"I would probably wash her."

Rick patted his shoulder. "Each of them has some hidden problem. For example, some are peeing in the shower at night."

"So what? All people have some hidden problem. Everyone here does everything the opposite way. As children. Probably we won't be any different. You and your colleagues will be very hard to take care of."

Rick paused.

"… What do you mean?"

"Tina said these poor patients' short-term memory does not work. For some reason they remember the past. They live in it. What have you been doing with your colleagues for years? Fighting fictional monsters. Try to imagine if all of you were put into such a nursing house. I suppose you would demolish it. You'd catch anything that resembles your weapons and you'd play heroes."

Rick was silent for a moment. Then he went away and returned with a plastic bucket and broom: "Do you mean this for example?"

At that moment, I came to the dining room and saw Rick with the broom and bucket: "What the hell are you doing?"

Rick shrugged his shoulders and stroked the plastic broom: "Nothing. I'm dusting off some of my weapons. I'm preparing for tomorrow's fight."

Peter laughed and I praised him: "Very good idea, but this time this won't help you in the fight."

Rick artfully said: "You will help me. I hope."

I nodded. "Worse part yes."

"Worse."

I remarked: "The dark box is a very powerful weapon."

Rick agreed: "Powerful it is. But I have a strong weapon as well."

"Hmmm. I see. Do you mean this plastic fake?" I knocked on the plastic broom: "We'll see. First, you wash your granny. Okay, let's go to work."

Rick returned the plastic broom back where it belonged and thought for himself: *You'll see how this plastic fake will work. Damn woman!*

After lunch, Rick followed me from room to room and helped putting the patients in beds. They were like children. Here he saw the real human misery. The human being actually ended at the beginning. Naked. Defenseless. Relying on help for all things like a small child.

When we finished, I send him to lunch: "You can go to lunch. We will continue in the afternoon." So, the guys left for lunch. Will and Andy couldn't wait to teas a bit the freshly trained nurse.

"So how do you like your new job? Is it a good feeling to move up a level?"

Rick was getting angry: "Sure. Higher level. Still not getting it? We would be screwed without cleaners."

Andy continued: "That's for sure, but, we're wondering if the nursing career is more exciting than the cleaning one."

Rick replied: "It's really very exciting. All of it."

"For god's sake! Stop! You're disgusting."

Peter defended him and Andy agreed: "We're disgusting again. We've been here for a long time."

Will continued with a question: "Did Tina show you how to wash a grandma?"

"Yeah, she did. It's not like...super hard."

Peter asked him: "What about that grandpa?"

"I have seen it once before. But today we came too late, he has been already clean. We have to wait till tomorrow."

Will shook his head in disbelief. "I can't believe that you would agree to such stupidity."

"You should try it too. Every person on this planet, even us, will end up like this. Probably."

Will waved his hand. "I'm glad I have normal, uncomplicated females in my collection. They are happy with gifts, flowers, jewelry, and so on. I don't have to do such a stupid thing. Washing grannies and so on."

Andy agreed: "We need the visible things, that's true. However, as if the invisible ones were diminishing from the world. Damn, we're still playing that in our movies."

Everyone was quiet. After the hard days in the nursing house, they started to realize it. In addition to material wealth, humanity also needs the spiritual one to survive. The invisible one. Even Jesus said, "Collect treasures in heaven. Not on Earth."

What's the point of having fat bank accounts when our hearts and souls are starving? Some human beings have spent all their life collecting wealth on Earth. Nevertheless, if they won't share that wealth with anyone, their heart and soul will starve. Helping even one human being managed to correct the disturbed balance. Although only partially. Love is not just about perfect beauty and perfect sex. It must go through all four levels associated with the four elements of creation. Fire, water, earth, and air. Because as soon as the initial passion fades away and our bodies are destroyed by the time, we will be left only with a higher level of love. The unpopular level that includes helping other human beings. Those whose fate didn't spare one of their loved ones from disease, know that. If their love didn't pass through all these levels, it would perish. Unfortunately, disease, death, and time were still present on Earth. So, we had to learn to accept the unpleasant aspects of human life. We've already had to fight for our survival. We've sometimes complicated it with our futility and cowardice. So far, we haven't invented a versatile cure for our bodies. However, we had a universal cure for the diseases of the soul and heart, but because we were afraid of pain, we often decided not to use it. We were afraid of disappointment. Fear made us weak. We were overwhelmed with the fear of not being loved. Well, many human beings didn't feel that way. We didn't know how to love. How could we know if instead of praising ourselves we would only look at our mistakes? Criticism spewed easily from our human mouths. It was harder to praise. Moreover, it didn't matter if we criticized and praised ourselves or someone else.

Peter looked very important when he released the next words: "Well, in this place we were for a short time saving a small piece of the world with small deeds. In movies, you saved the whole world. The world needs both ways of saving. Someone has to remind people."

Rick agreed: "We are doing that but maybe it's not enough. Maybe it should be remembered that the world is being saved every day, like this. With ordinary people, employees. We are all important."

Andy asked: "When this punishment ends, what will happen then?"

Rick explained: "Then there will be answers to the next three levels of love. The world needs these levels too."

Will laughed. "Well, it's you who mainly need them. Not us."

Peter said to him: "Maybe you'll be surprised. Maybe the answers will apply to you as well."

"I'm satisfied with my beauties. I'm glad I don't have to make such unusual things."

Andy patted his shoulder: "Well, be careful what you say. The Law of Attraction works. Do you remember Octoberfest and how you attracted the grannies?"

Will teased Rick: "How about you? Have you also attracted a nurse who makes such stupid things in her spare time?"

Rick approved: "Not only in her spare time. All the time I'm afraid."

Peter asked him: "Are you sure the answers are worth it?"

Rick was silent for a moment, then said: "I don't know. But I'm going to risk it."

Peter picked up: "Why?"

"Maybe anything that is at least somewhat related to any level of love is worth the risk. Look, we were even praised for how we've been cleaning up the whole nursing house. Would it ever happen? In our movies, most of the time people die suddenly as a result of various big disasters. In here people die slowly, and the catastrophes are happening daily. This is happening all over the world. Why we are fighting those disasters, big or small?"

Andy replied: "Probably because of the higher level of love?"

Will was quiet. Heroes on the screen could sacrifice themselves for the sake of the world at any time. Ordinary people who go to normal work admire them and try to mimic some of their characteristics. They use them in their daily life while saving the world. With tiny, small deeds of love. Then they remembered that when there was a real catastrophe in the world, whether war or earthquake; there were always human beings who went without hesitation to help. Why then in recent times, it seemed that love was diminishing?

The guys continued to work for a few hours in the afternoon and Rick was with me as a trainee-nurse. When he found out Tim was on duty with me in the afternoon, he asked me before the service ended.

"What if I stayed until the evening?"

"Don't you have enough?"

"No. I have nothing else to do anyway."

"Okay, you'll help Tim with preparing the dinner. I guess you know how to spread butter on bread."

"Of course, I know. I can do other things as well. I mean not only in the kitchen."

"I'm glad. If you wash your granny, there will be answers. We'll need it."

"What?"

"You will see."

I went down to the kitchen for the dinner. I've put all the plastic containers in the kitchen and opened them. Tim laughed as I pulled a large piece of strangely curved salami out of one of them. It was served regularly, and the patients liked it. I was laughing as I held it in my hand as I always did when we were preparing dinner from this strange piece of salami.

This time I said it in English: "Look, Tim. We have a girl's dream again. It's just a little bit big." Tim laughed heartily. He knew my sense of humor and my statements.

"Are you serious?" asked Rick with a surprised look on his face.

"For god's sake! That was a joke! Can't you see how it looks like? That's what we say in Slovakia."

"What? What you say?"

"Did you know that Slovaks, that small nation in the center of Europe, are hedonists? I already told you how they like to eat. In Slavic mythology, unlike in the Greek one, every god and goddess are considered, in addition to their main area of power, gods of sex and passion."

"You said it didn't matter, that only names are different."

"Yes. Names, but some mythology stories are often different." Tim understood what we were talking about and smiled quietly.

I told Tim in German: "Explain to him what to do. I'm going to get the medicaments and drops."

So, Tim explained to Rick what to do and they prepared the dinner. The guys were in the kitchen and I was happy that since my education was accepted in Germany, I could at least sometimes escape from the kitchen to the medicament's cabinet.

I was just about to leave when Rick came to the staff room. He sat down on the bench: "Do you have something for me there? For example, something special?"

"You men don't need anything special. You need a filled testosterone code. There's no love tablet. Nor against love. Luckily."

Rick asked: "Why? The blue one exists."

"It's not for love."

Rick attacked with his male weapons again. "But it's one of the levels of love, isn't it?"

"Many men just want friendship with benefits. Later when they fall in love, sometimes it's too late."

"What do you mean?"

"The right moment. I know a story of such a friendship. A woman loved a man and was waiting for him to fall in love with her. One day she gave up and left the fight. He lost her. He knew he loved her. He even bought a ring for her. She already loved another man. He lost her again. Forever. His love and emotions came too late. I have heard many stories of such friendships. With benefits. Some women were in love with them. From the beginning."

Rick defended himself: "You can't blame us. We are created this way."

"You are. I mean, sometimes people are hurting themselves with those friendships with benefits. Men as well, they just don't want to say it."

"Are you sure?"

"Yes. You have hearts too. You don't open them often though. We women almost always do. I still believe my sister is wrong. She says men are like drones. When they do their job, they need to be thrown out of the hive. I'm a naive romantic and I believe that men deserve our love."

Rick laughed. "Thrown out of the hive? And who would take care of you then? How about you? If there was such a tablet or some love drink, would you give it to me secretly?"

"No. Such love would be fake. There is no love drink. In our reality. I'm fighting with other weapons."

Rick confirmed: "Yeah, I've already found out. Washing grannies, spilling dangerous words. Earthly Olympus, gods. My head is really burning."

"More difficult things will come. Not just words."

"Well, now I'm curious."

"The granny first. Mrs. K told me once she wanted to be touched by a handsome guy before she dies. Will you fulfill her dream?"

His eyes widened. "Dream? Isn't that your dream as well?"

"I've been alone in all levels of love for some time now. It's possible."

"You can't be serious."

"I am. Nobody can make you happy unless you are happy with yourself. I've spent half of my life alone. It's difficult to love yourself. With all the mistakes, with an imperfect body, imperfect heart. It's a tough fight. Sometimes it doesn't work, and the human is sad and afraid."

Rick was silent, not knowing what to say. Yes, we all furiously want to be perfect on the outside. How many of us practice and strengthen our hearts and souls, not just the body? We have anti-wrinkle creams for the body, but we can't heal the wrinkles and scars of the heart. We don't know how. Is it even possible to heal those scars that harden with time until they are so hard that we can't open our hearts again? Some men with crooked hearts often don't give women a choice. Because of their own frustration and lack of love, they hurt them. Then a woman must run away to save herself and her children. Sometimes it is the other way around. They say one should not think of negative things so we don't attract them. It isn't always possible, because there was always polarity in the world and the free will of human beings. As it was impossible to make someone to love, it was impossible to make someone to hate.

I interrupted the silence: "We're going to give out dinner."

We came to the kitchen, Tim went to feed the lying patients, and I stayed in the kitchen. This time I had Rick, the trainee nurse, with me. He observed us while working and was surprised at how much work just two people had to accomplish. He didn't have an idea how much more when something went wrong with a patient and we had to call a doctor or send him to the hospital. Tim returned from one of the rooms where two patients were lying and told me: "Mrs. G is not looking good."

"You stay here I'll go to see her. Did you give her painkillers?"

"No. I just moisturized her lips."

I went quickly to her room. She was pale and hardly breathing. I went back. "It won't take too much longer. Finally, after many years of suffering, her time has come."

Yes. In these cases, it meant *finally*. These people lived their lives with love and without love, and it was time for their soul to return to where it belongs. After dinner, Rick collected dishes with us, and then we began to put the patients in beds. I took one of the old ladies back to her room to feed her, she couldn't eat alone anymore, the poor thing. After that, I took her to the bathroom to clean her. Rick sat on the shower stool to see what I was doing, and suddenly the old lady was afraid. "Are you going to sleep with me today?"

"Why? Are you afraid? Being alone in the room?" I was surprised.

"Yes. I'm afraid that the devil will come."

I was shocked. Rick tried to capture what we were talking about. I was wondering what to say to her.

"The devil does not exist. Only God."

The patient, who was lost in time and space, continued seriously: "He exists, believe me. I saw him. He has a beautiful face."

For a moment my heart stopped. Yes. People with dementia speak nonsense sometimes. Still, I was afraid. I was comforting her. "If there is a devil, then there must be God. He gave you a guardian angel to protect you from the devil."

"I was very bad."

The patient sunk her eyes. "No person is completely bad or completely good. We are all learning."

I objected and put her in bed. Rick asked with interest: "What have you been discussing so much?"

"She said she was afraid of the devil with a beautiful face."

Rick looked at me: "So, it's not a being with hooves, horns, and tails?"

"Not according to her. This idea of how the devil looks like people took from pagan Baphomet. Oh, let's not talk about it. I don't like to speak about the other side."

"So, not only Apollo is beautiful? Even the devil?"

I was confused. "I don't know. I didn't see any of them."

Rick smiled at me. "What if the devil looks the same as Apollo?"

"Be quiet. He doesn't."

"You said you didn't see them."

"Listen, you Apollo, the dishwasher is whistling. Can you go and do another good deed?"

"Yes, boss!" I was desperate. I didn't know how to defend myself. Although Apollo wasn't here the situation was worst. A living man who, in my opinion, resembled him was here. I had to resist him in order not to mess things up. Is it even possible not to? How? There are no problems with the paper picture. Although we, naive and romantic fans, think our idols from Earth's Olympus are perfect, it was not true. They also have to battle with mistakes, fears, and all sorts of things. We finished work and Rick sat on the chair near us in the staff room.

I sent Tim home and told Rick: "You can go now. You have enough for today. You have a tough fight tomorrow."

"Do you think I can't do that?"

"You can. I'm afraid of what's coming after."

"Why? Because of your boxes?"

I continued: "It's my fault. I should have been silent and just smiled. It's more than enough for the lower levels of love, isn't it?"

"That's not true! You made me wash an old woman!"

"Me? You decided so. That's your choice."

"You didn't give me another choice."

"There are always two possibilities. Fear or love."

"Yeah… The highest level of love. What about tonight?"

"Nothing. You need to rest. Today, no date at the Rabbit."

"So, it's a date now? That means you got a little lower."

"Shut up. I'm still in higher levels of love and you're still pretty low. We have to meet at the right time. Somewhere in the middle."

"Can't we meet down? What about the dark box? I already know your Pandora's box."

"You're wrong. You haven't seen anything from Pandora's box in my head yet. Go to sleep. Good night."

"How can I sleep after all this."

"That is not my problem. See? You're still at the bottom."

"When will you come down?"

"When will you come up."

"You said I was very high."

"You are high according to your career."

"Sure. According to my career, I look like Apollo, whom you haven't seen, or a savior."

"Go! Please. I can't concentrate. I don't want to make mistakes again."

"What are you going to do tonight? Alone?"

"Dance."

"Can I watch? Could you show me shimmy?"

"No, you can't. It's not the right time. Man must deserve it. There are millions of professional belly dancers on YouTube. There you can see shimmy."

"I'd like to see the splashy, curvy Bunny dancing."

"I'm just an amateur. I told you we're just pretending to be dancers and actors."

"When will I see it?"

"You have to create the right circumstances for the answers."

"And for the shimmy too?"

"I don't know. Shimmy is dangerous. Good night."

Rick was already leaving when he remembered the entertainment room. There the grannies had activities with the assistants during the day. In the evening splashy Bunny hid there to dance away the sugar and the stress. But she won't let him. He opened the door of the room. It was dark. The floor was perfect for dancing and was big, which was a paradise for Bunny because she could use the dance props that needed a lot of space. Rick looked at the coffee shop, which was next door. A makeshift wall separated the coffee shop from the hallway. He sat down at the table in the corner. He couldn't be seen. He was waiting for Bunny. Suddenly she came out of the elevator and hurried to her paradise. Nobody disturbed her there and she could be whomever she wanted to be.

I entered the room and with great difficulty, I did the dancing routine. It was even harder after so many hours of work. I stopped for a moment and put on my dancing props, the wings. Then I just sat on the floor wrapped in the wings and I was sad. I didn't know what to do. I really opened my Pandora's Box and brought the other one, the dark box, into great danger. Men were strange beings. I always believed they were full of love and goodness. I couldn't understand why they think and act in love in a completely different way than women do. How do I prevent damage? Damage. I got up from the floor and decided to finish the last piece of choreography. I was weak from ever worse shifts, so it wasn't easy for me.

Rick sat in the coffee shop and heard the music. He came to one of the doors and thought that because of the loud music Bunny would not hear him opening them. He quietly opened them only a little bit, because he didn't want to disturb her. He waited to see the shimmy. Instead, he saw only Bunny with wings. She only wore a training costume. She danced the same piece of choreography all over again. Every time adding more small steps to it. It was painstaking work. Her dancers often couldn't imagine how difficult it was to create a choreography with wings for such a strange, fantasy music. When she danced, she was completely detached from the real world. She really felt like she was up somewhere between her Olympus gods, angels, and fairies. The music sounded like that. She, an inconspicuous, ordinary nurse just pretended to be a dancer. The dance was not just about perfect, flawless performance with perfect-looking professionals. It was also about emotions. Bunny thought about it all in the long hours of loneliness. Most people in the world don't have the opportunity to develop their talent due to circumstances. So, they remained only amateurs, but it was very important. These were the moments when they returned to their childhood dreams. When they made themselves happy even though on the amateur level. They did it for joy. They knew that the human world allowed only a small percentage of people to fulfill their dreams at the highest level. Only the exceptionally gifted managed to reach the Earthly Olympus. The rules were regularly changed to make it increasingly difficult. Only a small percentage of very talented human beings managed to walk the path to the top. Even that small percentage paid often too high a price for that noble and magical reality. Few of us wanted to see the other side of professional life. These people worked really hard and many times went beyond their physical and psychological limits. Because in all these realities it was no longer just about the joy. It was about success and millions. About prestige and fame. We, ordinary people, were envious of them. Only occasionally did we get some information about anorexia and bulimia problems that ballet dancers, models, and actresses had. Because if they didn't look like a skinny doll, they had no chance in that shiny world. No matter how hard the doctors tried to warn them. Without hesitation, every model says she loves vegetables and a healthy diet. Sure, vegetables are healthy. Therefore, at times, these beautiful women gained weight and lost it again. Just to give themselves and their bodies a bit of pleasure although just for a short period of time. Out of love to themselves. This was love too. And men? They had to work out really hard just to look like Olympus gods. This way humankind fought for success and perfection. Out of love. Out of love for what? For our bodies? Because loving a perfect flawless body was easy? For the love of glitter, that time has ruthlessly turned into dust anyway? All that could be fine. The exercise, the healthy diet. We need to exercise and take care of ourselves.

We need to eat healthy. Mankind has lost the balance in all areas. Sometimes we torture ourselves with diets or with overeating. With food, we actually mitigate the pain of our souls. As if we were afraid to admit and realize that not all that is modern is the best for human beings.

Both Bunny's grannies, her sister and her mother-in-law, were excellent cooks and they always said, "Fed guy is a good guy." She learned a lot from them. Bunny understood that when she started her project Aphrodite's Balance and began to learn herself. Then, at an amateur level, she passed her knowledge to dancers of different ages. From little girls to 50-year-old women. She was just an amateur, so her little girls didn't have to perform flawlessly. She wanted them to be pleased when they learned something, and they turned into little fairies for a while. Bunny realized that even ordinary women, mothers, troubled because of their imperfect bodies, needed moments to transfer themselves to another reality. To turn into dancing goddesses. Although they won't be ballerinas anymore they can dance anyway. Of course, professional ballet dancers couldn't weigh much because of the lifts, balance, and dancing on their toes. That would be impossible with imperfect weight. In fact, nothing in life could be reached without sacrifices. Nothing but hard work was behind a few moments of luck and success. Hard work filled with tears. Dancing on the toes wasn't possible with overweight.

Bunny thought of all of this when she floated with the wings and didn't know she wasn't alone. Immersed in her thoughts at these moments she didn't need anyone. She had herself. She knew her role was to give a chance to dance and play theater to those who weren't gifted with such extraordinary talent that would be enough to take them to the higher spheres of art. She never refused anyone and along with her friend Barbs, tried to give a chance to everyone. Together with all the members, they created a rare living cell that lived mainly for the love of dance and theater. The money wasn't much but it was enough to survive. However, there were many rare invisible gifts in that group. Gifts that had been feeding it for years. Love. Friendship. Enthusiasm. Joy. Dedication. Bunny was often desperate when, due to lack of time, mistakes happened during the performance and sometimes something went wrong. However, Barbs comforted her: "What did you expect? We are amateurs. Mistakes always happen."

Bunny remembered some of these mistakes. During one performance, they danced with fire fans and somehow almost burned down the hotel. Fortunately,

Barb's husband was there, and he took the fans and soaked them into the snow. Once one of the dancer's scarf got on fire. The scarf was around her ass, and the morons in the audience started to shout: "Look, fire show! Fire show!" Those fools thought that the fire on the ass of a beautiful young dancer was deliberate. To enhance the effect of the shimmy movements. Bunny, who was already married, had no illusions about how men think. Desperate and very scared she knew why those men were screaming. She saw that one of her best dancers was really burning. They quickly quenched the flame on her ass and men were ecstatic. Even Bunny was ecstatic but in a different sense. Since then, whenever somebody booked the group and asked for a fire show she was afraid. The real fire burned. In addition, those screaming guys were burning as well. Not only due to the real fire on the ass of the dancer. There was also a fire in the lower parts of their bodies, a bit of alcohol, and they acted like wild animals. Then she understood why men, husbands, and partners were jealous of their partners and wives – belly dancers. She sighed and was almost crying. The guys didn't care about any choreographies. The important thing was that everything was shaking and waiving. Choreography? What for? She wanted to quit belly dancing. She never had a partner for a pair dance. Most of the guys already had their partners. Others probably didn't have the courage. Regular guy when asked to dance rather hides under the table. Bunny had no other choice but to continue with solo dancing and to teach choreography that no one really needed in this kind of dance. After that, all the young male dancers and actors left the group. They went to study. Except Bunny's son and the main actor. That is when the strong mother's personalities set the direction for the group and matriarchy prevailed. He adapted himself to the matriarchy. He liked them and they liked him.

Then Rick closed the door quietly. He saw Bunny in a different light this time. Here she wasn't the commander-general like at work or in the dancing group. She was a fragile, vulnerable woman who, at times, needed help and protection herself. All people around her expected help and protection from her. For many years, she had to manage everything by herself. All her life she served other people in the most humble way. In all areas of her life. After some time, her younger son decided to join her group. Therefore, Bunny often had to fight a rebellious teenager who often didn't want to rehearse. At the end of the day, he obeyed her. She didn't want to give up on him. Even more, because he was her child that she loved above all.

Chapter 8

Rick got home; Andy welcomed him with a remark: "That was a long shift. You were at the Rabbit again?"

Rick was nervous. "You're curious like an old aunt at the market."

"We just want to know how you progressed. Ah, I see, you didn't. Unless you wash your old lady, you don't have a chance, do you?"

Peter asked: "Why don't you guys talk about something else? Why are you interested in an ordinary nurse, hmm? Will, you said you were happy with your uncomplicated females."

Rick replied indifferently: "Leave them. If that makes them happy. I don't mind the idea of washing an old woman. I wanted to try it anyway."

The guys burst into laughter. Will continued to tease him: "Certainly! Every young guy burns with eagerness to wash one old, shabby, grandma, and grandpa. Do you think we believe you? You have no choice! She pushed you into the corner. So far she's winning."

Rick was upset, but he didn't show that. "Stop talking nonsense. If you are such a macho, then try it yourself."

"No thank you very much. My females don't have such crap requests."

Peter confirmed: "No. I guess not. They're okay with the good old methods of conquering women. To stun them with gifts and sweet words. Who knows what else."

At that time, Rick realized that love couldn't be bought. There will be never enough gifts. It will always be necessary to buy new ones. One deed never disappears. It's an invisible gift that's worth the price of a necklace with emeralds and pearls.

He only said: "Just shut up. Once you will be able to do it yourself then you can talk."

"I just don't want you to be disappointed. You're used to a different level of women, aren't you?"

Rick wasn't provoked and spoke quietly: "Does that mean we are better? Look where we ended up! At the lower level. Although for a short time. Does the fact that we are famous means that we belong to a higher level? And the others to the lower one?"

Peter watched Rick's blood rage. This was human pride, priggishness talking. The truth was that all those who had millions in their bank accounts belonged to the higher level. Because their account enabled them to live the luxurious life of celebrities. Occasionally, celebrities realize that without their fans from those lower levels, they wouldn't have their millions. They needed them. The fans needed their celebrities to be able to secretly adore someone.

Peter interrupted their teasing game: "Hey, guys! Please stop arguing! None of us will change the world order or its rules."

They went quiet and Rick left for his room. Peter wasn't sure if he was supposed to follow him. He didn't want to upset him more than he already was. Moreover, he didn't know what was going on inside of him. The whole situation was more than complicated. Bunny was really inconspicuous until she opened her mouth. That was her strongest weapon. Except with Rick, this weapon was imperfect because of the language barrier. However, he saw her deeds. Besides, today he saw her again in a different way. A woman who was pretending to be a dancer. Peter finally decided and followed him to the room.

"Forget about them. Look you'll survive it somehow. I mean washing the old woman."

Rick said thoughtfully: "Do you think I'm afraid of that?"

"Aren't you?"

"No, I'm not. Surprised? I'm beginning to worry about her answers. I saw her dancing."

"Where?"

"In that entertainment room. She didn't see me. She didn't even hear the door open. She was in another world."

Peter laughed. "Perhaps she is using the dance as a travel channel to the Olympus gods, saviors and I don't know who else."

"Exactly that's it. I'm afraid of that."

"Why? Do you think she wants to hurt you?"

"She doesn't. Maybe those answers can hurt us."

"Sometimes you must sacrifice if you want something. You can still call it off. No one is forcing you."

"Well, after today's amateur dance, I'm wondering what Bunny will come up with."

"Do you really want them?"

"Which guy wouldn't want them?"

Peter thoughtfully answered: "A coward? Someone who is afraid of…"

"Of what?"

"Risks?"

"It's not possible to live without taking risks. We risk our whole life."

"She is a little older than you. She has children…"

"Is that a problem?"

"I don't know. You must know."

"She already told me that men are young and beautiful much longer. Is that what you mean? Anyway, I have no idea what's coming. I'm not going to deal with the issues ahead. What for? Even so, everything will turn out differently than we plan."

"Yes…and we have to use plans B. Even our sentence in this nursing house wasn't planned."

"It wasn't. We got to know a higher level of love up close and personal."

Rick told to Peter: "I have a headache from those experiences. Really. You won't believe what one demented grandma said today. The devil has a beautiful face."

"Really? That's crazy!"

"She has dementia, you moron. Tina said they all live in other realities, not in the present one. You can't blame her. She hallucinates."

Peter contemplated: "It's good that modern medicine can justify such statements. Hallucinations. Let's go to sleep. Tomorrow unusual fight awaits you."

"Fight? With a grandma?"

"No. With pride. Even if you're a very good guy, a piece of pride is in each of us. In everyone."

The guys went to sleep. I went to sleep in my little room too. While sleeping, the souls of sleeping people separate from their physical body. They are transferred to a beautiful land where the dreams of every human being are fulfilled. However, in the morning, they can't remember. According to scientists, dreams were just reflections of the experiences of the previous day. Mostly we didn't remember our dreams when we woke up in the morning.

Maybe in one of the dreams, one of the patients saw a devil with a beautiful face. No one knew for sure, whether hell existed. Because information about hell has often originated either from human imagination or the vision of different human beings. It has been described in various religions as the opposite of heaven. And it was allegedly the devil, who at any cost tried to take over the earth. Or had he already? Nobody knew for sure. Nobody had evidence of his existence.

Devil with a beautiful face was now sitting on his golden throne. He was celebrating his little victories because more and more real and invisible waste and dirt were accumulated on Earth. Facing him was his most faithful servant Fear. He stared at the beautiful creature with cold eyes: "So far everything is going very well, my lord. Human beings are slowly but surely losing faith. Even in themselves. That's good for us."

Devil smiled coldly. "Losing faith in whom? In the one who is up there? Or in me?"

"In both, my lord. In both. The fact that people don't believe in your existence is amazing. It allows us to sow fear in their hearts more easily. Instead of faith, we put fear. Out of fear, people start to take wrong decisions after a while. The wrong and cowardly decisions make them unhappy. They don't have the courage to change something in their lives. They are like stupid sheep, who are really easy to control nowadays."

Devil said dryly: "Do you mean with technology?"

Fear continued: "With some technologies. For human greed and lust, over time they will use every new technology against each other. Those morons are using even social networks against each other. They scold and slander each other there more than they praise each other or confess their love."

Devil objected: "They still say beautiful words. They send each other hearts and likes instead of meeting in person. They hide behind those words. Moreover, they are splitting and getting back together over mobile phones and social networks. Some are connected there for 24 hours and they live other people's lives. They think they're happier this way."

Fear agreed: "That was the purpose of it! It encourages them to have more grudge against each other and to envy each other even more. Instead of detaching for a moment and starting to look again for the way back to themselves and then to the other people, they envy their lives. We couldn't come up with a better weapon! They're all connected and at the same time divided by an unattainable wall."

Devil continued: "They're no longer talking to each other. They write words without emotions behind them."

Fear laughed. "Oh, there are emotions believe me! They attach pictures to the words. It's amazing, amazing. Something that was originally created to connect humanity turned into the world's worst mass weapon because of the unjust system on that poor planet full of stupid, priggish people. Because human beings have destructive tendencies. They would rather hurt each other than praise each other. After some time, admiration changes to envy. Love to hate. They can't cope with their own pride, arrogance, and longing for power. They will forget that ruling others means to help others. Those social networks often help them in all that. That's great for us."

Devil paused for a moment.

"... That doesn't apply to everyone. There are still a lot of people on Earth who use this powerful weapon for good purposes. That's not so amazing. Do you have information on what it looks like on their Fields of Pearls? Did they manage to gather enough light from their miserable deeds of good, which have been so drastically diminishing?"

Fear replied: "Apparently, the situation has never been as bad throughout the history of mankind as it is today. We have never been as close to the goal as we are now. In fact, in the poorest areas of Earth, human worms multiply without thinking, like mice. They're waiting for somebody to rescue them. They don't care about the state of their beautiful, blue planet and its situation when they leave it to their offspring. Some struggle for survival and they're frustrated. Those who are well off and are helping the poor are frustrated as well. For they cannot save them all. What can be better for fear than their imperfect system of functioning? They are constantly worried about their miserable lives."

"Don't get so excited yet. You know that those up there have never given up on humanity. Maybe they have some backup plan B."

Fear objected: "They don't! Even Zeus is as desperate as he has not been ever before! Angel of compassion, I won't say peak his name, begged the guardian angels to speak and whisper in their hearts. But those weak human worms have lost faith in the most important thing. That they are made of love!"

Devil shouted angrily: "For the second time, you have mentioned the word *love*!!! I am sick of it. Finally, when we thought we were winning it crossed our plans!!! So, it won't be mentioned here!"

"Excuse me for my temerity, my lord, but we need to know thoroughly what kind of weapon our enemy is using."

"You don't have to bother yourself with that. I know it more than well. Even its dark side. The hate. Now go to work! You've got a lot to do. There are still enough of those open-hearted, merciful fools in the world, and that doesn't suit us. They need to be destroyed. Especially those need to be destroyed!"

Fear said uncertainly: "There is faith in their hearts. That's why they are open. They can tolerate any kind of pain. That makes them stronger. They get up from the ground over and over again and don't give up."

Devil started screaming furiously: "What the hell! Destroy their damn faith! They will believe in nothing; do you understand? Nothing! Not even in that one up there. Not even in faith. Not in hope. And especially not in love! Not in gratitude. Not in me. Let them keep thinking that nothing else exists. Only they themselves, the proudest beings in the vast universe! You have to build on their pride!"

Fear contemplated: "You have said the word *love*, my lord. I'm still trying to build on their pride. Those human worms carry a little of Him inside. Faith, hope, love, gratitude, compassion, forgiveness. These are His gifts. He encoded them in every human being and they still don't get it. Luckily. They don't know that. He loves them the way they are. Even with their mistakes. He is not punishing but loving. When they understand that, we'll be finished! Because they won't be afraid of Him anymore. They will try to approach Him through their small acts of goodness. For they will no longer fear Him. Though they will sometimes feel pain in their imperfect lives, faith will help them to believe that there are good things in the world. Some religions have made Him a being to be feared from. He doesn't punish. People are punishing themselves. Because these fools don't understand that, if He wanted to enforce their love with punishment, He would not give them free will. He's waiting for them to come back to Him. He doesn't forbid. It's up to people to decide. Whether for fear or for…you don't want me to say that word. His…hmm… I shouldn't say the word, complicates our intentions."

Devil said more quietly: "Fortunately, not everyone believes in Him. Luckily, some who believe in Him will sometimes blame Him when they are unhappy. That's good. Let them blame Him. The pain also plays in our favor. They're weak. They don't know how to endure pain. Any kind of pain."

Fear explained: "Pain, disease, and death are part of their lives. They can't destroy them yet. Sometimes pain lifts them to higher levels. Sometimes."

"Shut up! If there is too much pain, your work will be easier. So, try harder! Gifts from Him must be destroyed. Faith. Hope. Love. Gratitude. Compassion. Forgiveness. If this will be successful nothing will remain. Only that pain."

Fear was uncertain. "Your servants are working the best they can. As you see, they're doing pretty well."

Devil was displeased. "What does *best* mean? If only pain remains on Earth, then it will be good for us. So far, it's not like that. So, try harder! Let them constantly doubt each other, let them live in fear. Fear for their life. For their work. For everything. Fear destroys faith. Show them that the fear is real and destroy them! All of them!"

Fear knew that the gifts of the Creator could never be destroyed, and fear would not be sown in all hearts. The polarity had to be preserved for the time being. Devil didn't like that. Half of the planet was not enough for him. He wanted everything.

The next morning, I had a morning shift, which wasn't often due to the number of hours I had to work. We started with the morning washing and when the handsome cleaners came to work, I gave them their tasks. They tried not to make any more stupid remarks about Rick and his determination to wash a granny and a grandpa. The coincidence probably wanted it, as he said, to be finished. Man and woman. A couple, who no longer had beautiful bodies and unfortunately, their mind, was no longer working properly as well. Rick followed me. We took all the needed tools and entered the room. Mrs. K welcomed us with enthusiasm, and she was certainly anxious to see her dream come true. Rick was somewhat pale but determined to fulfill the unusual task given to him by the stubborn, splashy Bunny.

I started: "I'll do the talking. You will work."

Rick noted: "It's starting pretty well."

I smiled at him. "Don't worry. You'll be the boss in your reality."

"What do you mean?"

"Now let's start to work. We will talk later."

First, I washed the worst part of Mrs. K's body. The private parts. In her own bed. Rick sat on a chair and just watched me from a distance. I didn't want to imagine what he was thinking. I told him he can wait outside but he decided to stay. Maybe he just didn't want to look like a coward. When I put on her the netted, white panties, whose only task, unfortunately, was to hold the diaper well, Rick asked with a smile: "No whole today?"

I laughed. "You mean *Schnellfickerhosen?* No. Today they are without a hole. Common, help me put her in the wheelchair."

Mrs. K was smiling at Rick and she would look at him and then at me. Then we took her to the bathroom and placed her on the shower stool. I ordered him: "First, disinfect the sink."

Rick waited for the disinfectant solution to dry. I continued: "Open the water and soak the face washcloth under the running water. Give it to her. She can clean her face alone."

Rick waited until Mrs. K handed him the washcloth. Then the difficult part came. I told him: "You have to take off her nightgown."

Rick smiled at Mrs. K and she encouraged him with her wide smile. Rick took off her nightgown whose role was to cover the body at night. Any erotic role of such a piece of cloth would be useless.

Rick looked at Mrs. K's huge breasts and suddenly as if she could read his thoughts she sang in German: "They're real. Not fake."

I pointed at her shoulders. "Start with her hands."

Rick washed her hands. He dried them and started to wash her upper body. As he found out, it wasn't that easy. Mrs. K was a beast and had him struggle for a while. She watched how he struggled with her big breasts in order to wash the skin beneath them. I tried to look serious. Finally, Mrs. K felt sorry for him and said in German: "See Martina? These are typical guys. They do everything with brute force. Sometimes all they need to do is involve reason. Or humbly ask a woman for help."

Rick didn't understand, so I just told him: "Mrs. K says you can ask her for help."

Rick didn't speak German, he put his hands together as if he was praying. She immediately understood and with a smile, she lifted her big breasts. Rick looked at me and I shrugged my shoulders. "Sometimes we have to improvise. Use plan B." Rick dried Mrs. K's upper body and then washed and dried her back.

"Now take the body lotion and apply it to all her body."

Rick obediently did that. When he came back to the skin beneath her breasts, he reconnected his hands as if praying again and looked at Mrs. K. Once again, she helped him by lifting her breasts. Rick was glad he finished half of her body. He quickly dressed her upper part. I warned him: "Now wash her legs. Be gentle. They hurt her."

Rick washed Mrs. K's legs and thighs, which were much rounder than the thighs of the splashy Bunny. He rubbed them with body lotion. When she was done, we dressed her and placed her in the wheelchair. She smiled at her personal nurse and said with humor: "So, Tina. Now I'm ready to die."

I translated it to Rick and he just stroked her hands and smiled at her. He gave a rare touch to a woman who no longer looked like a movie star. It was a touch of higher levels of love. It was an act of love as well and therefore it was also saving the world. We walked out of the room, sorted the used stuff, and I said: "Now we're going to Mr. D."

I pushed the trolley to Mr. D's room. As we entered the room, Rick's face paled and he twisted his nose.

I ordered him: "Stay outside until I do the job."

The bathroom looked like in a horror movie. Tiles, toilet, everything was dirty from...you know what. In the toilet, the...you know what...was floating. Rick was still standing near the bathroom and I asked him: "Why are you still here? Where is your mask?"

"That will help me shit. But I can stand it."

"Your face is green. Open the window. Why do you want to be here?"

"I want to see it."

"What the hell do you want to see? You never saw a shit on the wall?"

"I want to see how you clean it."

"Okay, it's up to you. When you get sick, here's a bowl. Unfortunately, the toilet is currently out of service."

Rick's color improved only a little bit after the window was opened.

"I don't understand why you're not going out. There's really nothing nice about this kind of cleaning."

Rick took a deep breath: "There is. The result."

I was taken aback.

He then watched from a distance as I cleaned the mess with disinfectant wipes. In the nursing house, we were grateful for the modern hygienic aids.

This is one of the cases where modern technologies are used for a good cause. When I imagined such patients in the Middle Ages, I was sick. I was on my knees and couldn't understand why Rick was so harsh on himself and didn't leave. Watching this scene for men was worse than fighting in a battle. My older son often said he couldn't do this job because he wouldn't stand it. While cleaning, I was thinking that positive thinking and feeling do not give a universal recipe for how the world should function properly. Well, if I wanted to run such a nursing house, I would like to be a few levels higher. However, to do every day work, to keep those defenseless human beings clean and fed, I would need ordinary people, employees who would do the job for me. It occurred to me that hard-working guys, other admirable heroes, were sometimes freezing on construction sites. Doctors, soldiers, and, indeed, all human beings with their ordinary jobs also contribute to the functioning of the world. In every company, in every supermarket, in every hospital, ordinary, normal people who are not called celebrities created values because they lived their ordinary life, which is probably not worthy of a celebration. In each job, there is always a boss who manages these employees to avoid chaos. Yes, there was plenty of everything in the Universe and Earth. Surely, there was. We must finally take responsibility for it and for the future. We need to start changing the system from the ground up. We must start with ourselves. One particular deed of love is enough. One. Fortunately, some people are already doing it, but they feel it is Sisyphus' work. They only do what is most necessary. Positive thinking and feeling somehow do not help globally. We have failed to solve the real, big problems of our world. For example, in monasteries and churches, the troubled grannies and nuns are praying for the salvation of the world. They too have realized that something on our planet has not worked well for years. With their prayers and with their faith they are trying to save our world on the spiritual level. The only thing left for us, ordinary people, is the belief that there are still honest and good businesspersons, managers, directors, and politicians whose rule is based on serving people. That they are trying to create for the not-celebrities decent work conditions and give them decent wages. With love. Because the not-celebrities' only desire is to live in dignity and without fear. However, this belief is probably false. In fact, all over the world, the not-celebrities are in constant rebellion because their living conditions are not that good. Creating a business is fine. However, we always need ordinary people to put every business in motion. Designers wouldn't do much without a tailor. The doctor relies on a nurse to perform his or her tasks. The director gives orders to the actors. Almost everyone on the planet always has a boss. Every business is a living cell where employees need each other. Yet, in many cases, those who rule don't appreciate us, the ordinary people, the not-celebrities. Why? Because money is missing everywhere. Well, this is our human imperfect system that we can't handle. Therefore, at that moment one handsome celebrity watched me, the not-celebrity, as I was scrubbing and removing the consequences of the fact that Mr. D went to the toilet by himself. When I finished, I took a large green bowl that we used for watering flowers. Sometimes I was forced to get rid of the floating you know what with this bowl. Especially when the flushing facility in the toilets wasn't working properly. Rick watched with astonishment as I poured hot water into the big green bowl and tried to remove the floating something that remained in the toilet. Rick couldn't stand it anymore and started laughing: "What are you doing?"

"It's easier this way. It's not the first time."

Rick continued laughing. "This is how you fight...with...shi...?"

"Don't laugh! You fight with fictional monsters. You have your weapons. I have to fight with shit. I have mine. They work. See?"

Rick stopped laughing for a moment, though it was very difficult because maybe it was the first time that he saw a nurse fighting shit with a bowl used for watering flowers. This nurse wasn't watering flowers but something else.

"How can you do that?"

I looked at him while I was disinfecting my hands and asked: "How can you do your job? You must occasionally do things that you don't like as well. I think. Same as us, down here."

"What you mean *down here*?"

"We, ordinary employees that no one celebrates."

Then Rick contemplated. Every person on the planet should occasionally be celebrated, even if he or she doesn't have millions in the account. Because we all really need each other.

"What do you mean? Don't celebrate?" I laughed.

"The whole world knows about your work. I'm stressed out because of a dirty bathroom, but nobody knows about my bathroom. You have stress because of fans and critics. You, the actors must be in public. Otherwise, we wouldn't go to the movies. Some of us even more than once. Fame must be also stressful. I think."

"Yes, it is …big time."

"But you're still happy at work. I think."

Rick agreed: "I'm, but everything has its negative side."

"What about you? Are you happy at work?"

I replied sophisticatedly with the toilet brush in my hand: "Even my job has a negative side. I'm actually a pediatric nurse. I wanted to work in a neonatal department. As you can see, I do work in the neonatal department, but the one that starts from the other end."

Rick burst into laughter and then he asked: "Have you worked with kids before?"

"Long time ago. In the ophthalmology department. We've been playing for days. I organized entertainment for them. The head nurse didn't like me because of that. My head is full of nonsense. We played theater, we danced. Everything. Sometimes at night. I had to go to another country. Because of the money."

"Tell me more."

"Better not. It's not the right time."

"So now I'll wash Mr. D's private parts and you wait in the room."

"I've seen it before."

"Once is enough. Or do you want to do that? Then I'll wait in the room."

Rick reluctantly went into the room waiting for me to call him. He then under my guidance washed the other human being. A man. As he said; now it has been finished. A couple of human beings who were grateful for another kind of touch. For the touch of a higher level of love.

"We still have to shave him."

"Does he have a razor?" Rick asked.

"No. Just a terrible, cheap, dangerous razor blade. I'll do it. You have to be very careful."

Rick watched as I shaved the grandpa, put on his slippers, and told him: "So, Mr. D you can go for breakfast." Mr. D went out with the rollator to the dining room and we sorted things up again.

"You have completed a very difficult task." Rick smiled triumphantly.

"Now it's your turn. Now the answers. All of them."

"All of them? I don't know. It depends on the spark."

"How do you know it's not burning already?"

"I don't know. We must be patient. The result is uncertain."

"When will you answer me?"

"I will explain everything to you at the Rabbit tonight. Now you have to decide whether you'll go back to cleaning the cabinets or you'll continue washing patients. You still have to work a few more days."

"One offer is more attractive than the other."

"You have the choice."

"Honestly? It's a tough choice."

I made it easier for him. "Look, you don't have to wash the patients. You don't have to look at the negative part of my job as well. Your color was green."

Rick approved: "Perhaps we men like the smell of another type of fight."

"Yeah, blood, corpses, and so on. You need to fight sometimes. That's why you're probably working out all the time, boxing, and so on... Because of testosterone."

Rick thought: "What about you? Don't you like dumbbells?"

"A little. Yes, I know, we have to work out as well, but we should dance more. Fight with tenderness and work out more with dance. You guys with the male force. We'll talk about that later."

"Why later?"

"Because we are still in ordinary work and my shift didn't finish yet."

"So, I'm going with you."

"Okay, so come on."

Rick went with me. When we finished, he asked: "Tell me, what it is like in the children's department? The one from the other side? With you, everything is on the other side."

"That's just because of you and the circumstances. Because you're a being from another reality."

"Do you think it's a better reality because of the money?"

"Maybe. Mainly because you do what you like."

"And you?"

"Sometimes yes. Sometimes not."

"Because of..." I laughed.

"Don't say that expressive word! We don't use it here. You heard the boss."

Rick agreed: "Is it possible not to?"

"No. Not really. Now go to lunch."

Rick waited for his colleagues. When they were sitting at the Rabbit, they were all eager to hear if he had done the task. Rick didn't wait for them to ask and told them: "Can you believe that I have washed my grandma and grandpa?"

Will shook his head: "It seems that you have been seriously damaged by your stay here. In the beginning, you were like a macho and ended up as a temporary nurse. Nobody will believe you have done that."

Andy asked him: "Was it bad?"

"What do you mean? Bad? There are even worse things."

Andy teased him: "Worse? Worse than the body of an XXL granny?"

Rick answered mysteriously: "Try it. You'll see."

Andy objected sourly: "I am happy to clean. I don't long for such a career path."

Will added: "Neither did he. If he wants to finish baking the Bunny, he has no choice."

Peter remarked: "There's always a choice. The question is what we are willing to sacrifice for it. We always have to pay for each option."

Andy continued: "Did she tell you what's next?"

Rick sighed: "Why are you so nosy? Not yet. She'll tell me tonight."

Will provoked him: "Shall we go away somewhere tonight?"

Rick replied calmly: "I don't think it will be necessary. I think it's not going to go so fast. Bunny has strange things in her head."

Andy was curious. "Aren't you afraid?"

Peter answered instead him: "A coward would be afraid."

In the afternoon, they returned to work. When Rick's working hours ended, I sent him home. He decided to stay: "It's quite interesting here. Nothing special is happening at home now."

"I'm not sure if that's a good idea."

"Are you afraid now?"

"Yes. You're even more dangerous now."

I looked in his eyes for a moment. "Okay, as you want." He walked with me and gradually started to understand what I was doing. If there was a disaster in one of the rooms, I asked him to wait outside. I told him that he doesn't have to live my reality with all its details. We went to the room of one of the patients who was in a difficult condition. She was crying like a little baby all the time, except for when she slept. She was oblivious to her surroundings. Every manipulation was stressful for her.

Rick asked: "Why don't you give her medication?"

"Because she can't swallow anymore. She gets a tablet under the tongue. To calm her down." Rick stared at the unhappy being who really looked and behaved like a defenseless newborn. He watched how we lifted her with our lifter, which I called Thor or Zeus, and put her in the wheelchair.

"Why don't you leave her in bed?"

"We have to make them move as long as it's possible. It's prevention from lung inflammation and bedsores. Look at this woman. We care for her. She is old. Somewhere on Earth, men are hurting women. For different reasons, they cause them terrible pain. Men should protect women and love them. Not hurt them."

Rick was getting sad. "Nobody can save everyone."

"No. That's terrible. That helplessness."

Rick told me after a moment: "We're saving some people."

"Everybody is saving somebody. Even with little deeds. Like you do."

Rick confirmed: "And you."

"See how much misery is here in this little place? There are so many places in the world like this. Fortunately, saviors and heroes live in these places as well and they save other people with small deeds."

We stared at each other for a while then I turned quickly because I felt that everything was beginning to fall under me. I left the room. For the rest of day, I tried not to speak anymore. What will happen next? Actually, I have nothing to worry about, I told myself. Rick is a star loved by millions of women all over the world. I'm just one of them. He wants answers, but there is no guarantee that we will get through all the levels. So, I was comforting myself. Men want to have only fun. Especially fun. He has no idea how much fun awaits him.

In the evening, we met at the Rabbit and I put down my dictionary on the table: "The communication again."

Rick didn't care. "So. These answers!"

"We need appropriate circumstances. It can't be here."

Rick was impatient. "So, what do we need?"

"Many things."

"Things? You said they were invisible gifts."

"You should be happy because maybe you won't need to fight with breasts."

"You're a witch!"

"Every woman is like a witch. Each with her own charms."

"What are yours?"

"Don't be so nosy. So, let's go to business. I said that a divine man needs divine answers. That's not possible here."

Rick was very wise and immediately realized where I was heading. "All right. Do you want to take these answers to Olympus?"

"First. How much money costs a party at your Earthly Olympus? I heard that you have your own amusement park."

"Do you want to go to an amusement park?"

"I love amusement parks, but no. We'll create our own amusement park. One big party. When was the last time you played? I mean creatively with fantasy."

Rick grabbed his head. "You want to play? Are you serious?"

I watched as his eyes glowed in dark: "Not a doctor and a nurse game. That's boring."

"Boring?"

"Yes, boring. Everybody plays that. We'll play other games. We'll need other circumstances and friends who will play with us. With these games, we'll try to ignite the spark. The passion."

"Then it will be the game of the doctor and nurse."

I rolled my eyes. "If you don't stop, I'll leave."

"Okay, okay. I'm quiet. Continue, nurse."

"You wanted to buy jewelry. Those games will also be expensive. Like that jewelry. Memories will remain forever. Human life is created from experiences. We need some friends who like dreams and fantasy. We'll play. We'll dance. Not like professionals but as amateurs do. Like ordinary people."

Rick began to understand. "Do ordinary people make crazy things like that in your country?"

"And in yours, they don't? Creativity is very important. Even fantasy. Not only for us but in Hollywood as well. Everywhere."

"What we will need?"

"Too many things. Unfortunately, it will be expensive fun. Without emotions, the answers will be lost. We have to live them. As you did. Now you understand my reality differently. Because you lived it. Not only read about it. You experienced emotions. The good and the bad."

Rick observed me for a while then he wondered: "Do you do everything so complicatedly?"

"What does it mean 'complicated' to you? You are a professional actor. Acting is not only your profession. It's fun as well. I want to show you my answers in those games. Fire. Water. Earth. Air. Four elements of love. Four levels of love. If I just tell you about them without emotions, it will be boring."

Rick thought for a moment, and then asked: "Okay, so tell me, what do we need? Where are they going to take place? Those games?"

I shrugged my shoulders.

"Well. I don't know. We need to exist somewhere. Games will last for 16 days. There will be four of them. We need four days to prepare each game. Space for training and for fun."

Rick watched the splashy Bunny with astonishment. Then he realized that people spend a lot of money on expensive holidays and entertainment. He understood what the ordinary nurse was all about. She was about experiences. These are the fragments that creates the human life. The more experiences, the more emotions that form human beings. Recently, people were having fun mostly in a passive way. In movies, in front of computers or computer games. In order to forget about their everyday problems. Going for a holiday or having another experience allegedly helped ignite the extinguishing passion for couples who had crises in their relationships. That's why a team of animators took care of that part of creative entertainment on holidays. So that human beings can experience joy and positive emotions. That's why there were many enthusiasts, amateurs in the world who produced art or sport. Although with mistakes but they gave the audience the emotions. Professionals, on the other hand, earned their living out of giving away the emotions to the audience. Amateurs did that only to be able to go through their ordinary realities. Thanks to the amazing technology, human beings have been able to transfer themselves through a virtual journey to the realm of dreams and fantasy at any time. Therefore, computer games and social network creators have been earning millions. From the human desire to live their dreams even for a while. But it started to turn against human beings. Cold computer characters couldn't replace real human tears or laughter. Only real people could. Whether they were actors, singers, musicians, athletes. Nevertheless, they were real people. Some people who couldn't reach the Earthly Olympus full of professional athletes, artists, and all those who have made money from what they always wanted to do, gave up after some time. They thought amateur art wasn't worth it. It wasn't true. Splashy Bunny understood that. For years, she has supported her amateur theatrical dance group with her enthusiasm. Sometimes she was desperate for having to improvise because of lack of time.

Rick interrupted the silence: "We have to exist somewhere. How do you want to achieve that?"

Again, I had to think hard, how to explain everything to him. Because of the language barrier, I couldn't use my biggest gift. The gift of the word. Former members of our group, the swordsmen, have often made fun of that. They would say that with only my words I could make anyone do what I want. They meant it in a positive way. Now I felt helpless. The gift of word was not applicable in this case in its full power. I was forced to improvise all the time. I took a deep breath and said: "We'll need a big, really big room with a floor that can withstand the consequences of a real fire."

Rick teased me: "Ah. Damage. After fire."

"Real fire. Not the one that we have in our bodies. We'll need real flames as well." Rick grabbed his forehead.

"Isn't the entertainment room good enough for that?"

"What entertainment room? You can't use real fire in the entertainment room. I want to live in a garden house for the time being. I don't need a lot for living. I used to live in a garage or a basement. We're going to be neighbors basically."

"What?"

"I don't have much space in the nursing house. I'm used to that. Bunny sometimes needs her cage."

"Wait. So, you need a big room and a huge list of different things for some crazy games and you still need a garden house for all this? I don't get that."

"The room will be a temporary place where we'll create real emotions and dreams. Those will stay forever. For that, we need people and lots of props and many other things."

"For god's sake! What do you want to do?"

"We'll play my answers. We'll dance. Not like professionals. Just for creativity and fun."

"Have you ever done anything like that before?"

"No. However, I never had a muse like you before. You can see that those circumstances are expensive."

"So, you have no idea how it will look?"

"A little bit. You're going to be the director. The boss. Every game is about one element. You, the men will act. We women will dance. We'll play stories with punchlines."

"Oh, my god!"

"It's your decision." Rick was silent for a moment and watched me with a thoughtful look. This nurse wants to tell him her answers in a way that is very close to him because he does it every day. It's his work. Why does she make everything so complicated? First, her words, which she released randomly with the terrible Slavic accent. Now those crazy games. He was a man and men are curious creatures. Moreover, until now he saw the splashy Bunny only in the highest levels of love.

"What will I get if I arrange it all?"

"Answers. I told you my gifts are invisible but expensive."

"Will the list of things be very long?"

"Very long. Very."

Rick repeated: "So, big room. A lot of things. You want to live in a garden house? Is this garden house really necessary?"

"There I'll be secure for a while. The games will be hard. Very difficult. I have to have a place where I can hide."

"From what?"

"From fire."

"Which fire?"

"Both of them."

Rick was silent. Then he asked: "What should we play?"

"I have to prepare themes. I have to ask for help. I can't come up with them myself."

"Why not? You can speak words randomly as you have done so far. We'll understand somehow."

"You'll speak I'll do other things."

"That sounds interesting. We'll talk about this garden house. When are they going to happen, those...games?"

"When you'll have the room and a lot of other things... And friends who want to play too."

"Ah... Do you have any more requests? In addition to lots of crazy things?"

"I don't know. I'll know probably on the spot. I'll prepare themes and you those things."

"And a big room. I haven't experienced anything like that ever. Olympus style answers."

"Exactly. We'll experience the stories. We'll try to link between what is your work and what's just fun for me."

"Link. So, this is your dangerous way of flirting?"

"Are we flirting? We are friends. Friends can also have fun, can't they?"

"Friends. We'll probably never forget about this fun."

"We don't know. We don't know what's coming. We decide every second of our life. We have free will."

"You're a dangerous Bunny."

"I don't want to hurt anyone. I just want to show you the answers. To keep a promise."

"Okay, let's start writing that list. How many people will we need?"

"We need to fit in that room."

Rick watched me with his eyes, and he knew there would be trouble. Maybe even fun. So what? Why can't they have fun as friends? Friends. How ridiculous this word sounded, after all that he saw and experienced in the nursing house. He went through the heavy, unpopular highest level of love. The highest. The one that hurts from all levels probably the most. Its pain is so big that sometimes it can't be handled. Pain was hard to manage at all levels. All of them.

We started to write the list of things. Rick shook his head with astonishment, at the fact that the price of those things might climb to the price of the jewelry necklace. Then he understood the difference. Bunny preferred the invisible gift to the shiny stones. She knew that from her amateur group and he and his friends knew that from their work. Now from the cleaning job. He already saw in his mind the sarcastic smiles of his friends. How they would tease him because of how Bunny wanted to answer the questions. Friendship, kindness, humor, joy, enthusiasm. Maybe love. Emotions. Positive emotions.

When we finished writing, I said carefully: "I don't know, it's probably not all."

Rick was surprised. "It's not all? Oh, my god. Well, these are going to be pretty expensive games."

"Yes indeed. Don't forget the food. For many people. Four games, four big celebrations. We need food for us. We will prepare it ourselves."

Rick added: "We don't really know each other yet and we want to organize such huge games? We go from the end again. What will be the name of your games? They should have a name, right?"

I said with a mysterious smile: "Yes. The name can be The fight of intimacy." Rick burst into laughter.

I explained quietly: "That's what my son invented when he made fun of me because of you. It's a good name. Men and women fight in the war from the beginning of time. At all levels of love. We will include that in our play. Small parts of the war."

Rick got serious. "Well, that'll be a war."

"People fight for everything. Maybe we have to learn to fight occasionally with the most powerful weapon that the Creator gave us. Love. Because we can't always use it properly."

Rick was speechless. Bunny made his head spin from all the words she said. She forced him to experience the highest love for the sake of a broken human being who can still feel. His emotions were still alive. I interrupted the silence: "Tomorrow we will continue with the list. And the topics. And so on."

We left the pub and I said goodbye.

"I knew you have a rare and special heart. From the first day. Good night."

Chapter 9

Rick went back to their male nest. The guys were sleeping already but he couldn't fall asleep. Crazy Bunny. What the hell does she have in her head? Games. Answers. Oh, my god. Despite everything, he wanted those answers. Neither he nor she knew where they would lead them. But any such answer may have been worth the risk. Because everything related to love in any way was always worth the risk.

Just as Rick was thinking, Bunny was thinking. Recently, many people have become cowards, and some men who should fight for emotions and love as knights in armor have become cowards. They chose friendship with benefits, without love. Just to protect their hearts. Then they wondered why women had to become much stronger. They had to survive without men's love and protection in this world, where mostly men dominated because of their ego. Feelings were no longer in fashion. Sex was. Sex didn't go out of fashion. Women often didn't understand the justifying words of some wise men. They would defend themselves. They would say that they are poor creatures, it's not their fault, they've been created this way. Women, however, went into everything with their heart. Men didn't. That was the difference. In their boxes. How was suppose love to exist? Was it again in women's hands? Woman would set the direction at the beginning of a relationship. She was not allowed to succumb to passion too soon. Otherwise, the relationship will be spoiled. She set the direction in the family. What about men? Fortunately, if they were finally ready to open their fragile, vulnerable hearts, some of them tried to take care of their wives and families. So what? Even the animals do so. They supposedly don't have higher feelings. So where did our human higher feelings go? Unfortunately, sometimes it was the other way around. Where are the men, the knights, willing to make the impossible for love? Yes, they exist. However, some relationships were still falling apart like a house of cards. Why? Rick had no idea that for many years Bunny was looking for answers to this question.

She wanted to know how love works or doesn't work. She looked for these answers when she was away from home and heard many real stories from different countries. Moreover, she read many history books where infidelity was a common thing and unfulfilled, unhappy love as well. Someone who couldn't love somebody else in return would unintentionally break the other human being's heart. It wasn't the fault of any one of the two. It was chemistry. The sparkle. When it wasn't there, it was impossible to create love. It just wasn't. It was something that no human being could create. As if it was a gift from above. The scientists tried to find an explanation for it, but they couldn't. What was that? Fragrance? Perfect body? Eyes? People have suffered from love the most and were happiest from love as well. From the begging of time. Great, unfulfilled emotions have accompanied artists like nightmares. Later they would turn them into their art. These pieces of art have become precious jewels over time. Bunny loved and hated these jewels at the same time. She hated bad ends. It seemed to her that the amount of negative and sad emotions was more than the positive ones. Why? Did we really do it ourselves? Because something invisible has destroyed the faith in our hearts? She couldn't explain it. People longed for love, which according to some psychiatrists, didn't exist. However, because of love history has often changed. Behind the mighty men who ruled, were often women who influenced their decisions, sometimes even the bad ones. Was really love just a bunch of hormones that's only purpose was to make people reproduce?

All this was going on through Bunny's head. The next day at breakfast, Andy asked: "So, was Bunny's answers worth washing a granny and a grandpa?"

"You'll be surprised, but I still don't know."

Will did not understand. "Really? You fulfilled the task. What else does she want?"

Rick continued: "We're going to play the answers. As actors. We'll go back to childhood."

Andy put down his cell phone: "Childhood? But that's what we do at work, we act."

Rick continued: "Bunny wants to organize small scout camp. For adults. With entertainment activities. Invited will be those who want to recognize these four levels of love."

"What? A scout camp? For god's sake! Explain it!"

Peter started to understand. "All right now I get it! This is the friendly service she mentioned she would want from us for helping us then. She needs us as extras."

"Extras? Are you insane? I don't want to be an extra. I have already advanced in my career!" Will was offended.

Rick told him: "Don't worry you'll have a role in these games as well. Tina said that in addition to few men, she needs also women. I don't know exactly what it is going to be. She called it an adult vacation with creative entertainment."

"I don't get it. Why she needs other people to tell you those crazy answers? Why can't just the two of you play?"

Peter responded instead of Rick: "Because even a movie without extras wouldn't be a good one."

"Shut up! I'm not going to be an extra or a clown!"

Andy looked at him with a smile: "You won't? You didn't want to be a cleaner either. You didn't want a grandma. Look how we ended. The more you don't want something the more the circumstances will make you experience it."

Rick said calmly: "I'm not forcing anyone. Who wants to join in is welcomed."

Andy continued with a question: "How many people does Bunny want to have there?"

"You mean how many extras she'll need?"

Rick asked cheerfully and continued: "I have to have a large room with a floor that can withstand a real fire. We'll see how many would even dare to try."

The guys went quiet.

"Are you sure you're going to do those crazy games? You said only a few sentences and it sounds…"

Peter added: "Crazy and creative Why not?"

Rick explained: "Supposedly adults don't play enough. Few create their own, active entertainment. We need experiences. Just joy. In our work, in every job, we are all under tremendous pressure. Will fans like the movie? What will people say? What will the critics say? Few realize how difficult it is to be a professional. Ordinary people are stressed out of other things. Everyone who has a boss is under pressure from them. The more money is in the business, the more pressure is placed on the employees. Unfortunately, this is how it goes."

Andy contemplated: "If I understand it properly, we all want to play some games."

Rick agreed: "The answers to Bunny's four levels of love. The first game, Fire. The second game, Water. The third game, Earth. The fourth game, Air."

Will blurted out: "I hope she's not some kind of witch!"

Rick comforted him: "Witches don't exist, don't worry. Only in fairy tales. However, women have something that sometimes forces us to make such foolishness. These games for example. They have a dark box. It's their biggest weapon. For a few seconds, they can beat a really strong opponent with it."

Andy looked at Rick. "Well. That's right. So, we're going to play. Like kids."

Rick added: "Like kids and like amateurs, who, according to Tina, produce art without the professional stress we have."

Peter smiled. "Wow! Why she wants to answer you in such a difficult way?"

Andy understood: "For emotions. Look at us! Although we knew, that people work in places like this, and that their work is difficult, we didn't get it until we experienced their reality and did part of their work. She wants to partially understand our reality. Although just for fun. Stress from failed scenes and angry director Wait! Someone has to manage it all, direct it. If it is going to be such a spectacular game."

"Rick will do it! Am I right?" asked Peter.

"For god's sake! I don't want to see that. He accommodates a strange woman who makes crazy games that she can't do just with him and then he'll spill the frustration of this crazy madhouse on us!" Will explained scornfully.

Rick laughed. "She would like a garden house. Perhaps to hide in her cage when it is…"

Andy added: "Unbearable. It probably won't be easy."

Peter remarked again: "Love is difficult. Even this higher one."

Will continued to tease Rick: "Higher. Higher. So, Bunny is still not baked. Instead of answering, she invented these crazy games for which she needs the extras. Oh, god! I don't envy you. Why the hell you want to do this?"

"As I said. I want to see what weapons she will fight with. Maybe I'll see something better than scrubbing dirt and that annoying higher level. In addition, people are willing to spend a lot of money on entertainment. So why not?"

Andy turned to Will: "What we do for living is entertainment for ordinary people. To distract them from their ordinary reality. It's a different story when they sit in the movies and just watch what we do to when... when they have to invent it and play it themselves. Even if just for fun."

Rick thought: "When we are at work preparing a movie, we are friends as well. Not just actors. She also has a group of friends. The difference is that we are professionals at the highest possible level. In what she cosinders to be an Earthly Olympus. On the other hand she and her group live in ordinary reality and they act only when they have time. They neither have the time nor the opportunity to move up. Some of them are mothers with children. I've seen the pictures. They have to divide their time between work and family. Instead of watching TV or being on the phone, they use what's left of it to act."

Andy asked: "Are the answers worth your while? When what she wants it so complicated?"

Rick shrugged his shoulders. "Sometimes we have to risk, even if the result isn't always what we expect. Maybe the complications are important. If she just gives me the plane answers, they would be just words but she wants those deeds and real emotions."

Peter spoke to them sadly: "People are afraid of emotions. Because the bad ones are increasing on Earth. Only few wants to talk about it. As if it was increasingly difficult to create those positive emotions. The ones that will touch us deeply."

Rick ordered: "We must go."

When the guys came to work with strange smiles I knew why: "You already know, right?"

They laughed and Andy was curious: "Well... These will be a hell of a games. Do they have a name?"

"You didn't tell them? They do. The name is... But hush... don't say it aloud... copyright ... you know." Everyone laughed loudly.

Peter asked curiously. "Who invented the name? You?"

"No. My older son did. It's perfect for these games."

Who knows what Will have had in mind when he heard the name, but he agreed: "I'm in."

I was pleasantly surprised. "Are you sure? Love is difficult. Love is not meant for the cowards. The name hides other levels of love as well."

Will confirmed: "Yes, I am."

"Great! We'll play then. This is the friendly help I meant when I cleaned your apartment."

Peter added: "It probably won't be easy either. Like cleaning our mess wasn't ."

"No, it won't. In these games, we'll try to clean something else. Our hearts and souls. We'll try to understand why we all need each other. That we still don't help each other enough. Now let's go to work."

Guys got their tasks as always, and I thought what a pity that in a short time they'd leave forever. Grannies liked them, employees, almost all women, too. At least for a short time, we, ordinary women could dream. All close up and personal. As my son said, even we, ordinary people, need Earthly Olympus, because a world without professional artists would be sad. Himself he couldn't imagine the world without music.

Rick didn't want to go back to cleaning the lockers and he was looking forward to never having to do that again in his life. He was with me. He was changing bed sheets and did many other things with patients. Except for washing and changing diapers. Both genders should complement each other. Unfortunately, as if the world still didn't understand it and women had to fight for centuries for their position. It was very difficult for women to survive among men who ruled this Earth for years. Emancipation helped us only partially. Each of us is constantly deciding between love and fear. Men often made senseless acts out of fear from women that actually hurt both genders. Why? Though men are driven by their strong sexual and hunting instincts, they also have hearts. Many of them brave and worthy of love.

Peter also got used to the grannies. The grannies were ecstatic, even though they forgot the second day that they had such a luxurious service. Some of them didn't know why the guys were there the next day. Therefore, we answered them the same questions all over again. From where they were, and so on. We were used to that. These people really understood the law of attraction. They rejected their unpleasant reality and lived in the one that gave them positive emotions. In the one, they chose for themselves. They were trying to forget the bad things every day. So, this was the reality full of suffering and at the same time full of the precious highest level of love. The reality that was needed to sustain not only love relationships but all relationships on our planet. Well, by getting the gift of free will we could not always understand. The imperfection had its charm. Perhaps the Creator knew why he gave it to us. If we didn't have it, we would show our love for Him unwittingly. He wants us to do it because we want to. Because we feel it. Not because someone ordered us to do so.

God is the universal principle of love, part of which he has given to humanity. We don't understand. We are scared. We are afraid of His love because if we understand it, we will also feel the pain. We fear pain. Doing a deed of love to a particular person was the manifestation of love that reflected in human beings, what was probably meant in the Bible. God created man in his image. He has given humanity many visible and invisible gifts and was waiting for the deeds of love. The feeling that every human being felt when helped another human being was the divine spark of love. The feeling that the other one was grateful for the help that reflected the Creator in us. Some understood it. They understood the price of service and sacrifice. First, they also had to move to high levels of love and accept themselves with mistakes. Learn to love themselves. Only then, could they begin to help other human beings. No one could save the whole world at once. We could only do it gradually. That was very difficult.

Rick and I walked into the room of two patients. One bed was empty.

"Where's the grandma?"

"She died. At night."

Rick asked sadly: "In sleep?"

"Yes. She fell asleep. Forever. We'll all end up like this and yet we hurt each other."

Rick added: "We also help each other."

I smiled at him. "Yes, we do. Let's go to work. By the smell I can tell that the other granny is okay, you can stay."

Rick laughed. "Fragrance? Smell?"

"Fragrance."

We gradually cleaned and fed all grannies and grandpas. Some had to be guided to their rooms because they constantly would forget which one is theirs.

Rick stayed with me, but I couldn't talk a lot during work because the workload was growing. The state of grannies sometimes didn't improve. It headed for the end. In the evening, I sent Mr. D to the bathroom and told him that I was coming later. We went back to his room and we found him scared to death sitting in his wheelchair. We didn't understand why. The light in the room was dim but then we saw something behind the bed. That was the reason of his fear. A granny who crouched by the bed and was trying to get to his bed. That was a scene. Desperate Mr. D was afraid that she wanted something special from him, but he didn't dare to beep. When we stopped laughing, I told the her: "Okay now, let's go to your room. This is not your room."

"He said I can stay." she defended herself.

Poor Mr. D who normally didn't talk much in this woman's madhouse, objected: "That's not true. Go away." With great difficulties, we convinced her to leave. We put her in bed and then we placed Mr. D in bed as well. Rick couldn't stop laughing.

I sighed: "This is how some relationships work."

Rick added: "The other way around too."

"Yes, that's true. Okay, let's continue with work."

"We need to finish the game-planning in the evening."

"Yeah, we have to. If we want to play those games."

"We want."

"Will I have that garden house?"

"Isn't a room enough?"

"It won't be safe. The house will be."

"Why isn't the room safe?"

"Because you're a man."

"Ah, and you're not dangerous?"

"No. I'm a nurse."

"Why do you think you're not?"

"Why do you think I am?"

"Women are sometimes almost like witches. Will you also cook love potion?"

"Maybe. I'll put it in your dinner."

We both laughed and I said seriously: "I said to you, there is no such a thing like a love potion. Only a spark exists and it's not always ignited. Chemistry. Free will."

Rick was silent and I interrupted the silence: "I'm glad we will play. I hope it will be fun, lots of fun."

In the evening, we sat at the Rabbit again and continued to plan the craziest amateur games. We didn't notice that a bunch of tourists entered the pub. They had a dangerous age and were looking at us constantly. When I realized that I said with concern: "These young people are looking here. We have to leave before they start taking pictures."

Rick sighed: "Where do we go?"

"Well, we can go to the room where the grannies are playing."

"Where the splashy Bunny dances in the evenings with wings." Rick laughed and didn't realize he'd revealed himself when he said that.

I was surprised. "How do you know? Wait you have to explain!"

"Now we must disappear. I don't know where we're going to eat tomorrow. Luckily, we are leaving in a few days," he said quickly to cover up for his mistake.

We left quickly and we really didn't know where to go. It was cold and snowing outside. I realized that if I ring the bell on the night service, they'll see that I'm not alone. Even if I could hide him somehow when entering, how would he leave? We felt like two teenagers who have nowhere to hide from people to steal some kisses somewhere on the stairs. But we needed to finish the plan. I remarked: "I'm really like a rabbit in a cage."

"Then come to my place. We'll finish it there."

We both laughed and I objected: "That sounds awful. I'm not going there."

"Don't worry. They're fine. At least we can plan together. Maybe they'll have a few ideas."

I was afraid. "That is not a good idea. It will create stupid rumors."

"Rumors maybe will be created after this evening in the pub. Who knows if the people there recognized me?"

"Okay, let's go." I finally agreed. When we came to their male nest, the welcome was even worse than I expected.

Those fools started laughing like crazy, and between the laughter, Andy teased Rick: "So, shall we leave you alone?"

Will continued: "So instead of baking, splashy Bunny probably got burned right? That's why you couldn't stand it and brought her here?"

Rick ordered them: "Shut up! We're going to plan our games. There's so much work that needs to be done."

I was glad we had nothing to explain. I was really shy and now I was not in my uniform, which was my own armor. In a sense, it was my protection against certain things. Now I felt very vulnerable. I didn't know what will happen and at the same time, I was shocked that all these people agreed to participate in those crazy games. Maybe there was nothing special about it. People like to have fun to gain strength for everyday life full of problems.

When we were in the middle of planning, Peter wanted to know, why we came here: "What happened that you had to come here?"

Rick replied: "The winter tourist season began, and Christmas is coming. Although this town is dead, skiers are everywhere. Some tourist came to the pub. I'm afraid they recognized me."

Andy calmed him. "I doubt they would believe it. What would you do here? In this godforsaken place?"

Will answered instead Rick: "Well, he started washing all sorts of boxes, proceeded to wash grannies and grandpas and ended up planning crazy, expensive games to…"

Rick shouted at him: "Please, can't you just keep your mouth shut? None of this would happen if you kept your mouths shut in front of those cops then."

I knew how Will would finish it. But there was nothing certain. Because Will didn't know anything about my life and faith. That's why I had to become a complicated person. Because my destiny taught me to believe only in human deeds. Words which, especially from the mouth of male beings, changed into lies of cowardice and excuses after a short while, made me really the shy Bunny. A Bunny who believed that perhaps good men still existed, but at the same time forced her for many years to rely only on herself. That was why I liked heroes. The muscles were no longer so important to me. Those deeds. I believed there were still men who had at least some of the rare features of the savior.

I told Will: "Nothing is certain. Everything is a risk. As these games. Even your movies… Love… Everything… We never know the end… Free will…"

I disarmed Will. After that, the guys were having fun with planning the games. What they did in their daily work now they used for themselves and their partners. This time with no stress. Just for the sake of having fun and emotions. It was too late, and I had to go. Rick went with me and when I saw the nursing house, I said quietly: "I'll go alone."

"No. I'm going with you." The sky was yellow because it was snowing heavily. I felt I broke in half inside. I was panicking. This will end. That's exactly it. We never know how and we're forced to risk.

"Really. Good night." I literally ran away. I was scared. To keep such a man as far from me as possible? No way!

Rick stood in the street for a while and said to himself: *So that's why you need your garden house. Not because you are scared of me but because you are scared of yourself!*

He returned to their temporary accommodation. I was in my tiny room watching the snowflakes falling from the sky. They often reminded me of the frozen tears of all the etheric beings of light trying to keep Earth alive, but not everyone believed it.

Meanwhile, in the heavenly Olympus, the situation was boiling. Zeus kept checking the angels collecting precious white and pink light from the white and pink pearls. He was not satisfied with the result.

Apollo was furious. "Why do you care so much about those cocky pricks proud creatures? Look! They don't believe in anything. Not even in themselves. Everyone thinks millions in the bank account will make them happy. They want to own everything in the world."

Zeus replied quietly: "That's the problem. Some don't believe in themselves anymore. They don't believe in love anymore. In nothing, but not all people are like that. There is still enough of pearls."

Apollo laughed mockingly. "Do you want to convince me or yourself? We were both at all the battles that these stupid creatures have no idea about and yet they proudly claim to be masters of creation. Never before there were as few pearls as now. It's over, Zeus. Honestly? Maybe they deserve it. Why should we save them again? Why? On one hand, they save some of their lives with the latest technologies they celebrate, and, on the other hand, they kill their own brothers and sisters with them. Zeus, people are the Creator's failure. Excuse me, and may the Creator excuse me as well. They are a failure, failure. Nothing more."

Zeus looked at Apollo and smiled mysteriously. "So why you use all these complicated ways, sometimes behind my back, to help them fulfill their desires?"

Apollo spat off angrily: "Because I'm crazy."

Zeus resisted: "Because you haven't lost faith in them either. Until they have free will, we can't do anything else but try to save them. We must believe that they too believe that true love is a better choice than fear. All evil deeds come from fear."

Apollo was angry: "Even from fear for their lives? I wonder what these creatures from bellow will come up with this time. Zeus, I don't feel good about this battle. I know we can't afford to lose faith, but there is not enough of pearls. There is not! We can't continue convincing ourselves otherwise."

Zeus spoke mysteriously: "You created with Petal fairy your unsuccessful love potion. Eros unwillingly poisoned the poor man's heart because of your personal war. Despite the fact that the potion worked the opposite way, what is the result?"

Apollo sighed: "We thought you didn't have time to deal with stupidity while Earth is burning. That's not related to the state of pearls, right?"

Zeus corrected him: "It is, my dear Apollo, it is. What just happened with that potion confirmed that humility could clear human hearts. Therefore, you actually did well. What is lacking in humankind is just humility. Especially those who rule are not able to be humble in front of those who contribute to the functioning of the world with small tasks and deeds. Four famous men have shown that saving the world should be the only task for every human being living on Earth. That it can be done in small parts. Deed by deed means pearl to pearl. An open human heart means many pearls. A lot of light."

Apollo asked: "So, you won't punish me for violating the rules of our work?"

"For the sake of love, we all violate the rules. You need love, Apollo. You're alone. That doesn't do you good."

Apollo looked at the giant plain full of white and pink light: "What about Hera? Is she okay with you cheating on her all the time?"

Zeus didn't know what to say. Then he replied with a heavy heart: "Even we, living in Heavenly Olympus aren't perfect. Only the Creator is perfect. Sometimes even we break the rules. Maybe with our mistakes, we show humanity that mercy, compassion, humility, and gratitude help to forgive."

Apollo reluctantly considered: "If we were perfect, I wouldn't argue with Eros and he wouldn't shoot that poisoned arrow. It did the purpose. Mistakes show humanity and us the right direction."

Zeus patted him on the shoulder: "Definitely. Maybe, the Creator wants the polarity to be preserved. Good and evil. Only some of the heavenly ethereal beings are getting closer to Him. They gave up free will for the love of Him. Oh, Apollo. I'm scared. I really fear for Earth. I know I shouldn't because it's my duty to believe in a miracle, but you're right. Earth is falling down faster."

Apollo looked at the beautiful Fields of Pearls: "It's happening also because people are multiplying rapidly in places where there is nothing. Where the planet suffers the most. For the greed of others who plunder those places. They don't want to see it; they don't want to hear it and they don't think about it responsibly and with love for their planet and for themselves. They plunder and destroy. Only a few voices are talking about it loudly, but their voices are disappearing because they are not strong enough. In a short time, those silly human worms will have to eat real worms, so they won't die from hunger. What the birds will eat then, they don't care. Sure, they'll breed those worms so there will be enough of them for the birds. Oh, I forgot, they managed to create something like artificial meat as well. Oh, god. Just imagine it, Zeus. Artificial meat. But no wonder. People have created so many artificial things on Earth that it is nothing unusual. Artificial breasts and legs and so many other artificial things. Soon they will grow everything in the laboratories. Even themselves. Do you understand their human thinking, Zeus? First, because of their greediness, they destroy the planet that is supposed to feed them, and then they have to move to the lab. On top of that, they're celebrating this as their amazing progress."

Zeus rebuked him: "Apollo, what are you saying? They help themselves with those artificial things as much as they can. Don't be so hard on them. They do what they can. I was hard with the Petal fairy because of her artificial… You know that…"

"Hard? What a shame we can't send Ambrosia and nectar to Earth, maybe it would help. Some of them create too quickly too many new human beings in conditions that don't provide new human beings with safety, home, food, and clothes. That is not a manifestation of love. It's a manifestation of selfishness. New beings should be born into conditions suitable for them. Not at any cost, just because people think that the only completion of love and the sense of life in pairs is to have a child. Children are a real gift. A gift for adults to take care of. How can they take care of children when they are unable to take care of themselves in many cases? I don't mean only securing material things!"

Zeus objected: "Earth has enough for everyone. Universe has enough. Only people could think a little bit more."

Apollo disagreed: "Here is our main problem again. They think they must have everything. They want to have everything they can get, Zeus. At any price. They don't know the price of the sacrifice. They still don't get it. They don't want to hear and see the problems that are at the other end of the planet where they don't live. They don't look at things from a broader perspective. They see only the small area around them. Those who have opened their hearts to allow the entry of higher levels of love suffer from within. They feel endless pain because they can't destroy the cause of the suffering of other human beings. They can't cope with the imbalances. They can't even rule. Neither does the flame of faith is helping them. They live in fear."

Zeus continued: "I told you. Earth has enough for everyone, Apollo. Well, we must not lose faith. We have to take care of them on a spiritual level and try to save them."

Apollo was not satisfied: "Zeus, how long are we going to try to rescue them when they're not willing to sacrifice almost anything for their own rescue? They don't realize that although they can fulfill their dreams, they have to learn to live with these dreams! They are involved in nonsensical wars that hurt them, yet they are losing the most important battle of saving the planet that was given to them as a gift. Because they are greedy and voracious!"

Zeus convinced him: "Not everyone, Apollo, not all. Look, we haven't lost yet. There are still people in the world who are kind, good and loving their children, families, and friends. Everything big, Apollo starts in small. People must understand that. If they find their way to their hearts again, they won't make decisions out of fear but out of love. Then they will create new people responsibly. Because they will understand the price of the sacrifice. A child is a gift and a sacrifice for life. Children deserve security, love, and home. They must learn to behave responsibly. Then they will know whether they are able to provide themselves and new people with good conditions. Everything starts in their hearts. They can attract everything they want. However, only the mature, cleansed heart will know how to use the gifts that it will attract. How to deal with new people. First, they have to save themselves. Then they can save others."

Apollo said indifferently: "Ah, so let them try to save their imperfect hearts, and we'll figure out how to pull their half-destroyed planet out of shit. Because that's where it is, Zeus. I know you hate it when I talk like this, but it's true. Earth is in deep shit. In real and virtual one."

Zeus shook his head. "Apollo, please. You have to feel and imagine we're already winning. You have to feel it."

"Go to hell Zeus with your advice!"

Zeus spoke his next words very seriously: "Oh, Apollo. That's the problem. We're going there…"

Apollo disappeared in order to fulfill his duties – fulfilling the crazy wishes of human beings, and Zeus said to himself: *You wouldn't see everything so rational and black if you had a female being next to you. Because only female beings can abrade aggression and brute force. Only they see the light where male beings no longer see it. Unfortunately, you have to wait, Apollo. First, we need to save Earth. Then we will solve your problem.*

Zeus watched the angels of healing who were collecting the light from the pearls. Human beings have not believed in themselves anymore. Let alone that there can be something in the higher dimensions. Beyond their ability to perceive with their senses. They were deaf and blind and were constantly looking for evidence because their hearts had lost faith. They didn't understand that everything was related and connected. They didn't know and didn't want to understand that they were not alone in the infinite universe, where a lively life was pulsing. To save them. To save their planet, which they, unfortunately, destroyed more than they loved. As they often did to each other. Yet Zeus knew their imperfection made them unique.

Laying in my bed, in the dark a kept thinking for a while. We people living on this planet are longing for the love of other people all the time. We love others. However, often we are not able to love ourselves. Because we want to be perfect. Because we are comparing ourselves to others. Self-love is the most difficult thing in the world. We make mistakes for which we are forced to seek forgiveness in other human beings. In addition, throughout our short life, we can't forgive ourselves. We haven't been given the gift of perfection. We are dying of diseases; we have partially poisoned our planet and our hearts. However, we still believe there is love. The most powerful magic in the world, which, even in our material reality, creates the greatest wonders in the world every day. Love is the only salvation of humankind. Nevertheless, we sometimes didn't understand it or didn't want to understand it. For fear of the pain that it sometimes brought.

The next morning, I didn't let Rick clean cabinets and other parts of the nursing house. Changing bed sheets and helping me with the patients was much easier. He didn't mention that to his friends, so they won't think that I favored him. The truth was that I actually did. He managed a difficult task and

I didn't want to bother him anymore. I knew the hardest part was yet to come. We were in Mrs. K's room and she asked disappointingly: "The young beautiful man won't wash me anymore?"

"No, he won't. Once was enough. Washing patients is my job. He only did it because he had to sacrifice something to get something else."

Mrs. K, who had already forgotten but was smart: "You?"

"No. Only some answers and they are rare. They are not for cowards."

Mrs. K looked at me. "Oh… So, he had to struggle with my big breasts to get the answers! Why?"

"Only a man who can serve a human being only with inner beauty can understand that love is not always pleasant."

"What do you give him in return?"

"Gifts. Invisible. It's up to him if he accepts them."

"You are a very special person. You have high demands."

"I had them low all my life. After years, I realized that if someone has high demands on himself, he or she could demand something special from others. Something that has a price that can't be paid with money. He managed to experience my world for a while. He was able to humble himself to the lowest point possible in my real life. I'll have to, though only for a while, experience his. Although only through games. His real life is sometimes harder than my diapers. Trust me. Even in his real life, one can't survive without humility. Nothing works without humility."

Then Rick accompanied Mrs. K to the table, which made her very happy. Peter poured her coffee and water. He already knew what the grandmothers wanted. They were shining with satisfaction. Such fans could only be obtained by pouring coffee and doing small deeds. They wouldn't have understood much if they saw some of those men playing in their movies. They understood their smile and willingness to serve them. None of them had to sacrifice their lives for them here. A smile and a touch were good enough. I sent the guys to lunch and Rick told me: "I don't know if it's a good idea to go to the Rabbit. After yesterday. I guess we have to improvise."

Andy said: "Okay, let's order something here."

"Go down to the entertainment room," I suggested.

Peter asked: "And you? Don't you have a break?"

"I have. I would rather stay here."

Will added: "The plan for your crazy games is not finished yet."

Rick wondered: "Yesterday you didn't want to participate. I still don't understand, why this sudden change?"

Andy replied instead of Will: "He wants to see how we're going to make idiots out of ourselves. Free of charge."

Peter disagreed: "Not free of charge! There will be no salary, but Rick will have to pay dearly."

"I washed a granny with huge breasts. Nothing worse can happen to me anymore!"

I looked at him with an innocent look and said to myself: *How wrong you are. Typical guys. Whenever there is even a small chance of something related to the lowest level of love, they plunge into the fight and don't think about the consequences. About the damages.*

I told quietly: "I hope you are right. We will finish the game schedule in the evening. You will have to execute them."

The guys went to the entertainment room where I used to hide in the evening to forget the daily stress.

While waiting for food, Rick whispered to Peter: "Here she comes. Evening—"

Peter wanted to add something, but Andy interrupted them: "What are you whispering about? Do you have any secrets?"

Rick replied: "Why are you so nosy?" Will looked around the room.

"Guys. You won't believe me, but I'm going to miss it a little."

Andy looked at Will with a smile.

"You mean that pretty blonde? The trainee?"

"So what? I didn't do anything. I was sticking to your advice."

Peter remarked: "We are all somehow different."

Rick agreed: "We cleaned the nursing house. Some of us washed a granny and a grandpa. We can feel that there is more room left in our hearts."

Andy asked with interest: "More than before our punishment?"

Peter was very serious. "More. Definitely. Because seeing something in the picture or in the movies is one thing. Then we become part of what we see only passively. If we feel and experience it on our own, then we become active."

Rick understood. "That's why Bunny wants to answer with deeds. Deeds are words transformed into reality. If she'd just answered me with plain words,

I wouldn't have experienced those answers, and wouldn't understand what she wanted to say. Thanks to all of us, we will give emotions to these deeds."

The guys didn't know what to say. Some of them have breathed life into their movie characters, but it was only a picture. It was a movie. If they play it live, even with mistakes, they won't only feel the emotions of the movie, but they will experience them as well. It was exactly what some advisors would tell adults when advising them on how to overcome the unbearable problems in their lives. We've all become too real. Too rational. We stopped even trying to fulfill our dreams. Only even if partially. We thought games were just for kids. That's a big mistake. Even adults have to play. The actors play in the movie or the theater all the time. It's their work but there they are under pressure. Therefore, games for adults need to be created. There they can be free to create space for their dreams with their own efforts. Rick remembered what Tina told him about her amateur dancing group. She said they were just pretending to be actors and dancers. They produced precious emotions. Especially for themselves. Although with technical, acting, or other types of mistakes. Sometimes their props would fall, sometimes they would forget the scenario, and dancers would turn to the wrong side or move their hands in the wrong direction. They don't have as much stress as professionals. On the other hand, even a small mistake of professionals is not forgiven. Sometimes the film fails; critics and fans scold them everywhere and are ruthless. Rick had no idea that for Tina all the movies were in some way good. She forgave the mistakes and she found something good in everything. People have forgotten that the same imperfect human beings with mistakes create professional art and movies...

Meanwhile, I was thinking. We are to blame ourselves. We created Earth's Olympus. We consider them to be perfect gods. We love them but when the poor creatures go wrong, we attack them with all our force. Let them know what kind of trash they have created. We deserve that. We think they are gods living on Earthly Olympus. That's not true. They are normal, vulnerable people who want to please us, increasingly demanding fans. Demands from both sides soar to the heights. Only our hearts often remain somewhere down.

It took me a long time to admit that male beings didn't give a damn about choreography. Everyone will find his favorite dancer in the group. They were interested in how the woman's body was waving and shaking only. This was one of the oldest dances in the world. The most dangerous and controversial as well because it's closely related to sexuality. Unfortunately, or, fortunately? I often wished to see what's happening inside the male brain when watching this dance. One of the group's faithful members told me: "Brain? What kind of brain are you expecting to see during this type of dance? It's somewhere else. In the lower parts of their bodies."

I was planning to create a group of female dancers who would want nothing else but to please their male heroes and I was feverishly wondering if it would be possible. The future dancers will perform only for fun and joy. On an amateur level. The guys who are used to the perfection of professionals will be transferred to the amateur level for a while. So that, as Will would call it, they will make goofballs out of themselves. Free of charge. Friendship, humor, and love should help them in that.

I didn't want to be alone with Rick in the evening because it was getting pretty hard. That's even before the games started and before the answers. *How it's going to be later?* I was wandering. Will the garden house save me for some time? We agreed to complete what's possible in the game planning in their male nest. A few stupid notes will be less dangerous than me being alone with him. Although I had no idea what was going on inside him, the hunting instinct was boiling in every man and that complicated the situation.

Rick didn't like it very much. While we walked down the street to their apartment, he asked me: "Why do we have to go there? We can be in the entertainment room."

"No, we can't."

"Are those crazy games really necessary?"

"Yes, they are. Do you want the answers or not?"

"Yes, but why in such a difficult way?"

"Because according to everyone and that includes my boss, I am a perfectionist. Even when I make a mistake, it's a perfectly complicated one. Everything I do must be perfect."

Rick laughed. "Including stains."

"Be quiet. We are almost there. I hope you can go through the games."

"Sure, I can and I won't be green."

"No, you will be red. From anger." Rick laughed heartily: "Why?"

"Don't you know?"

"No. I have no reason to be angry."

"The reason will come. It will be me."

"What? Do you want me to be angry?"

"No, I don't. The circumstances. The games won't be easy."

"I don't understand you."

"That's good. Come on. What about that garden house?"

Rick observed me in the darkness and asked: "Is it really necessary?"

"It is. Believe me. You'll appreciate that little house. Later."

"Jesus! You are such a complicated woman."

"My life is complicated. Maybe. I want to eliminate the damages."

"Okay. I'll try. I'll arrange the house, the hall, a lot of crazy things, friends and…"

"We'll see what happens. We never know. Never."

We were silent. Rick didn't know why he had agreed to all this craziness. The strange thing was that his friends were intrigued as well. Even though they laughed at him. There was no reason to laugh. They will do the same thing as they do for a living. Only this time it will be just for fun.

They didn't laugh when we came this time. They knew that organizing something like this really needed more heads and ideas. Even Will was no longer wondering why Rick was going to create something that he called a crap for the sake of the complicated Bunny. So what? They are only going to play. Nothing more. Innocent entertainment, with points that should reveal how the four elements of love work. Crazy idea? After all, they earned their money from crazy ideas that someone first had to create. The only difference was that this time they had to create them themselves. Not only that, they had to play and dance those ideas as well. Just like everyone in Bunny's group did. They all did what was necessary.

I was becoming tired. "I'll be going. You all know what you have to do. See you on Monday. The last day of your work. You were great. All of you. Thank you for your help."

On the way to the nursing house, we were silent. "Sorry to be silent. The barrier. It's very, very difficult."

Rick said: "The words. Sometimes to be silent is enough."

We reached the entrance. I looked in his eyes. "You'll be missed a lot here."

"We'll meet. In your crazy games."

"Well yes."

"I'm excited. Although you said, I'd be angry."

"You will. I can't do it another way. Maybe it's a huge, big mistake. I feel that I'm selfish."

Rick listened with interest, then asked, uncomprehending: "Selfish? In your reality? It's impossible to be selfish here!"

"Sometimes the deeds of love are very selfish. They cause damage. There is always damage. You're a good man. I have to go. Good night."

"Wait! Why do you think you are selfish? I want to know."

"No. There is no time. Patience."

"God! I'm patient! I'm doing everything you want!"

"No. You're doing what you want. It's your choice. Nothing is a must. We only need to bear the damages that come after our decisions. There are always some damages…"

Rick contemplated. Yes, we blame the circumstances. We often blame others or ourselves for our wrong decisions. We don't understand that for each and every decision, even the one that we think is a good one, we will pay a price. Nothing is for free. We're basically beings controlling the most powerful magic. We just don't realize it. We have emotions. These are the spells that create our world. Price must be paid for everything in our imperfect lives. The higher the goals, the higher the price. That was the reason why many of those who made it to the highest spheres on Earth were sometimes more unhappy than ordinary people, living even in diaper realities. Because not only they had more rewards, but they took on themselves more stress and responsibilities. As well as fear for themselves and their loved ones. Sometimes we didn't realize this in our ordinary realities. Where there were huge rewards, people seemed to really have to turn into Earth's Olympus because they wouldn't have done it otherwise. Sometimes they had to learn to use one bad feature. To be selfish. Otherwise, they would not survive in that shiny, merciless world. That was the cruel truth. Rick said quietly after a moment of silence: "Each of us has a dark side."

"Everyone has. I have it, too. We will finish the details tomorrow."

I left. Rick walked down the snowy street.

Chapter 10

The most beautiful holidays of the year were around the corner. It was the time when people's hearts seemed to wake up and were more open and much more good deeds were done. People needed Christmas. It didn't matter if some of them would associate it with the birth of Jesus, or those who didn't go to church, with Santa Claus. The believers felt offended and would tell it's all turning to one kitschy marketing event. We didn't realize one important thing. Both of these archetypes served humanity as an example of perfect self-sacrificing love that should give people joy and do deeds of love. It doesn't matter what or whom we believed in. If the beings we believe in show the path of love and sacrifice, it is the right faith. Every religion in the world is true as long as the deeds made by its followers, not just words, created love and its tracks. Looking into the past, we reveal the cruel truth. From all that the Creator has given us, we wanted to take only what was good for us. We did it with everything. With religions, our imperfect governments, our imperfect system of functioning of the planet. We have been trying to ignore the uncomfortable parts of it. We have forgotten that this world lost perfection because imperfect beings with free will live in it. It is precisely the gift of free will that makes the uncomfortable part wait for us somewhere around the corner. Waiting for us to fight it and win over it with the most powerful weapon we have. With love. It won't help us, or any positive thinkers, if we ignore the problems so that we don't attract them, or give them, as in some countries, noble names. Only a fair fight will help us. Very special fight. To stand up to the problems and forgive our own mistakes first and then to forgive the others. We often see the mistakes of others only. Therefore, we often are not able to forgive ourselves. We swear at our governments and we don't realize they are a reflection of our thinking. We failed in that because pride and desire for superficial glitter and power settled in our hearts. That suited someone. Someone from whom people laughed and didn't believe in. They forgot that polarity was present not only on Earth but also in other dimensions. That is why he had such an easy work. Because no one believed in him.

Rick went to his temporary male nest and I fell asleep in my tiny room. Our souls left our bodies to visit dreams that have not yet materialized.

Meanwhile, in their invisible dimensions, Aphrodite, Eros, and Psyche sat together and were discussing the current situation.

Aphrodite was angry at Eros. "Eros! How could you even think that the failed love potion will work?"

"What about your regular love potion? Do you think it would work? How? Successfully?"

Aphrodite continued to measure Eros with a stern look. "It's none of your business. Love potions don't concern you. You should take care of your arrows."

"I care, mother. What do you want from me? After all, did you see how greatly the potion is working? The guy was able to humble himself, just to be able to…"

Psyche laughed. "To do what? Finish it, Eros. Just finish it. A double dose of that stupid dill seeds! What was that good for? To attract the hearts?"

Eros sighed: "Where is the problem? Men don't need dill seeds anyway. They have a surplus of it. That's why love is so complicated."

Psyche retorted: "Or rather it doesn't work. So, what? He washed a granny to get her…"

Eros completed: "To lower levels of love."

Aphrodite was disappointed: "We wanted to get him to the higher level! And now? Men will move heaven and earth to get what they want. We must hope that the potion, or its remnants, will disappear as soon as possible. Otherwise, everything will fail."

Psyche was afraid. "We never know if it will be successful. Eros is right. Essentially, such a high level of dill seed's effect is circulating in male beings' blood that they don't need anything else. Now it's all going to be complicated."

Aphrodite asked seriously: "You think it would be easier without the potion? In their situation?"

Eros answered: "We just don't know, mother, we don't know. We just show and give chances. It is up to human beings to do what they want with them. I shoot, yes, I shoot my arrows, but they don't have to eat and tear all the fruit that I put in their way."

Psyche told him: "Exactly that's what you are doing! You're complicating things for them."

"I have to. They have free will."

Aphrodite grabbed her forehead. "That makes them think that they can have everything even in love. Men want to tear and eat all the fruits. Some women just cry because of that. Sometimes it's the other way around. It's all…"

Eros laughed ironically. "Imperfect. Hmmm. Imperfect. Is there a recipe, mother? Shall I put away my bow, so there will be no more pain? Then there will be no physical love. The one who bears my name. Mine! Not yours, mother or yours Psyche. You're in charge of the soul and heart. I'm in charge of the body. The sex. That's the way it is. I will shoot until the end of the world. The same way as they are. Imperfectly."

Psyche was disappointed from his words. "Well, that's your ego speaking. Now, tell me what's next? We have a lot of pain in the world. Few deeds of love. Little pearls. Even fewer pink ones because you always throw other fruit in their way."

Eros laid his feet on the table and stoically shrugged his shoulders. He took a sip of the nectar from the glass in front of him: "So what? Life will be boring otherwise. The truth is, actually, no one is interested in those higher levels of yours. Everybody in the world is crazy about… How did the nurse call it? Few seconds? Because of them, they are willing to create such stupid things as that fool. He washed a granny and a grandpa. I haven't seen anything like that before. As I see it, men, too, have evolved. Because of those few seconds, they no longer have to kill each other if they ever go to the garden to take that fruit. Instead of using swords when fighting, for example, they can fight by washing grannies."

Aphrodite warned him: "Are you excited about this amazing progress? Don't you see what's happening on Earth, Eros? Sometimes there were wars because of these few seconds! Wars! Whole governments have fallen, and revolutions started! And that's been happening for centuries!"

Eros laughed.

"Are you talking, for example about one stupid king who didn't care about ruling and listened to women's advice instead? Regarding my erotic love? He gave away all his fortune to his mistresses, and his offspring ended up pretty bad. That's the proof of the level where these human beings worthy of love are. Almost always down."

Psyche didn't give up. "Not all of them. Some do deeds of mercy. What about those beings who, because of the higher levels, will give up physical pleasure and do just the deeds of sacrifice?"

Eros continued: "Well, yeah…yeah… You're right."

Psyche thought: *Maybe because of their prayers, many things have turned into good things. Only history books don't write about it. Because these beings don't care about fame. Because they were all dressed up in humility. Eros, we need all levels of love. People have to learn again not to be afraid to ascend higher.*

Aphrodite told Eros: "Every human being if he or she turns his or her faith into deeds of love, helps to save the world. No matter where he or she belongs to or what he or she believes in. And you Eros, you go to Apollo and humble yourself. You must apologize to him. For everything. Even for the bad love experiences that you sent to him."

Eros stroked his curly hair and said reluctantly: "Hmmm. I hope he won't cut me with his most precious weapon, his sword. Part of the light of the Creator is hidden in it. To help him fight the beings from below. However, its rare blue light had begun to fade. That is somehow related to the waning light from the pearls."

Psyche was sad. "Less pearls means less white light and the extinguishing Apollo sword. That's not good. With deeds of love, people should reflect that divine in them. The weapon against evil is not a fight where people have to die. It is love. Only she can alleviate the consequences of evil. The light in the blue sword fades away because people have lost faith in themselves and thus in the Creator. They refused to be worthy of higher love. With that, they have also rejected the divine in them."

Aphrodite thoughtfully continued: "Zeus knows that. He knows. People are trying to cover their dark side, ignore it, and they seek superficial perfection that does not exist. Because with the imperfections they pay for the gift. The gift of the free will."

All three stayed quiet. For years, human beings were born and died on the planet, trying to fight for everything. They also tried to fight for love. They wanted to get it for themselves. They didn't understand its basic principle. They must begin to love themselves and not only work on physical perfection but also on the less popular, mental one. It hurts more than exercise. Suffering is the nightmare of humanity. Until the polarity remains, it won't be otherwise. True love will begin to emerge from the hearts of people who will accept themselves the way they are. Including their dark side. Then they will no longer have to fight for love or ask for it from others. When love starts to emerge from one's heart, it begins to spill over on the human beings around them and love can find its way. That is the hardest task and at the same time the easiest.

It looked like someone, who was on Earth or near it, knew that. He also recognized the key to saving the human's hearts. He was constantly destroying their faith in everything. Made them bitter and blaming everyone around them. He encouraged them to envy and hate. He deceived them with a lie that only perfect people can be rich and happy. That the only possible mean of human happiness is superficial perfection and material wealth. If that was true, in the poorest countries on Earth, food, or a piece of clothing would not be enough to create basic happiness. Yet, in these places, happiness was present. In these places, even small things were enough to make human beings happy. So little was enough. Many human beings have already understood this principle and started to teach those other beings. Quietly. They teach them that anyone was able to create the most precious spring, the greatest magic that busted the walls of prejudice and pride. It was not necessary to fight for it. It existed and will continue to exist. Just like the Creator. Nobody had to fight for her. One just had to find the key and open his or her heart. Those who did divide and reign in the world didn't want to do that. The human beings were afraid that if they opened their wrinkled hearts with the key, they would die of fear. Fear of what they committed. To themselves and to others. Such human beings hid the key as far as possible to see and hear nothing of their evil deeds. That key was the conscience. That was the silent voice we sometimes heard. Those who believed in the existence of ethereal beings of light claimed that it was their voice. Human beings didn't always do the right things, but it was possible to correct the balance with deeds of love.

Aphrodite interrupted the silence: "Eros, go to Apollo. I beg you."

The words she spoke caused a miracle. The god of love said: "When I'm dead, chopped by Apollo's sword, you'll have to take on my role of shooting arrows Psyche. Then, I'm afraid there will be terrible boredom in the world. The chaos that arises for these few seconds is just…divine… As I know you, you will think million times before you will shoot an arrow. Just because you want to avoid causing any damage. By the time you decide to shoot, people will be living in monasteries and will just pray."

Aphrodite was irritated. "Oh, shut up, Eros! Human beings need all levels."

Eros disappeared and went to Apollo to humble himself. He found him sitting in a desolate state on his chair at the table, where pending human wishes accumulated. He tried to fulfill them with his Earthly team in various ways. Many other wishes have been stored in many other rooms. Apollo tried to fulfill those wishes according to time and difficulty. It was a hard job because although he was a god of divination, no one ever listened to his warnings.

He greeted Eros with grumpy words: "What do you want you feathered snake?"

"I came...eh...to apologize...for having poisoned the poor man's heart, but look, he washed a granny and a grandpa. So, the potion worked fine!!"

After a moment of Apollo's staunch silence, Eros continued with fear: "I'm sorry for the crap I've sent you as well. Love is imperfect. Only love from the One who is above is perfect."

Apollo told him more amicably; "Eros. Look at me. I don't have time for love. I'm busy. I'm burnout because to fulfill the wishes of some human beings requires precise and hard work. In addition, some wishes are... Well, listen... God, I wish to have a new car. I beg you for a new house with a pool. I have a new job. I want to be a millionaire. I want my rival to burn up in hell. You know the one who stole my husband. God please, let my neighbor finally ask to marry me. God please, give me a promotion in the company. And so on. These are the less painful ones. Then there are those that I can't even read. From those dying in wars, from hunger and diseases. Yet, Zeus wants to save them. They can't even share the food. They'd rather throw it in the bin. Because of hygiene. I'm sick of them. I'm sad, Eros. Very sad. You know why Eros? Shortly they will have nothing to share because they will destroy their planct as well. However, Zeus believes in their hearts and miracle. Back to you, what do you want?"

Eros asked gladly: "You won't cut me in half with your sword?"

Apollo laughed sadly. "I don't know if the sword can cut anything. The blue light begun to diminish. That which is supposed to reflect the divine in human beings, which is to create love and positive emotions, is disappearing. I don't know, for the first time in millennia I don't know what will happen."

Eros tried to comfort him: "Don't lose faith, Apollo. Keep the faith. Everything will settle down somehow."

"Somehow. Somehow. So, do you want anything else?"

"I want to thank you for your help. For the chances you create so some human dreams can come true. For the ordinary nurse. You helped me and I didn't listen to you. Please forgive me."

Apollo finally smiled at him. "Not at all. I'm just doing my job. However, sometimes I am not able to fulfill everything that people want. You have to admit that some wishes are meaningless. Hardly anyone wants to have an open heart, courage, or ask for more humility. They just want to be rich and beautiful. They want such superficial values. Such a horrible system that human beings invented does not exist in the entire universe."

Eros added: "This is what He wants. The One who created it all. Until He takes away their free will, the system will work even when it is not perfect. You see not all of them are superficial."

"But their system stopped working, Eros! It stopped! That's why we're going to fight for them again. Oh, god. Even the weapon He gave me is not helping me."

Apollo disappeared for a moment and came back with a beautiful blue sword, radiating a beautiful blue, light. However, Eros saw that it was shining less than before. The deeds of people have less and less reflected the divine spark in their hearts. Apollo placed his sword carefully on the table, and both looked at its beauty. As if through the dark, blue light, they felt the Creator's presence. Eros touched the sword. "Look, it's still shining. Weaker, but shining. We must not lose faith."

"Eros, look! Its light is weaker day by day. The divine spark in human hearts began to fade away. The one who is down knows that and this time he will attack in full force. This time he has a better chance. Remember, Eros, the Creator wanted the balanced polarity to be preserved in the universe. Now there is more negative emotions on Earth. That's why Earth is falling. Hate often prevails over love. Pride prevails over humility. Pride is the strongest weapon of that one who lives down. Because of pride, people have torn our invisible dimension. They seriously damaged what had to remain connected and balanced. Because of their human pride, they claim that the little pieces that they have picked out from the torn parts is their true faith. Faith, Eros. If they just believe in love… They wouldn't need anything else. They can believe in what they want, but they must do good deeds."

Eros stared at the sword. "Love reflects the Creator. Hate reflects the one who is down. Eternal struggle taking place at all levels of Earth and the universe. Only the highest levels are not involved in this struggle. Apollo, why does the Creator always want to save everything? Why doesn't he just stop?"

"Because he loves everything he created. He doesn't judge, he doesn't punish. People are punishing themselves. They have created their own hell on Earth and now they are afraid of it."

Apollo stroked the precious sword, created to fight evil, and whispered: "Let's go, we have a lot of work to do. You with shooting arrows, so that humankind continues to get crazy for those *few seconds*. Otherwise, life would be boring, as you told your mother Aphrodite and Psyche. I will try to fulfill at least some of the wishes of those stupid worms. Before they start eating the real worms."

Eros laughed. "Apollo, what are you talking about? What worms?"

"Oh, nothing, forget about that, Eros. Now they think they have enough. In a few years, when they will eat those worms, their silly and senseless wishes will look completely different."

Eros started to think that Apollo was getting insane. Who wouldn't?

"Apollo, do you feel good? What do you mean by that?"

"If they don't save themselves, they'll end up wishing for the basic things. Food, water, and a place to live. When they lose all the luxury and shine and everything goes so bad that earth will no longer be able to produce grain and the wells will begin to dry, they will understand that the most precious gifts are not diamonds. You can't eat them or eat gold. They'll be useless for them if they won't be able to buy anything with them. They are still not very grateful. They didn't understand anything. They repeat the same mistakes all over again. Anyways, let's go to work."

Eros disappeared and Apollo stared at the beautiful sword for a long time. It was a gift from the Creator. Then he returned it to its place.

The goddess of fate, Tyche, looked at Apollo. "Does it still make sense? To fight for them?"

"Yes, it does. There are still human beings who are trying to create deeds of love. At all levels. The problem is that the deeds of love that are related to the highest level are waning. Oh, Tyche, I don't want to work today. I need to be alone and think."

Apollo closed himself in his most important room and sent the goddess of fate away for a while. Nothing will go wrong if they don't see the human desires that have accumulated at least for a while. Because the number of new human beings grew daily. As soon as any of them started to think, he or she had desires.

I woke up in the morning in my tiny room and realized that I was sad. Soon the four handsome guys will leave forever. They will no longer need to work on their career as cleaners. Although they did very well in it.

Throughout my whole shift, I thought about how I'm going to teach with my terrible English foreign beautiful women one of the most controversial and oldest dance in the world. A dance that was perfect for women of all ages and they didn't need a partner for it. Partners mostly looked at them while they danced. In those moments I wanted to look into their male brains to see what they were thinking. Thinking... Well... They think and feel differently. Women sometimes don't understand them and neither do they understand us. As I expected Rick appeared in the evening. He said he had nothing to do and besides, we didn't finish the game plan yet.

I started: "It seems you like spending your time with those grannies."

Rick mysteriously agreed: "Grannies are perfect. They don't need much and they live. You care for them."

I corrected him: "We care for them now. Together with you and your colleagues."

We laughed. I told him: "I have to stay till nine today."

"It doesn't matter."

I asked him: "What happened to you all?"

Rick fought with my weapons. "Now our hearts are purified even more. There is a lot of empty space left. It needs to be filled—"

I interrupted him: "Okay let's go then. You can start filling the empty space with mercy and compassion."

Rick was impatient.

"When will you come down?"

"I told you. Everything has the right time."

Rick said nothing, and once again my colleague was happy that we won't waste our time with the kitchen devil, the dishwasher. We liked it because it was able to wash the dishes, but because of the lack of time and staff we were loading and unloading it all day long. Every helping hand came in handy and we were grateful. By eight o'clock the other colleagues had already left, and I was left alone. I didn't care what would they think anymore. I understood during my difficult life that there would always be rumors. People were nosy by nature.

The department went silent. Those were the beautiful moments for us, stressed out nurses and caretakers. I still had to put one rebellious granny on a couch protected by a rubber bedsheet and give her a sleeping pill.

I told Rick: "Now please, don't say anything. Otherwise, I'll write nonsense again."

Rick smiled and sat quietly while I tried to focus on writing and checking the patient's reports. I often wrote notes on my hands, so I won't forget something. There were many other notes all around me. That's why all my colleagues laugh. I've never been perfect. I always managed to make some small mistakes. Well, with all that I had in my head that was understandable. I thanked God that the head nurse didn't see what's inside my head. She wouldn't understand. My head was full of unnecessary things. Oh, who would remember all those boring things like which cabinet to lock? I could change diapers, wash people, and disinfect everything. Other things were not that important. Except preparing the medicaments and drops. But the writing? Oh, god! Rick was quiet, but it was still hard for me to focus. Fortunately, he couldn't see what's in my head. Neither could I see what's in his. When I finished writing the reports and prepared the medicaments for the next morning, I said: "I have to check our grannies and grandpas. Some often sleep in the wrong rooms."

Rick laughed. "So what? We sometimes sleep in the wrong rooms as well."

I explained: "Eros is to blame. He shoots his arrows as he wants. Then there is chaos. Come on, let's go."

We started checking the rooms and came to the room of Mrs. M, who once we found in the room of terrified Mr. D. Positioning pillows were on the floor as well as cookies and chocolate pieces. One sock was in the bin. The basket that she used to carry with her was full of sweets, magazines, and newspapers.

Rick couldn't stand it and started laughing. "Jesus! What did she do?"

"It is normal."

"And, where is she?"

"Definitely with Mr. D."

"How do you know?"

"Some human beings never give up."

I was right. We entered Mr. D's room and saw an amazing scene. Mr. D was covered up to his nose with the duvet. He was terrified. His eyes were wide open, and he looked like a child who just saw a monster. By his bedside, that cheeky grandma sat on a chair and was sleeping. Although the room was dark, they could see that her mouth was dirty from chocolate. She was satisfied that she was not alone and didn't want to leave the room. Rick was laughing like crazy because this scene expressed everything. So little was enough for the granny to be happy. She didn't want to be alone in the room, so she found a solution. She kept searching for her late husband. Since she could no longer find the love of her life, she had to improvise. She sat quietly in that darkness, on that chair happy just knowing that she wasn't alone. I tried to get her out of the room, but it wasn't easy.

"Come on. We have to go to your room. You can't sleep like that."

"I don't want to sleep. I want to stay here."

"Please. Come on. Can I clean your mouth? It's dirty from chocolate."

Granny loved chocolate and sweets, and she was curvier all her life. Nevertheless, she said that her husband loved her, and she loved him. She wanted to be with him. But her time hasn't come yet.

I cleaned her mouth and we managed to take her to her room. I put her in bed, and she started crying: "You're so good to me here and I am complicating your life."

These were the moments, those tiny flashes of light in the already broken minds of seriously ill people that were most important to all the employees of this kind of institution. These flashes of light let in humility into the hearts of both employees and patients. These moments gave strength to imperfect human beings who cared the best they could for other human beings, thus helping them to endure it all. They came in moments when employees felt endless despair and helplessness. When they felt they were not doing their job well and wanted to escape. Where did these flashes come from when demented people didn't recognize either time or space? Was it a coincidence? Or were they glimpses of the divine in us? Humility was what humanity still lacks the most. Sometimes even I was at the edge and I hated and blamed myself for that. Then came a little moment, a faint flash of light, and I continued. For years and years. Instead of small, innocent children, fate arranged for me to take care of people destroyed by life and illness at the end of their lives. To learn at least a bit of humility. Four handsome men have also learned it and survived. They proved they can be heroes in real life as well. They understood that the world can be saved even with small deeds.

Rick watched the granny laying in her bed and when we went out, he asked: "Will she stay there now?"

"Probably not. Maybe five minutes." We continued and checked on other grannies. Then we came to the room where Rick helped us with a restless patient whom I could disarm at least for few seconds with air kisses. Once the few seconds had passed, he was furious again. Now, thanks to the pills, he slept like a baby.

Rick watched my movements in the darkness and said quietly: "I would like those few seconds."

I froze inside.

"It's not possible yet. Everything would be destroyed. There would be ruins. Trust me."

"How can you know?"

"Very bad experience. Sorry, but we must protect your heart first."

Rick looked at me blankly. "Excuse me? Did you say my heart? Not yours? How do I understand this?"

"The fact that you don't know is a proof. We're not ready. Neither you. Nor me. Please. Let me get the answers first. Please. Patience."

Rick disagreed impatiently: "Why are you making this so difficult?"

"Because everything in life is difficult, Rick. People sign pre-nuptial contracts for money and infidelity. They won't sign contracts for other things. Sometimes they don't know what hurts the other. Once they sit with the therapist it's usually too late. Maybe some things need to be addressed at the beginning. Not after."

"I don't understand why you mentioned my heart. Only mine."

"That's the problem of all of us. We often think only of ourselves."

"Why do I feel it's the opposite with you?"

"I have the same feeling about you. Feeling. I don't really know much about you. It's a feeling. Please, let's go."

Rick was a little angry. He didn't understand why I acted so strangely. Men never understood that. They could not understand that in the chaos of our relationships we must not only think of our hearts. But also, about the hearts of other human beings. We've forgotten that lately. Because sometimes we didn't love ourselves enough. That's why we were so worried about our own, fragile hearts.

We came to the staff room and I said quietly: "Those games will be very complicated, Rick. Decide. You'll need a lot of strength to complete them. Really a lot. Me as well."

Rick asked: "You don't trust me?"

"Not after what happened a while ago. I'm not a woman of your reality. The huge barrier. I'm afraid of it. A language barrier."

Rick was silent for a moment and then spoke: "We will occasionally improvise."

"All right."

"Wait for me down in the cafe. My colleague doesn't have to see you."

Rick went down and I handed over the work to my colleague. In my room, I took off my uniform quickly and put it in the laundry basket. I already had everything there to save precious time.

We walked down the street and we were silent. I was tired of the never-ending shift. I had to work the prescribed number of hours. The language barrier was also strenuous. I did what I could. I interrupted silence suddenly: "Too bad you don't know German."

Rick repeated: "Too bad you don't know English."

I laughed, and desperately, between the laughter, I asked: "How will I communicate in those games?"

"As you always do. You're going to speak random words. And show with hands, legs, and other parts of the body. Wings."

"I don't have wings."

"You do."

"Let's go. Here we are."

We were finishing the details of our crazy games. They began to realize that people really needed occasionally to think and perhaps act as children. Especially, to create new and more positive emotions. For mankind was not only threatened with the famine of the body. But even a mental famine, because our souls suffered as well.

On the penultimate day, the plan was almost finished, and Will announced: "Well, guys. It's going to be a madhouse. I'm so excited. That will be so much fun! We'll probably never forget that."

I looked at him and said to myself: *Yes, that's right. Nobody will ever forget about that madhouse. That's the point.*

Andy remarked importantly: "Well, we all know that it's not easy at all to organize something like that. We have to do it ourselves. No wonder there are those endless credits at the end of the movies."

Peter thought: "That is to not forget a single human being who contributed to that million-dollar madhouse."

Rick added: "Sometimes even billion dollars madhouse."

"I want to thank you. You worked amazingly and it wasn't easy for you. Really thank you. For the games as well."

Peter told me: "We thank you. For this stay. What looked like a punishment, in the beginning, will be missed in some sense."

Andy immediately corrected him: "Well, not all will be missed. We won't miss the monster attacks from the bags for sure."

The guys burst into laughter and Will brought his surgical mask and put it on. "This didn't help us anyway."

We laughed again. They were the shining stars of their Earthly Olympus, but here in this tiny dot on the map, they showed that they could humbly save even with small deeds. They showed that they had brave hearts in real life as well. To withstand any suffering, whether in a real war where weapons are used for destruction or in our small everyday wars is just as difficult. Here, invisible weapons were used. They often had a different, invisible force because at least occasionally they could defeat the real evil.

I was about to leave. I explained to Rick: "Colleagues from the night shift will be upset again that I am disturbing them. They must open the door for me."

"When will those games begin?"

"When you will arrange the garden house and the big hall."

"And a lot of other, unnecessary things. Dance and theater props, for example."

"Exactly."

"It's hard to fight with you."

"Are we fighting? We're friends."

Rick nodded. "Sure. Friends analyze different boxes and so on."

"I'll wait for the garden house."

"Garden house."

"Good night. See you tomorrow. Your last day. Are you glad?"

Rick paused. He realized that despite the frightening reality that hadn't spared him, sometimes it was a good thing for human beings from the higher levels to experience the life of the lower level. Perhaps then people would stop looking at cleaners with arrogance.

He replied: "Yes and no."

"Good. Tomorrow then."

In the quiet dark night, all four world's finest cleaners slept. I slept too. Only our guardian angels watched over our hearts and whispered to us love decisions.

The guardian angels of the four extraordinary men and my guardian angel sat in the dark on the roof of the nursing house. They watched the thick snowflakes falling from the sky.

Chasariel, Rick's guardian angel started: "I wouldn't really expect my protégé to do such a heroic deed."

Nolachiel, my guardian angel was surprised: "Why not? You know his heart the best, don't you? By the way, which of the many deeds do you have in mind?"

Mechiel, Will's angel said in awe: "Well, washing his granny and grandpa, or?"

Ameliel, Andy's angel rebuked them: "What's funny about that? Such action also requires humility. Just as when someone sacrifices his life for another human being."

Avariel told Ameliel: "Come on, don't be so serious. Look, our whispers were efficient. Now our voices will be heard even more. They have more space in their hearts to do more deeds of love for other human beings."

Nolachiel agreed: "Yes. Every human being can save the whole world in his or her way. When they finally understand it, there will be paradise on Earth."

Chasariel objected: "Well, that may take some time. As long as people have the freedom of choice, then… I don't know."

Ameliel disagreed: "This is what people should understand. With their love decisions, they create their own paradise or their own hell."

Avariel warned them: "Don't mention hell, please. There is enough of that in the world. The one from bellow is happy. Because he is doing great in his work. He is destroying the Creator's gifts in human hearts. Faith. Hope. Love. Gratitude. Compassion. Forgiveness. People stopped listening to us."

Nolachiel comforted Avariel with faith in his voice: "That's why we have to do our job even better."

Chasariel smiled mischievously at Nolachiel. "Ah! So, it was you who whispered to your protégé this crazy idea of games?"

Nolachiel shook her wings. "Don't be nosy. Who searches, will find. Who believes in us will get ideas."

Chasariel shook his head.

"If all goes wrong, what will we do?"

Ameliel responded thoughtfully: "Well, we will saw. Their torn hearts. That's what we will do. As always. Angels of healing will heal the scars with pink tears from the Flower islands. This is also an angel's job. Because their way of stitching patches on their tattered hearts doesn't work anyway. Patches tear over time. They just don't know that."

Mechiel laughed.

"As Zeus said, 'they do what they can.' They already have artificial hearts, don't they? If their real hearts can't be stitched, only artificial ones will help."

Chasariel rebuked him: "Shut up! Artificial hearts. Artificial hearts. What about their feelings?"

Avariel explained: "What feelings? Scientists say feelings are just hormones. Apollo is angry with artificial meat. You are bothered by the artificial heart. And so, what? They are imperfect, but they have an excellent gift."

Ameliel asked: "What gift?"

"They can improvise when they're in distress. They'll use plan B."

Nolachiel contemplated: "They are amazing creatures. Really. Their imperfection and ability to improvise make them human. We're going to work, and we must believe that Zeus has a plan B. It would be bad if they didn't exist anymore."

Chasariel was scared.

"Oh, don't even say that! We would lose our jobs! I don't want to collect pearls! I'd be bored."

Avariel added: "Me neither. So, we have to whisper even more in their imperfect, yet still real hearts."

The angels disappeared and the last morning came. It was the day when the punishment of the four cleaners from high reality was coming to an end. The manager called them to the office to praise them and thank them for their help. She explained that she also had her hands tied and had an exact key used in recruiting. Cracked key. Money was missing everywhere and that was the result. In that ordinary reality, those ordinary people, those noncelebrities had to improvise. Then something happened that no one expected. Medical control came. Nightmare of every nursing house. Because the work of the inspectors was to look for and find as many mistakes as possible. Every time they entered the building, chaos broke out. Everyone was running around like headless chickens. I went back to do my job. I looked at the head nurse's face and I knew things were not going well. The inspectors found some mistakes. I myself have forgotten to dispose of one expired medication. My head was somewhere else, and some expired drug was not my priority. My colleague Tim wore a white plastic apron in which we all looked like slaughterhouse workers. The poor man forgot to take it off and almost entered the dining room with it. That was forbidden because germs could be transferred in this way.

Fortunately, the head nurse saw it before the strict inspector. He looked important as if the whole world belonged to him because he had to. It was his job. The boss had sent the four temporary cleaners to clean the lower floors, not wanting the poor guys to run in the chaos that had occurred.

I asked the head nurse: "What should I do? Can I go and wash Mrs. S?"

She was one of the most difficult patients because of the weight and the care she needed. As the inspectors chose to check her, it was good that she was scheduled for that unfortunate Monday. I was stupid enough to want to eliminate the damage Mrs. S always made in the bathroom when she was washed in the net with the help of the Thor lifter. You know what fell from her continuously. It wasn't her fault. This time I didn't use Zeus or Thor, but another lifter. With a woman's name. I relied on a woman and that was a big mistake. I put her in a wheelchair, and everything went great. Only the most important thing I waited for and why I didn't use Thor's net was still not happening. Then it happened. The clean and beautifully groomed patient did what I expected but at the worst moment. It happened when I picked her up from the shower stool and wanted to put her on the bed. Mrs. S did her job.

Perfectly. Not only she was dirty, but everything around her. The clean bed, lifter, the shower stool. Great damage was on the floor as well. I was almost crying. Whenever we rushed and were stressed the most, we attracted even more disasters. The impatient inspector wanted to check how we take care of this patient. Hmm. So, I started cleaning the damage. When I finished, I found out that my snow-white uniform was dirty as well. I cursed and started to clean myself with disinfectant wipes in front of the bathroom mirror.

Damn shit! Jesus! I look like… I thought when I saw myself in that mirror and laughed at myself in despair. The plastic apron didn't help me. The negative part of my work manifested itself in the most unfavorable time. I managed to partially remove the spots. There was no time to change my clothes. I had to improvise. My uniform was in a dilapidated state. When Tim saw me in the kitchen, he asked: "Why are you all kind of…wet? And speckled?"

"Don't even ask."

Tim replied with a laugh because he knew it very well: "Mrs. S made shit on herself, didn't she? She always does it when she's already cleaned."

"Oh, Tim, kill me! See how I look?"

Tim shrugged his shoulders.

"You cleaned yourself well. Almost nothing is visible."

"Almost. I will have to get my uniform." Then I felt terribly sorry for everything that had happened. The head nurse and the boss were angry and stressed out because the inspectors found some mistakes. For us these mistakes were irrelevant, but not for them. For a moment I hid in the bathroom, where every morning I divided the tasks between four temporary cleaners. I cried and that made me feel better. Oh, now we will be blamed so much for being incompetent and inattentive because we forgot to do this or that. So what? The inspectors must also live from something. It occurred to me that even the actors had such annoying inspectors. Paparazzi who sniffed like dogs and waited for their mistakes. They also have to live. Fortunately, I had a short shift. When I finished, I went down to the entertainment room. Luckily, the guys had already finished their lunch.

I said to them: "The boss said you can go…home…" It was very difficult for me to say that.

Rick smiled. "To prepare many things for the games… Then I'll see you."

The men stud up and without a word, went out of the room to leave us alone for a while. Rick stared at me, and then noticed my still wet uniform and the marks of stains on it. Luckily, they were tiny and almost impossible to see.

"What happened?"

"Nothing," I lied.

"How, nothing? You're all..."

"You mean speckled?"

"Not. Sad. Why?"

"I'm not sad. Everything is okay. When everything is prepared even my garden house I will come, and I'll try your reality."

"You mean because of the games?"

"Because of the games. Even the other things that you have to do to be so...perfect..."

"We're not perfect." We were silent for a moment, then I thanked him.

"Thank you for showing me part of your heart. It's a precious gift. Your heart. I'll be looking forward to it."

"For games or garden house?"

"For everything."

Rick asked with a smile: "What about the testosterone code and its filling? Would you try that too?"

"We'll see where the games will lead us..."

I abruptly walked away. I couldn't be in his presence any longer. It was very difficult. Because I wasn't wrong. His heart shone like the sun. So, the guys went to pack up to return to their reality and me too. Into my ordinary but also important reality. A lot of work was waiting for me. Not only at home, with my artistic group and the little girls who because of their innocence still believed in fairies when they danced with me. I had to come up with themes and stories for the craziest games that should give Rick answers for all four levels of love. Four answers. Four games. Because I believed that, like Earth and the universe needed all four elements of fire, water, earth, and air, to function properly, love also needed them. Love was just like us in our imperfect human world. Imperfect, but beautiful.

Imperfect and beautiful was love in the heavenly Olympus as well. Apollo thought about the imperfections of love and tried to work. He was in the room that was in the red tower that ruled action. He gazed out at the magnificent flame of faith that emerged from the divine vessel. Its colors ranged from light orange to red and poured out from the red tower of his palace to Earth. However, human beings often used the flame of faith incorrectly. Such energy from the flame of faith could not go back to the precious vessel. Human beings lost faith and that was bad. Suddenly his sister Artemis stepped into the room.

"Are you losing faith, brother? Until now, you never doubted."

Apollo smiled at her: "Do I have a reason not to lose it?"

Artemis came closer to the flame of faith: "If we lose faith too, how can human beings find theirs? The world needs to believe in good and in love."

"Yes, that's true. We need help."

"Apollo, the help comes at the right time only to those who don't lose faith, you know that."

"Look at the flame, Artemis. It pours out of this vessel continuously. Even though because of their free will human beings often misuse it."

Artemis stroked Apollo's shoulder. "That's true, but they don't misuse all of it. Part of the energy people used to do good deeds is coming back. Not all is lost yet."

"You see the light where there is not. Mine is fading away somehow. My sword, Artemis, a gift from the Creator. Its light is disappearing. That never happened before. Zeus relies on my powerful weapon against evil, and I just look helplessly at its weakness."

"Because you see everything so negatively. Yes, human beings make a lot of mistakes. Try looking for the positive things in them as well. Not only their mistakes."

Apollo laughed sadly: "Zeus also sees the positive in them. They say they do what they can. Lately, they're doing everything the other way around."

"Not all of them, Apollo, not all of them. Look for the goodness and faith in their hearts. Not their mistakes. We're not perfect either. Only the Creator is perfect. He gave them the invisible gifts they have in their hearts. While there are still human beings who use these gifts even though partially, everything is fine."

"Only a small part of them, Artemis, only a small part. Look, the light in my sword, which is supposed to reflect that divine spark in their hearts, is diminishing and I can't stop that!"

Artemis thought: *Maybe it's not your job to stop it. Maybe you just have to restore the light. Ignite it again. You still have enough of it.*

Apollo shook his head.

"Oh, as if I heard Zeus say we have enough of pearls. Yet their light is diminishing."

Artemis said: "Don't look at how the pearls are waning, but how they are increasing. There is still enough love in the world with all of its levels."

"Enough? What does it mean, Artemis?"

"While there is only one heart left on Earth that won't lose faith in good and love, it can ignite a spark in another heart. Look at your heart, Apollo, and on the light in your sword. It's still there. That means there's no reason to lose faith. Remember that. Don't lose faith!"

"It is hard."

"Maybe it's not that hard. Look at what the four famous men of the most exalted reality had to try on their own. In this place where you unexpectedly sent them. Of course, by mistake as always, right? They understand that help and humility is needed in any reality. You also help those human beings. We all help them."

"Help."

"You have led four noblemen to recognize the power of humility. Humility, Apollo, rules forever. Pride only for some time. Don't lose faith, Apollo."

Apollo looked at his sister and thought about what she had told him. Artemis continued: "Nothing is as it seems at first sight. Not all is good or bad in the imperfect realities. Wherever we see the darkness, there is a piece of light, and a piece of darkness hides where we see the light. Polarity, Apollo."

Artemis looked at Apollo and then disappeared. Apollo stared into the magnificent flame of faith. A flame that he gave to human beings to help them look for light in their reality. But without darkness, light could not exist. People could find the light only if they experienced the darkness…

CPSIA information can be obtained
at www.ICGtesting.com
Printed in the USA
BVHW052136270522
638317BV00007B/61

9 781647 501969